I strained against the duct tape, knowing it was useless.

"Russell, DeSade was merely the Homer of Cruelty. I am its Aristotle. Its Newton. Its Tesla. I'm not just a fucking artist, I'm a *scientist*." He stood up, walked around behind his chair and rested his hands on its back, still keeping the bound and helpless Nika covered with his gun just in case she decided to fling herself bodily across the room at him and try to chew through his Achilles' tendon. She looked mad enough to try. "But I admit," he said to me, "that I'm as proud of the uglinesses I've invented and catalogued as any human artist could be of the beauties he creates. Like Leonardo, I want my work to live, for the ages. I like the idea that five hundred years after my death, my name will be enough to make strong men pale and children weep."

I saw a logic problem. And then all at once I got it, and shut my eyes so tight I saw neon paisley. "Oh, no. Dear God, no, don't say that. No?"

Twinkling eyes. Puckering anus smile. Bashful nod. "It's true. I have a website."

I heard myself giggle. "Of course. Of course you do."

* * *

"I just read VERY BAD DEATHS . . . and it scared the living shit out of me, thank you very much. Definitely one of the worst, baddest, most creatively awful villains ever, and wonderful heroes and heroine as usual. I read it in one swell foop, and laughed out loud lying here in bed several times, and was transported up there to the San Juans and Victoria and such."

—**David Crosby**, musician (Crosby, Stills & Nash) and author of *Stand and Be Counted*

Baen Books by Spider Robinson

Very Bad Deaths

SPIDER ROBINSON

VERY BAD DEATHS

Copyright © 2004 by Spider Robinson

A Baen Books Original

Baen Publishing Enterprises
P.O. Box 1403
Riverdale, NY 10471
www.baen.com

ISBN 10: 1-4165-2083-X
ISBN 13: 978-0-4165-2083-2

Cover art by Stephen Hickman

First paperback printing, September 2006

Distributed by Simon & Schuster
1230 Avenue of the Americas
New York, NY 10020

Library of Congress Cataloging-in-Publication Data:
2004016880

Printed in the United States of America

*This book is dedicated to Daniel Finger
for the Jura Scala Vario,
and to Guy Immega
for keeping it alive this long*

ACKNOWLEDGMENTS:

This book would not have been possible without the generous and knowledgeable assistance of two of my neighbours, noted Simon Fraser University Criminology Professor Neil Boyd, author of *The Beast Within* and the forthcoming *Big Sister* [Greystone], and his wife Isabel Otter, who since graduating from Osgoode Hall Law School has been an advocate assisting—at various times—physically, mentally and/or emotionally handicapped adults and children, prisoners, and people having trouble with Worker's Compensation. Additional valuable aid was provided by my good friend Guy Immega, as usual. Walter and Jill, proprietors of Vancouver's superb mystery store Dead Write Books (<www.deadwrite.com>) as well as the equally superb SF/Fantasy bookstore White Dwarf books (same URL), have long been my native guides through the worlds of mystery, suspense, thriller and detective fiction, and were of enormous help to me with the writing of this book. The books of Lawrence Gough, police procedurals set in Vancouver, were a particularly fruitful recommendation of theirs; I hope you'll try one. At least one other substantial contributor of relevant information has specifically declined the honour of being identified here; my heartfelt thanks nonetheless.

As always, none of these people should be held responsible for the way I've misunderstood, misrepresented, mistyped or forgotten what they told me, unless it's the only way to get me out of a lawsuit.

—Howe Sound,
British Columbia
6 February, 2004

2003

Trembling-on-the-Verge
Heron Island, British Columbia
Canada

I was fifty-four years old the first time a dead person spoke to me. Wouldn't you know it? It was the wrong one.

To be fair, he did manage to save my life. Just for openers.

I don't actually believe in ghosts. I stopped believing in them even before I stopped believing in the Catholic church, and that puts it pretty far back. Not that many years after I stopped believing in Santa. It's just that a few decades later I stopped *dis*believing in ghosts, too. My wife Susan told me that when she was in her mid-twenties, at a time when she was awake and not under the influence of drugs, her dead father appeared to her. She said he asked for her forgiveness, and she gave it.

I never knew Susan to tell a lie unless it was to spare someone's feelings, and she had fewer delusions than just about anyone else I ever met. She had been dead herself for five years now, and I still hadn't given up hoping to hear from her. She didn't need my forgiveness, and I'd had all I was ever going to have of hers, and like I said I didn't believe in ghosts. But still I hoped. So I guess I still didn't entirely disbelieve in them either.

It was about the time they are traditionally reputed to appear, too, somewhere between three and four in the morning. Despite the hour, I was, as Susan had been for her own visitation, wide awake and not under the influence of drugs unless you're enough of a purist to count coffee or marijuana.

This was normal for me. All my life I've been a night owl, and now I had a job that allowed me to get away with it, and with Susan gone and our son Jesse on the other side of the planet there was absolutely no reason not to do so. I write an opinion column called "The Fifth Horseman" that runs twice a week in *The Globe and Mail*, Canada's national newspaper, so basically I think hard for a living. What better time to do that than the middle of the night, when there's nothing on TV and nothing that isn't mellow on the radio, nobody comes to the door, the phone doesn't ring, and nobody anywhere in earshot is using a chainsaw, swinging a hammer, practicing an electric guitar, or riding a motorcycle?

And what better place than my office? It's a small outbuilding that was originally a pottery studio, well-heated, soundproof enough to permit me to scream obscenities in the small hours if that's what the job calls for, though that's less important now that I live alone. The noisiest thing in it is my hard drive. It sits a whole six steps away from the house—overgrown cabin, really—which, now that Susan's not living in it anymore, is basically just the place my coffee and food come from and go back to, and where I spend the daylight hours in a coffin of my native earth. The noisiest things in the house are the furnace, fridge compressor and cat. House and office sit together on a secluded bluff at the end of a long tire-killing pair of ruts that wind through thick woods, in an out of the way corner of an island that's forty minutes by ferry from North America, and contains a bit over two thousand permanent residents, two sidewalks, and not a single street light or traffic light. The noisiest thing on it in the middle of a weeknight is generally an owl, or a cat in love with mine.

Given this unusual tranquility, stillness and peace, this near-perfect opportunity for contemplation and reflection, naturally I play a lot of music. Jazz and blues CDs, mostly. Sometimes I sing along. Contemplation needs a little challenge, the way cookies need a little salt.

All things considered, I have an ideal existence for someone of my temperament and tastes.

That night, however, the stillness and quiet were lost on me.

That night nothing, anywhere, had any salt, or any other flavor. I wasn't writing a column, or trying to, or even trying to dream up an idea for one. I wasn't surfing the web, for either research or amusement. I wasn't reading. The walls of the office were almost totally obscured by a couple of thousand cherished books; not one contained a line I wished to reread. I wasn't even listening to music. Nearly three-hundred CDs lay within arm's reach; not one of them held a single track I wanted to hear. The telephone hanging on the wall beside my desk connected me directly to everyone else on the planet; I could think of none who were any use to me.

I was no longer trying to decide whether to kill myself—only how and how soon.

A perfect life without Susan in it simply hurt too much to bear. I had been denying that for over a year now, waiting doggedly for the pain to recede to a tolerable level. By now I knew it was never going to recede at all, even a little. Maybe there are no good deaths, I don't know. I know Susan had one of the bad ones.

I estimated I had at most another day or two in me.

It would call for a bit of cunning. The only thing left I could possibly give my son Jesse that he would accept from me was my life insurance benefit—and there was an antisuicide clause. So it would have to look like an accident. I was going over a short list of three finalist methods, weighing their respective pluses and minuses, when the knock on the door startled me so badly I backhanded a cup of coffee clear off the warming plate and onto the floor.

An unexpected knock in the dead of night is alarming even if you have a clean conscience—or so I imagine. I had my brain do a hasty search for Things This Could Be That Wouldn't Be Catastrophic. By the time it reported failure, a small pipe and a gray plastic film can had been rendered temporarily invisible, and I was up out of my chair, halfway to the office door, and my fist was unobtrusively wrapped around the trackball of my TurboMouse, a solid plastic sphere about the size and weight of a cueball. I can only wonder what organ directed all these actions, since my brain was fully occupied in the fruitless search for harmless explanations. Spinal cord, maybe.

Silly, isn't it? I was planning my suicide . . . and ready to kill in self-defense. No wonder humans own the planet.

The knock came again as I reached the door. It was depressingly loud and firm. I could think of perhaps a dozen acquaintances or neighbors who might conceivably bang on my door in the small hours, but any of them would have done so softly, apologetically. They are, after all, all Canadians. There was a short list of maybe four friends who might feel entitled to whang away that assertively at that hour, secure in the certainty that I would be both awake and willing to fuck off for a while. But for one reason and another I was fairly certain none of them could be on-island just now.

That left only discouraging possibilities. A raid of some kind. Someone bringing the news that a loved one was dead or badly hurt. A neighbor who wanted to tell me my house was on fire. The first home invader in the history of Heron Island.

Number four was a joke; we did have a full-time RCMP officer on the island, Corporal McKenzie, but he'd never made an arrest. Numbers two or three would be bad news, but the kind I would *want* to open my door to. It was number one that had me hesitating at the threshold.

I had little to fear from a legitimate police raid. Nothing, really, except annoyance and brief indignity. My house and office were always scrupulously free of any seditious, proscribed, or obscene materials, My hard drive never contained anything remotely questionable whose encryption I did not trust absolutely. And the contents of the little gray plastic film can, while outstanding in quality, were of a quantity nobody could reasonably call anything but personal use. By a cheapskate. If part of your job description is pissing off the powerful in the public prints, you're wise to keep a tight ship at all times.

But one of the things this knock might be was a mistake. Heron Island is about half an hour from Vancouver. The drug squad, a right bunch of cowboys, loved to make surprise busts. The trouble was, they were notorious fuckups. You probably read about the time they kicked in the wrong door, and the twenty-year-old college student inside was unwise enough to be caught with a TV remote control in his hand that, in a certain light, looked not too much unlike some sort of Martian weapon; he had to be killed to ensure the safety of the officers. Who then learned that the guy they actually wanted lived next door, or rather, used to; he had moved six months earlier. If you missed that story, you must have heard about the squad that crashed their way into a house they had been surveilling continuously for days, were startled to find a child's birthday party in progress inside, and were forced to blow the family watchdog into hamburger, in front of a room full of horrified kids and terrified parents, for trying to protect them. There turned out to be no drugs or drug users present.

In both cases, an internal inquiry totally exonerated the cops of any improper actions.

If, thanks to some totally typical typo, it was those guys out there knocking on my door, I definitely did *not* want to open it with a weapon in my hand, even one as low tech as a plastic trackball.

But what if—as seemed more likely—it was some sort of nutbar out there? An insomniac Jehovah's Witless, say, or a tourist ripped on acid. Or a belligerent drunk, or the new boyfriend of an old girlfriend in search of karmic balance. In that case it might be better if I *didn't*, literally, drop the ball. I'm skinny, frail, and no fighter: any edge at all was welcome.

Most likely of all, of course, was the secret nightmare of any opinion columnist bright enough to get published: the disgruntled reader who decides to make his rebuttal in person, with a utensil. There is no opinion you could conceivably express, however innocuous, that won't piss off somebody, somewhere. It was comforting to be in Canada, where there are almost no handguns, despite everything the government can do to keep them out.

But that didn't mean that the guy who was even now knocking on my door for the third time wasn't doing so with the butt of a shotgun. Or the hilt of a butcher knife, the sweet spot of a Louisville Slugger, the handle of an axe, or for that matter the tip of a chainsaw. Maybe, I thought, I should forget my silly trackball and start thinking in terms of turning my half-liter can of Zippo fluid into a squeeze-operated flamethrower, or some speaker wire into a noose, or—

"Owww," whoever it was out there said. *"Cut it out."*

The voice was muffled; I could hear it at all only because he was speaking loudly. And the words were baffling, when I'd thought myself as confused as possible already. Cut it out? I was standing still, frozen with indecision—what the hell was it I was supposed to stop doing?

"Being so paranoid," he called.

I stood, if possible, stiller. A comedy voice, somewhere between Michael Jackson and a Mel Blanc cartoon character.

"You didn't used to be so suspicious."

That voice tickled at the edges of memory. Deep

memory. Twenty years? No. It felt like more. Thirty, maybe. Which would make it—

Oh wow. The trackball fell forgotten from my hand to the carpet. I opened my mouth—and hesitated, caught by a ridiculous dilemma. I thought I knew who he was, now . . . and for the life of me I couldn't recall his real name. Just what everybody used to call him, and I certainly wasn't about to use that. But screw names—how could it *possibly* be him out there? I wanted to fling open the door, and couldn't bring myself to touch the knob.

"It's me, all right, Slim."

I stepped back a pace. For the first time I began to wonder whether I was having my own first encounter with a dead person, like Susan's visit from her father.

"You didn't used to be this superstitious, either," he said.

My words sounded stupid to me even as they were leaving my mouth, but I couldn't seem to hold them back. "How do I know that's you?"

Silence for five seconds. Then: *"You never did the Bunny. But you* would *have."*

I gasped, and flipped on the outside light and flung open the door, and gaped like the cartoon character he sounded like, and still faintly resembled.

"Smelly," I cried. "Jesus Christ, you *are* alive."

No question it was him. He looked much the same, only balder—but far more significant, he smelled just as unbelievably, unforgettably horrible as ever. My eyes began to water.

"I wish I could say the same for you," he said. "My God, you're at the end of your rope."

I felt I should be offended, but couldn't work up the

energy. "How the hell could you possibly know that?" I demanded. "You just fucking got here."

He frowned and shook his head. "I'm going to have to fix you, first. And there's no *time*. But you're no use to me like this."

"Why would I want to be of use to you? Do I owe you something I'm not remembering? Look—" His name came back. "Look, Zandor, I ain't broken, and even if I was, I didn't ask to be fixed."

"I don't care. I need you to help me prevent the torture, rape, and butchery of an entire family," he said, and stepped into my office.

Flashback:
1967

St. William Joseph College
Olympia, New York
USA

1.

I felt like the Wandering Catholic.

Wandering Apostate, anyway. Wandering around the campus on the first Sunday of September 1967 and of my sophomore year, looking for my room. It wasn't where it was supposed to be. Or rather, it was where it was supposed to be, Dabland Hall, room 220—but there were two other guys' names on its door. And two guys with those names inside, already unpacked, totally uninterested in my dilemma.

As I said, it was Sunday. There was no one anywhere on campus to consult. And nothing for it but to wander the whole dorm, squinting at the 3x5 index card on every single damn door, looking for one that read *Russell Walker/Sean McSorley*. The only consolation was looking forward to seeing Sean, knowing what a meal he would make of this screwup. His sense of humor was almost Krassnerian. I knew he would have me laughing.

15

My faith wavered when I finished the whole dorm without finding either of our names.

Could I have missed a card? Certainly. Did I want to recanvass the building for it? Not a whole lot. Sighing deeply, I checked on my VW—still not broken into, still packed to the consistency of a rubber brick with my stuff—and trudged uphill to the other men's dorm, Nalligan Hall.

I never did find a card with my name or Sean's. But on the third floor, near the front, I found a door with no card. Instead there was an envelope affixed to it with Scotch tape, and my name, only, was written in ink on the envelope.

I pulled the envelope off the door, leaving a Scotch tape tail, and tried the knob. Locked. The envelope contained no keys. Just a brief note:

> Dear Russell,
> Please report to me before checking into your room. Your situation has changed.
>
> > Cordially yours,
> > Ivan Lefors,
> > Resident Advisor
> > Room 345

What the hell did that mean? Nothing pleasant, I suspected. My instincts have always been good.

"Sean's been drafted," Lefors told me.

"Oh *shit*."

He nodded. "That's exactly right." He was way too old to be in college. His bearing, his haircut, his dress, his room, *everything* screamed that he had, in the immediate past, been in one of the armed forces. I correctly assumed Vietnam. "He failed one too many courses last year, and last week the draft board pulled his deferment."

"Oh, the poor bastard—"

He nodded again.

"You don't understand," I said. "I hate to see anybody get shot at. But this is like they drafted Oscar Levant."

He looked pained, but said nothing.

Does it seem strange to you that I heard the news that way, that Sean didn't phone me? This was a long time ago. You wouldn't believe what long distance cost, back then. Sean had doubtless written me the news; for all I knew the letter was even now being delivered to my parents' house back in New Jersey.

I wanted to cry. Sean in the jungle was as unimaginable as Mr. Rogers buying smack. After a while I said, "So what happens now? Is there, like, a list of guys in the same boat, that I get to select a new roommate from?"

Now he looked constipated.

"Actually," he said reluctantly, "he's already been selected."

"The hell he has."

This time he looked nauseous. "Look, Russ, I'm going to ask you to help me out, here."

Now *I* started feeling nauseous. Any time the administration asks your help, it's time to change your name and move to someplace with no extradition. "Yeah? How?"

"I've looked over your record. You're an unusually tolerant man, do you know that?"

"As a matter of fact I do. Right now, I'm tolerating being dicked around when I should be unpacking in my new room . . . somewhere."

"The school needs an unusually tolerant man, just now,"

he said, ignoring my sarcasm. "I'm hoping you're that man."

I thought I saw light in the undergrowth. "Oh my God. They actually admitted a sixth Negro?"

He paled. "Uh, no."

I snorted. "Sorry—I got carried away there for a minute." Out of a student population approaching a thousand, exactly five students were black. All male. That's another clue how long ago this was.

"No, this is in regard to a student who's already enrolled here."

"Then what's this about—"

I broke off, blinded. The undergrowth had suddenly burst into flame.

"Jesus Christ. You want me to room with that crazy Serbo-Croatian. With *Smelly*. That's it, isn't it?"

He had gone from pale to brick red. "With Zandor Zudenigo, yes."

"Son of a *bitch*," I said. I couldn't even ask why me. He had already told me.

Zandor Zudenigo was a campus legend, and deserved to be. Not for his mathematical talent, which was rumored to be better than first rate, nor for his striking ugliness, which was of clock-stopping magnitude, nor even for his habit of wandering around the campus in pajamas, mumbling to himself and writing on an invisible blackboard. These things, by themselves, would have made him a colorful campus character, a figure of fun, a kind of mascot. But what promoted him from risible eccentric to worldclass whackadoo and hopeless outcast was his smell.

No. "Smell" doesn't begin to touch it. Even "stench" is inadequate. Another word is needed. Perhaps "reek," or "miasma," or possibly "fetor." You could have planted beans in his body odor. Some said it would show up on radar. Paint discolored as he walked past. Flies dropped from the sky behind him.

This elicited plenty of reaction, of course. But Smelly did not seem to realize it. If someone asked him why he didn't bathe, he simply stared, blank-faced, waiting for them to say something. If someone became offended enough to scream at him, he literally failed to notice, didn't even flinch. If someone got mad and punched him, he didn't seem to notice that, either: simply waited for the blows to stop, and then walked away as if nothing had happened. Or if necessary crawled.

Hell, in his way, the guy was as weird as *I* was.

"Okay," I said. "What's our goddam room number?"

It was a pleasure, watching Lefors's jaw drop.

How can I begin to convey to you just how *long* ago this was?

The Beatles were still together. They would always be together. They'd just performed "All You Need is Love" and "Hey Jude," live for the whole world, that July. Forget Altamont—*Woodstock* hadn't happened yet. Brian Epstein was dead, but Brian Jones was still alive. So was Che Guevara.

There was not a single footprint on the moon, and most adults believed there never would be. All educated people knew that the Cold War would, in our lifetimes, culminate in an apocalyptic nuclear exchange that would sterilize the planet. Some of us railed against it, some fought to prevent it, some accepted it, but none of us doubted it. Nobody, I mean nobody, anywhere, would have thought it conceivable that the Soviet Union might ever simply . . . stop. It wasn't possible enough to be the premise of a science fiction story.

Bobby and Rev. Dr. King were both still alive. Charlie Company had not saved My Lai. LBJ was president, and it was unimaginable that he would not run again. Nobody knew that Chicago cops were vicious thugs and Mayor Daley was a monster except black people who lived in Chicago. Paul Krassner had not yet coined the term "Yippies" for the people who would go there to protest the war.

You could smoke a cigarette just about anywhere except church or schoolroom. Nobody realized they minded it yet, and the dread dangers of sidestream smoke had not yet been faked. You could smoke on an airplane. No— here's how long ago it was: you could buy a plane ticket under any name you liked, with cash, and board without showing ID or passing a metal detector. The term "terrorist" was not yet commonly heard outside Israel.

That's how long ago it was for the world. Here's how long ago it was for *me*:

I was entering my sophomore year at St. William Joseph, a Catholic college run by the Marianite order in Olympia, a medium-sized town in northern New York state. Only my third year as a free human being. My parents still believed I was a Catholic. And a virgin.

I could still count my lovers on the fingers of one hand . . . and give the peace sign at the same time. I had been drinking alcohol for a little less than a year, smoking pot for six months. I'd never taken any other drug, and didn't expect to.

I wasn't sure whether I wanted to be a lawyer, an English teacher, or an anarchist. One of those.

Long time ago.

Maybe this will convey something. I basically had only two heros, at that time. Ed Sodakis, and Paul Krassner.

You've probably heard of Krassner. Youngest violinist ever to play Carnegie Hall, at age six . . . Lenny Bruce's roommate, uncredited editor of his autobiography . . . took acid with Groucho Marx. Publisher since 1958 of *The Realist*, an underground satirical journal dedicated to outraging as many people as possible, ideally to apoplexy.

He had in fact just that summer pulled off what was probably his greatest prank. A writer named Manchester had written a controversial book about the Kennedy clan, and their lawyers had managed to force the deletion of a few chapters before publication. *The Realist* ran a piece purporting to be some of the suppressed material. A dazed Jackie Kennedy is wandering around the plane, in search of a bathroom where she can wipe her husband's blood from her, when she opens the wrong door . . . and finds LBJ having carnal knowledge of the corpse, in an apparent attempt to make an entry wound look like an exit wound . . .

It's probably hard to imagine now, but back then if you merely said—in print—that the president of the United States had sex with the corpses of his enemies, some people got all upset. A shitstorm of rage descended on Krassner. There was some talk of having him nuked. He spent the next year on the lecture circuit, unapologetically reminding audience after outraged audience: "Who are we to judge? It may have been an act of love."

Anyway, that was one of my heros. The other was Ed Sodakis. Him I don't think you know.

In the Catholic all-boys high school Ed and I had attended, you were *required* to receive Holy Communion with the rest of your homeroom at Friday afternoon Mass. That meant that most of us spent Friday morning lined up for Confession. Terminal boredom, with the prospect of humiliation at the end of it, the only consolation being that the humiliation would be about as private as possible.

One particular Friday, the apprehension level spiked. A new priest, Father Anderson, had recently rejoined the faculty, after several years as a missionary in Kaohsiung, Taiwan. Rumor made the place sound worse than the Walled City of Hong Kong. Father Anderson himself looked just terrifying, bald and hatchet-faced, never smiling, with thunderclap eyebrows. Nobody wanted to get in his line for Confession, that morning; a Brother had to assign guys to it. Ed Sodakis was one of them. Until that day he had been, in the judgment of one and all, student and teacher alike, just another asshole. He had no particular rep, one way or another.

Then he stepped into Father Anderson's confessional, and became immortal.

Outside all went on as before; that is, nothing whatsoever went on. Pin-drop silence. Totally bored adolescent males fiddled with their neckties and silently struggled to think of anything interesting besides sexual fantasies, and of course there was nothing. Sound of grate sliding shut. The light above the left-hand side of the confessional went out. A student pushed aside the heavy curtain and exited, trying not to look relieved, and failing. Sound of a noisier grate sliding open on the right side. Silence resumed, for thirty eternal seconds . . . then was shattered

by the voice of Father Anderson. He screamed so loud
he required a full chest of air for each word.

"You . . . did . . . WHAT?"

The last word seemed to blow Ed from the confessional like a cannonball. The curtain couldn't get out of
his way fast enough, so he took it with him the first few
steps and then tossed it aside. His face was absolutely
expressionless, but the color of a ripe plum. In seconds
he had left the chapel.

The kid waiting his turn on the other side of Father
Anderson's closet emerged only seconds later, looked
around at us, and got in another line. We looked round at
each other in slow motion. Then a beehive buzz sprang
up, which the Brothers allowed to go on a little longer
than usual. Then everything returned to normal. Except
that nobody went into Father Anderson's confessional,
on either side. No Brother made them do so. A few minutes later he emerged, poker-faced, white as a sheet, and
left without even glancing at any of us. Five months later
he was killed in a car crash.

Ed, sensibly, never told anyone what it was he'd done.
Bribes, threats, and appeals to his compassion all failed. I
never saw him again after graduation, doubt I ever will.
But to this day I wonder what he confessed that morning.
And so, I imagine, does everybody else.

Anyway, that should give you a rough idea of how young
I was, that first day of sophomore year. My two heros
were Paul Krassner and Ed Sodakis. I was as ready as
anyone alive to meet and move in with Zandor Zudenigo.

2.

The room was about as isolated as a dorm room can be. It was at the far end of a hallway in the north wing of Nalligan, on the third or top floor. Next to it was not another room, but the stairwell. So, no neighbors on either side. And the room across the hall was not just uninhabited but uninhabitable: it had no door, and you could see fire damage inside.

I was not surprised at the remoteness of the place. By that time I could already smell him, through the closed door. Even though someone had wedged the hallway window open.

You probably think you have some conception of his smell, but you're wrong. You're thinking of very bad body odor with the volume turned all the way up. Smelly smelled *way* worse than that. Body odor was a component, to be thoroughly sure. Rank armpits, fetid groin, cheesey feet, unwashed undergarments, inadequately wiped ass, all were there. But they struggled to be noticed among so many stinks. Death itself was in there, faintly, coming and going, like when there's a dead rat inside the wall. So were spoiled milk, meat turned green, and rotting vegetables—in particular, rotten celery. But there was something else, something I couldn't identify. It was as bad as all the others, but worse, too, because it wasn't even organic. It was a chem lab, industrial plant kind of bad smell. The kind that would make a cat leave the room.

This was before I even opened the door. Standing in a well-ventilated hallway, outside a room he had inhabited for at most a matter of hours. I braced myself for something five times worse, unlocked the door, and walked in.

It was at least ten times worse.

It seemed to take a small effort to walk through, as though the air were Jell-O on the verge of setting. Part of the smell made the eyes water, but another part dried them, so they canceled out. Each breath had to be a conscious act; reflex refused to take in *this* air without constant confirmation that it was really okay. It is possible to totally isolate the nose and nasal passages from the act of respiration, but it usually takes years of yogic training to learn how. I reinvented the trick on the spot. It didn't help enough. It is possible, I learned to my dismay, to smell with your tongue. Tastebuds work even on air, and they have no off switch.

"Hi," I said, to be exhaling.

His appearance was less startling than his aroma, but not by much. He stood no taller than five eight or nine, and weighed close to three hundred pounds. He didn't seem to have shoulders. His skin looked like bread dough that wasn't going to rise. Facially, he looked like the fetus that would one day be Alfred Hitchock. With five-o'clock shadow.

"Hello, Slim," he said.

I stopped short, halfway to the obligatory handshake. I didn't want to; irrationally, I wanted to be a moving target for that smell. But I was struck by what he'd called me.

Physically I was the backwards of him. As I had since the sixth grade, I stood six two, and weighed maybe one forty-five. Fully dressed, after a long walk in the rain. "Slim" was what I had always secretly wished people would call me. But no one ever had. My actual nickname throughout high school had been "Rail." The printable one, anyway. Somehow, I'd managed to get through freshman year of college without picking up any nickname at all. But I knew my luck was due to run out.

"What do people call you?" I asked, as if I didn't know.

"Zudie, usually," he said, as if he didn't know. "But friends call me Zandor." He pronounced it not like *manned oar*, but like the last half of the name Alexander. For all I knew it was the Serbo-Croatian equivalent.

His voice made me think, *Tweety Bird has finally conquered the lisp*.

Something about his eyes caught my attention. Not the eyes themselves. They were ordinary, hazel, a bit moist. Nor was it the way they met mine steadily. This was 1967. A *lot* of people looked you square in the eye and didn't look away. It was the *way* his eyes looked at me.

They said that he forgave me.

In advance. For whatever. If I despised him for who he was, he would accept it. If I needed to be cruel to him to tolerate his presence, he was prepared to work with that. He was used to it. If I preferred to be polite to his face, then say cruel things about him behind his back, that was okay too. If I simply couldn't bear him, and had to go back and scream until I got assigned some other roommate, he wouldn't hold it against me.

I was very young. But even back then, I dimly sensed that it might be a worthwhile thing to know somebody who was good at forgiving. It was a skill I wanted to learn myself. And I'd probably never get a better student project.

So I unfroze, took that last couple of steps forward, and finished bringing my hand up into handshake range. My nose wanted me to grimace, but I suppresed it. "Pleased to meet you, Zandor."

"Pleased to meet you, Russell." We shook.

Go for it. "I think I like Slim better, actually." His hand didn't *feel* particularly slimy, or greasy, or encrusted with anything. His grip was not strong or aggressive, but neither was it weak or submissive. His fingers were a bit on the thick side. His skin was very warm.

"Sure." He broke the handshake, stepped back, and gestured. "Look, Slim, I'm open to discussion, but I thought we both might be more comfortable with things arranged *this* way. What do you think?"

For the first time I took in the room. It was almost a generic dorm room. A rectangular box the approximate dimensions of a cargo container. Total contents: two single beds (thin mattress on metal spring frame), two maple desks with matching maple chair, a desk lamp and a short maple bookshelf on the wall above, and two maple dressers. The only thing that kept it from being exactly like every other one in the building was that since it was a corner room, it had windows on *two* walls.

But Smelly—I was determined to call him Zandor, but I already doubted I would ever think of him as anything but Smelly—had changed the room even more, by rearranging the furniture. The standard pattern was that, as you came in the door you passed first a pair of closets on either side, each capacious enough to hold three sports coats at once, then a dresser on either side, and then a desk on either side, and then a bed on either side, and then your nose hit the window.

Smelly had moved things. As you came in, there was a bed on the left—clearly his, already made, with some of his stuff piled on it—and on the right, a dresser that was just as plainly his. Then at the foot of his bed, there was nothing but space, until you reached a dresser at the far end of the room. Just to the right of it was the other bed, turned sideways, its head end flush up against the wall on the right. This put it right up against the radiator that was the room's principal source of heat, and right below the main window. Along the right-hand wall, between the bed and Smelly's dresser, were the two desks facing each other below the second window.

The net effect was that my clothes would be as far as possible from his—and the places where I'd be spending most of time, my bed and desk, were both within the cross-breeze that would be generated if we were to leave both windows slightly open at all times. As they were now. That could get chilly in winter, but my bed, at least, was right next to the radiator. I could see that on cold nights I'd be warm in that bed, with plenty of air circulation just above me.

It was a most thoughtful and practical arrangement. Given that one of us stank like Death in a garbage can. And it had been most tactful of him to just go ahead and do it before I arrived, and present it as a fait accompli neither of us needed to comment on in any detail. "Looks good to me, Sm . . . Zandor," I said. "Aesthetically satisfying." Think of a reason why it's good *other than* how it will minimize his stench. "Uh—"

"And we'll both get sunlight at our desks."

"Right!" I blinked. "Hey, how did you know my name was Russell? There's no name card on the door."

He shrugged, and took that steady gaze away from me for the first time since I'd come in the door. "Look, there's one other thing I want to get clear from the start."

Oh shit. I braced myself. This was the part where he was going to tell me what he considered the law, and under what circumstances he would be laying it down. The house rules, his version. "What's that, man?"

Those fearless eyes locked on me again. "I'm pretty square."

"Oh hey, look—"

"Let me finish, okay? I don't drink, or smoke, I don't go out much, I like music you've never heard of, and I study all the time. But I don't expect the same of you. You can drink whatever you want in here as long as you don't puke on my part of the room. You can smoke as much as you want. You can smoke as much *pot* as you want, or take any drugs you like, as long as you never ever leave anything illegal in my part of the room. The only place I draw the line is: no parties in this room, and no sneaking girls in here. Can you live with that?"

"What kind of music?"

"Ray Charles."

I felt myself starting to grin. "Which do you prefer? The Atlantic sides, or the new Columbia stuff?"

His turn to blink. "Well, they're both great. But my favorite is his big band instrumental stuff."

Big grin now. "Really? Never heard any."

He smiled back. "Then we're going to have to hook your stereo up. Mine died on the trip."

On the way out to the car, and all the way back again, I kept intercepting looks, from friends and strangers alike. First they'd gape comically, at the sight of Smelly and me going by together with our arms full, obviously room-mates. Then they'd throw me a look of sympathy, or pity, or amusement, depending on their disposition. Then when my own expression told them I didn't agree I was a victim, thank you very much, they'd get mad at me.

Ray Charles's *My Kind of Jazz* albums turned out to be incredible.

It didn't take long for word to get around campus that I not only had drawn old Smelly for a rooms, *I didn't mind.* I had always been considered weird in the extreme . . . but this immediately weeded even my oddball circle of friends down by a good twenty percent.

I regarded it as something of an achievement. The people I hung out with, loosely known as the Boot and Buskin Gang, were a hard bunch to shock. They were the ones who usually did the shocking. Theater people. Poets. Philosophers. Musicians. Behavior that had been deemed borderline acceptable if not necessarily admirable, the previous year, had included soft drug dealing, gross sacrilege, treason, sexual relationships involving odd numbers of participants, pipe-smoking (by a female), chastity (by a male), blatant plagiarism, being kept by a forty-five-year-old divorcee with two kids who called you Uncle Bob, semipro porno work, pro vandalism, pig drunkenness, shoplifting food, reading poetry aloud, nervous collapse, attempted suicide, and even voting Republican. It was a point of honor with my crowd to be unshockable, nonjudgmental. Most of us would rather have lost our pants than our cool in public.

But coolness lives in the forebrain, and aversion to morbid stench lies further back, involves neural circuits that were laid down millennia before the forebrain evolved. Even the hippest had trouble dealing with Smelly. And some of them, it developed, had a problem with me because I didn't have a problem with him.

"Man, I don't care," Slinky John Walton said loudly in the dining hall, a few days later, "Understanding is far out and everything—but if you can live in the same room with that guy and not kill him, you're as sick as he is."

I sighed. "Slinks, you of all pots have no business criticizing how other kettles choose to live their lives." Slinky John wore, at all times, a wrinkled black ankle-length coat beneath which lurked God knew what, a Mephistophelean black beard with greased mustachios, and a black eye patch which kept moving from eye to eye. He was an anarchist and saw no reason to hide it. Nobody would have been much surprised if he had reached into that coat one day and pulled out a cartoon anarchist's bomb, a black ball with a lit fuse sticking out, and hurled it at some politician's passing motorcade. This year he had added to his costume a button, pinned to his lapel, which he'd obviously made himself by crudely painting over some other slogan and hand-lettering his own message. It now read, "GO LEMMINGS, GO!"

"There's a difference between healthy, therapeutic weirdness and pathology," he said stiffly.

"Nice to see you and Dean Dizzy agree on something," Bill Doane said.

"Fuck you," he riposted, and I knew Bill had reached him with that shot. Slinky John and Sidney Disraeli, our universally despised Dean of Men, had tangled more than once over the subject of decorum, and would again.

"You think you're man enough?" Bill said. He was a big shambling rawboned guy with a red beard as big as his head, curly red ringlets of hair down to the base of his shoulder blades, and a booming laugh. He and Slinky John were close friends.

"I think I'm right, and Russell has gone over the edge," Slinks insisted. "Granted, I frighten small children and some adults. But I do not cause plants to wither, small birds to fall from the sky, and strong men to weep. Russell's roommate does."

"I hate to admit it, Russ, but he has a point," Bill said. "I tried talking to Smelly, once. You know, stand upwind, breathe in through my mouth, out through my nose. I gave him ten minutes; that was all I could take. Forget it. Cat wasn't a bad conversationalist, really—but rancid, man."

"A walking pestilence," Slinky John said. "No, a waddling pestilence."

"Do you stop noticing after a while?" Bill asked. "I've had that happen with some bad smells, that's why I gave him ten minutes. But Jesus, it never got any better."

I shrugged. "You do get used to it . . . a little, anyway.

And I get a good breeze in there. I bought a fan. And look, you guys remember what I roomed with *last* year, right? Anything's an improvement over the Drink Tank." My freshman year roommate, Brian "Tank" Sherman, had been a *major* asshole. He'd once drugged my beer at a clandestine room party so that he and a bunch of his jock friends could cut off my long hair and beard while I snored. Let's say it strained a relationship which had never been good.

"Fuck all that," Slinky John said. "I want to know how you can stand living with a *Stink* Tank."

I glanced quickly around the dining hall, then gestured Slinky and Bill closer and lowered my voice. "Listen, I brought a little something from home. Panama Red."

"Jesus," Slinky said. Bill said nothing, but a broad smile appeared in the midst of his beard. A fair amount of the time we'd spent together in freshman year had been in fruitless search for a local connection.

That's how long ago this was. At a medium-size college, there were fewer than a dozen heads, and no connection. Not even in town; there weren't enough jazz musicians to support one. We had to make do with whatever we could bring from home. And, we had to be discreet to a degree probably unimaginable today: pot was considered a narcotic, then——both legally and culturally—and possession of one joint could draw you a class A felony indictment if the DA was politically ambitious.

"So what do you say, John?" I went on. "Shall we go to your room and do some up?"

He flinched. "Oh man, not *there*—are you nuts?"

"Why not? Your roommate's cool, isn't he?"

"Lukewarm—but he's not the problem, man, it's

everybody else. Even if we put a towel under the door, sure as hell somebody would rat us out."

"Ah," I said. "We can't burn a bone in your place . . . because people would smell it. Is that the problem?"

"Well, sure they'd—" he said, and broke off.

"So I guess we'll have to go back to *my* place, then," I said.

Bill's broad smile became a broad grin.

"Holy shit," Slinky John breathed.

So we went back to my place, heaved the sticky window all the way up, and between the isolation of the room, and the tendency of all passersby to voluntarily stop smelling when near it, we did up a couple of fatties without attracting the slightest attention. By the time Zandor got back from dinner, Slinky and Bill were ready to be polite to him.

They didn't get much chance, though. As soon as he saw I had company, he said he had to go right back out and do some studying at the library.

"Zandor?" I said quickly, before he could make his escape. "Look . . . is it cool with you that we smoked in here? I figured, the window's open, and . . ." I trailed off, unable to find a diplomatic way to say, *and I thought your stink would mask ours*. "It's your house too, man. I won't get high here if you have a problem with it."

He looked at me without blinking for several seconds. Then he made a little smile and said, "Slim, as long as you don't leave any of it in my part of the room, I'm just fine with it. I told you that already."

I relaxed slightly. He hadn't just said it; he'd meant it.

"You want some?" Slinky John asked him.

"Thanks for offering, maybe another time," Smelly said, and fled.

As soon as he was out of earshot, we all broke out in stoned giggles.

Bill, who happened to be holding the roach, relit it, and passed it to me. " 'Slim,' huh?" he said reflectively, and looked me over carefully. I held my breath. Well, I was already holding it, but you know what I mean.

He released his own. "I like that. Slim Walker. Cool."

I mentally blessed my malodorous roommate. "I guess." Like I didn't care one way or another.

Slinky John snorted. "Don't bogart that joint, Slim."

"Wow, man," Bill said a moment later. "I can actually *see* his smell."

Slinky lost his toke and coughed. "Holy shit," he managed to croak, "Me too. Pale green, right?"

"Like a zero gravity lava lamp."

By golly, they were right. "It's actually a little easier to take, that way," I said.

"You know, Slim's right," Bill said. "It's not so bad, *seeing* it."

After several seconds, Slinky John said, "True—but hearing his face was a little hard to take," and all three of us got the giggles.

Within a few days, most of the people whose opinion I cared about had managed to find at least a little compassion and tolerance for Smelly in their hearts, and lungs. And the rest stayed as far away as if a restraining order were in place, which suited me fine. Privacy is a rare and sweet commodity in a men's dorm. It was worth a little stink to have peace and quiet.

3.

In a movie, Zandor Zudenigo and I would have gradually but steadily become good friends. I'm honestly not even sure we ever managed to became good *acquaintances*. Maybe by the end of that year we had become good strangers.

He was just too weird to befriend. And I speak as one with a higher than normal tolerance for weirdness. He was away a lot, and when he was there he rarely spoke voluntarily, and when he did it was often in monosyllables or grunts—but there was more to it than that.

It reminded me of Gertrude Stein's famous crack about Oakland: "There's no *there*, there." You couldn't get a purchase on him; it was like trying to make a snowman out of bubbles.

Hundreds of times I found myself wondering what was going on behind those moist squinting eyes of his. Not once did I ever have a clue. I not only never knew what he was thinking, I rarely knew even in the most general terms what he was thinking *about*. In freshman year I had been dismayed to discover that the roommate relationship could enforce a high degree of intimacy even with someone you couldn't stand. Now I was a little startled to realize how little intimacy it could provide even with someone you kind of liked.

And I did kind of like him. He was low maintenance. He had a knack for erasing himself. I'd forget he was in the room, or fail to notice when he arrived. His shoes didn't seem to produce footsteps. His clothes didn't rustle when he moved. He never seemed to be in my way, or make sudden or unexpected moves in my field of vision. He never complained about anything I did, and seldom did anything that bothered me. He didn't seem to get drunk, depressed, high, homesick, or horny. Or bored, even when he was just staring at the wall. Unlike his miserable predecessor Tank Sherman, he never played practical jokes, or said cruel things, or threw tantrums, or vomited on my bed.

His *only* downside as a roommate, really, was that our room reeked so badly it made no perceptible difference whether he was present or not. Noseplugs, some incense, and I learned to handle it.

One thing I noticed. Math majors frequently asked me what it was like to be his roommate. Math *professors*, too, even. They always listened carefully to whatever I said, and then they usually just nodded and thanked me and walked away. It happened often enough to make me wonder if maybe the reason I couldn't seem to connect with whatever he had going on behind his eyes was simply that I was too dumb and innumerate to understand it.

For whatever reasons, connection was impossible. I gave up trying early, probably in the first day or two I knew him. And I'm not sure I can explain exactly why. It wasn't that he discouraged conversation, exactly. You would start to say something to him, and as the very first syllable left your lips he was already looking your way, giving you his full attention, and somehow you found yourself reviewing what you'd meant to say, and deciding it was dumb. Or trivial. Or shallow. Or something. So all that ended up coming out of your mouth was a sigh. And by the time you had patted your remark into acceptable form, you no longer had his attention, and the moment was seconds past.

If I've given the impression that Smelly himself never spoke, that's not strictly true. He did say things occasionally. Just seldom, and as economically as possible.

I once saw him stop a riot with a two-sentence telephone call, for instance. No shit.

It was the year when, all across North America, young men with long hair, beards, and no girlfriend somehow simultaneously decided, like scattered lemmings marching to separate seas, to band together and take over their campus's library building. It was generally agreed that this would shorten the Vietnam War. Also, it was as much fun as a panty raid, but you *didn't* have to feel like a total jackass.

There was nothing like an official SDS chapter at Saint Billy Joe; the administration would never have permitted anything so radical. But that year our campus longhair supply finally reached critical mass—fifty or so. And so one sunny fall day, the same sort of migratory instinct that brings rural young men with mullet-head haircuts into 7-Elevens with cut-rate pistols led those fifty urban young men with Buffalo Bill haircuts, and two or three of the more adventurous girls, to march on the Chaminade Memorial Library together with guitars and antiwar banners and a pound of purported Acupulco Gold. They tried to set an American flag on fire in front of the main doors, and though they failed, they did manage to literally raise a stink, and the word spread round campus *like* fire. A crowd materialized in time to see the intrepid demonstrators announce that they were Liberating the Library, then disappear inside the building. Everyone backed off about half a football field, in case of gunplay or an air strike, and began taking sides.

I was one of them. The spectators, not the demonstrators. I was as opposed to the war as anyone my age—even though I knew for certain the draft would never get me. But in the first place I had never voluntarily joined anything in my life. And in the second place I could not for the life of me imagine what good it would do to capture books.

Still, I was definitely in the half of the crowd that was applauding the demonstrators. Over the next ten minutes or so the building slowly emptied of non-demonstrators—students, faculty and staff—adding to the crowd. Those who chose to stick around and watch events unfold also seemed to split about evenly between pro and anti. Arguments began. Volumes were raised. Immoderate language was heard. Campus Security showed up, raising the crowd's density and lowering its average intelligence; the arguments became less intellectual in character. I remained an observer, present but passive, uninvolved.

Suddenly I remembered that Smelly usually spent time in the library at this time of day, when it was least populated. I had not seen him come out. By now the library windows were mostly either broken or full of gleeful freaks hanging banners with defiant slogans on them. I scanned them anyway.

And saw him. At a window on the second of three floors. He was in some office, talking on the phone, and looking intently out the window at us all.

No. Past us.

I glanced behind me and saw nothing remarkable, at least in that context. But Smelly was still staring out at the campus and frowning as ferociously as if something were there.

Then something was, and suddenly I wasn't having fun anymore. A group of guys came into view from behind the chem building, heading our way, and I knew at first glance it was Easy Company.

It is a clue to their intelligence and their philosophical orientation that they chose to name themselves after a comic book about a combat unit. (*Sgt. Rock* of Easy Company, a DC comic written by Robert Kanigher and drawn by the great Joe Kubert.) They were a pack of thugs, archconservative upperclassmen, most of them either engineering majors or jocks. They fervently supported the Vietnam War, almost enough to enlist, and found everything about the Age of Aquarius offensive, and liked to express their displeasure by beating the mortal shit out of any longhair they could manage to corner alone in a dark corner of the campus. Good Americans.

This was the first time they were coming out in the open, in broad daylight, where they could be identified.

But I knew it was them the moment I saw them. There were something like twenty of them. They *looked* like I'd pictured Easy Company: big, fit, smug, arrogant, and mean. I knew a couple by name, and wasn't surprised to see them there. Since they did not have their prey outnumbered twenty to one, this time, they had brought utensils to help shape the flow of discourse. Axe handle. Tire iron. Brass knuckles. Louisville Slugger. Crowbar. Car antenna. Like that.

I glanced back at the library and noticed Smelly still in that upstairs window, just hanging up the phone. I waved to get his attention, but couldn't seem to catch his eye.

I turned back to Easy Company. Even Campus Security had noticed the approach of a heavily armed mob looking for trouble. But unlike the shouted arguments they'd been having with other bystanders, the discussion they were now having with Easy Company was muted, damn near chummy.

With a sinking feeling I looked back at the library again. Except for Smelly upstairs, the demonstrators seemed oblivious to their doom—to everything but how much fun they were having. Several were leaning out of various first floor windows, hanging banners, bellowing unintelligible things through a bullhorn, throwing Frisbees and leaflets to girls, having a swell time. Nobody was guarding the entrance. They'd settled for chaining the two big glass doors shut, overlooking the existence of things like crowbars and baseball bats and people disposed to use them in defense of the sacred honor of a library. I looked for Smelly, was relieved to see he was gone from the window. I hoped he was smart enough to be looking for a good place to hide.

A few minutes later, Easy Company finished their palaver with the authorities and walked past me on either side, on their way to the library a few hundred yards distant. I looked hastily around. Not one Campus Security officer in sight. Maybe they'd all been beamed up to the mothership.

I felt a powerful impulse to yell, "Hey! Assholes!" at the backs of Easy Company, as loud and challengingly as I could. They would stop their advance at least briefly and turn around to look at me. The goofballs in the library would hear, look, and be warned. Then they'd have a minute or two to prepare themselves, or flee out the back way, while Easy Company were busy kicking the mortal shit out of me. I thought of a very persuasive reason not to call out, which I can't seem to call to mind just now. The goon squad was a hundred yards from the building. Fifty—

Five men came walking around the corner of the building. They didn't seem to be in any hurry, but they covered ground fast. They stopped in front of the library doors, spaced themselves a few feet apart, and folded their arms across their chests.

All five of St. William Joseph's black students.

Easy Company, startled and nonplussed, milled to a stop.

The man in the middle of the five, a giant named Charlie Sanders, shook his Afro from side to side slowly, so that he met each pair of vigilante eyes at least briefly. In a voice that was gentle and surprisingly high pitched, yet carried clearly, he said, "No you don't, either."

Easy Company looked at one another. They had the black guys outnumbered four to one, with hundreds more white people watching. They were nearly all heavily armed, and the black guys were showing only hands. On the other hand, you could see rednecks deciding, that didn't mean they were unarmed. All Negros carried knives, right?

Wheels turned. You could almost smell the smoke of thought. At least one of the five black students was known to be a goddam *ballet dancer*, for Chrissake. Then again, the son of a bitch *did* have thighs like Captain America. Arms too. Another was a nerd . . . but nerds could sometimes be tricky little bastards. All five appeared to be carved from blocks of obsidian.

One of the most overlooked and underappreciated details of the Sixties, I believe, is that a baseball bat or tire iron is vastly less effective against a man with an Afro.

A few of the goon squad tried to open a dialogue, but were all unsuccessful. Charlie and his friends didn't seem aware of their existence any more. Or inclined to move away from the doorway anytime today.

Demonstrators had finally noticed the storm gathering at the portal, and began to shout various helpful things down from nearby windows. The thugs began to realize they were vulnerable to attack from overhead as long as they stood there.

It didn't happen all at once, but over the next little while, each of the members of Easy Company recalled pressing business in another part of the forest, and within a minute or two there didn't seem to be any of them left.

Nobody ever did find out how the 'Fro Five, as Bill Doane named them, had heard of the incipient massacre. Nor did anyone have a clue, or even a plausible theory, about why they decided to put themselves on the line to prevent it. Nobody white had the stones to ask, and nobody black was talking.

I asked. For all the good it did me.

That night, when Smelly got back to the room, I said, "You phoned Charlie, didn't you?"

He sat down at his desk and bent to get a Coke. He drank the stuff literally by the crate, at room temperature. He got a bottle, used a drawer handle to pop the cap off, and took a long gulp. I figured he was stalling. But after the belch, he said, "Yes."

His admission took me slightly aback. I'd expected him to lie, or at least duck and weave a little first. I wanted to ask why he'd done it, but the question suddenly seemed silly. He'd done it because it was the right thing to do. What I really wanted to know was—

Because I was hastily thumbing through the script trying to catch up, what I blurted out was, "How?"

As the word left my mouth I knew he would now say *How what?* and I would say *How did you know?* and he would say *How did I know what?* and I would say *How did you know Easy Company was coming?* and he would say *I saw them,* and I would say *How did you see them through a solid building?* and he would—

"I just knew," he said.

"You smelled them coming," I said, and then wished I could cut out my tongue. "I'm sorry, man, I didn't mean that the way it sounds." Yeah, and my vocal cords, too.

"If you're Serbian, and you were born in Croatia, you learn to smell violence coming, yes." This was so long ago, I had no idea what he was talking about—but I got the gist, and it did seem to explain things, sort of. He turned away, set the Coke down on his desk, sat down, opened a text and began studying. It was the first time I could ever recall him voluntarily coming any closer than ten feet from the nearest person.

So I did the same. Sat right beside him at my own desk, and opened a textbook. It was a kind of penance. Through some yoga technique I invented on the spot out of sheer necessity, I was able to make the eye on the side away from him do all the watering. After a few silent minutes, he made a long arm and opened the window a little more, and it helped. I think we kept it up for over an hour.

The next time I spoke was just before we turned the lights out for the night. "How did you know Charlie Sanders' phone number?"

"There was a campus directory in that office."

"Ah." We clicked our bed lights out.

Odd, I thought. Each floor in every dorm had a single payphone, hanging on the wall just outside the RA's room. There was indeed a college-published directory of all of them widely available. But to use it, Smelly would have had to know just what floor of which dorm Charlie lived on. "Hey, Zandor?"

His answer was a snore. I gave up and went to sleep and it wasn't until I was alone in the john brushing my teeth the next morning that I thought, *Smelly doesn't snore.*

The second question, why Charlie and his friends had done what they did in response to Smelly's call, I asked Charlie the next day, when I found him alone in the cafeteria. He looked at me in silence for ten or fifteen seconds, and then changed the subject.

That happened to me a lot when I tried to talk with black people in those days. Come to think, it still does, sometimes.

That very evening, however, the whole subject was driven right out of my head for good, along with any other thoughts that might have been lurking in there. An incalculable number of thoughts deserted nearly a thousand heads in Olympia that night. Every thought but one, really.

For that was the night the Bunny walked into Wanda's Rest, and into legend.

4.

Wanda's Rest had been, by all accounts, one of the best bordellos in the state of New York—a remarkable boast—when the Society of Mary of Geneva got a terrific deal on the hundred acre parcel just up the hill and built a large Catholic college on it, back in the late 'Forties.

Wanda was a realist, and had many powerful friends, including more than one whose collar was worn backwards. Negotiations were undertaken; conditions were sworn to; an accommodation was reached. The upstairs business was shut down forever. The bar downstairs became the whole business. It was the only bar remotely within walking distance of the college, and it was agreed that no other bar would ever be granted a license near there.

The change suited nearly everybody, really. A monopoly bar just down the hill from a large college is, oddly enough, *more* lucrative than a good brothel, so Wanda was content. Her girls were much happier selling beer than themselves. And the powerful people who now would have to stop coming to Wanda's were, if the truth be known, getting just a bit long in the tooth to keep up a reputation in a whorehouse anyway.

By 1967, just about the only lingering clue as to the previous nature of Wanda's Rest was that every one of Wanda's employees and staff was a hard-boiled softhearted woman in her fifties, who took drunken college boys absolutely in stride. Contrary to what a cynic might expect, not once was it ever even rumored that one of Wanda's gals had reverted to her former ways, even for a night. I'm sure it would have been hugely lucrative, and now that I'm in my fifties myself I begin to see how appealing some of us brash cute shit-faced randy boys could have been. But Wanda had given the bishop and the mayor her word, and Wanda could make a cage full of lions leave a fresh steak alone if she wanted to.

So for the hundreds of desperate lonely yearning bursting young testosterone slaves who passed through Wanda's door every Friday and Saturday night, their only faint hope of sexual relief—dream more than hope, really—was virgin Catholic girls. Classmates, who already knew exactly what jerks they were, and furthermore were being looked out for by uncannily wise barmaids and waitresses. Hope springs eternal within the human pants, of course. But I'd have to say that the underlying mood in Wanda's on any given weekend evening was a blend of manic optimism and maudlin despair, and the sexual tension was always thick enough to sink pitons into.

A lineup of the most desperate guys would hover along

the bar just inside the door. (Bill Doane called the process by which this line sorted itself out "peckering order.") It was exactly like a line of taxis waiting outside the terminal door at the airport. *Climb aboard, dear lady, I will be giving you a most particularly enjoyable ride.* Each time a girl came in the door, whoever was first in line would leave the bar and go hit on her. "My name's Jack, and you're the prettiest girl to come through that door all night—can I buy you a drink?" Something over ninety-five percent of the time, he would be shot down, and would slink to the tail of the line, while the girl went on to join her girlfriends in the back room. Once in a long while she would nod, and they would stop briefly to collect drinks and then head for the back room together.

It could have been any one of us. A junior named Fred Speciale happened to be the guy Fate selected to be on deck at Wanda's Rest, the November night the Bunny walked in for the first time.

She was unremarkable in Fred's opinion. Average height and weight. Her body looked okay, though it was hard to be sure with a winter coat over it. Blonde hair, long and straight, caught back in a ponytail. Her face was quite nice, beautiful in a way, and missed being pretty only because of the strange expression on it. She looked like somebody brave reporting for her mammography. She stood just inside the door and scoped the room, dubiously.

As long as they weren't actively vomiting or brandishing a knife, it was all the same to Fred. Baring his teeth, hoping against hope as always, he approached her. Guys just after him in line monitored his progress with a mild professional interest. "Hi. I'm Ace Speciale, and you're the best-looking woman to come in that door all night. May I buy you a drink?"

She looked him square in the eye, unsmiling. "No," she said, in a voice that carried to the end of the bar, "but you can fuck me."

And before he knew it she was leading him by his necktie out to the parking lot, and directly into the back seat of a car, where without preamble or foreplay of any kind she pulled down both their pants and fucked him three times in a row without giving him a chance to lose his erection in between.

At some point he found himself lying on gravel with his pants down. She had pushed him off her and out of the car. He saw her get out, pull up her pants, and zip them up. "Jesus," he croaked, "that was incredible." She tossed a large sodden wad of kleenex to the ground beside him, stepped over him without a glance, and walked back into the bar on unshaky legs.

Fred gave thought to lying there until he died, but his ass was cold. He managed to climb up the open car door until he was on his feet, pulled his own pants up, and set off for Wanda's front door, tacking a little against a sudden wind. By the time he got there, the girl—it suddenly came to him that he did not have even a first name for her—was already coming back out again, leading Tommy Flaherty by *his* necktie this time. She ignored Fred as she passed him.

She fucked twenty-three guys that night.

At some point after the first dozen or so, old Wanda herself, a slim redhead pushing seventy, came out to talk to her. They walked off to a corner of the parking lot together and spoke in low voices for maybe five minutes.

Then Wanda went back inside, and the guy whose turn it was went back inside, and the marathon resumed.

Of the twenty-three, it later turned out that seven had thought to ask her name. None had gotten even a first name out of her. By the time Wanda's closed that night, she was known to everyone present as the Bunny.

By lunchtime next day, every single person on the campus—male or female—was either talking or thinking about the Bunny.

Everybody had an opinion, even if they kept it to themselves. *Nobody* had fact one. Attempts to elicit a useful description of her, from the almost two dozen closest witnesses, proved largely frustrating. No clear consensus could be reached on any individual feature of her face, which didn't surprise any of the girls much. But they found it baffling that nobody who'd been with her in that humid back seat could positively state even the simplest basic parameters of her body—breast size, ass size, waist-to-hip ratio, thigh flab, quantity and placement of hair—with any degree of confidence . . . *except* for one specific body part, about which each of the twenty-three proved capable of writing sonnets. Even those who had actually had some authentic previous sexual experience (everyone claimed to) agreed hers was in a class by itself.

One in particular, Eddie Faulkner, was such a notorious cocksman he was comfortable admitting his own unique experience—at least to us guys. "Fellas, I was so damn drunk, and tell the truth, put off a little, I went limp before I could get it in. Didn't make the least bit of difference. I swear to God it sucked me inside—*thwppp!*—and wrung me out *twice* before I even had a chance to think of something sexy to think about. You ever want a diamond dildo, give her one made of coal."

"I was next-to-last man in," Bobby Joe Innis agreed, "and even by then, she could have made the batteries fly out of a flashlight." Suddenly his expression was strange, almost sad. "Funniest thing though. Just about the time she had me thrashing and squealing like a throat-cut dog, I happened to open my eyes and see her face, and it was like she was alone in the gymnasium, doing jumping jacks."

All around campus, guys met each others' eyes, and then looked away. And then they began to talk loudly to one another. Some spoke a lot of words, and some only a few short ones. But all of them were spoken with a curled lip, and what they all boiled down to was, *Eww—gross*. Guys who had girlfriends said it most emphatically, especially if their girlfriend was present. But the rest of us, too, felt an odd need to reassure one another of how disgusted and repulsed we were by the Bunny's conduct, what an incredible skanky pig we considered her to be. We made cruel and stupid jokes about her, and about the twenty-three losers who had disgraced themselves by consorting with her. God, how desperate could you *be*?

And then we all made our excuses, went back to our rooms, and spent long periods of time looking at ourselves in the mirror, frowning.

The Bunny had appeared on a Friday. Needless to say, the following night the line to get into Wanda's Rest stretched around the building and two blocks back up the hill.

Fistfights occurred over place in line before anyone even knew for sure she would reappear that night. When she arrived, a little after nine, three guys stepped forward simultaneously and said in chorus, "Hi, can I buy you a drink?"

"No, but I'll fuck you, you and you, in that order," she said, then took her first choice by the necktie and led him back out the door to the parking lot.

The place went nuts. Wanda had to come out from her office in back and restore order. The shotgun she held casually down at her side helped. She required a line to form, of those interested in visiting the parking lot with the Bunny, and decreed that anyone leaving the line lost his spot, and anyone cutting in was 86'd forever.

That night the Bunny accommodated thirty-seven guys. By the third man she had dispensed with the social formality of coming back in the bar each time to get the next one. It became more like waiting in the confession line: it was your turn when the guy before you came back.

Except that now he had a goofy grin on his face, and walked funny.

The Bunny established two rules.

First: no voyeurs. She kept her car parked around behind Wanda's, and passed the word that if she ever saw so much as a single face peek around the corner, she would drive away and never return. One or two clowns naturally tried to get away with it, but found themselves significantly hampered by having the living shit kicked out of them by a vigilante squad.

Rule two: no oral sex. In either direction. In extreme cases of wagging wand she would, reluctantly, offer limited manual assistance for as long as thirty seconds. After that, they said, you were on your own.

It will not surprise you that no one ever admitted to impotence. But I think that was the simple truth. That *is* a bit hard to believe . . . but if anyone *had* failed conclusively, I think she would have kicked him out of the car well before his five minutes were up. That never happened once.

All part of her legend.

She did not return on Sunday night. It didn't surprise anyone much; Wanda's bartenders, all former professionals, had assured us that nobody could sustain that kind of pace three nights in a row. Much beer was consumed in sorrow nonetheless.

She did not return on Monday night. Or any subsequent weeknight. By Wednesday everyone understood and reluctantly accepted that the Bunny was a strictly weekend phenomenon.

The next Friday, the crowd around Wanda's was so thick and intense it was difficult to see the building, and the line stretched all the way back up the hill.

The Bunny showed up at 8:20, this time, and took on fifty-two guys. Someone worked the math, and reported she had it down to an average of five minutes a man.

The next night, she only managed forty-six. The cops showed up at around ten, and her private negotiations with them used up a whole hour, while the men of St. William Joseph waited inside in wild impatience.

She again failed to show on Sunday night. But there was a related incident. A lot of guys had showed up purely on the hope that she might change the pattern this week. When she didn't show, they became surly and frustrated. So they were feeling territorial when some guys showed up from another college, ten miles away, drawn by rumor. The riot squad had to be dispatched, and the emergency room was full that night.

Next Friday night, I found myself getting ready to take a stroll down to Wanda's.

It had taken me that long to fold.

I can't tell you how many hours I devoted to debating whether or not to bang the Bunny. And there were countless others like me in both men's dorms. The antinomy was exquisitely agonizing for a young man.

It will be hard for you to grasp, but our problem was *not* fear that she might be diseased. This was 1967. The Sexual Revolution was just dawning. None of us even knew anyone who might know someone who had ever had a venereal disease. We had certainly heard about them—and what we had heard was that they could be totally cured with a simple series of shots. That long ago, it was true. It did not bother anyone much at all that the Bunny flatly refused to let anybody use a rubber; if anything the quirk was endearing.

The dilemma was more than just a matter of taste, too—although that too was clearly a factor.

What it came down to for a lot of us was a question of pride. Of self respect. Of identity.

Am I the kind of guy who would bang the Bunny? And equally important: *If I am, do I want everybody to know it?*

Certainly there could be no trace of cocksman's glory in it. Anyone with a pulse and a penis could have her. There'd been one or two candidates that many observers had expected her to reject, but she hadn't. She didn't require flattery, handsomeness, wit, charm, sexual expertise, or even basic hygiene. Breath was not a factor; she never kissed. Nor was performance anxiety a serious factor; by all accounts the Bunny simply did not permit failure.

The central question was, *what would a real man do?*
Did not a real man take advantage of every single recep-
tive vulva he encountered? Or did he maintain some sort
of minimal standards? Was some sort of chase, some sym-
bolic conquest, some kind of surrender won, *essential?*
Did it matter to a real macho stud *what* was going on
north of the warm moist contracting tube?

Would it not be degrading, disgusting, to wallow where
so many others had wallowed? Would it not be embarrassing, shaming, to reveal yourself before the whole
school as someone who *accepted* the description of himself as a penis with a pulse? What girl was going to go out
with you, after you had publicly revealed yourself to be a
rutting animal, willing to make use of any vagina with a
pulse?

In those days if you were Catholic or even ex-Catholic
and wished to partake of the sexual revolution, you were
required to tell yourself and any co-ed who would listen
that what you wanted was not mere animal *sex* but *making love.* This was a profound, magical, deeply beautiful
and spiritual thing, a deep sharing and growing-together,
a natural expression of love, a . . . a hard stance to maintain after you've been seen lining up for the Bunny. A
man could end up trading his total and entire prospects
at a four-year college for a single five-minute interlude in
a ripe and humid back seat.

And were the other girls wrong to be revolted? (As
they surely and loudly were.) Was not what was being
done to the Bunny a degradation of her womanhood, even
if she solicited it? Was it not a kind of desecration of the
whole concept of the male-female relationship, a blanket
insult to women? If other girls watching took it to mean,

this is what they would all *like to do to us, if they could,* would they be wrong?

Finally, what of the Bunny herself? If she derived even a morsel of pleasure from what happened, and happened, and happened, in that back seat, nobody had caught her at it yet. Was there not clearly something wrong with her inside, some volcanic self-hatred or corrosive self-disgust that drove her to so debase herself? And if so, was it then not dishonorable to take advantage of her affliction?

All that on one side. And on the other side:

. . . *but Jesus, man, it's a* guaranteed lay!

It was, as Bill Doane called it, a dilemma of the horns.

5.

Timing was important. And damned tricky.

Ideally you wanted to be as close to the front of the line as possible. Get it over with as quickly as possible and crawl back up the hill to the dorm. Certainly it was essential to at least be in the first forty or so: to stand on public display as a lecher all night long, *and then not get laid*, was simply unthinkable.

The problem was, some guys had absolutely no pride whatsoever, and would begin lining up well before the sun went down. If you wrestled your way into their midst . . . there you stood in broad daylight, in line for the Bunny. For hours. Being harangued and berated by flying squads of what were just then beginning to call themselves feminists.

But if you waited for sundown and the anonymity of darkness, by then there'd already be at least two dozen guys ahead of you in line.

So, half an hour before sunset, that third Friday night, I was in my room, checking my appearance in the mirror before departing.

The long hippie hair that I'd spent all summer growing in the face of ferocious pressure from my parents was pulled hard back into a ponytail. The ponytail was stuffed up under a watchcap that looked nothing like my trademark Aussie bush hat. My beard had shortened by an inch, and lost its pathetic attempted sideburns. Instead of my usual brown imitation-vinyl imitation bomber's jacket with imitation kapok falling out of the seams, I wore a big grey parka borrowed from Bill Doane, with enough furry collar to satisfy Liberace. My whole silhouette was different. I'd swapped my customary bell-bottom jeans for the pants my mother had packed for me. They had *creases*. And instead of Frye boots with heels that brought me up to six three, I wore loafers that changed my height, stride and style.

I turned a few times before the mirror, in the dance of the nitwit who hopes for a glimpse of himself from behind. I added a scarf to the ensemble for flexibility, and took my glasses off and tucked them in my shirt pocket.

Perfect. I couldn't see the mirror. Break a leg on the way downhill.

I put the glasses back on, and affixed clip-on sunglasses. Better.

I wished I could detect in my innermost self even a particle of sexual arousal. Partly for reassurance, and partly for distraction from the queasy churning a few inches higher up. My cunning brain, the result of millions of years of evolution, had sampled the mixture of anticipation, fear, guilt, excitement, and repulsion I was running through it, realized I would shortly need to be in peak condition to deal with this crisis, and promptly abdicated control to my gut, which sagely decided that whatever the hell was going on up there between the ears, what would best help me right now was equal measures of nausea, heartburn, and gas. Bad gas. Half a joint of Panama Red had failed to quell the situation, and I needed to save the other half. For afterward.

Enough. Time to go. If I was going. I tried to smile at myself in the mirror and failed and turned to the door and it opened and Smelly walked in and stopped in his tracks and stared at me.

Well, we stared at each other. And that's the weird part, because I swear from the moment he came in the room his eyes never left mine. He didn't have any opportunity to really take in my altered appearance. And yet somehow I was sure that he knew instantly—*knew*—what I was planning to do. His eyes squinted, in what I took to be disapproval. For maybe ten seconds, we stood there in silence.

Then I glanced at my watch, and he nodded and stepped away from the door, and I left.

The direct route to Wanda's from my dorm was to go out the front door, straight across the center of the campus commons, past the gym building, out the north gate, and then three *steep* blocks down Dreier Street. I slipped out the back door, planning to go out the *west* gate (rarely used because it didn't go anywhere useful), and walk around most of the perimeter of the campus. Nobody would see me until I got to the top of Dreier.

But as I was nearing the gate, a female voice I didn't recognize said, "Russell Walker?"

For a wild instant I fantasized that the Bunny had been unable to wait for me, and had come up the hill to get me. But even I couldn't sustain that one for more than a microsecond. Whoever this was, she was doubtless as far from being the Bunny as she could be. And whatever she had in mind, she was a distraction I could not afford, threatening to make me late. It had taken me two weeks of rationalization to get myself this far. I knew if I didn't go through with it tonight, I never would. Even as I turned toward her voice I was already saying, "Look, I'm sorry, but whatever it is you want to—"

And then the breath I would have used to finish the sentence left me in a little silent *huff*. I stopped walking and stopped thinking about walking and stopped thinking and stared.

The Italians are wrong. It isn't anything at all like a thunderbolt. It's like getting slapped in the face with pixie dust. Your cheeks tingle. Time seems to slow about ten percent. Your vision sharpens about ten percent, but your peripheral vision shrinks an equal amount. Somebody turns the treble way up, and everything takes on a slight echo that lets you know the recording devices have switched on.

"You roommate said I could catch you here about this time tonight. My name is Susan Krause," she said. "I'm in your Lit 205 class."

"No you're not," I heard some incredible asshole say, using my voice.

She blinked.

Good, contradict her. That's endearing. "I'd know," I insisted.

Her face went through that little evolution where the

mouth opens just slightly wider, and the eyebrows go up and down a few millimeters, and it means *ah, I get it*. "I just transferred in."

Demonstrate capacity for inferential reasoning. "Ah. You were in Cassidy's class."

"Yes."

Mr. Cassidy had been colorful even for an English teacher. Picture a Peter O'Toole built like Jimmy Cagney, gloriously pickled most of the time. About a third of his students fiercely loved him because his wildly rambling lectures taught them so many fascinating things. The other two thirds found him wildly frustrating because the things he taught them almost never had any noticeable connection to American literature (which, after all, they were, in effect, paying him to teach them), and very often undercut their most cherished misconceptions about life.

"I had him last year," I said. "They treated him shitfully." It was important to me that she know which side I was on. I knew which side she was on. I knew a lot of things about her. Already. Just from that first look.

That October, Mr. Cassidy had totalled his beloved Triumph one night, and racked himself up so bad they said anyone sober would have surely died. And his department chairman had waited until he'd been in hospital for thirty-one days to visit him. And tell him that the fine print said a medical leave of more than thirty days without advance notification and approval was grounds for loss of tenure, and Mr. Cassidy might want to use this period of recuperation to reflect on how to make the best use of the *next* phase of his life.

"Yes, they did," she agreed fervently. As I had known she would.

We looked at each other in silence for . . . how long? Five seconds? Five minutes? Even momentary conversational lulls usually make me anxious, but looking at her seemed to require my full attention and be a perfectly acceptable use of my time. It was she who finally said, "If you were on your way somewhere—"

I tried to think where I might be going, out the west gate—but it was all residential that way, out to well past walking distance. "Just out for a walk."

"Oh." She took a half step back.

Put a stop to *that*. "Was there something—?"

"Well . . . yes. Did you write a paper on *Red Badge* for Boudreau?"

A grenade of pleasure went off in my stomach. Dr. Boudreau had not only given me an A for a recent essay on *The Red Badge of Courage*, but had taken steps on my behalf to have it published, in a critical journal so prestigious that contributors were paid *three* complimentary copies. "You heard about that?"

"Your roommate and I were talking about the war. Zandor, is it? He mentioned your paper. I can't *believe* nobody ever interpreted *Red Badge* as an antiwar novel before," she said.

"I can't believe anybody ever read it any other way," I admitted.

"Me either. It's so obvious. I mean, the only times the guy ever succeeds as a warrior—"

"—are the times he goes nuts, loses his humanity—"

"—loses or *abandons* it—"

"—right! Exactly—"

"—that scene right before the first battle, when he feels like he's in a moving box—"

"Would you like to walk with me?" I asked.

And then I'm not sure about the choreography of what happened next—who did what, who went first—but when it was over her arm was in mine and we were walking out the west gate together.

"So what was it you . . . I mean, why . . ."

"I was hoping I could ask to borrow a copy. I've only heard about your paper, and I'd like to read it for myself."

"Are you a Crane freak?"

She shook her head. "Peace freak."

"Ah. Were you there when they liberated the library?"

We basically walked and talked all night—with intervals of doing neither, sharing silent companionship beside the reservoir, and again on a hill overlooking the state highway—and it wasn't until after I'd dropped her off at her dorm and was halfway to my own, whistling, that I remembered the existence of the Bunny.

When I did, I grinned wryly. It was like remembering my boyhood intention to be a cowboy when I grew up. As far as I was concerned, the Bunny was history.

I didn't know how right I was. Until I got back to my own dorm, and found the entire building in mourning.

The Bunny had failed to show the night before. People had waited—a few were reportedly *still* waiting, down the hill—but there'd been no sign of her.

Nor was there any that night.

Or any subsequent night. As mysteriously as she had appeared in the first place, the Bunny had vanished for good.

What did I care? I was in love. For the first time in my life. And, I could already sense, for the last as well.

Flashforward:
2003

Trembling-on-the-Verge
Heron Island, British Columbia
Canada

1.

Yes, his words should have held my attention. But I was distracted. By the sudden realization that my first assessment had been completely mistaken. He did not smell as bad as ever.

He did not smell bad *at all*.

He smelled just like most people, which is to say he had no detectable aroma of any kind. That first blast of stench when I'd opened the door had been completely imaginary, a product of memory association.

I realized I was openly sniffing the air, to confirm that—and was instantly mortified.

"It finally didn't help any more," Zandor Zudenigo said, as if replying to some remark I'd made. "I got too sensitive." His voice no longer sounded like that of Tweety Bird. It had deepened. It now sounded like the voice of Marvin the Martian, the little guy who wants to blow up Bugs Bunny and the earth with his Illudium

71

Q-36 Explosive Space Modulator.

I nodded as if I understood what the hell he was talking about. I couldn't seem to get a handle on my thoughts; they careened around like a cloud of drunken gnats. "You want some coffee? Something to drink? Are you hungry? Do you still like Oreos? Come on in the house with me, and we'll—"

"I'm fine."

"I can't believe it's really you," I said. "I heard you were dead."

"I nearly was. They almost had me. Playing dead was the only way I could get clear."

"Clear of who?"

He looked at me. Charlie Sanders had looked at me that way, thirty years and more ago. His expression had said, *If you really need me to tell you, you won't understand the answer.*

"You know who," Zandor said.

Instantly I was on the defensive. "No, I don't."

"You know," he insisted. "You knew when you heard I was dead."

My heart was hammering. "How would I know?"

"You knew most of it thirty years ago. You put the rest together thinking about it, later. By the time my death was announced it didn't surprise you much at all."

"*I don't know what you're talking about.*"

"Yeah, Slim. You do."

Mouth dry, breathing fast and shallow, knees trembling. "God damn it, Zudie, you show up here without knocking after thirty fucking years, and the first thing you do, you—"

He laid hands on me. Physically touched me. Grabbed me by the lapels of my shirt, hard enough to pop a button.

He had never touched me before. Or anyone, to my knowledge. *"Did you hear what I said when I came in the door?"* he shouted. That cartoon voice, shouting, was ludicrous, but I didn't laugh, because he had his hands on me, and because yes, I had heard what he'd said when he came in.

He had asked me to help him prevent the rape, torture, and murder of a whole family.

"That was serious? For real?"

"Serious enough that you don't have the time to waste on denial, okay?" he said, and let go of my shirt. "I *know* you are a good man. Everybody knows you're smart. But I know how smart you really are. I know how much you hate to admit the existence of anything you can't explain. But I also know you've had it proven to you that such things exist. That there are things in this world, in this life, you'll *never* be able to explain."

Reluctantly, I nodded.

"So *deal with it.*"

"You want to dump something spooky on my lap."

He nodded. "And if you can think of a better lap to move it to, great."

I closed my eyes for a second.

The worst thing was, I *did* know what he was talking about, sort of. I didn't want to, but I did. He was absolutely right: over the last thirty years I had been working it out in the back of my mind. I knew what he was. And I didn't want any part of it.

When I opened my eyes again, they met his. The years melted away and it was once again the afternoon we met, and those moist eyes were staring right into mine, just as they had back then.

Forgiving me.

Unconditionally. Blanket absolution, for anything I'd ever done or left undone and whatever I was about to do, for everything I'd said or left unsaid or might say in future, for who I was and who I could have been but wasn't and whomever I might become.

I was aware of my breath and pulse slowing. With each breath my shoulders settled a little lower. It was *way* too late to lock the barn door. And nothing was going to be stolen, anyway. There was nothing left to steal.

With an effort, I broke eye contact. "Let's go in the house."

"I'd rather not."

I was surprised. "There's no good place for you to sit down in here. And nothing to eat or drink. We can—"

"It would be too noisy in there for me," he said.

I understood what he meant at once. I didn't want to admit that either.

He was right, too. I sighed. "Well, I've got to have some coffee, if we're going to be talking about *this* kind of shit. Take my desk chair, there. I'll bring another out for me. Coffee for you?"

"No, thanks."

"You sure? If you like coffee, even a little . . . well, mine's special."

"Another time," he said, in a tone of voice that suggested the other time would postdate the glaciation of Hell.

"Anything? Tea? Soda? Juice? Thirty-weight oil?" No hits, not even a smile on the last one. "At least take some water? It's pure."

He nodded. "I'll share water with you."

I shot him a quick look. Was he referencing Heinlein's *Stranger in a Strange Land*? Impossible to tell from his bland Baby Huey face.

I left him there and went in the house and made coffee.

It didn't take much time, or require any of my attention. A German radio baron was once so pleased by something he read in a column of mine that he sent me, out of the blue, as a token of his appreciation, a Jura Espressa, the Scala Vario model. It is a Swiss machine the size of a portable TV, and requires a converter the size and weight of a truck battery to operate on Canadian wall current. It lists for US $2,000—very roughly CAN $2,700—and is worth every damn penny. It makes the best possible coffee, instantly.

You keep it loaded up with a couple of liters of water, and half a pound of coffee beans. That's it. Any time you push the Go button, it grinds some beans, makes coffee by the French press method, dumps the grounds into a hopper for disposal, and rinses itself. Once a week or so you empty the hopper—that and keeping it stocked with beans and water are the total work involved.

So making superb coffee was a matter of pushing a button and waiting for the cup to finish dripping. The aroma of fresh-ground filled the room while I wrestled with myself, inside my head.

I saw my cat Horsefeathers sprawled on the living room floor, staring at something invisible in midair, tracking it as it moved across the room. Could I say for sure there was nothing really there? Everywhere I looked, just out of my peripheral vision, were little ghostlets of Susan. Was I absolutely positive they were imaginary? Not five minutes ago I had been planning my suicide. Did it matter where this craziness might lead me?

If you believe only in reason and empirical truth and the material world . . . no wonder Susan hasn't contacted you from beyond, you dumb shit.

The coffee finished dripping. I stirred in some sugar. I got cream and a half-liter bottle of filtered water from the fridge. I put some cream in my coffee and put the rest away again. I started to take my coffee and his water back out to the office, but before I was two steps out of the kitchen I stopped and backtracked. I tipped half an inch of coffee out into the sink, and replaced it with brandy. Before resealing the brandy, I took a big fiery gulp, and coughed. Then I put away the bottle, and brought my coffee and Zandor's water and a folding chair out to the office.

I set my coffee mug down on a bookshelf, and turned my back on him to set up the chair. As I was doing so, without warning I tossed the plastic bottle of water back over my left shoulder in his general direction. I finished arranging the chair to my satisfaction, retrieved my coffee, and when I turned around and sat, he was just as I had left him except that he was drinking water now. The sudden appearance of a flying bottle of water had startled him not at all.

"You're right," I said. "I thought about it a long time. And you're right. I *did* figure out a few things. I know the three most important things about you. I'm not so sure I didn't know them back at St. Billy Joe."

He waited.

"You read minds."

He nodded.

"There's no off switch."

He nodded again.

"And it *hurts*."

He sighed and nodded a third time. "Christ, yes. More than I can tell you."

Holy shit.

"Well," I said, "I was going to ask how you managed to track me all the way across a continent, but I guess that wouldn't be too much of a challenge for—"

"I didn't have to track you anywhere," he interrupted. "I was here when you got here. For the last twenty years I've been living on Coveney Island."

Extremely holy shit.

The coastal waters of southwestern British Columbia are overgenerously supplied with islands, ranging from the leviathan Vancouver Island—nearly twice the size of Massachusetts—all the way down to Coveney, which is about twice the size of the average high school grounds. It made my little island of 3,000 souls seem like Metropolis. There was no ferry service to it at all, not even a foot-passenger-only water taxi as far as I knew, and until now I had believed it to be uninhabited. If Zandor lived there, he owned a boat. And must be uncommonly skilled in its use—even horny teenagers tended to avoid Coveney Island because there was no easy place to come ashore, and no beachfront. I only knew of its existence because the ferry between Horseshoe Bay and Heron Island passed near it, and I once idly asked a ferry crewman if it had a name. It was basically just a lumpy rock bristling with trees. From a certain angle, if the light was right, it looked like a sleeping green hedgehog. I could not recall ever seeing chimney smoke rising from it, or a boat moored there.

"And basically what you've been doing there all this

time," I said, "is hiding out from the CIA. Right?"

He didn't flinch. "And the FBI, the NSA, Treasury, CSIS, the horsemen, Interpol—yes, they're part of what I've been hiding from."

"Jesus, who else *is* there to hide from?"

"Everybody."

"Oh."

"Back in college, I could stand having most people as close as ten or twenty meters away from me. Smelling terrible helped keep them outside that range—but it also made me noticeable and memorable."

I noted that he'd said "meters" instead of "yards." He *had* been in Canada longer than I had. I also distinctly recalled that he had seemed comfortable having me within a meter or two of him for long periods, back then. I decided to be flattered.

"You should be," he said. "But now . . ." For the first time, I noticed lines on his face that hadn't been there in college. A lot of them. "Ah Christ, being within a hundred meters of just about anybody is agony, now. My range and sensitivity have both increased to where there's just no point in smelling bad anymore: it doesn't keep people far enough away. And being that noticeable stopped being good strategy, anyway." He had one of those thousand-yard stares. "It became time to bail out of the world. Or end up chained up somewhere in Langley or the Pentagon basement or RCMP headquarters. As I said, they very nearly got me."

"So you jungled up. On Coveney. Jesus. How did you know I was here on Heron?"

"You mention it in your column sometimes. I tracked you from there."

"You can't get *The Globe and Mail* on Coveney Island. Hell, I'm the only person on *this* island who gets it home delivered, and only because I'm on staff."

"I read it online."

Suddenly I felt myself blush.

"Yeah, that's right," he said. "All those years ago, every time you called me *Zandor*, inside you were thinking *Smelly*—and every time I knew it. Big deal."

"I—" What was there to say? I was busted. "I'm sorry, man. Really."

He waved it away. "Don't worry about it. Most people called me Smelly to my face. I appreciated you taking the trouble. Just like I appreciate the fact that you haven't once thought of me as Smelly since you realized I'm not anymore."

I blushed again. "Look, I—"

"Don't worry about it, I said. Zudie is fine."

"Zandor just sounds like the name of the secret agent in an episode of *General Hospital* to me."

He nodded. "My uncle used to call me Zudie when I was a boy. I kind of like it." Pause. "No, really, Russell."

I finished my coffee and set down the mug. "All right, Mr. Sensitive Mind Reader. You probably know my situation as well as I do, right?"

"Better."

"You poor bastard. Okay, fine. So what's wrong with me, that you need to fix? Grief? How the hell do you fix grief?"

He didn't hesitate. "You're in deep clinical depression."

"Oh, horseshit. I don't believe in depression. It's the modern equivalent of witchcraft, complete with a magic potion."

He continued as if I hadn't spoken. "You're about two days from suicide. Maybe less. I don't need to be a mind reader to know that."

"Oh yeah? What was your first clue, Dr. Freud?"

"You haven't asked me a word about the family who are going to be butchered. You haven't wondered about them. For all you know, they're neighbors of yours. Your heart is switched off. Your soul has shut down."

The strangest thing happened to me. Without warning I found myself crying, sobbing full out—except no water came out of my eyes. *I cry dry*, I thought. *I cry dry*.

"What are you doing, counting in German?" he asked.

I was startled enough to giggle, in the midst of my crying. In all the time I'd known him, I could not recall Zandor Zudenigo ever attempting a joke, let alone a pun, much less a multilingual pun.

"Do you know why shrinks *love* to see a patient come in the door with clinical depression?" he asked me.

I shrugged. "Nonviolent?"

He shook his head. "Nearly all their patients are nonviolent."

I shrugged again. "Why, then?"

"It makes them feel effective. There are about a thousand things that can go wrong in the functioning of a human brain. Depression is the *only* one that can, to ninety-five percent certainty, be completely cured by prescribing a pill."

"Horseshit," I said again.

And again he ignored me. "The trouble is, you have to take them for at least a couple of weeks before they start to kick in. We don't have that kind of time."

Oddly annoying dilemma: if you're crying, but no water

is flowing, what are you supposed to *do*? Pat your cheeks with an imaginary tissue? "That's easy," I said. "You're a telepath. Just wander around until you find somebody who's got a time machine, and that—"

"Do you trust me, Slim?"

"—way all we have to do . . . say what?"

"Do you trust me?"

"What do you mean?"

"I mean, do you trust me?"

I wasn't crying any more. "That's not a simple question, Zandor."

"Yes, it is."

"Well, in what sense? Are you asking, do I trust you not to boost anything while I'm in the house making coffee? Or, do I trust you're not an al Qaeda mole? Or do you mean, do I trust you never to be mistaken about anything?"

Those shiny eyes bored into mine. "You know that I walk around inside your head, privy to your innermost secrets. Yet you have made no attempt to kill me. So I know you trust me to that extent."

"I know you *can't help* walking around inside my head. You'd stop if you could."

"You 'know' that because I told you."

I lifted an eyebrow. "Good point." After a moment, I lowered the eyebrow. "You're right, I must trust you. Hell, we lived together once. Yeah, I do trust you."

"*Everybody* is at least a tiny bit telepathic. In your heart of hearts, you know I mean you no harm."

I looked around for my heart of hearts, but couldn't locate it. So I thought, instead. "Yes. Yes, I do."

He took a long drink from his water bottle and twisted

the cap back onto it. "All right. You trust me to wander around inside your head. Next step: do you trust me to make a few small changes, while I'm in there? The equivalent of—" He glanced down. "—straightening up a desk just a little? Before everything on it lands on the floor?"

I stared. "Zudie, you think you can really do that? Like, instant Prozac—by Vulcan mind-meld?"

"More like one of the tricyclics," he said. "But yes."

I couldn't decide how I felt about it. Which I realized was weird. All my life, the very idea of this kind of mental invasion, someone else making alterations in my personal mind, had been a special horror of mine, featuring some of my worst nightmares. Tonight I was so apathetic, so burned out, I couldn't seem to give a shit anymore. There was just enough of me left to realize intellectually how alarming that ought to be. But my intellect got hung up on the absurdity of doing something that *should* frighten and revolt me, *in order to* regain the power to be frightened and revolted again. I would know it was working if I found myself starting to freak out.

"It won't be like that," he said. Not arguing, just furnishing information.

"Will—?"

"No. It won't hurt." A promise.

"Will I—"

He looked mildly exasperated. "How can I know that— before the fact? There's no *telling* what people will decide to regret, after the fact."

I couldn't argue with that. "Well . . . have y—?"

"Yes, I have. A total of six times, so far."

After enough time had passed I said gently, "You *know* my next question."

He sighed and nodded. "Of course. Three of the six were reasonably happy with the changes I made. Another was wildly happy. But one was angry, and over time learned how to undo everything I'd done."

"Huh. How l—?"

"It took him about a month."

More silence. I didn't prompt him, this time.

"The sixth killed herself," he said when he was ready.

"Ah," I said.

"Yeah," he said, and sighed heavily.

I thought about it. "So if I let you do this, the spectrum of possible reactions runs from, I get really high to I kill myself?"

"Well, on the plus side I suppose it's possible you could achieve true enlightenment and become the next Buddha, but basically that's it, yes."

"Whip it out," I heard myself say.

"You're sure?"

"Bring it. Either of those is way better than where I'm at now."

He got up, wheeled my chair out from behind my desk and into the center of the room, and made me sit in it. He turned out the desk lamp, leaving my Mac the only significant light source in the room. He moused around that until he located iTunes, opened it, and activated its visual display. The screen exploded into psychedelic lunacy, whose nature, colors and speed changed constantly. My eyes were drawn to it, and found it hypnotic. He pulled his chair beside mine, sat facing me. I offered him my hands, palms up, but he waved them away.

"Is there anything special I should be thinking?" I asked. "Or thinking about?"

"Ideally," he said, "you should not be thinking at all. Not even thinking about not thinking."

"Terrific. How long does *that* take to learn?"

He spread his hands. "It varies. Some Buddhists spend their lives working on it, very hard, and never achieve it."

"Wow," I said.

"Just watch the screen."

"Okay."

And then—without thinking about it—I stopped thinking. About anything at all.

2.

"It didn't work," I said.

"No?"

"Hell, no. I still have my grief. All of it. I mean, it hurts just as much as it did an hour ago. God still sucks. Nothing's changed."

"Ah."

"I don't feel any different at all." I opened up my eyes, and there he was beside me, looking at me with no expression. The screen display on my computer had been shut down. I snorted. "Look who I'm telling. You probably know it better than I do."

He shrugged. "Well, I tried."

"Now what about this family? Where are they? How many? And who wants to kill them? What are you smiling about?"

"Nothing."

"Why can't we just go to the police?"

"Maybe we can. I can't."

"What do you mean?"

He frowned. "Russell, I've known you for a long time. I always liked you, and I still do. You have an unusually tolerant and sensitive mind, a kind heart, and a gentle disposition. You can stand next to someone you know is reading your mind, and not want to kill him. After all this time, you remembered I like Oreos. I can't think of anybody I'm more comfortable with." His frown deepened to the point of becoming a grimace. "And I can barely stand to be this close to you. I'll have to go, soon."

"*Oh.*"

"You were only part right before. Reading minds doesn't just hurt. It . . . it *degrades*. It forces you to know things that you know you're not supposed to know. I came here in the dead of night . . . and even then I almost didn't make it. You have no idea how loud some people can dream, Russell. But in daylight, forget it: I'd have been catatonic before I got halfway here. And this is a sparsely populated island of peaceful rural people. If I were to try and make it to a city police station, let alone walk inside it . . . or even get within a few hundred meters of a single beat cop—" He shuddered. "Some kinds of mind, it hurts me even to think about. Cops are high on the list."

"You could call them. I'm sure you don't have a phone out there on Coveney, but you're welcome to use mine."

"Think that through."

Okay.

I'm a police desk sergeant. Someone calls up and wants to report a whole bunch of murders that haven't happened yet. He won't say how he knows about them. He has no hard evidence. He won't come in and be interviewed. He won't say why not. He'd rather not give out his address. He says his name is Zandor Zudenigo. And he sounds like Marvin the Martian.

Click.

"Okay," I said. "Let's start over. Who—" I stopped, thought for moment. "No, let's start at the beginning. If we can locate it. When did you first become aware something was wrong?"

He nodded. "That's the right way to approach it, I think."

"I'm a columnist. I know where the lead belongs."

He paused a moment to collect his thoughts, or perhaps to consult his memories. "Okay. I selected my home for privacy—for obvious reasons—and it usually works pretty good. Strangers almost never get near enough to come to my attention. And when they do, there's always plenty of warning, because they have to come slowly, by boat, picking their way through the shallows. A seaplane won't take off or land near Coveney, because the water's too treacherous there. So if a plane does pass overhead, it's high up enough to be way out of my range.

"All of which is just to explain why I was taken so completely aback, when suddenly there was a monster in my head, one night. For a horrid second I almost believed I had *invented* him. Which would make me one sick fuck."

I stared. I had never heard Zandor use the word "fuck." Not even in the worst of the Sixties.

"But a second later I realized what was going on. See, maybe that's a clue: in that first instant of contact, *who he was* was more important to him, more prominent in his thoughts, than what was happening to him. Which is amazing because, as far as he knew, he was dying. His seaplane was going down, fast and shallow. Some mechanical defect I understood perfectly just then, and can no longer remember how to explain. As I became aware of him, he was already passing over my head, about thirty meters up.

"And I agreed with him. Who he was was a lot more interesting than his imminent death. Certainly way, way more horrifying. He was . . . monstrous."

Zandor caught himself, and paused.

"No," he said, "I'm not saying it right. You're picturing a combination of Ted Bundy, Bela Lugosi and Arnold Schwarzenegger. This guy is a thousand times worse. What makes him terrifying isn't even so much what he wants to do. It's how small a thing it is to him."

As I thought of opening my mouth he said:

"You're right, I'm rambling. Sorry. Okay, if I'm going to convey it, I'm going to have to confront it. God, I hate this."

He closed his eyes, let his features go slack. In repose his face looked like that of a pouting, remarkably ugly baby. After a moment he took a deep breath, and continued.

"A guy is in your head. Has no idea you exist. He's about to die. He *knows* that. He's been dealing with that for over a minute already, and it's coming up on showtime. Is he making his peace? Gibbering in fear? Trying to bargain with God?

"No. Not this guy. He's laughing. Contemptuously. He's thinking, *You think you can scare me into believing in you again? Screw you. I would have killed a thousand, if I'd had more time. Worse deaths than anything even you've ever dreamed of. I'd do it now if I could—I had a terrific one planned for next week. Do your worst, Yahweh old boy: you'll vanish the instant I do."*

He opened his eyes and sought out mine.

"You see? What he's got left is measured in seconds, and he's using them to congratulate himself on remaining atheist. On not selling out his intellectual integrity for even a few seconds' final comfort at the end of a life of psychotic savagery. And how does he do that? By telling an imaginary God to go chase himself, and throwing mortal sins in His face. That's funny to him."

He broke eye contact, looked down at the floor.

"And then whatever it was—a plugged fuel line, that was it—just fixed itself, at the last possible moment. He got enough control back to get the nose up, hit the water hard, skipped back into the air like a flat rock . . . and a few seconds later he was out of my range. I've been trying ever since to come to terms with what I learned during those twenty or thirty seconds I was connected to him."

He swiveled his chair, turning his back to me, and gripped his upper arms as if he were hugging himself. "All right!" he said, responding to what I had been thinking of saying. "I still haven't gotten to it—I know, okay?"

"If you like," I said, "I can go take a nap, and you can tell me later how this conversation came out."

He turned back around to face me, still clutching his biceps. "His first name is Allen. I don't know any others. He wrote a piece of software only programmers have ever heard of that made him roughly as wealthy as Alberta. He never has to work again and never will. His hobby takes up all his time these days. His hobby—" He closed his eyes, took a deep breath, let it out. "His hobby is suffering."

"Sounds like me," I said.

His eyes snapped open and captured mine. "Not experiencing suffering. Causing it."

"Jesus."

"Studying it. *Cultivating* it. Learning how to maximize it, refine it, enhance it. Prolong it."

"I don't understand," I said. "What kind of suffering?"

"All kinds," he said. "Every kind. Physical, emotional, mental, spiritual, philosophical. I really don't think he discriminates."

"But how—"

"If you were to meet him, within two minutes' conversation Allen would know what you fear the most. Within four, he'd know who you love most, and what it is they most fear. Within five minutes he could make you burst into tears by speaking a single sentence. And probably would, for the pleasure of your embarrassment.

"But the moment he laid eyes on you, he would already know just about everything there is to know about how to make your particular body experience maximum *physical* agony. That's a given."

"What th—"

"He could, for example, dig the second joint of his index finger into a certain spot on your body—not hard, certainly not hard enough to break a shortbread cookie—and make you beg him to kill you."

"Oh bullshit."

"No." He shook his head. "And that's first-grade stuff. He's a Ph.D. He's been studying the subject for a long time. As long as he can remember, really. Suffering is, to Allen, what art or music or literature are to others. And he is a gifted artist, a once-in-a-generation talent."

"So what are you saying, he's like, a serial killer? Hannibal Lecter?"

His shoulders slumped. "Killing is about the kindest thing he does. He puts it off as long as possible."

"How many has he—"

"I don't know exactly. Enough that he's lost count. Many dozens. Somewhere in the general neighborhood of a hundred and fifty."

I heard a loud buzzing sound. I could feel a headache coming on, and my stomach was cramping. "Dear Jesus God."

"Russell, you have to help me stop him."

"*Me?*" I felt my jaw drop. "What the hell can I—"

He overrode me—hard to do with that voice. "Listen to me! Let me give you just one single small example of why this man has to be erased from the planet at once. Allen buys gas masks by the crate."

"Gas masks?"

"Vintage WWI and WWII gas masks. He especially likes the ones that cover the whole face, if he can get them."

"I don't—"

"That way, when he sets someone on fire, they don't get to have a nice quick merciful death from smoke inhalation or scorched lungs. They remain conscious long enough to feel themselves c—"

"*Jesus Christ, that's enough!*"

A short silence ensued, in which I tried to wrap my mind around what he'd just said.

"What is it you're asking me to do?" I said finally.

"Did you ever read a Larry Niven novel called *Ringworld?*"

I shook my head.

"Mistake. Well, in Niven's universe there's an alien race, giant cats, very vicious and aggressive—so aggressive that in their wars with humanity they always lose, because they *always* attack too soon. Anyway, they're so xenophobic they refuse to concede that any other race is truly sentient, so the title they give to their ambassador to the human race translates literally as 'Speaker-to-Animals.' "

I smiled. "Nice phrase. I like it. You're saying he's that ferocious and alien?"

"No. I'm saying I want you to be Speaker-to-Cops."

My smile went away. I retrieved the mental movie I had created earlier of Zudie calling the cops, and replayed it—this time with *myself* in the starring role. It actually got less funny. "Uh . . ."

"You are the closest I can get to a cop. Even if I did find someone closer, I'd never convince them of what you already know. Certainly not in a week, which is the most we've got." He got up out of his chair and came to me. To my surprise, he touched me with his hands, put them on my shoulders. "There *is* nobody else, Russell. I'm very sorry, but you're elected. By random chance, the same way I was. Your two choices now are to help me, or to go to your grave knowing that you could have saved the lives of a blameless harmless couple and their two sweet children, and declined. It is not necessary to know you as well as I do, to know that the second alternative is simply not in you." He let go of my shoulders. "The decision is already made, man. Catch up with reality, okay? We really don't have much time."

I was beginning to realize that he was right. One of my favorite Charles Addams cartoons depicts an elderly portly man in black tie and tails, wearing a monocle. He is on skis, in midair, hundreds of feet above the ground, descending, and the expression on his face says clear as print, "How the bloody *hell* did *this* happen?"

I wished I knew.

"How much time *do* we have? Exactly."

He frowned ferociously. "I can't be sure. His plane went down Monday—two days ago. The words he used in his head were 'next week.' But that's not very specific. He could have meant first thing next Monday morning . . . or any time before a week from this Friday. I got the sense that there was something preventing him from doing it any sooner than . . . whenever it is next week, something he couldn't help, but I have no idea what it was, or how firm it was. What I'm saying is, we could have anywhere from five to nine days . . . or, he could have been inspired by his near-death experience to clear his calendar and get cracking: for all I know, he's out there now, doing—" He stopped speaking and shuddered.

"Doing what?"

He folded his arms atop his head, like a prisoner of war. "Are you sure you want to know the specifics?"

"I'm sure the cops will want to know. Better if I don't make them up."

He lifted his hands straight in the air, then let them fall. "Yes." He took a deep breath, let it out. "But are you sure you want to know?"

No. "Yes."

He nodded and turned away so we wouldn't have to see one another's eyes.

"It's a rather ambitious scenario. His requirements are fairly specific, but he's already located what he considers the perfect victims in Point Grey. A family of four, son pubescent, daughter not quite, all four of them beautiful and kind and decent—the most picture-perfect, Hallmark card, Norman Rockwell sort of family he can possibly find.

"The mother is most important of all to him: to fit his fantasy she has to be June Cleaver, Ma Walton, whatever the hell the name of Timmy's mom on *Lassie* was . . . God, I just now realized I can't think of a single warm loving sexy married mother figure in all of contemporary television, I have to go back to the Stone Age." I started to argue, and squelched myself. "Never mind, I'm stalling. The point is, he wanted a happy homemaker who respects her husband and adores her kids and cares about her community and has never had a mean impulse in her life. And has big breasts. And a strong but kind and loving husband who deserves her, and two sweet kids they've done a great job of raising together, who haven't yet been driven completely insane by the hormone storms of puberty."

"What does he plan to do with them, now he's located them?"

"They apparently have a weekly family ritual. Every week on the same night, and God I wish I knew which night, they order pizza and all eat together. Next week they're going to get a special pie. The last truly free choice any of them will ever make in their lives will be whether to fall on their faces or land on their backs."

"Jesus Christ," I murmured.

"A couple of minutes after they make their choice, he'll enter their home. He'll cut each of them out of their clothes, superglue the backs of their hands to the outsides of their thighs, and wire their ankles together. Once he has all four secured and gagged with tape, he'll pack them into his van, and drive it up the Sea to Sky Highway to a tract of woodland he has, miles from anywhere. He'll drive a few miles into the woods, carry them one at a time from the van into a small log cabin, and hang them up on the hooks meant for that purpose. And then he'll wait, controlling his eagerness, for them to wake up."

"Zandor," I said, "I think we can stop here, okay? I don't think I need those specifics after all. I think I've got the picture. As much of it as I need, anyway."

"Almost," he said. "I will spare you the details. In part because if I try to s-s-speak them I believe I will vomit on your carpet. Repeatedly. But the general outline of the . . . event, at least, I believe you have to know. You do not yet grasp the kind of mind I am talking about. You are imagining mere de Sadean nightmares. This man is much worse. You need to have some sense of how much worse."

"Okay," I heard myself say.

"You are thinking in terms of torture, rape, murder, perhaps some sort of gruesome post-mortem mutilation." He shook his head. "Think horror. Think maiming—physical and mental. Think total psychological breakdown, annihilation of the personality, catastrophic ego collapse. Think heartbreak, despair.

"And when you think of mere physical pain, think first of the absolute maximum agony that a human nervous system can endure before dying. And then square that, or cube it, because he has drugs. Magical drugs—blackest black magic. Some he found in the more obscure parts of the standard pharmacopoeia and adapted to his purpose, and some he developed himself. A drug that makes it impossible to lose consciousness, to pass out from pain.

A drug that keeps the heart strong under sustained stress. A drug that makes pain *hurt* more—two or three times as much, he thinks. Another that enhances fear, promotes panic. Another that makes time pass much more slowly than normal. Whatever was the worst excruciation ever visited on any human by another since the dawn of time, that is where Allen *begins*."

I closed my eyes and probed at them with my fingers until the rainbow kaleidoscopes came. "Jesus, Jesus. Zandor, I can't—"

"Broad outlines only, we agreed. All right. He will take two full days to kill each one. First the father, then the daughter, then the son."

I opened my mouth to say, *stop, no more,* and he abruptly stopped talking.

He was silent for so long I stopped rubbing my eyes and opened them. He had *his* eyes closed, and was rubbing them with his fingers to make the kaleidoscopes work.

"Saves the mother for last," I said, just to be saying something. "Let me guess: he takes *three* days to kill *her*."

He let his hands fall to his lap. "Oh, no. No, not at all. I'm telling this wrong if you take him for so kind a man. No, he doesn't kill her."

I felt my stomach shriveling up inside me. "Aw Jesus— the dirty, dirty, *dirty*—that's sicker than—how can he possibly take the risk of leaving her alive? Is he that scary? Can he really break someone so totally that for the rest of his life he can absolutely rely on their silence?"

"Probably he could," Zudie said. "But why depend on it? He will use a combination of injury and drugs to render her permanently quadriplegic and aphasic. How ironic, the highway patrol will think: she managed to leap from the family vehicle just before it went over that cliff, and then ruined herself for life when she landed. And she won't be able to tell them any different. She will be placed in some institution somewhere, with absolutely nothing to do but go over her memories. For years and years. Allen plans to visit her regularly—"

The thing about having a swivel chair in your office, you really don't actually *need* the swivel feature a whole lot, but then when you do, it's gold. I managed to get nearly all the vomit into the wastebasket.

"Now, you're getting it," he said. "I'll stop now."

"Thank you," I said, and heaved again. "Really."

"You're welcome."

I wiped my mouth, drew in a big breath, and screamed, "What kind of a—"

And stopped, stymied.

"Yes, that's the worst of it," he said after a while. "You want to use a word like 'animal' or 'reptile' or 'beast' . . . but you know no animal is capable of such behavior. It's hard to admit, but the only word that applies is 'human.' So your question is, what kind of a *human being* can do such things to another human being?"

"Yes, I guess it is." I cracked a fresh half-liter of bottled water and rinsed my mouth.

"The only answer is to point to him and say 'That kind.' There is no kind. He's one of a kind. We all are, but he more than most. He may very well be literally one of a kind. If that kind of brain mutation is a one-in-six-billion freak, then he's probably the one we have this season. If it's only a one-in-a-*billion* freak, there could be enough of him to form a basketball team. Or perhaps it occurs once every ten trillion births, and he's the only one in recorded history. I doubt that.

"But I don't know. And I don't think it matters. He is the one I know about. He is the one we have to stop."

I took another long drink of water, wiped the neck of the bottle, and offered it to him. He took it, drank deep, handed it back. I looked over at the empty top of the bookcase just to the left of the office door. It is the place where I used to keep a large framed photo of Susan, back when I could bear to. Removing the photo had probably been pointless, because every time I saw the bare top of that bookcase I thought of the photo. And therefore of Susan. I could imagine what she'd have made of all this. She'd have been as horrified and demoralized and sick at heart as I felt now, of course. But underneath that would have been a substratum of a strange primitive excitement. The thrill of the hunt—all the cleaner because this prey *needed* killing. She'd have turned us into Nick and Nora, or Simon Templar and Patricia Holm, insisted that we make laconic wisecracks as we went along, made the whole thing an adventure. Thinking about that, I started to feel faint stirrings of that excitement myself.

"All right," I said, "let's bag this bastard. Tomorrow I'll go into town, downtown to the cop shop, and start what I confidently predict will be one hell of a lot of talking. We'll have them run his background—if he's as sick as you say he is, there *has* to be something there—and we'll make up enough lies about things we've supposedly seen in his house to let them get a search warrant—God knows what they'll—what?" I had finally noticed the expression on his face.

He cleared his throat. "I didn't say this was going to be easy."

3.

I closed my eyes, took in a long, slow breath, let it out. "What's the problem?"

"I can't . . . you don't . . . it isn't like . . ." He stopped talking until he had a sentence he was prepared to go with to the end. "What I did, what happened to me was like looking over somebody's shoulder as he works at his computer. He may have twenty gigabytes of data in there, but all I can see is what he's working on—the couple of hundred megabytes or so that's the maximum his computer can keep in RAM."

"What are you telling me?"

"I got a *lot* of information about Allen. But all I got was what he chose to think about, during the half minute or so I was reading him—plus some of the inferential and referential links to other things. I know a great deal about his relationship with God, tons about his idea of the perfect sexual experience, and enough of what he calls his philosophy of pain to gag Hugh Hefner.

"But during the brief time he was in my range, he never happened to think his last name. Or his home address. I know where his remote forest horror hideaway is—but not where he lives. I know the full names of some of his most recent victims—but not his last name."

"Shit." Then: "Shit!" And: *"Shit!"*

"How often do you think of *your* last name?"

"Okay. Okay, you said he was a software designer with some success. We'll get somebody to give us a giant stack of mug shots and wade through them until . . . you've got that look again."

"During that minute or two I was in his head, he *did* place himself in a fantasy more than once—but when he did, he never bothered to fill in his face. Actually, his whole body was really just a sketch. Except for the—"

"You're telling me you don't know his last name, his address or what he looks like. Just that he butchers people with extreme savagery and ingenuity. And has issues with God."

He nodded. "That's what I'm telling you."

"And you want me to tell this to the police for you."

He nodded again. "I'd do it myself if I could."

"What's wrong with the mail?"

He shook his head. "It's hard enough to believe a story like this if someone looks you in the eye and tells it with great sincerity. On paper . . . they wouldn't read past the first page. Not to mention the fact that we probably don't have a week to wait while Canada Post transports a piece of paper ten miles. And e-mail gets even less attention and less respect from cops than regular mail."

I noticed for the first time that I'd had a pounding

headache for several minutes now.

"Zudie, I literally wouldn't know where to begin."

"You're a journalist."

I sighed. "A lot of people make that mistake, because my work appears alongside that of journalists. What I am is a columnist. I don't break stories, investigate leads, cultivate sources, or any of that crap. What I do, I read the papers, and when I notice something that pisses me off, I think about it awhile, do a little research, and then write a thousand words about it and get paid. The paper I write for is the national newspaper—but it's published in Toronto. I don't have a single connection in local government, either municipal or provincial, and I don't know a soul in the Vancouver police force or RCMP, and I don't have any savvy reporter buddies to ask. If I did, all they could tell me is how such things are done in Toronto. I don't—"

He raised his voice slightly; the effect was as if any other man had bellowed. "God damn it, Russell, *stop dodging and let's get this thing done.* Okay?"

I was not used to this aggressive and proactive a Zudie. But then, I wasn't used to a stenchless one, either. In my memory Zudie was a figure of fun, not someone who told you to be a man. Most annoying of all, he was right.

"I will if you will," I said finally.

"What are you—*oh,* no! Forget it."

One thing about conversing with a telepath: you don't waste many words making yourself clear. "Who's dodging now?"

"I *can't,* Russell."

"Dammit, be reasonable! If I want the police to go on a snipe hunt for the Marquis de Sodom, I have to bring them *something.* You are absolutely all I got."

"I told you, I—oh. *Oh.* Brilliant! I see what you—"

"You said you have satellite web access out there on your island . . ."

He nodded. "And a webcam. I could put together a software package and e-mail it to you. It'll let us set up a closed two-way, live video and audio. Oh, shit. Really? *Why?*"

I shrugged. "What can I tell you? I'm a Macintosh guy."

He grimaced. "Okay, I can still do it. Take a little tweaking, that's all."

"So if I can—*somehow*—persuade a cop to talk with you—"

"As long as I don't have to physically be anywhere near him, yes, I can manage that. Very good thinking, Russell. You see my problem. I'm not used to thinking of ways of communicating with people. I think of ways to avoid it."

I had my eyes closed. I was running a little mental movie of Zudie in closed circuit converse with The Man, and it did not please me. "Ah, you know, cops are freaked out by good computers, maybe it might be better if, just to start, we kept it to audio-only—or maybe even just text, for the first—"

I opened my eyes and found him glaring at me.

"Russell, what is the point of trying to be diplomatic with a mind reader? I'm not offended. I know what I look like. And sound like. And you're right, put them together, I come across like *exactly* the kind of guy that calls up the cops and says I can read people's minds, you gotta arrest this rich guy. Text it is."

"No, I'm wrong," I said. "Text-only is worse than nothing at all. Why do people communicate online by text-only?"

He saw my point at once, of course. "So they can lie if they want."

I nodded. "Even cops know that by now."

"Would it help if I altered my voice?"

I flinched. He had asked the question in Bill Doane's voice, still instantly recognizable over a gap of decades. "Maybe. But don't alter it that much, or it'll sound phony. A slight variation on your own voice is the way to go."

"Okay. So we avoid the internet altogether, and just do this by phone then, right? Aw jeeze, Russell, make up your mind, okay?"

"I know, I know. Forgive me: you'd think by now I'd have a simple thing like connecting mind readers to The Man down pat."

"I'm sorry. I know this must be—"

"It's just I was thinking that disembodied voices on the phone don't carry much more weight with cops than a chat room typist does. If your testimony is going to count for anything, it'll be because you delivered it to his face, looking him in the eye, prepared to answer questions about your story."

"Even if I do look like Baby Huey and sound like Marvin the Martian?"

He was right: there was no sense even pretending to be diplomatic with a telepath. I spread my hands. "Yeah. That makes it tougher, but yeah."

"Okay, I'll send you the software tonight. What time is it?"

I glanced up at the clock over my office door. "Half past broccoli."

Susan found the clock at a yard sale on another island, even more remote than ours. The numbers are all represented by farm products. One is a carrot. Two is a pair of onions. Twelve is a dozen eggs. And so on. Four o'clock is represented by four little clumps of broccoli.

Anyone else would probably have stared at me as if I'd lost my mind. Zudie just nodded, of course. "I have to be out of here by a quarter to turnip at the latest."

Turnips are five. "So soon?"

He nodded. "People start getting up by then. I want to be in my boat, pooting home, when they do."

"Where are you moored? Not down at the marina."

"Of course not. I tied up to a sheltered little dock at an empty house not far from here, about a mile up the road that way." He gestured.

"How could you be sure the house was . . . I withdraw the question with as much dignity as I can muster. What kind of boat do you have?"

He looked at me. "Would the answer mean anything to you at all?"

He had me there. "Not a thing."

"So why ask?"

"To keep the conversation going. That way after you're gone and I think of the dozen intelligent questions I *should* have asked you, at least I won't be remembering any gaping holes in the conversation during which I could have asked them if I'd thought of them yet."

He rummaged on my desk and located one of those little pads of white notepaper that no handheld computer is *ever* going to replace, found a pen and started scribbling. "I already have your private and work email addresses, and your phone number." Well, of couse he did. "I'll give you my e-mail, a couple of URLs, and my phone code. Anything we forget we can deal with later. I presume you have broadband?"

"Just," I agreed. "They only got the cable out here to us a few months ago. I still can't get over how fast everything loads. You must have some kind of fancy satellite rig, eh? How does it . . . you're right, forget it, the answer would mean nothing to me. Is it expensive? That's what I do want to know, I guess. How well off are you, Zudie? How do you pay for things? I seem to remember your family had money."

"They're all gone now, and so is that money," he said. "I support myself."

"Do you mind if I ask how?"

"Not when you phrase it that politely. These days I gamble online."

My eyebrows rose. "Ah. I see."

He reddened slightly. "I don't cheat. Exactly."

I nodded. "But you know a hell of a lot more about the mathematics of probability than anybody else in the game—including the house."

"A hell of a lot more. Thank God for the Indians."

"I don't follow."

"Most of the online gambling outfits are the same people that own casinos in Vegas and Atlantic City. They share information. As soon as one house notices that your luck is literally incredible, they all know it, and what you look like and your Visa number and your ISP. But lately some of the Indian tribes with casinos of their own have been going into online gambling too, in a big way. And they *don't* share information. They hate each other more than they fear people like me. I exploit this error."

I nodded. "Terrific. That's going to really impress the

cops. You're Bret Maverick, the riverboat gambler of cyberspace."

He shrugged. "I'm also a theoretical mathematician affiliated with Oxford, knee deep in honours. People have written their dissertations about me. I'll win the Nobel if I live long enough."

"Ah," I said. "A flake."

He nodded. "Yes, I do see the problem. None of the things about me that are impressive will impress a policeman. I'm sure you'll come up with a brilliant solution." He stood up. "I have got to go, now. It's getting on turnip."

"Some coffee for the road?"

He shuddered. "Thank you, no. Not my drug."

"What is?"

He smiled that weird wonderful Crazy Baby smile of his. "Nitrogen and oxygen, mostly. It's a great high."

"Withdrawal is a bitch, though."

His expression sobered and he nodded. "That it is. That it is." He stood up. "Good night, Russell. Thank you for helping."

"I haven't yet. I'm not convinced I can."

"Thanks for agreeing to try, then. We can do this, you know."

Uh huh. "Well . . . I know we have to try."

"Yes. We do." He turned and began to leave. But he stopped in the doorway, and turned, and after a pause he said, so softly his voice sounded almost normal, "She really was special."

I swallowed, hard. It stung just like a hard slap, made my eyes water and everything. But only like a slap. Not like a punch to the heart. "Yes, she was. Why she chose me I'll never understand."

He nodded. "That's right."

He turned to go again, and this time I stopped him. "Zandor?"

"Yes?"

I felt stupid, but I went ahead anyway. Basically the story of my life. "You really think I would have done the Bunny?"

"I know so," he said.

That wasn't the way I remembered it. But I had a sneaking feeling that he was right, that the way I remembered it was bullshit. "Huh. God, I haven't thought of her in years. I wonder what the story was with her."

"Oh, I can tell you that."

"No *shit*!"

"I was out for a walk early one Sunday morning, and she drove past me on her way back to the school of nursing. All she could think about was why she was doing . . . what she'd just been doing."

"*Right*," I said. "I remember now. The year after that Bill Doane dated a nurse, and he mentioned seeing a picture of the Bunny in their yearbook from the year before." I frowned. "It never seemed to make sense. I mean, you'd think a nurse of all people would be more likely to appreciate things like hygiene, genetics—"

"She didn't want to be a nurse," Zudie said.

"No? What did she want to be?"

"A housewife."

I grinned. "No, really."

"A farm housewife. She was daffy in love with her high school sweetheart, who was two thousand miles away at agricultural college studying to become a scientific farmer, and all she wanted to do in the world was marry him and populate his farm with fat kids. Unfortunately, he had failed to knock her up by the end of the summer, and so her parents had forced her to go off to nursing school at the other end of the country. The first week there she suddenly thought, what if I *were* pregnant, and just found out now? Why, her parents would have to let her drop out of nursing school and let her boyfriend make an honest woman out of her, that's what. All she needed to do was become pregnant—"

"Oh my *God*—" I began to giggle.

"—So quickly that all concerned would readily accept her boyfriend as the father. Since there was no telling why they had failed to conceive so far—it certainly had not been from lack of trying—she had to assume at least part of the problem might lie with her. So she felt it would be good to attack the problem with maximum force, take every step she could to maximize the chances of conception . . ."

I was laughing now.

"She was prudent enough to choose a college bar, rather than some bucket of blood downtown, where the men might have been more virile but definitely would have been more volatile. And a Catholic college at that."

"I will be God damned." I had control of the laughter now, but I couldn't stop grinning. "And it worked. Right? That's why she disappeared?"

He nodded. "Tested positive, and she was literally on the next train smoking."

"Jesus." My smile went away. "Jesus. So . . . if I'd—"

"Yes. If you had made up your mind to go down and see her a week earlier than you did, you would have been one of the candidates for father of her baby."

"Wow." The thought of a second human being

wandering the planet burdened with my genetic short-comings was weird. On the other hand, it would be nice to have a child somewhere who didn't hate me yet.

"There's time to fix that, you know," he said.

"Good night, Zandor." Enough is enough, for one night.

"Yes, it is. Good night, Russell. Thank you."

"For what?"

"For being who you are."

I thought of several flip responses. Instead I said, "You're welcome. It has not come without effort."

He nodded. "I know." He turned and left.

I watched the office door shut behind him. I sat there staring at my computer desktop for a minute or two, trying without success to take a comprehensive survey of my mental and emotional state. The only thing I was reasonably sure of was that I was alive. And had not been, for some indeterminate time.

Finally I said aloud, "Now, *that* was passing strange." I put the computer to sleep, shut off the light, and went into the house, and along the way I noticed that I was not exhausted. I was tired, very tired, I could tell I would be asleep within minutes of lying down in bed. But I was not exhausted. I realized I had been, for some indeterminate time. And was not any more.

Tentatively I thought of Susan . . . and allowed myself to *feel* about her, as well. The familiar wave of sadness and yearning crashed over me, so intense I caught my breath and broke step. But when it had passed, I was still standing. And the yearning had receded, was now like the wave receding back into the sea, a tugging at the legs that was powerful and insistent, but endurable.

I went to bed and as I had expected I slept at once.

4.

You might expect that I'd have awoken the next morning with a feeling of unreality, more than half wondering whether the whole Zudie episode had been a sustained hallucination. I didn't. The moment I opened my eyes, I remembered everything that had happened, and didn't doubt a second of it.

But I didn't think about it right away. I was distracted by how it felt to wake up. It had been a long time since I'd woken up. I'd just been regaining consciousness. This was much better. I was surprised when I got my glasses on to see by the clock on the VCR that it was 1:00 P.M.— that I had, for the first time in months, slept for eight solid continuous uninterrupted hours. The sleep had not been dreamless, but I didn't recall any of the dreams, retaining only a general impression that none of them had been distressing. I felt good. Rested.

Hungry.

I had not awoken hungry in at least twenty years.

An omelette and two cups of coffee later, I was sitting on the sun porch between the house and the office, enjoying the sunshine and the clean foresty-smelling breeze and the distant sounds of less fortunate souls laboring with things like chainsaws and mowers. And trying to think of some viable alternative to simply walking into a police station and asking to speak to a detective about some murders. When I came up empty, I tried to think of anything I could bring with me to the police station that would make my story even slightly more plausible. After a while I went into the office, fired up Netscape and sent Zudie an e-mail:

> Zandor,
> 1. Did you get the sense that Allen has used that particular site before?
> 2. Could there be physical evidence there of previous kills?
> 3. Do you think you could spot the site from the highway?
>
> —Russell

He responded so promptly I knew he'd been waiting to hear from me.

> Slim,
> 1. yes
> 2. perhaps
> 3. maybe—in theory. But only if there were some way to get me there without covering the intervening distance. I couldn't endure the journey. Racing

past that many minds in quick succession . . . no.
Sorry.

> Zudie

I thought of suggesting we go in the middle of the night,
when traffic up the coast was negligible. But how would
he be able to see anything in the dark? There was no point
in even asking if he'd be willing to wander around the
Point Grey section of Vancouver at random, trying to spot
a member of the target family from Allen's mental picture of them. Ah, but maybe—

> Zudie,
> Suppose I could get you in touch with a police
> sketch artist. Need not be in corpus; phone should
> do. Could you produce a sketch of any of the four
> victims? Did he picture them clearly enough?
>
> —Slim

His answer was again immediate:

> Yes. I think I could do that. All four. Good one,
> Slim.

That was something to go on, at least. Not much, but
measurably more than nothing at all.

So now the question was, *which* police station? And
now that sense of unreality I'd expected to wake up with
finally began to kick in.

I *did* know that the question was not a simple one.
Law enforcement in the Lower Mainland of B.C. is so
complex a patchwork of jurisdictions that it may be the

best possible commentary on how insignificant crime in Canada is: the cops can afford to run a Chinese firedrill 24/7. But I thought it was something I could at least make a start on by phone. Two hours after I began, I knew better.

The city of Vancouver itself, or Greater Vancouver as it wishes people would call it, has its own police force—though it's not as big as those of some of its suburbs like Surrey and Burnaby. But the whole Lower Mainland, which encompasses all three, is also the jurisdiction of the Royal Canadian Mounted Police—the Mounties, or federal cops—and just where and how RCMP interfaced with VPD was a mystery to me. In the land of my birth, it was the FBI that took the biggest interest in serial killers, but whether or not the analogy held in Canada I did not know.

I was also pretty sure that the scattered geography of the crime itself was going to complicate the assigning of jurisdiction. According to Zudie, the victims all lived in Point Grey, one of the better districts of Vancouver. But the crime was going to take place at some indeterminate point along the Sea to Sky Highway—which is over two hundred miles long (310 kilometers, to a Canadian. Or indeed, to anyone on planet Earth but an American). I did not know whether any one police agency took responsibility for the entire highway, and some of the towns along its length, such as the famous ski town Whistler, might easily have their own local heat as well.

All this seemed to suggest that the RCMP might be the logical choice, since its mandate was unbounded. But I didn't *want* it to be the RCMP. If it was, I was going to have to make my report to Corporal McKenzie, Heron Island's sole peace officer. In the first place the most shocking crime he had dealt with in his entire tenure was the theft of a barbeque, and in the second place he was famously the clumsiest human alive, so uncoordinated that two or three times a year he knocked himself unconscious by slamming his own car door on his head. That was why he was finishing out his service on Heron Island. If he sent a file as flakey as this one over to the mainland it would be shitcanned for sure. But if I went to any other RCMP office, I would be insulting the poor old man.

On the other hand, there was certainly little point in driving all the way into town, walking into a police station, and then being told it was an RCMP matter.

Which police station, for that matter? I vaguely remembered hearing that there were half a dozen or more "community police stations" scattered around Vancouver, but I had no idea what that meant: whether they were real police stations like the precincts I remembered from New York, or just places for kids to meet Officer Friendly.

I decided that I wanted if possible to get this right on the first try. It was going to be hard enough to tell this story once. So I tried to get an answer by phone.

To avoid committing myself for as long as possible, I decided to present my question as a hypothetical one that I was asking as part of a column I was writing for *The Globe and Mail*. Suppose a person on one of the islands has knowledge that a man of unknown residence plans to kidnap someone in Vancouver and murder him somewhere along a 300-klick highway: how would such a tangled jurisdictional problem as this be worked out in real life? If this person were to call 911, what would he be told to do?

Two hours later, I was fairly confident that I had set a

new world's record for pointlessly climbed telephone trees, and spoken to several of the most surly incompetent intransigent obfuscatory uncivil-unservice toads in the Lower Mainland, but those were my only accomplishments. The official media spokesperson for the police department, my first choice, was away from her desk, at two in the afternoon, and her answering robot suggested only that I try calling back during business hours. I wondered what those might be. The main administrative switchboard operator, a woman with an unmistakable honk of a voice, divided her time between giving me numbers to try that did not work, and stoutly denying that she had ever given me any such numbers. The police non-emergency operator maintained that a) only the 911 operator could answer my question, and b) I would be committing a serious criminal offense if I were to call 911 and ask it. And the community relations number I tried in desperation produced a phone machine that required me to select one of nine options, none of which applied to my situation, and declined to take a message; I wasted some time confirming to myself that the three options that came *closest* to matching my problem all led to *other* phone machines that went nowhere. *For a list of ways in which technology has failed to improve life, please press one, or stay on the line for other options. Please do not hang up: your humiliation is very amusing to us.*

I managed to stop short of throwing the phone to the floor and dancing on it. I put it very gently down on its mothership, and breathed deeply until the impulse to bang my head against the wall had receded. Then I got dressed and fired up the Accord and drove down to Bug Cove and got on the ferry lineup. In half an hour the ferry arrived, and when it had finished disgorging about a hundred pedestrians and fifty or sixty vehicles, and a few dozen foot passengers had boarded, our lineup of cars rolled slowly down the hill and onto the ferry with the bored competence of something most of us had done hundreds of times. As usual there turned out to be just enough cars to fill the boat, because all us islanders knew the point at which, if you had to line up behind that, you weren't going to get aboard for that sailing—and if some ignorant tourists got in line behind that point, someone was usually compassionate enough to tell them they were wasting their time. Unless they were loud or in some other way obnoxious.

Most Heron Islanders make a great point of being jaded with the ferry ride. They sit in their cars and read the paper. I've never been able to get over it. I always get out and gawk along with the tourists. It's one of the few times you'll ever encounter tourists who aren't making a sound— even the kids. That half hour ride is simply the most beautiful journey I know. Dead ahead: the lower mainland of British Columbia, a gorgeous mountainous coast covered with a thousand shades of green and capped with snow even in July. Look left, and you're looking up the passage to Alaska, at a succession of islands and mountains that recede infinitely like a grey-scale poem. Look right, and there's open sea, gleaming in the sun: the mouth of mighty Vancouver Harbour can be glimpsed further down the coast, and just visible on the far southern horizon is some part of the state of Washington. Turn and look behind you, and there's Heron Island rising from the water in your wake, bursting with green growing things and happy people—and beyond it, vast Vancouver Island, which is to Heron as a whale is to a goldfish, and beyond that . . . well, Vladivostok, I guess. Pleasure craft are visible in all directions, but not in great numbers. The sky seems huge, a cloud painter's largest canvas. There are almost always small planes in the air, but rarely more than one or two.

I can see I haven't conveyed it, merely inventoried the furniture. I don't know if the words I need exist, and if they do I don't know them. Just let it stand that to ride a ferry to any of the Howe Sound islands is to take a magical mystery tour through a place of timeless beauty so *large* that no lens will ever capture it, and so poignant that no heart will ever forget it.

Half an hour after we pulled out of Bug Cove I drove off the ferry into Horseshoe Bay—strictly a terminal town—and half an hour after that I was in downtown Vancouver, hoping for a parking space where the cars on either end of me would be more expensive than mine. I did not expect this to be a major challenge. My Accord was an '89—so old that the last time I'd needed to replace a headlight, it had proved impossible to fasten it in place in the normal fashion, because the retaining frame was too corroded to hold a screw anymore. I'd ended up using Krazy Glue.

In my ignorance and pitiful naivete, I had presumed that because both the Vancouver Police Department's website and the municipal listings in the phone book gave the address of police headquarters as 2120 Cambie Street, I would find police headquarters at that address. Silly me.

I pictured a vast brick and stone mausoleum with big white globe lights on either side of the doors; inside would be dozens of uniformed cops, benches of despairing perps, walls festooned with wanted posters, and a big U-shaped counter behind which a fat, cynical, old desk sergeant would hold court. He would be full of skeptical, probing questions, but if I gave him the right answers and persuaded him I was a serious man and not a whack job, he would pass me on to a detective. And then the hard part would begin.

Just finding the fucking address proved to be a nontrivial problem. I won't bore you with the details that would be necessary to make sense of this, but just take my word for it that although the address was nominally on Cambie Street, it was actually located *underneath* and beside the very heavily traveled Cambie Street Bridge, at a place where, perhaps God knows why, 2nd and 5th Avenues intersect. It can only be approached from one of the four points of the compass, and then only if you ignore what the map says. About the third time you drive helplessly past it, cursing and beating the steering wheel, you catch the trick.

Once I solved the maze, parked in front of the giant block-sized building, and got out of the car, I began to understand why the place was as difficult as possible to reach: it wasn't police headquarters at all. Oh, one end of it was a police property of some kind—but as I fed coins into the meter I could clearly see that ninety percent of the structure, a vast office building, in fact constituted the headquarters of ICBC. The Insurance Corporation of British Columbia is a semiprivate company with an absolute monopoly on auto and collision insurance in the province of B.C. It is internationally renowned for its compassion, generosity, efficiency and competence, and I am Marie of Rumania. This was where you came to file your appeal, begging for at least some token fraction of what you deserved and desperately needed, and they were in no hurry at all for you to find the place.

Apparently the police felt the same way. And once you had made your way to "headquarters," down at the ass end of the building, and pushed through the glass door with the police logo on it, where were you?

In a cheesey and entirely empty lobby, strikingly like that of the Olympian, the crummy hotel in downtown Olympia, New York, one step above a flophouse, in which Susan and I had surrendered our virginities to one another. No milling cops. No suspects cuffed to D-rings. No crying babies or people screaming in foreign languages or hookers in abbreviated costumes. Off to the left was a wide counter, again much like the front desk of the old Olympian, save that back in those days front desks were not yet enclosed with bulletproof glass. The only people visible behind it were two middleaged women in civilian clothing, both of whom ignored me. On the right was an office that appeared to be unused.

At the far end of the lobby I could see elevators. Curious to see how far I would get before I was stopped and asked for my ID and an account of myself, I wandered down there. Nobody tried to stop me. The elevator alcove *finally* made a stab at pretending to be part of police headquarters: All the elevator doors bore the VPD crest, with the word SERVAMUS above it in some large bold chancery font, and above them hung sixteen large portrait photos memorializing officers who had been killed in the line of duty. The most recent was from a good five years ago or so. I could still remember the details of the story. Probably most Vancouverites could. As I looked over the photos, two uniformed cops came out of one of the elevators, walked past me and left the building. Neither looked at me.

Once I established that if I felt like getting on one of those elevators and wandering around headquarters, knocking on doors at random, I could, I retraced my steps to the glassed-in front desk. My story was more than flakey enough; I didn't need to start out by pissing them off.

For which reason I let the women behind the counter keep their backs to me for as long as they felt necessary to establish their authority and importance. By the time the alpha female was ready to acknowledge my existence, a courier with a parcel under his arm had arrived and lined up behind me. He gave off an air of being in a hurry, and I did not feel like trying to sell a complicated, tricky story while an impatient man waited at my shoulder. I waved him ahead of me. Both he and the woman behind the counter stared at me. After a short hesitation, he stepped around me, slid over his parcel under the bullet-proof glass, and left, looking over his shoulder at me to make sure I was not going to turn violent before he cleared the door.

The woman behind the glass was now the picture of skepticism. In size, shape, and general facial appearance she bore a strong resemblance to Lou Costello, but the hair was more evocative of Larry Fine of the Three Stooges. I introduced myself, and produced a business card, a press card, and a few print copies of recent columns I had published in *The Globe and Mail*, as evidence that I was gainfully employed in a respectable profession not noted for raving lunatics. And also to clearly make the point that I did not work for the local *Vancouver Sun* or *Province*, which routinely raked VPD over the coals, but for the *Globe*, which being published out of Toronto rarely felt any pressing need to do so.

She declined to so much as glance at my exhibits, and the moment our eyes met I knew I was dead in the water here. No matter what, I was not going to get anything I wanted from this woman if it lay within her power to withhold it from me. I have no idea why, but the gaze she fastened upon me was unmistakably the Evil Eye. Instantly I was catapulted back through time thirty years: she was the Assistant Dean of Women, and I was a raggedy-ass hippy, and no explanation I could possibly concoct for my presence on the third floor of the girls' dorm at 3:00 A.M. was going to be adequate.

I did ask her some of the questions I had prepared on the ferry ride—I had come this far—but at the last moment I decided to phrase them as I had on the phone, as hypothetical inquiries for a work of prose, to avoid committing myself as long as possible. It was immediately clear to both of us that I was wasting my time. When it finally began to dawn on her that I was wasting *her* time too, I did manage to elicit a single fact: that *if* the allegedly hypothetical questions I was annoying her with happened to actually be actual questions, what I would need to do was be interviewed by "an officer from Major Crimes."

A detective?

"An officer from Major Crimes, sir."

"So I'd just go upstairs—"

"You cannot go upstairs, sir."

"Ah. I see." That's what *you* think, lady. "So this officer would come down here, and—"

"Major Crimes is not located in this building, sir."

"It's not?" You obviously have never been in an auto accident in this province. "Where is it?"

"I won't tell you that, sir."

I stared at her long enough to blink several times. "The Major Crimes division is not located at headquarters. And citizens are not permitted to know where it is located."

"That's correct, sir."

I nodded. If you react, you only confirm that they've insulted you. "Mind if I ask why not?"

"Not at all, sir."

Blink, Blink. Blink. Ah, of course. "Good one. Why not?"

"Was there anything else I could help you with today, sir?"

"If I did want to see a Major Crimes officer, how would you suggest I locate one? Random questioning of the populace?"

I was surprised when a slight edge came on her voice; I hadn't expected her to recognize sarcasm without tone-of-voice cues. "*If* you convinced me a Major Crimes officer needed to speak with you, you would sit down on that bench right over there and wait, for as long as necessary, and eventually an officer would speak with you."

I glanced behind me. Sure enough, there was a bench there which I had overlooked. "Group W, I presume," I muttered. But of course the reference went over her head. She was too young to know about mother-stabbers and father-rapers and an envelope under a half a ton of garbage. I wished she were with it.

"*Was* your question hypothetical then, sir?" How do public officials manage to make such a deadly insult out of the word *sir*? "Or did you wish to report knowledge of a homicide?"

I looked into her piggy little eyes and knew that I did not wish to report to *this* woman knowledge of an attempted jaywalking. "You've been most helpful," I lied. "And I for one have enjoyed this brief interlude."

She looked down too late, and found that I had just retrieved my ID and my old columns. "What was your name again, sir?"

"English, on my mother's side," I said. "Hard to know about Dad until he's identified."

"Can I have your name, sir?" she persisted.

"Why, I'd have to think about it. Can you cook? Are you fertile?"

She reddened, and glanced around for a cop, but I was already backing away from the glass, and anyway what would a cop be doing in the lobby of police headquarters? "Sir—"

"I could talk to you all day," I said, "but I'd prefer to set myself on fire. Besides, today happens to be the Feast of Ali Ben Dova Redrova, and I have sworn to carry the Sacred Domestic Utensil beyond the Lion's Gate Bridge before darkness stumbles and falls, so—"

"Sir—"

"Fuck you very much—have an ice day, now."

I fled.

5.

Driving away from there, I suddenly remembered the building that I'd thought 2120 Cambie was going to turn out to be—a structure much more like my mental picture of what police headquarters ought to look like. Now where the hell had that been? Oh, yes. Catty-corner from the Firehall Theatre, on the corner of Main and . . . what, East Cordova?

The Firehall is one of the better dance venues in Vancouver. I hadn't been there in over a year, since before Susan's death. Some of the fun of attending a modern dance performance had faded once she was no longer around to be dragged along kicking and screaming. (Perversely, I'd been to several of the poetry readings she used to drag me to in revenge.)

But I was able to find the place without difficulty. It was largely a matter of following the junkies. By the time I reached it I thought I understood why it was not police headquarters, even though it should have been.

The Main Street police station does indeed look exactly like a police headquarters ought to look—massive, monolithic, medieval, proof against anything short of nuclear attack, surrounded by copmobiles. And it lies exactly one block from the single worst open-air drug supermarket in North America: the gaping, glistening open sore that begins at the corner of Main and Hastings.

I've always thought of it as the Corner of Pain and Wastings. It is a 24/7 rolling-boil riot of junkies, crackheads, crystal queens, dragon-chasers, pill freaks, drunks, winos, whackos, and the dealers who love them all. Elsewhere, they are whores, pimps, muggers, pickpockets, panhandlers, squeegee guys, dumpster divers—everybody has an occupation—but when they get near Main and Hastings, they're all just customers, anxious to score whatever it is they need to get over. The whole area throbs with a desperation that transcends even despair, an ugliness that has no choice but to flaunt itself. It didn't matter how suitable the physical structure might be: to have had police headquarters one block from that international disgrace would have been unthinkable.

I thought it was amazing luck that I found a parking space right next to the front door. Then I got out and discovered that the parking meter was "broken"—it ate my money, but continued to show time remaining as "00:00." It was obviously the cops' way of assuring themselves a space at need, when they were too rushed to go around back and use the underground garage. Cursing under my breath, I got back in the car and found another space a block and a half away. I checked the interior of the car very carefully before getting out, to be absolutely sure that nothing pawnable was visible from any window, and that tape cassettes were visible to make it clear this car held no CD player. Even so, I more than half expected to find the car gone when I returned. I guess that's a clue as to just how foul the area around Main and Hastings is: there are people there who would steal an '89 Accord.

This lobby *looked* like the lobby of police headquarters. For a start, it was full of cops, on their way in or out. To my left as I walked in were windows with signs saying things like RECORD CLEARANCES, DOCUMENT SERVICES, and TAXI DETAIL. (This being normal business hours, all of them were closed.) On the right were doors labeled FINGERPRINT ROOM and POLICE-NATIVE LIAISON. (I couldn't help wondering if any Indians had liaised with the police lately—voluntarily.) And directly ahead of me as I entered was a glassed-in cage much like the one back at Cambie Street, similarly inhabited by female civilians—but *these* looked much more like the kind of women a sane person would hire to run a *real* cop shop than the trolls back at the Potemkin police station.

The alpha female here clocked me as I came in the door, and by the time I reached the counter she was waiting for me, with a pleasant smile. She was a tall slender brunette in her sixties, and exuded competence and calm. I introduced myself, and presented my cards and columns as before. This woman looked at them all politely, and nodded. "How can I help you, sir?" were her opening words.

"I'm working on a novel, and I have a hypothetical question," I said. Neither of those statements was a lie; it was only together that they became misdirection. "It's about jurisdiction. Suppose a Heron Island resident, like myself, came in the door and told you he had certain knowledge that next week, say, a person of unknown address is going to kidnap a Vancouver resident, take him an unknown distance up the Sea to Sky Highway, and . . ." I hesitated. " . . . and shoot him. For a start, who would have jurisdiction in a case like that—VPD, or the horsemen?"

She nodded. "If you actually came in and told me that, I'd refer you to a Major Crimes officer and let him make the call—but I can tell you what he'd say. Barring other complications, the operative factor is the address of the victim. So yes, it would be our case. Of course, we might very well interact with the RCMP, or with other police agencies along the Sea to Sky, depending on the circumstances."

"I see."

"And if your hypothetical murderer were from another country, say, we could also end up interfacing with Interpol, the FBI, or the like."

I was mildly stunned. She had given me the information I'd asked for, just as if I had a right to it. "So basically if my hero came in with that story, you'd tell him to have a seat and then you'd send for a—"

"I'd just send him upstairs to Major Crimes and have him speak with a detective."

I blinked. "Major Crimes is—"

"Third floor."

"You're allowed to tell me that?"

She frowned. "Why not?"

"Never mind. And what the detective would probably say is, the address of the victim controls, so it'd be his case."

She nodded judiciously. "If, as you say, the victim resided in Vancouver itself, and not one of the suburbs with their own force, like Surrey or Burnaby."

I suddenly realized, to my horror, that I was fresh out of questions, and could not think of any new ones. The rotten bitch had been unforgivably helpful, and now the moment of decision was upon me, way before I had been expecting it. Here, now, was the point at which, if I was ever going to, I should clear my throat and say, well actually, it isn't hypothetical and I really do need to speak with a detective.

I wanted to. Why else had I come into town, for Christ's sake? I'd promised Zudie. And some fucking lunatic wanted to butcher a whole family, for the sheer artistic symmetry of it. No matter what, I couldn't let that happen, and continue to live with myself.

But I pictured the conversation ahead, with the detective.

Let me see if I've got this, sir: you're sure Mr. Zudidoodi can read minds, because a long time ago he used to smell really bad? And last night, armed only with the knowledge that you're a widower, he divined that you're depressed? That seems conclusive, all right. And you say all we have to do is find a rich fella that lives somewhere within flying distance of the Lower Mainland—or a family of four somewhere in Point Grey—or a quiet spot somewhere along a three-hundred-kilometer highway? No problem: we have a special department for that. You want to go down and talk to a woman behind the desk at 2120 Cambie Street. . . .

"Uh . . . well, I guess that's all I needed to know, for the moment. Thank you, you've been extremely helpful."

"You're quite welcome," she said.

I started to leave—then stopped. "Can I ask you a personal question?"

She looked me over. "How personal?"

"How have you lasted this long as a civil servant, being so helpful?"

Her smile had been pleasant, but her grin was glorious. "People are generally too grateful to rat me out."

I grinned back. "I'll bet they are."

"Have a good day," we chorused at each other, and grinned some more, and I left.

I don't know about her; my grin didn't last as far as the sidewalk. The whole trip had been a waste of time. I *had* to tell the cops. But I had not been able to. And it was not ever going to get any easier. I felt like a fool.

I was in such a sour mood I was perversely almost disappointed to find my car still where I had left it. I told myself I deserved to have it robbed, for being such a coward. I got in, and put the key in the ignition, but didn't turn it. The car behind me started up and drove away; now would be a convenient time to back up two feet and then pull out myself. I just sat there.

I thought about getting out, going back to 312 Main and completing my report. That lady behind the counter had been so polite, she might actually pretend to be surprised when I told her my question hadn't really been hypothetical after all. A car took the space behind me, and a blonde woman got out and walked away. Pedestrians passed. Every so often, one would stop and bend down slightly to check me out. I was sitting in a car on Main Street with the engine off; was I selling, or buying?

I ignored them all and tried to persuade myself I was glib enough to sell my wacky story to an experienced detective. I wasn't glib enough to sell that to myself. In my rear view mirror I saw a gaunt bald man get in the car behind me and bend down out of sight. It seemed to me that what I needed to do was find some way to *demonstrate* telepathy to the police. That meant I would have to somehow bring Zudie close to one of them—but I believed him completely when he said he couldn't survive coming to town. And I had no plausible excuse to haul a Vancouver cop all the way out to Heron. For some reason I don't understand, it's harder to get people to take a half-hour ferry than to drive an hour out of their way in traffic.

Behind me the engine started, and the bald man reappeared behind the wheel. A glimmering of a possible solution occurred to me then, but it would be a good five minutes or so before I had time to examine it closely, because an instant later the penny dropped, and I was way too busy finding my key in the ignition and starting the car and putting it in reverse and stepping slowly but firmly on the accelerator while leaning on the horn.

Bump. HO-O-O-O-ONK!

When it was clear to the bald man that I was not going to let him drive away in that stolen car, he got out, leaving the engine running, and came toward me. Belatedly it occurred to me that car thieves are criminals, and as such are generally aware that most citizens oppose their actions, and for that reason will often bring to work with them implements designed to win arguments. I stopped honking my horn, slammed my transmission from reverse into drive, floored it, and of course the Accord stalled out. I looked frantically around its interior for something deadly. No luck. I rolled up my window and made sure all the doors were locked. I was reasonably sure he did not have a gun—we were in Canada—but that didn't mean he couldn't be holding a knife, or hiding a tire iron up his sleeve.

The bald man arrived, bent down and glared in at me. He made a roll-down-your-window gesture. I responded with a go-fuck-yourself gesture.

"What do you gotta be a prick for?" he called bitterly. "You think I picked this from a list of exciting career opportunities?"

I couldn't think of a thing to say in reply. I tried to restart the car, failed, and waited to see if he would smash in my window, produce a weapon of some kind and kill me.

He looked as if he were thinking about it. But as he pondered, he glanced behind him, said, "Shhhhh-*it*." and took off—in the same direction I was facing, and at considerably better acceleration than I would have been able to manage with the Accord.

He had reason to. She was right alongside me in the street when she decided it was hopeless and abandoned the chase—but running so fast, she was four cars ahead of me before she could manage to put on the brakes. I think she could have caught him, in fact, but made the reluctant decision that the prize would not be worth the energy expenditure. She stood with her hands on her hips for a few moments, breathing hard, then turned and trudged wearily back my way. I rolled my window down.

"Thanks," the blonde woman said when she reached me. "That was nice of you." Her breathing was already back to normal.

"You're welcome."

Her hair was cut short in what, back in my day (late Bronze Age), was called a pageboy, and for all I know still is. On a lot of women who wear it, that style looks just too goshdarn pixieish for my taste, but it suited her. The knee-jerk reaction would have been to call her butch. She was not, quite, but there definitely was a certain androgeny to her features, and to the way she was dressed—grey cutoff sweatshirt, blue jeans, black sneakers—and indeed in the way she carried herself. She could have passed for an extremely pretty boy. But only from the shoulders up. Even under a sweatshirt, her breasts were impressive enough that I knew I must not let myself be caught looking at them.

"I really appreciate it," she said. "Really."

By now I had noticed that her car was an Accord, like mine—a few years more recent, but in even worse condition. "Sentimental value, eh?"

The left corner of her mouth twitched slightly. Somehow I knew that meant she thought what I had said was hilarious. "It's not the car. My badge and gun are in the glovebox."

"You're a cop!" I blurted.

"Police officer," she suggested.

"Yes, of course, I'm sorry," I said, flustered. "I was born in New York." That sounded silly even to me. "Uh, so you're a police officer."

Her right eyebrow lowered a quarter of an inch. Somehow I knew that meant I had said something painful. "Sort of."

"Well, I'm pleased to meet you. My uncle and two of my cousins are c . . . are police officers. My name is Russell Walker."

"Nika Mandiç," she said. Arm muscles defined themselves concisely as she offered her hand.

I shook it. Somewhere else, I *might* have said, "A pleasure, Nika." But I might not . . . and a block away from the police station, and given the circumstances, I knew what she would find more comfortable. "A pleasure, Constable."

I realized I was hoping I'd guessed wrong, that she would say, it's "Detective," not "Constable." Then this movie would be back on the rails: I'd have located a sympatico detective. But no. All she said was, "The pleasure's mine, Mr. Walker." Oh well. Not much good a beat cop could do me.

"Let's check the damage," I said, and got out of the car.

But it turned out there was none to speak of. Though our Accords were of different years, the bumper heights matched.

Our own heights nearly did as well. I'm six foot one, but she came within an inch or two of me. (I've lived in Canada long enough now to have copped to the metric system in most things—it really is a more sensible scheme, generally—but here I make my stand: I am not 185.5 centimeters tall, I'm six one, and she was five eleven, not 180.5, and there's an end to it.) And there was no question which of us weighed more. I'm bony and frail, and she was neither. But all her extra weight appeared to be muscle; the more I saw her move around, the clearer it became that she was fit enough to run up the side of a building and kick in a third floor window.

And almost agitated enough. She seemed mad at herself for not having been fast enough to run the perp down.

When she discovered that her rear bumper had not fared quite so well as the front one, and she would be talking with ICBC after all, she pulled a flat of Pepcid, the antacid nostrum, from her shirt pocket with a practiced gesture. It comes in rectangles of stiffened foil, on which a dozen little pills lie sealed under individual plastic bubbles; when you want some, you push on a pill until it bursts through the foil and pops out. As she did so now with the last pill on the flat, I could not help but notice that on every one of the previous eleven holes, the little leftover flap of torn foil had been pulled completely off and thrown away. I've never done that in my life. She did the same with the twelfth as I watched: peeled off the scrap of foil, rolled it into a tiny ball, and dropped it into her shirt pocket along with the now-empty flat. I was sure enough to bet on it that all eleven previous foil balls had made it as far as an approved garbage receptacle. This woman was so tight-assed she probably broke wine glasses every time she farted.

So she was exactly the wrong sort of person to try and sell a story as wacky as mine to. And even if I did somehow convince her, she'd be little help; there simply wasn't anything in her book of rules and procedures—the software she ran on—to cover the situation. And finally, she had minimal clout. She was a mere constable, a uniform cop, probably a beat walker—somewhere in her first five years of service, and for all I knew fresh out of the academy. What I needed, at minimum, was a detective constable, a senior investigator, ideally from Major Crimes. A sergeant or an inspector would have been even better.

On the other hand, Constable Mandiç was here, she

was talking to me, and she sort of owed me a favor.

As Bill Clinton found out, a bird in the hand is worth two George Bushes. If you can't be with the cop you want, cop to the one you're with.

Next question: would the logistics work? People who live on islands tend to keep track of the tides; I thought about it, worked the math, and it seemed to me that low tide tonight would come around 3:30 in the morning.

"Are you coming off duty, or about to go on?" I asked her, as she was taking down my particulars so I could be her witness with ICBC.

"I come onshift tonight at 1900 hours," said Constable Mandiç. For some reason saying that made her glower. "Why?"

"I seem to remember you guys . . . excuse me, you officers . . . work eleven-hour shifts. So you'll be on until 6:00 A.M., right?"

She nodded grudgingly.

I took a long deep breath—and decided to go for broke. "Constable, I'd like to ask you for a favor. It will require that you trust me a little bit. I need about twenty minutes of your time tonight . . . and I can't tell you why just yet."

Her shoulders dropped slightly. "Mr. Walker—"

I tried to hold her eyes with mine. "I'm asking you to trust that I'm not an idiot, not a clown, that I'm not wasting your time. After twenty minutes, you'll understand why I had to play it this way . . . and you'll be glad I did, I promise."

She tilted her head slightly and looked me over. "What do you do, Mr. Walker?"

"I write a column for *The Globe and Mail*," I said proudly. Then, seeing her expression, I said quickly, "I'm not a reporter, honest. I'm barely a journalist. I just comment on the stuff reporters dig up—the national and international stuff, at that. I've never yet had occasion to say a single bad thing in print about the Vancouver Police Department. I have often had unkind things to say about the Toronto Police Department."

As I'd hoped, that got me another of those quick corner-of-the-mouth twitches. But no more. "Mr. Walker, I am grateful to you for your help. But you seem responsible enough to know why I can't be doing personal favors while I'm on city time."

"Constable," I said, "I'm responsible enough that I wouldn't ask you to if it wasn't really important. And not just to both of us."

She looked frustrated. "Does it have to be tonight? While I'm on duty?"

I nodded. "It needs to be three things. As soon as possible. Between midnight and 4:00 A.M. And at low tide, which is a little before four tonight."

"Why low tide?"

"Because I need to show you something you can only see then."

She actually turned her head and looked from side to side, as if to catch some Internal Affairs spook photographing her in the act of thinking about doing a civilian a favor while on duty. Failing to find one, she still hesitated.

I tried to think what argument might reach her. The promise of a major bust? Fame? Career advancement? "Constable, look," I said, "I give you my solemn promise. If you do this, lives will be saved."

She sighed. "That doesn't leave me much choice. You

sure you won't give me an advance hint."

"I *can't*."

Very slowly, she nodded twice. "Okay. Where is it you want me to meet you at low tide?"

"Spanish Banks," I told her. "Down at the far west end of it, the last parking lot. Call it 3:30."

She squinted at me. "Is this some kind of drug landing? Or illegal immigrants landing? Or what?"

I spread my hands. "All will be revealed at 3:30 A.M. But you won't be needing backup or firepower."

"Okay, Mr. Walker," she said reluctantly. "This better be good."

"It will be," I promised.

As I drove away I was frantically figuring out the logistics necessary to make this work.

6.

Low tide did indeed turn out to be a little after 3:30, which was nearly perfect from my point of view. A lucky break.

It was far from my last one that night, and I needed every one. The plan was complicated by the fact that Zudie didn't own a cell phone. Well, why would he? He did have a radiophone on his island, but it wasn't portable. His internet connection *was* portable . . . but mine wasn't.

So I had to go to Spanish Banks early. Out of sheer pessimism, I allowed a full hour and a half. That was my second lucky break.

At 2:00 in the morning, the shore was as deserted as I'd hoped, and the weather was pretty near ideal, overcast enough to hide the moon but not damp, cool but not quite cool enough to call for the leather jacket I'd fetched in case; I left it in the car. Spanish Banks is the name given by Vancouver to the last westernmost series of beaches that face the Harbour. Each has its own parking, and every couple of beaches there are washrooms and concessions. After that you can leave your car in the final parking lot, and keep following the rocky shore west on foot a ways—*if* the tide is low enough—until eventually after half a klick or so you round the point and come to Wreck Beach, Vancouver's famous clothing-optional beach and anarchist beachhead. It faces west to the sea rather than north to the Harbour, at the bottom of a near-vertical cliff with a rickety wooden stairway that leads up to the campus of the University of British Columbia. You're apt to find people on Wreck Beach at any hour of the day or night, albeit naked people, testing the latest batch of acid. But the sanitizing stretch of sandy shoreline between the alfresco anarchists and Spanish Banks doesn't really exist at high tide, and even when it does, is very sparsely populated by day—and pretty reliably deserted after midnight. Anyone coming on foot or by dune buggy can be seen from a long way off.

The last parking lot was the only one that wasn't at sea level; the road had begun the climb up to the UBC campus by the time you reached it. So instead of there being houses immediately across the street from the beach, here they didn't begin until several hundred meters further uphill, behind thick trees. That last lot in line was nominally closed after dark, but the barrier preventing entry had been destroyed by a drunk years earlier and never replaced. I was not worried about being rousted by the wrong cops—in the dozen years I'd lived in Vancouver, staying up pretty much all night every night, going for long walks, I had never once seen a police car or officer on patrol.

A short path took me down to the water. The tide was just low enough to let me continue past that last beach without getting my feet wet—another bit of luck as I had no spare shoes or socks or pants. The wind murmured insistently in my ear as I walked, but failed to dispel that familiar potpourri of iodine-y smells which the landlubber thinks of as the sea and the seaman thinks of as the land: the smells of land's end. The footing was lousy, this was where God kept his small rock collection, but I had a Maglite. Thanks to the overcast I failed to spot Zudie's little boat coming. Then as I was beginning to wonder whether he'd screwed up his navigation I heard its engine chuckling softly, and it was just there, no more than a few hundred meters offshore, moving very slowly east to west. I signaled with my Maglite, twice, and he signaled back with his, twice then once, as prearranged. So it was him for sure. His bow turned, and he started in—

—and the next ten minutes or so were an extended Abbott and Costello routine, sidesplittingly hilarious but only in retrospect, which ranged back and forth along the shoreline, and involved furious attempts to whisper at the top of our lungs to one another, and ended in our mutually conceding that we were *not* going to be able to beach that goddamned boat. We came within about eight meters once, three me-lengths, but that was our best shot, and we were too dumb to stick with it: in the end we had to settle for about fifteen meters. Across which Zudie looked at me and I looked at Zudie.

So then Abbott and Costello changed to Buster Keaton: see the funny skinny guy with the sad face walk like a cartoon ostrich through fifteen meters of surging icewater in his clothes, trying to scream in a whisper and brandishing a cell phone above his head. When I was still a good six meters from his boat, the water—or was it liquid nitrogen?—reached my testicles. I abandoned radio silence and called *"Catch!"* at normal volume, and it was as the phone was leaving my hand with what I could already tell was superb accuracy and I'd begun my turn back toward shore that I heard him say *"Don't!"* at the same volume.

Ever try to reverse a full-speed 180 on uncertain footing while crotch-deep in water? Here's what happens. You end up falling over backwards, watching helplessly as: your cell phone hits Baby Huey on the top of his balding head—rebounds, then falls—meets his hands coming up to help him say *ow*—is batted back up in the air—he sees it, tracks it, makes a wild grab at it on its way back down, misses it by a meter with one hand and a centimeter with the other—it comes down *just* inside the boat—he lurches forward, thinking it has fallen overboard—the phone, caught between the tip of his shoe and the side of the boat, squirts up into the air one last time, hits him in the mouth and drops into his shirt pocket—startling him enough that he falls over backwards and disappears from view, lands with a crash—and says softly, after a perfect Chuck Jones pause, "Got it, Ruffell. Fun of a *bitf*!"

There's no way you're going to miss a frame of this, naturally—and a good thing, too, because the overwhelming impulse to laugh you're left with is what keeps you breathing as the arctic cold tries to paralyze your diaphragm and stop your heart. But by the time the sequence has finished unfolding you've been floating on your back in ice cold, faintly greasy salt water for long enough that there's really no hurry at all about standing back up again.

Eventually we both got to our feet together, and looked at each other for a moment, trying to think of something to say. Almost at the same moment we shrugged, waved silently, and turned away from each other. His engine began chuckling again, then burbling, then receding. And I began groaning and shuddering and chattering as the wind chill started to hit, while wading then walking then running with exceptional stride at high speed, and swearing artistically and obscenely whenever I could get a breath. It left little to spare for sobbing.

As I said, it was very lucky I had allowed an hour and a half. I needed every minute left to me. And some further luck. I happened, for instance, to have enough gas in the car to keep the engine running and the heater roaring full blast the whole time. Once I was safely inside, out of the wind, and the windows were starting to steam up, I stripped naked, hung the items of clothing I deemed most crucial by the vents, and did the best job I could of drying myself with the lining of my leather jacket, an old scarf I'd found in the trunk, and half a box of kleenex. Then I put on the jacket, composed an extended castanet solo with my teeth, and rehearsed it until I could make it sound improvised, while smartly and repeatedly slapping every inch of skin I could locate until so much blood had risen to the surface I was in danger of organ failure. I remember wondering what I would say if the *wrong* cop came along before I was done drying my clothes. Not that the right cop would be all that much better. But at least there'd be an explanation I could give her, even if it *was* ridiculous.

At 3:25 I lost my nerve. My clothes were by no means dry yet, but I put them back on anyway. Constable Nika

Mandič had struck me as the type that would be on time.

She was.

In those last five minutes, vestigial core body heat trapped by my damp clothes and leather jacket had achieved a sort of wet-suit effect. I'd begun to feel . . . well, not warm, but less than maximally cold. Then I saw her headlights and got out of the car, and the breeze hit me, and I got chilled all over again before I had time to zip the jacket up.

Okay, it wasn't as bad as before. I wasn't cold enough to actually shudder or chatter anymore. Summer nights in Vancouver are generally pretty pleasant. It might not have seemed a cold night at all, if I'd been dry—I'd originally gone out in it without the leather jacket. I was really no worse than uncomfortable and miserable as I walked to her vehicle.

I'd been expecting her to drive something macho while on duty—a generic cop Plymouth or a Crown Vic or, given her personality, maybe even a Humvee. What I got instead made me smile a bit despite my discomfort. Her own private car, the same one I'd rescued for her that afternoon. A Honda Accord, the same anonymous grey as mine, and no more than a couple of years younger by the looks of the body. Why would she be driving her own ride on duty? She wasn't a detective. An undercover assignment, perhaps?

No, she was in uniform when she got out. "Good evening, Mr. Walker," she greeted me, and just from the tone of her voice I knew she was having second thoughts about this. Well, so was I. In fact, all of a sudden I saw a hole in my planning that might spell disaster.

"Good evening, Constable Mandiç. You have a cell phone with you, right?"

To my vast relief, she nodded and pointed to it on her uniform belt, next to the gun.

"Good. Come for a walk with me, please. It's not far."

To my pleasant surprise, she didn't speak her misgivings. "Okay, Mr. Walker."

I led her down to the water, and back along the shore to the point where I had come thrashing out of the water earlier. It was easier going now that the tide was at its lowest, and I knew where the worst patches of rocks were. And the overcast was letting up a little; armed with the knowledge of where it was, I was able to spot Zudie's boat this time, about a hundred meters offshore, making just enough way to hold his position, the engine sound inaudible in the wind.

I asked Constable Mandiç for her phone, and dialed my own. Zudie picked up at once. "Hey, Slim."

"How about it?" I asked without preliminaries. "Are you getting anything, or what?"

"Repeat after me," he said.

"Wait a sec—I haven't explained what I'm doing yet."

"She'll figure it out. Repeat after me."

"Okay," I said. I turned to her, and started repeating, one sentence at a time, what Zudie said:

"Your career is in the toilet . . ." Her eyes widened at that and she started to rebut; I overrode her.

"But it doesn't deserve to be . . . Your father and grandfather and your maternal aunt were all cops . . . Hero cops, all three . . . Yes, two of them were in another city, but still it should have counted for something . . ." She was frowning ferociously, but held her peace. "Your grades at the academy were outstanding, and between that and your performance since, you should be at least one pay grade higher by now . . . and getting much better postings.

"What *is* her posting?" I asked Zudie, because her frown had become a glare that was actually a little frightening.

He told me—and my heart sank. I hadn't expected much, I'd known she was of low rank, but . . . the words "Oh my God," slipped out of my mouth before I could stop them.

Now she was glowering.

"You're Constable Friendly?"

Even in the dark I could tell her face was beet red. "I drive one of the two Police Community Services Trailers."

"Full of 'crime prevention' displays donated by local businesses, right? Let me guess: lock displays, home alarm displays, a dangerous drugs exhibit, pamphlets full of worthless crimestopper tips—"

In my ear, Zudie said, "She's thinking of popping you one in the mouth. Stop pissing her off and start impressing her with our magic powers."

"—but what am I saying? I don't *have* to guess," I segued, and let Zudie feed me my lines again. "A Police Community Services Trailer is comprised of a 1996 GMC one-ton 'crew cab' style pickup truck . . . and an 8.5-meter or twenty-eight-foot 'fifth-wheel' style trailer . . . It was acquired by the Community Services Section in January 2003 . . . It was the second such facility; the first having been acquired in June 1996 . . . It serves as both a display unit and a mobile crime prevention office . . . All nineteen Community Police Offices use it occasionally as a mobile office for their own functions . . . the whole unit is fifteen and a quarter meters long, call it fifty feet, and as tall as two of the pickup trucks stacked . . . Jesus, what a behemoth . . . so you have to plan your route, and there are some places you just can't get to . . ."

By this point she had actually stepped back a pace. She put a hand on her gun, although she may not have been aware of it. "Mr. Walker, what is the name of this game?" she demanded.

"I am trying to show you that I know things I can't possibly know."

"Crap. You could have gotten most of that off the internet—"

"Listen to me," Zudie said through my mouth. "I know *why* you keep getting the shit postings."

"Crap," she repeated. "Nobody does. Nobody outside the department."

"I do. And it's not on the internet."

"It sure as hell isn't! Okay, go ahead: why am I driving a fucking Museum of Boredom?"

"Because you're not gay."

As the words were leaving my lips, I felt the rightness of them. One of the less widely known, and never discussed, facts about the Vancouver Police Department is that an unusually large fraction of the women on the force are gay. So what? you say, and I'm politically correct enough to want to say the same. But I had to admit it did matter. To be in that department, and look as macho and fit and, well, as handsome as Constable Nika Mandiç, and *not* be a dyke . . . well, I could see that it might not put her on the fast track for rapid career advancement.

"How could you possibly know about that?"

Zudie had me say, "The same way I know that all the

women in your family die of heart failure . . . or that you always put two sheets of Bounce into the dryer instead of one . . . or that your secret vice is Stallone movies, which you label something else on the videotape boxes so no one will know . . . or that you got your period about an hour ago."

She came up close, put her eyes only centimeters from mine. I felt their force. "Where are you getting your information, Mr. Walker?"

I moved the hand I held the phone with. "My friend."

"What's his name?"

I shook my head no, with some difficulty. "Maybe later."

"Where is he getting *his* information?"

Time to go for broke. "From you."

"*What?*"

Zudie prompted me again. "He doesn't just know your first boyfriend was named David. He knows that actually, David was just the first boyfriend *that anyone ever found out about*. He knows about Jamie."

"*Nobody knows about Jamie,*" she hollered, but as she was hollering she was moving, and by the time I realized that, she had already drawn her gun, put it to my head, and wrenched her phone from my hand.

The next bit of conversation I heard only her side of.

"Who is this? . . . Oh yeah? Whose? Not *my* friend . . . So? If that's true, quit jerking me around and tell me what's . . . what did you say? . . . Right. Uh huh."

Her eyes refocused on me again; she noticed I was wincing and backed off the pressure of the gun muzzle against my temple. "He says he's reading my mind," she told me.

Very carefully, I nodded. "He is."

She frowned, and her eyes went vague again. "Look,

pal," she said into the phone, "if you're reading my . . . what?"

And then she just listened to him talk, without saying a word—for something like three or four minutes. She stopped being aware of me, and since her face was close enough to blow on, I could follow it even in the darkness as it went through an extraordinary series of expressions. Once or twice she opened her mouth as if to speak, but each time it proved unnecessary after all. At one point she suddenly looked around in all directions, but she didn't seem to spot Zudie's boat.

Finally, either he was done, or she was done listening for a while; she let the hand holding the phone drop to her side, without breaking the connection. She turned to face the Harbour, and stared out at it for perhaps thirty seconds, facing about thirty degrees to the right of where I knew Zudie was floating in the dark. I left her alone with her thoughts, feeling one of us ought to.

She let out her breath in a long sigh, put the phone back to her head, said, "Hold on," and let it fall again without waiting for reply. Turning to me again, she began a series of questions mostly phrased as statements.

"He reads minds, you don't."

"That's right."

"He'd rather not. He can't help it. He can't turn it off."

"Yes."

"It hurts him. Bad?"

"If he could make it stop by something as simple as castrating himself or pulling out his eyes, I don't think he'd hesitate."

She nodded. "I can see how that would be. It's killing him to be this close to me."

"Yeah, I think it is."

"He's out there in some kind of little boat."

"Yes."

"You aren't going to tell me his name, or where he lives."

I spread my hands. "It wouldn't help you if I did. He's off the grid. No address, no driver's license, no credit cards or phone number."

A pause. Then: "You've known him a long time, Mr. Walker."

I nodded. "More than thirty years. Except we haven't seen each other for thirty of it."

She thought about that. "So he's been walking around inside your skull since you were in your twenties. And you're okay with that. You find him that trustworthy?"

I didn't answer right away. Finally I said, "Look, Constable, I'm going to be as honest as I can with you. I'm not sure I find *anybody* that trustworthy. I'd rather he couldn't see through my skull. What I can tell you is that in thirty-some years, so far I have never had cause to be sorry that he can. He's . . . he's been a good friend."

"Really."

"A better friend to me than I've been to him," I said, thinking back on some of the things I'd said about him behind his back in college. No, come to think of it, it *hadn't* been behind his back, had it? Nobody had ever said anything behind his back. It came to me suddenly that maybe first impressions are the most accurate: unconditional forgiveness must indeed be something he knew more about than most of us.

She lifted the phone to her ear, nodded, and reported to me, "He says you're wrong."

There, you see? I thought. "He would," I agreed.

She seemed to come to a decision. "Okay," she said briskly to us both. "I accept the premise. An hour ago I'd have bet cash it was nonsense but I accept it. You, Popeye the Sailor, what's your name?" He told her. "Okay. So you read minds, Zudie. Since you're telling me, and I'm a police officer, I infer that your talent has brought you knowledge of a crime of some kind. But it has to be something that you can't just dial 911 and report, for some reason. Excuse me?" She listened for a while. "Okay."

She put the phone down. "He says to find myself a seat, this is going to take a while. And he wants to talk to you."

"There are some logs over there," I said, and pointed with my Maglite, dialed way low. She nodded and gave me the phone.

"Why don't you go for a walk, Slim?" Zudie suggested. "You've already heard more of this part than you wanted to. She's going to need to hear more than that, to prove how tough she is."

I was reluctant to leave her, but he had a point. "How long will you need?"

"Stay within shout; I'll have her call you when she's ready."

"All right." I went to where she was seated, gave her her phone back, and said, "This is where I came in. Give me a holler when you've caught up on the What Has Gone Before." I started to turn away.

"Russell?"

It was the first time she'd used my ex-Christian name, and it startled me a little. "Yes, Nika?" I responded without thinking.

She didn't object. "A lot of guys wouldn't have done this."

"I admit it's a bit of a hassle," I said, "but it was the only way I could think of to do it. Zudie needed to be able to get clear, if you wouldn't go for it." Or, I didn't add, if you turned out to be the kind of cop who'd think that a telepath was a lovely thing to own.

She nodded. "That's my point. You thought it needed doing—enough to go out of your way. Most people don't get involved."

"Wait until you hear," I said. "Nobody could walk away."

"Okay. Still. Thanks for stepping up."

Why argue? "You're welcome. I'll see you in a while."

I wandered back in the direction of the parking lot. Even in near total darkness, and in damp clothing, looking out across Vancouver Harbour can't help but be magical. Large bodies of water are always soothing to the spirit. Far across the water are the twinkles of North Vancouver and West Vancouver, and beyond them the looming mountains. Straight ahead of me as I walked and sprawling way out to the left was the Emerald City itself, downtown Vancouver, with Stanley Park at its leftmost end. To my right trees marched off up a steep slope; here and there higher up the night lights of private residences could be picked out, as close as a few thousand meters away. A lot of harbours smell bad—Halifax's reeks—but so far Vancouver's doesn't. The footing was as much rocks as it was sand, but since I wasn't really going anywhere, it seldom got bad enough to call for my Maglite.

The view was so magnificent I was tempted to walk as far as the parking lot, get my pipe from the car, and have a few tokes, but it would have taken me out of earshot for a few minutes. It also would have left me with dope breath, and I intuitively felt that my new first-name basis with Constable Nika was not yet quite solid enough to be tested in that way. The Supreme Court had recently struck down the federal law against simple possession, and the legal right to medical marijuana had been cautiously established—but the various police agencies across the country had not yet quite stabilized on how they felt about it, nor had the individual officers within them. Nobody was lighting up in front of cops, yet, except a few flagrant activists like Marc Emery. I've been a head for so long that I didn't think I'd *ever* be really comfortable smoking in front of an on-duty police officer, whatever our relationship. In any case this was not the night to find out.

I picked out a stretch of easy walking between two rock farms and paced it slowly back and forth, like Hornblower on his quarterdeck. The image made me clasp my hands behind my back, and say "Hrrrrumph!" every once in a while. Each time I walked westward I tried to spot Constable Nika or Zudie, or hear her voice, but I never succeeded. After a while I found I was mostly dry by now, and no longer cold. Good old body heat.

I had to admit I was very impressed with her mental resilience. I like to think I have an unusually open and flexible mind, and on my best days it may be true—but it had taken me many months of slow accumulation of knowledge to believe my roommate Smelly was a telepath. And then thirty more years to admit it to myself consciously. She had accepted it almost at once. Granted, she'd been given convincing proof, an advantage I had lacked back in 1967, but still.

I saw her coming toward me. On that ankle-breaker

terrain, in extreme darkness, she moved like someone on well-lit pavement in a big hurry. It was good I happened to be facing her way or I wouldn't have known she was coming until she gave me the heart attack. When she reached me she handed me the phone without a word. I put it to my ear.

"What do you want me to do with this phone now, Slim?" Zudie asked.

I hadn't thought about it, which made me mad at myself. Now that I did think about it, all the options sucked—which didn't improve my mood. "Hang on to it," I decided. "I'll get another one."

He sighed audibly. "I really hate to own one of these. They *ring*, don't they?"

"Not if you leave them switched off."

"Then why have it?"

"Zudie, I don't know! It'll be useful down the line, probably. I can't keep swimming out to meet you every time you want to talk to someone."

"Won't it be a nuisance for you, telling everyone your number's changed?"

"Yes, god damn it, it will, okay? But not as much nuisance as swimming back out there to get it, or working out some way for you to stash it on Heron Island somewhere I can find it and nobody else will. In fact, not much nuisance at all, now I think of it: I hardly ever give out my cell number. Can we drop it?"

"Okay."

I glanced at Nika. She was pointedly ignoring my conversation, staring out to sea. Her body language was hard to read. She seemed to be breathing faster than normal. "So where are we?"

"Talk to her."

"Okay. Smooth sailing home. I'll call you tomorrow. As soon as I get my new cell phone."

"Good night, Slim."

I hung up and gave her her phone back. "Well?" I said.

She said, "We need a shitload of caffeine."

I shook my head. "We need a fuckofalot. That's three shitloads . . . or shitsload, if you're a purist."

She nodded and smiled at my feeble joke, the first smile I had ever seen on her face. Her eyes were bright. "When you're right, you're right."

The smile was my reward for pretending not to notice that she was scared half to death.

7.

We found a White Spot on Broadway, so empty it hummed, and by our manner convinced the waitress our need was serious. She brought us a full pot each, and even managed to turn up a couple of human-sized cups somewhere. Once she was sure we were liberally supplied with cream and sugar, she left us alone, without bothering to ask if we wanted anything else with that. I grabbed the check she put down, and set the amount plus a hundred percent tip under my saucer before adulterating my coffee.

Nika took hers black, so she was already refilling her cup by the time I took my first sip. She said, "This is whack."

"Tell me about it."

"Zandor has told you all about this . . . *Allen*?" She said the name as if it were a synonym for evil. Maybe it was.

I grimaced. "As much as I'd let him. And I wish I'd cut

him off sooner. I just didn't take in what I was hearing until I'd heard too much."

She nodded, staring down into her cup, only half hearing me. "Yeah. That business about using a drug that's a perfect painkiller . . ."

Frequently, when someone says something I don't understand, or something I think they must surely have got wrong, I just nod and let it pass. I wish I had this time. But she looked like she was starting to tune me out. Perhaps it offended my ego. "You mean perfect pain enhancer."

"No, I don't."

That's all she said. Just those three words, and she was willing to drop it and move on.

Not Einstein. "What would a sadist want with a pain-*killer*?" Then she looked up from her coffee cup and I saw her eyes. "Oh shit, you're going to tell me, aren't you?"

I think you have to clench your teeth to make your jaw and temple twitch at the same time. "Yes, I am going to tell you, Russell. I want you to know exactly what you've dragged us both into."

"Look, I've got it," I said frantically, "He's a monster, he studies pain, if de Sade was a Marquis he's the fucking King—"

"The drug utterly obliterates all pain, for twelve hours. He injects it in a victim. He works on them for eleven hours, doing his best to break every single bone they have. Then he tells them how long they have before the drug wears off, and sits back to savor the show. Sometimes he lies and says they have *two* hours, just to be—thank you."

She was thanking me because I had turned my head. By luck I happened to turn into the booth instead of toward the aisle. By even better luck there wasn't much in me but coffee, and not much of that yet.

Finished, I lifted my head and looked around dizzily. Nobody in sight. "It was a reflex," I said. I rinsed my mouth with the water I had not asked for, and added another five hundred percent to the tip under my saucer. Then we moved to another booth, bringing our pots and cups.

She said, "We're never going to take this guy if we can't even bring ourselves to think about what he is."

My dizziness vanished at once, but the ringing sound in my ears increased. "What you mean 'we,' paleface?"

I don't think she knew the joke, but she got the gist. "You son of a bitch, do you think you get to just drop this in my lap and walk away? You made your report, like a good citizen, and now your part is done?"

"Well—shit, Nika, you're a cop, right?"

"Why did you pick me up on the street? You wanted a cop, why didn't you just dial 911? Or walk into police headquarters?"

"Hey, let me tell you something about walking into police headq—"

"You didn't file a report because you don't have shit." She realized she was too loud, and drank off the last of her second cup of coffee in a gulp. Somehow it enabled her to lower her volume without losing any intensity. "You know what I mean. You don't have much information, and every scrap of it came from a mind reader."

"God damn it—"

"It's not that I mind looking like an asshole. Even if we assume every word is true—and Jesus, I'll be awhile making my mind up on *that* one—and even if somehow I could get a Crown Attorney to come down here some night and convince her it's all true, it wouldn't be enough for her to apply for a search warrant. It wouldn't be enough for my sergeant to authorize the manpower for an investigation."

"Why the hell not?"

"Investigate *what?* If everything Zudie says is gospel, what you've got is an allegation that a person unknown intends to commit felonies on other persons unknown at an unknown location on an unknown date. How horrible the alleged felonies are is irrelevant."

"Not to the victims," I snapped back. Sometimes even I myself am awed at my dumbness.

"That's right," Nika said. "That's why I can't drop it. And why you can't either. I'm an ordinary citizen in this. I'll have no police infrastructure behind me, no authority, no special advantages. Hell, with what I've got, I can't even get Zudie access to the sketch artist he wants. I'm going to have to work on my own time, and when that's not enough I'll have to take sick time." She leaned forward. "There's no way I can do it alone, Russell."

I was so agitated I forgot my stomach was tense and poured more coffee. This is actually interesting: it may give you some idea of what level of dumbness I mean. I decided not to add cream and sugar, because she took hers black, to show that I could be macho, too. And then with my next breath said, "Nika, look at me. Do you see a commando? A Navy SEAL? Travis McGee? Do you see even a good crossing guard? I'm two meters tall, I mass seventy kilos with my coat on, and I look like a newspaper columnist. Who's fifty-mumble years old. The nastiest weapon I've ever used was an ad hominem argument. The last time anyone tried to harm me physically was in a dodgeball game. I would have been a coward during Vietnam, but fortunately I was 4-F so it never came up."

She let me run down, waited patiently until I was done, and another several seconds to be sure. Then she leaned even closer, and said very gently, "A family is going to be butchered like pigs, to amuse a bug. You know it. You're either going to try and stop it, or you're not. The rest of your life, you'll either be someone who tried to stop it, or someone who didn't."

"But—"

She sat back in her seat. "Look, I am far from a mind reader, but even I know you're not going to walk away from this. So can we please stop dicking around now, and start getting some planning done?"

There was no help for it. I was just going to have to tell her. I took a sip of coffee—grimaced, and added cream and sugar. The time for macho posturing was past.

"You're right," I told her. "I'm not going to walk away. I'm going to help in absolutely any way I can. But for you to do your planning, you need to be clear on the ways I *can't* help. Not because I 'don't want to get involved.' Not even because I'm afraid of this clown, although I am. Just because I can't."

"So? What ways are those?"

I sighed. "Basically, pretty much anything physical."

She gave me the look cops give civilians who insist on making idiotic wisecracks in a serious situation. "What—"

I gave up and just spit it out. "I have collapsing lungs."

Now it was the look cops give civilians who start speaking in tongues.

"I am subject to sudden lung collapses. It's called spontaneous pneumothorax. I had my first one at fourteen, and I've probably had two or three dozen since."

"Nemoj me jebat!" She sat back in her seat and poured the last of her coffee. I could tell it wasn't hot enough, but she drank some anyway. "What's it like?"

"Like an elephant sitting on one side of your chest. Fortunately to God I've never chanced to have both go down at once. You take air in tiny sips, and each one hurts like hell."

"How long does it last?"

"It used to be a week or two of agony in a hospital, and then two or three weeks tottering around the house like a very old man made of cornflakes and Elmer's glue. Twenty years ago I had some major surgery, and now the worst it usually gets is two days of sharp pain, spent lying down at home, and the rest of the week getting back up to snuff. But for those two days, lifting a full cup of coffee to my mouth is a big deal."

"How often do you get one of them?"

"There's no telling. I've gone three years without one. Another time I was three weeks in hospital, then when they let me go, I blew the other lung in the parking lot."

"What brings it on?"

I shrugged. "Different things. Lifting more than twenty kilos or so. Straining to loosen a nut, changing a tire. Running more than a certain distance flat out. Sometimes it just happens, for no discernible reason at all, while I'm reading a book."

"What causes it?"

"Just lucky, I guess. I was born with bubbles all over my lungs, just like a bald tire. Every so often, one pops." I pointed upward, then let my finger droop while making a *tssshhhwwwwww!* sound, to indicate a deflating tire.

Her face was a tug of war. *You poor bastard* versus *terrific: a crip for backup,* pretty well matched. I didn't care which won; either was offensive to me. I made up my mind that whatever she said next, sympathy or disdain, I would use it as the pretext for a tantrum.

And what she said was, "Okay. Then you can be the brains of the outfit. What's the plan?"

My mouth dropped open. It was several seconds before words started falling out. "*Me?* You're the cop, for Christ's sake. Catching the bad guys is *your* area of expertise. What do I know about police work? Stories my uncle told me, almost certainly lies, and television. If I'm the brains, we're an idiot."

She shook her head stubbornly and began ticking off points on her fingers. "One: an idiot could not have figured out a way to convince me a man named Zandor Zudenigo can read people's minds. Two: there *are* no experts in tracking someone like Allen. He has nothing to *do* with normal police work. This is going to be more like disease control. Three: you've been thinking about this for a day longer than I have. You must have come up with *something* by now. So what have you got?"

Something about the way she'd pronounced Zudie's name caught my attention. I remembered her odd exclamation when I'd first told her about my lungs. "Nika," I asked suddenly, "what nationality are you? By extraction, I mean."

"My grandparents were all Croatian."

My eyebrows rose. "Wow, that's amazing. Did you know that—"

She grimaced and nodded. "Yeah yeah yeah, Zandor and I talked about it. A Serb and a Croat going after a monster together, big whoop. You civilians think irony is interesting. You ought to get out more."

I spread my hands. "My point exactly."

"God damn it, Russell, *what have you come up with?*"

I sighed, lowered my head, and rubbed the muscles at the base of my neck. It doesn't work much better than tickling yourself. "Okay. Sherlock Holmes said to start by eliminating the impossible. We have no way to identify or locate the intended victims that I can see. Clean-cut, good-looking families of four are thick on the ground in Point Grey."

She said, "If there's a way to identify or locate the perpetrator, I don't know what it would be. All we know is his first name is Allen—at least, we're pretty sure it's a first name—and he wrote a successful piece of software sometime in the last twenty years and he flies a small plane that may or may not be registered in his name and which he may or may not be licensed to fly under his own name and he knows a quiet spot along the Sea to Sky Highway.

"On TV I would type those five data into a computer, and in less than three seconds it would produce three possibles, or five if the show was an hour and a half made-for-TV movie. But there's no such magic database in the real world, is there? Jesus, I can't even interface with the computer systems of any of the other local police forces without a major hassle, let alone get RCMP data.

"Let's say Allen has a pilot's license. Big whoop: so does every fifth male in British Columbia, and there will be a lot of Allens. I know absolutely nothing about the computer industry, and even I know three rich software guys named Allen, and how long would it take me just to find out which ones have ever been in Vancouver? We have a matter of days, and maybe only two. Weekend days, when nobody's in the office."

She was right. I had not allowed myself to think through just how impossible this task was. I'd told myself all I had to do was find a cop, convince her, and then make supportive noises. "So you don't see *anything* we can do?"

"Well . . . not much. But it's just slightly better than nothing. I hesitate to say it, it's so lame."

"Give."

"We have no chance of finding the perp or the vics in any useful amount of time. But we've maybe got a hundred-to-one shot of finding the crime scene."

Flames danced in her eyes. "How? All we know is it's somewhere this side of Lillooet. After that, nobody calls the road the Sea to Sky anymore."

"I know this is nuts, okay? But Zudie told me he *saw* the place, in Allen's mind. *He saw the turnoff from the highway.*"

The flames damped themselves back to glowing coals. "Jesus Christ, Russell, you're talking about more than two hundred kilometers of highway. There must be a couple of thousand curb cuts along the way: logging roads and dirt roads and deer trails and country driveways and—"

"I know, I know."

She was exasperated. "Well, just how fucking good a description do you think Zudie's going to be able to give us of the fucking turnoff?"

I shrugged. "I told you it was a long shot. But think about it: for a start, he can tell us which side of the road it's on. That eliminates half your curb cuts right there."

"Fabulous. Now we're down to a thousand. I repeat,

you're talking about over two hundred klicks of—"

"I'm talking about maybe four hours of video, total," I said.

Her mouth fell open. Her face went blank for a few long seconds. Then suddenly the coals in her eyes burst back into flame, and she began to smile in spite of herself. "We make the run, I drive, you shoot, we get the tapes back to Zandor, he tells us where the spot is—"

"Then we just stake it out." I waited for her reaction.

Her smile froze in place—but her eyes kept crackling. "Go on."

I locked eyes with her. "We stalk him like an animal. We set up a couple of blinds in a crossfire, and we stake the place out with long guns. I can't shoot for shit so you better get me a shotgun. As soon as he steps out of his vehicle we kill him. We bury him and any evidence we want gone. At some point on the drive back to Vancouver, we end up having a conversation with the victims, and if we are very lucky they will all be smart enough and grateful enough to keep their mouths shut tight for the rest of their lives. Comment?"

She stared back at me in silence for a long time. Finally she said, "I don't think I can do that."

"Nika, I just don't see any other—"

"God damn it, neither do I! I still don't think I can do that."

"If we don't, if we just spring out of hiding and shout 'Surprise!' the worst we've got him on is four counts of kidnapping . . . and no good way to explain how we stumbled on it. Rich prick, good lawyers, he'd be back out in the world in a couple of years, pissed off and feeling he's got something to prove."

She shook her head slowly back and forth, once. "That's vigilante talk. I'm a cop. A cop can't think like that. A cop shouldn't think like that. I'm not even a judge, and I'm damn sure not an executioner."

I mimed clapping my hands. "I sincerely applaud every word you just said. You're talking to a no-shit card-carrying member of the Civil Liberties Union. Up until yesterday, I'd have agreed with you absolutely."

She was still shaking her head. "It's the kind of principle that's not situational," she insisted. "It's always true."

"And why is it always true? Why should a cop never take the law into her own hands?"

"Because she shouldn't," she said, her voice rising.

"Stop knee-jerking and *think* about it: *why shouldn't she?*"

"Because she might be wrong!"

I let that one hang in the air for a while. "Because . . . ?" I prompted finally, and waited until I saw her get it before I said it aloud. "Because she can't read minds."

She said nothing.

"This once, she *knows* she isn't wrong."

"God damn it—"

"Or am *I* wrong? Do you doubt anything Zudie told you is the gospel truth?"

She took a deep breath. "No," she admitted. "But I took an oath—"

"There's a higher responsibility than that oath, and you know it."

"Have you ever killed a man?" she snapped.

"Once." I could see that surprised her. Well, it surprised me. "A long time ago, when I was a kid. I didn't plan to. Another kid tried to kill me with a knife on the street. He had very bad luck. Have you?"

She looked down at her coffee. "No."

"But you're trained to. You've prepared yourself for the possibility. That puts you at least two steps past where I was that day in the street."

"How can we just stalk another human being?"

"If he were a human being, we couldn't," I said. "As it is, I don't see that we have any choice. If we let that bug walk away with a few years for kidnapping, everything he does after that is on us."

She had no reply, but I knew she was still unconvinced.

I said, "I'll tell you the truth: I don't think we're up to it."

She frowned. "You think he could shoot both of us dead while we're holding guns on him?"

"I think we might be incredibly lucky to get shot dead. Think about who we're talking about."

I reached her with that one. Too hard; I reached across the table and took her hand. After an instant's hesitation, she let me.

"Look, sleep on it," I said. "If you tell me we have to try and take Allen alive . . . well, I guess I'm willing to try, if you get me a shotgun and a good Kevlar vest. But I'll tell you right now, if I see you go down, I plan to shoot myself in the head. And then there'll be nobody to stop him."

"Anything else I can get you folks?" the waitress asked.

We mangled each other's fingers and turned together. She was no more than a few meters away; we hadn't heard her coming. That's why they call that kind of footgear sneakers. It was clear from her voice and face that she hadn't heard us; nonetheless we felt like assholes.

Nika recovered first. "We're fine, thanks."

I thought about telling her I'd barfed in the original booth she'd seated us in. Fortunately she was gone before I'd finished thinking. Either she hadn't noticed the booth switch, or she wasn't nosy.

"We're good at this," I said.

Nika said, "Let's get out of here."

"We'd be fools not to."

On our way out I stopped at our original booth and added another five hundred percent to the tip under my saucer. It's the sincerest apology I know.

8.

We weren't ready to separate yet. We stood together for a while in the parking lot, leaning against our respective, nearly identical Hondas. In the lousy lighting, the only way I could tell them apart was by the chip on my windshield that had spent almost a year threatening to become a crack, after which it would soon become a hole where the windshield used to be. I could tell she wanted to say something but didn't know how to start.

I said, "I'll call Zudie and find out which side of the road we want, and I'll spring for a good camcorder. I've been thinking of getting one lately anyway. What kind of shape is your car in?"

She grimaced. "Not great. Two bald tires, and the brakes need work."

"Then we'll take mine. When do you want to go?"

She checked her watch. "I get off at 0600. About an

hour from now. You said you usually work nights. Where are you in your cycle?"

I was startled, but game. "You want to start right away?"

"If we sleep, we lose most if not all of today's daylight. Tomorrow is Saturday. Zandor says Allen was thinking 'next week'—which could be as soon as Monday."

I was nodding. "And setting up a perfect ambush for a wild animal with clothes on might just turn out to be a nontrivial problem; the longer we have to cope, the better. Okay, well . . . I usually start finishing up work by 6:00 A.M., and get to bed by nine if I'm lucky. And it's been a long night. But I guess . . . yeah, I'm good for another eight or ten hours, easy."

"You're sure? Good to *drive* that long?"

"Definitely." I had a thought. "But I propose a compromise. I suggest we both nap somewhere until nine. I don't know any place I can buy a camcorder much earlier than that anyway. It still gives us a good seven or eight hours of good light. I probably won't be able to get the footage to Zudie before midnight anyway."

"I guess that makes sense."

"I presume you know a good place to coop."

For a moment she bristled automatically. I assumed it was because civilians aren't supposed to know cop slang, and tried to fix it by adding, "I told you, my uncle and cousins are on the job."

She nodded, and relaxed a little, but her body language remained stiff. And she didn't answer my question.

"Well?" I prodded finally. "Do you have a good place or not?"

She didn't answer for so long I had decided she wasn't going to, and when she finally did I could barely make out the words. "Yeah, I have a place," she muttered. "Follow me."

Halfway there I got it.

However lame, corny, dopey, cheesey or full of shit you may have imagined a Police Community Services Trailer to be, I assure you the reality is several orders of magnitude worse on all counts. I fell asleep on an air mattress under the dangerous drugs display, feeling genuinely sorry for her.

Surprisingly, the awakening three hours later was not really all that horrible. For one thing, I've reached the age where three solid consecutive hours can constitute an achievement. For another, my nose told me Nika had a machine that produced coffee-like fluid, and sure enough it proved nasty enough to jumpstart my cerebrum. The only really bad part was the total bodily agony. I hurt in places I was pretty sure I didn't *have*.

When I had evolved far enough to construct sentences I told her, "I have good news."

She was still at the grunt stage. Well, so are we all.

"When I went out to pee, just before I crashed, I phoned Zudie."

"Oh, was he back home yet?"

I failed to hear the question. In fact, I had caught him just as he was going to bed himself after sailing home to Coveney Island. But if I allowed Nika even a rough estimate of sailing time from Spanish Banks to Zudie's home, it would greatly help her narrow down where that would have to be. That was why I'd gone outside to make the call. "He told me the turnoff will be on the righthand side of the road, and just past one of those '*Passing Zone:*

slower vehicles keep right' signs."

Her face did something I found oddly charming: her eyes lit up with excitement at the same time that her eyebrows frowned in skepticism. "Great. There can't be more than half a million of those on the Sea to Sky. How *much* past it, did he say?"

"Well, he said when the turnoff first comes into view in the distance, the sign is also in the picture. So not more than . . . what? Half a kilometer?"

She nodded. "Five hundred meters is possible. And it could be ten meters. He have anything on just what the turnoff will look like?"

I made a face and finished the last of the liquid in my cup, which was backwards. "Like nothing at all, unfortunately. A gravel road that's just barely there, obscured by overgrowth. There'll be almost as many of them as *Keep Right* signs."

"Probably." She was in civilian clothes, the first time I'd seen her out of uniform. I had to suppress a grin. Pale gray shades. Pale gray baggy sweatshirt with the sleeves raggedly cut off, showing workout arms. Dark grey baggy jeans. White no-brand sneakers, clean yet not new. She was what Susan used to call me: a fashion paper plate.

She also looked fit enough to run the length of the Sea to Sky Highway and back. She could feed herself along the way by punching out the occasional caribou and gutting it with her nails. She was so perfect a classic caricature of the butch dyke that I could easily see how her heterosexuality could—dare I say perversely?—infuriate some lesbians.

I asked, "Have you signed out from your shift already?" She nodded. "Then let's get rolling." I put my shoes on.

She checked her watch. "Still time before camcorder stores will have opened up."

"I know," I said, "but there are already places open that sell coffee."

She said, "Oh, we have plenty of coffee here," and brandished a Mr. Coffee pot.

"No, we don't," I told her, and went outside.

"God damn it," she said behind me a few moments later.

"Hey, it's not one of *our* tires," I said, zipping up and turning around. "And it's not *my* fault VPD doesn't equip its Community Relations Trailers with a toilet. Exigent circumstances."

"Did you have to pick that particular vehicle?"

"No," I said happily, "I went to extra trouble." It was the Chief's car. It said so on the side.

But my grin faded and died under the withering blast of her glare. I could see she was really angry. "Look," I said, "it goes with my job. I'm a professional iconoclast, okay? That's someone who—"

"—attacks settled beliefs or institutions," she said. "Literally, 'image destroyer.' I understand the term, and the kind of mind that needs to do that all the time."

"Now wait a damn min—"

"You wait," she said. And I did, chopping off in midword, because she did *not* raise her volume or speed to top me, but spoke so softly I could just barely make it out, and somehow I knew that was very bad news. "You, Russell, have put me in a situation where I am going to have to spend the next few days systematically pissing on some of the most important things I live my life by." If she had been speaking in a normal voice, I would have tried to interrupt here. "So I am going to ask you, *please*." Her voice got so soft I had to fall back on reading lips, so slow I was able to. "Don't *you* piss on any of the things I live by. Okay?"

I felt sweat on my forehead. I could hear the things dogs hear, though not of course as well. "Okay," I agreed meekly. "That's fair."

"Fair enough," she said, loud enough now to be heard clearly.

I had to admit she had a point. But it seemed a bad omen for the whole enterprise. If we were starting out without even a sense of humor . . .

I thought about some of the things she might live by, and opened my mouth to ask a question, and experienced a sudden rush of brains to the head, and closed my mouth again. Plenty of time to climb those stairs.

We found a Bean Around the World outlet, and I tried to teach Nika the difference between what she had been drinking and fresh-ground Cuban peaberry. She didn't get it. Both were hot, black and bitter; what was the big deal? Rupture is what I call moments like that: a sudden unexpected gulf across which no communication is possible. I don't think it's as simple as just men being from Mars and women from Venus: I think so-called humans must come from at *least* nine different planets. It's a wonder we can interbreed. And a shame we don't, much.

We agreed over coffee that even though mine was the best car to take, Nika was the best qualifed driver. I gave her the keys and rode shotgun with the camcorder.

The Sea to Sky Highway seems like a perfectly normal highway until you're past a town irritatingly spelled

Caulfeild. (It doesn't irritate the locals a bit: until Mr. Caulfeild moved in, the area was called Skunk Creek.) Then, with inadequate and confusing signage, the road suddenly splits in three—and the center lane is the one that suddenly comes to a dead stop, at the toll booths for the huge B.C. Ferries terminus at Horseshoe Bay, which serves several major and minor ferry routes including the one I would have been taking home to Heron Island, if I'd been lucky enough to be going home that morning. The left lane enters the tiny town of Horseshoe Bay itself, and only the right lane forges on, relentless in its quest to unite sea and sky.

The next fifty kilometers or so of highway serve to separate the men from the helplessly screaming objects plummeting from great heights. Those fifty kilometers carry you through some of the most splendid scenery to be found anywhere on the planet, and ensure that you will not be able to spare a single second's attention to appreciate it. They seem to have been carefully designed by a crack team of brilliant sadists to provide every possible driving challenge . . . over and over, often in combination, and always by surprise. There are blind curves, double switchbacks, incorrect banks, inadequate shoulders overlooking horrific dropoffs, vanishingly rare passing zones, frequent avalanches—and on the rare stretches that do let you get a little speed going, there's usually a scenic-lookoff turnout feeding low-speed traffic back into the stream.

In fact little of this is bad design, it's mostly enforced by the terrain: you're basically clinging to the side of a cliff overlooking Howe Sound. It's a "dancing bear" sort of situation: it's so ridiculous for a road to be there that to demand it be a good one would be unreasonable. The only really dumb design decision was to build it in the first place; everything after that was inevitable. The pressing reason for building it was to allow enough people to move up inland so that there will always be some jackass behind you in a great hurry who is vastly more familiar with the road than you, cannot forgive your criminal ignorance, and expresses his contempt by tailgating.

You would think this would be much less of a problem when the person behind the wheel is a police officer. But no. Nika refused to wear her uniform hat, even though she had brought one—and without it she was just a woman in a cutoff sweatshirt. This being decidedly not an official investigation, she was determined to stay as low profile as possible. I understood the point, and agreed she was being prudent. But I couldn't have done it. Hell, I'd have pulled my gun. But then, I was born in America—which has ten times the population of Canada, and something like a thousand times as many gunshot deaths per year.

Even so, I was glad I had let her drive. The Sea to Sky intimidates the hell out of me. Nika treated it like a sustained high speed chase. She was good; the lack of lights and siren hindered her not at all.

Unless you need to pee very badly there are few reasons to get off the highway during that first fifty klicks of the Sea to Sky, and the only sensible one is Shannon Falls, a remarkable series of cliffs about forty-five minutes out of town in which water from something called, swear to God, Mount Sky Pilot falls 335 meters—call it a thousand feet. (And it's only the third highest waterfall in British Columbia.) It's a breathtaker at any time, but if you're ever near there during a very cold winter, don't miss it. Once every few years, *the waterfall freezes*. Whereupon enthusiasts come hundreds or thousands of miles to climb it, with axes and screws, and no way of knowing just when the whole giant icicle will suddenly detach from the rock face. Not a sight easily forgotten.

But that's about all the road has to offer besides McNuggets until it reaches the city of Squamish. Some claim the name is Indian, but I think it's just that by the time you've ridden the Sea to Sky rollercoaster that far, most people are feeling squamish. There Howe Sound ends, and Highway 99 finally puts the "sea" behind, and begins heading for the sky.

The next stop of consequence, quite a ways up the road, is Whistler. Forty years ago there was *nothing* there but mountains and trees. And a few people who liked it that way. Then a handful of rich imbeciles decided it would make a great Olympic Village, if only there happened to be a village there, and a road to it. Today there are thousands of rich imbeciles there, skiing—and waiting with barely concealed eagerness for the 2010 Winter Olympics to come destroy the ecology, economy and tranquility of the region forever for their aggrandizement. As a fair man I try to despise all sports equally, but it is hard not to feel an especial contempt for an allegedly athletic pursuit which combines high speed and zero protection, and whose one and only possible achievement is to not fall down. I like to think the late Senator Sonny Bono sums up skiing: evolution in action.

9.

We started looking for NO PASSING signs and scrutinizing a few hundred meters before and after them just as soon as we cleared Horseshoe Bay, but we were neither surprised nor disappointed that the first fifty klicks to Squamish had produced only a few even longshot maybes. Both of us were fairly sure that our target killing field lay somewhere in the stretch between Squamish and Whistler—or if anything further up, between Whistler and the old Gold Rush town of Lillooet. It just seemed to me, and Nika didn't disagree, that if you were engaged in activity that was going to result in people screaming at the top of their lungs, and you didn't *want* them to keep their voices down because you liked applause, you would want to be a lot more than half an hour or so away from a major city.

Nonetheless, Nika adamantly insisted I carefully video every even remote possibility. Each time, she slowed to

50 kph to assist me in panning, enraging the drivers behind us even though by definition we were in the slowpoke lane. Once when in her opinion I was sloppy about it, she actually turned around at the next scenic lookoff and doubled back and made me do it again, no small pain in the ass on that road. But all in all there really wasn't much to do but talk. So Nika put on the radio, and we listened to CBC. One day the scumbags and traitors who are systematically leaching every good thing about Canada into anemia so they can feed on the bones will finally succeed in cutting the budget of the Canadian Broadcorping Castration so far that it can no longer produce better radio than any station in America, any day of the week—but it hasn't happened yet, by God. So far the main focus of their attention has been dismantling our health care, education, and military. When they can spare the time to ruin a merely cultural industry it's usually film or television.

Once past Squamish we began hitting pay dirt. For one thing, there could *be* passing zones now that the road was no longer carved out of a cliff. When they occurred, the right-hand slowpoke lanes didn't always have curbs that would make a curb cut obvious. The terrain and soil became more hospitable to the sort of thick leafy scrub growth that might obscure the mouth of a dirt or gravel road. I became fairly proficient in the business of panning across a swath of country. It helped a lot to be able to see exactly what I was getting, both live and in instant playback. The technology is starting to get pretty slick. I can remember a time when I thought Super 8 was a great improvement over ordinary 8mm film. I still have a vagrant memory, from about age six, of the family's very first color

TV. Today, laptops have larger screens, with much better color.

I had asked the kid-clerk at the camera store that morning how much I might save if I opted for just black and white. He didn't know what I meant. Apparently even the ATMs shoot color, now. I'd ended up getting a midprice Sony model, and was quite pleased with it.

By the time the crisp mountain scent of money alerted us that we were approaching Whistler, about three hours after we left Vancouver, I had nearly used up a whole cassette—one hour at high speed, which I was using—and had exhausted the first battery pack through lavish use of the LCD screen. The clerk had offered me a car cigarette-lighter adaptor that would let me either run the camera or charge the batteries . . . but since I knew Nika's car was a Honda the same vintage as my own, I had presumed correctly that her cigarette lighter didn't work either, and sprung for a spare battery pack instead.

So I was still operational, with enough juice and extra cassettes to take us as far as Lillooet if necessary, when Nika pulled over into a tiny gas station on the outskirts of Whistler proper, shut the engine, and said, "I'm having trouble believing he'd go this far north, just to get guaranteed privacy. I'm thinking he'd stop way short of here. If he's a rich guy he knows other rich guys, and this is where they hang out, year round. His comings and goings would be noticed. Even remembered."

I nodded. "Rich people on vacation don't really have much else to do but note each other's comings and goings. That's why nobody's coming to pump your gas: they can't believe you aren't about to bounce out and do it yourself, so everyone driving past will know you're in town. My money's on somewhere behind us, too."

"But the trouble is . . ." she began, and trailed off.

"The damned parks," I finished. "They bother me, too."

"Yeah." I gave her some cash, and she got out and pumped the gas.

Seven large provincial parks lie between Squamish and Whistler, and the majority of them as well as the largest of them are on the righthand side of the road, the one we were interested in. They extend deep into the wilderness, and offer the usual variety of wilderness attractions—camping, hiking, walking, standing and staring, sitting and staring, boating, fishing, swimming, floating, picnicking, portapotties—and taken together they provide just enough action to support the occasional general store, burger stand, or gas station. There just weren't enough, or long enough, stretches of the kind of total, foolproof isolation we were looking for. Hikers are liable to hear a child screaming a long way. I had documented over thirty approaches to NO PASSING signs—but there were only four or five I had any real hopes for.

"Look," I said, when Nika finished paying for the gas and got back in, "it seems to me we have a manageable number of serious candidates. If we turn around now, we'll have enough time to drive a little ways up each of those gravel roads and see what we see."

She frowned and shook her head. "Negative. I changed my mind: I want to go on a ways. It gets emptier from here on. And I keep thinking about this Allen. From Zudie's description, he's so twisted I can picture him driving all *day*, if it gets him to a nice perfect playground."

"With four drugged vics in the vehicle?"

"No reason he couldn't stop and shoot them all up again, every hundred klicks or so."

"Still, that's a long exposure time."

She shrugged. "No cops. No cross streets. No small-town traffic lights or speed traps. Pretty safe exposure. I want to go another twenty or thirty klicks."

I gave up. "Okay, but let's at least eat first."

"Done."

We were able to find a place in Whistler that was willing to overlook our shabby attire long enough to charge us a grotesque amount of money for a gratifyingly small portion of horrible food. The view through the big windows was so eye-watering, I let the waiter live.

Nika was right: when she pulled over onto the shoulder another forty klicks or so further up the road, we had doubled our number of serious candidates. By now, however, we were a little over four hours from Vancouver, and running out of steam.

She said, "I think we've gone far enough. We should just boot it back home, and trust that Zandor can spot the right one from the tape. We go driving up a dozen gravel roads into the wilderness, and sooner or later I'm going to tear your muffler off or crack an axle."

"Or even just blow a tire or two," I agreed, and reached out and shut off the ignition.

"Hey!" she said, indignantly. "What are you doing?"

"Not sitting in a car," I said, and got out.

"We've got to get back," she said, getting out herself.

I left my door open. I put my hands on my hips and arched my back a few times, tried to touch my toes and managed my knees, walked like a stork for a few steps, cracked my neck a few times. At that point I realized my groaning was beginning to sound like I was fucking, so I made myself stop—a few seconds too late, from her expression.

"We've got a long drive ahead of us," she insisted.

"Think it through," I suggested. "If we leave right now, and make good time, we'll run right into the very worst of the rush hour."

"*Oh.*" Vancouver has, incredibly, nearly as much to be ashamed of as it has to be proud of, and one of its worst disgraces after its police department is its road system. Incredibly, it's all what Californians call "surface streets"—no freeways, no loop road around the city, no fast way *anywhere,* and a criminally inadequate number of bridges, a setup guaranteeing universal gridlock twice a day in the best of conditions. It would make for a perfectly rotten ending to a whole day of driving. We'd be bucking the flood tide of commuters trying to pour out of the city. The crucial Lion's Gate Bridge from North Van to Stanley Park is, unforgivably, a three-lane bridge: in evening rush hour, inbound traffic would get only one.

Right here, a car went by maybe once a minute or so.

"Stretch your legs, Nika," I urged. "Throttle back to idle. Smoke if you got 'em. Listen to the stillness. Contemplate nature's wonder in the heart of summer. That funny smell is called 'fresh air.' The forest surrounds and enfolds us. Right now, animals are browsing you with their eyes, like shoppers, judging whether they can afford you. Grok the fullness."

She left her own door open like mine and came around behind the car. She put one foot up on the rear bumper and leaned forward to stretch her thigh, repeated with the other leg. "I guess you have a point. It *is* good to be out of the city. I keep thinking about taking a drive out into the country, but I keep not doing it." She looked around her, too quickly at first, and then more slowly, letting her eye be caught here or there by this or that, the way you do in nature. "It *is* peaceful here. This is just what I was—Jesus *Christ*, Russell!"

"What?"

"God damn it, is that what I think it is?"

"Texada Timewarp," I said. "Why, you want a toke?"

She advanced on me. "You son of a bitch, put that fucking thing out. Right now!"

I made myself stand my ground, refused myself permission to turn my fear into anger, kept my voice calm and low as I said, "The Supreme Court of Canada says this is legal to possess."

"Federally, *maybe,*" she conceded, dropping her own volume down closer to mine. "For now, anyway. But the Chief says it's still against the law in Vancouver—thank God!"

I nodded. "Then I better be sure and destroy all the evidence before we get back to Vancouver," I said, and took a long deep toke.

She turned bright red, but within two seconds I knew she was going to let me get away with it. By the time I exhaled, so did she.

"You're out of your jurisdiction," I said. "The best you could do would be to place me under citizen's arrest and take me to the nearest RCMP detachment. Who would want to know why you're spending your off-duty hours chauffeuring a Boomer pothead with a camcorder through the Interior. Not to mention why you're wasting their time and yours on a possession bust for a single joint, which is not a federal crime. Are you *sure* you don't want a hit?"

"Get that out of my face!"

"Sorry. But you don't know what you're missing." I took another toke—but when I saw her expression, I had to exhale it to say, "Are you telling me you've never smoked dope? Never? Seriously? Not even before you were a cop?"

"That's right," she said.

I shook my head briefly like a fighter throwing off a punch. "Holy shit!"

She turned on her heel, went and got back in the car and slammed her door. The engine started, and revved. I was tempted to stay where I was and finish the joint. But a couple of hits of Timewarp is plenty. The world was sparkling as I got back in the car.

"Jesus Christ," she said as I was strapping my seat belt. "I was just going to ask you if you wanted to drive the return leg."

"I'd be glad to," I said.

"No thanks."

I reached down and caught her hand just as she was about to put the car in gear. She let me. "Back in college," I told her, "back on the East Coast, I did a lot of what was called work-study. I did odd jobs for the administration, and got a break on my tuition. One week I typed up the raw results of a study by the state Narcotics Addiction Control Commission, comparing the effects of alcohol and marijuana on driving. They'd had volunteers drive an obstacle course over and over, first sober, then at five successive stages of drunkeness, and finally at five levels of stonedness. Experienced users, mind you, not beginners."

She nodded. "So you know the facts."

I nodded right back. "But you don't. Only a handful of us do—because the state never published that study after all, and it was never replicated. The results were too clear. With alcohol, a driver's performance started to degrade right at level one, and bottomed out by level four. With pot, the first three levels *improved* driving performance."

"Bullshit!"

"Reaction time speeded up. Peripheral vision expanded. Subjects became mildly paranoid, looked further ahead for trouble, made conservative choices. And they tended to find the world interesting enough to keep them alert at the wheel. By level four, they were back to baseline, and at level five, totally blasted on several spliffs of the finest hydroponic sinsemilla sativa buds, their performance resembled that of a man with a couple of beers in him."

"Bullshit," she said again.

"I typed the results. The numbers were clear. I typed the conclusions: I didn't make them up."

"I don't believe it. Prove it."

"Prove it to yourself," I said. "Look it up."

She pounced. "Aha. How am I supposed to look up a study that didn't get published?"

"By listening to what the dog didn't do in the night," I said.

By God, she wasn't completely illiterate. She got the reference, I could see it in her face. She just didn't see how it applied.

"Do a Google search," I told her. "You'll find that every year of its existence, that Narcotics Addiction Control Commission produced something—a study, a paper, a conference, a brochure, something. All state commissions do, just like provincial commissions up here. They have to: it's how they pretend to have earned their salaries. In 1968 and 1969 that commission produced *nothing*, as far as the record shows. Yet they still got their funding for 1970, uncut. You figure it out. Check it out."

She glared at me and hunted for a good comeback and came up empty. "I will," she said, and snapped her gaze forward. Her hand moved abruptly under mine, putting the car in gear, and she stomped on the gas.

There was no time. No time to yell, no time to point, no time at all. As I moved, I was thinking that what I was doing was wrong, but fortunately my hand didn't care what my brain thought: it grabbed the gearshift as her hand came off it, thumbed in the button, and slammed it all the way forward into park. The transmission howled. We stopped abruptly enough to have deployed the airbags, if Hondas that old had airbags, and both banged our heads, she on the steering wheel and me on the dashboard. Everything but the left front wheel was still on the gravel shoulder. She had time to draw in breath, select an obscenity, and turn toward me to deliver it before the huge Peterbilt and trailer *w-w-w-WHUFF!*ed by and punched a large shiny hole through the space we had been just about to occupy. The wind of its passage rocked the car as much as the panic stop had. A second too late, its mighty airhorn blared, and dopplered away into the distance like Homer Simpson being told he couldn't have a donut. We sat in the sudden silence and blinked at each other.

"Peripheral vision," I said. "Reaction time."

She groped for rebuttal. "You probably screwed up your transmission."

"Yes."

"That's gonna cost you money."

"Not as much as dying. I priced it recently."

She made a face. I waited. Finally she forced the words out. "Thank you, Russell. Why don't you drive for a while?"

"All right. Until Squamish, anyway. You're a lot better at the rollercoaster stuff." I kept my face straight and my voice neutral. I could tell how much the concession had cost her, and I admired her for it. In her place I might have tried to take refuge in a smoke-screen tantrum.

We changed places and headed for home.

A few klicks down the road, I said, "What are you doing?"

She said, "What does it look like I'm doing?"

"Taping."

"Bingo. Slow down a little."

"Why? Are you taping."

"There's a *No Passing* sign coming."

"Yeah, but it's on the wrong side of the road." Nonetheless I eased off on the gas a bit. "Zudie was very clear: Allen's mental image of the turnoff was on the right. I mean, it's not the kind of thing you're liable to remember wrong, is it?"

"Maybe not." She kept taping until we were past, then turned round and faced forward again.

"So then . . . ?"

"Maybe it's on the right after you've driven past it and then turned around at the next convenient place—so you won't attract so much attention pulling off into it. Maybe it's on the right after you've landed your plane in a lake north of it and then driven south."

"How likely is that? He'd have to keep a car up there in the country just for that purpose."

She set her jaw stubbornly. "There's nothing wrong with having suspenders *and* belt. It doesn't cost us anything to be thorough."

I decided to let it go. She was right on both counts, when you came down to it. And she had let me have the last one. "Okay," I said.

"I've been trained to cover all the bases, assume nothing, and believe nothing I'm told until I've confirmed it."

"Okay, okay," I said. "Did anybody ever tell you you've got a slightly rigid mind-set?"

"Yeah," she said, "I hear it from potheads and junkies all the time."

10.

We drove several klicks in a silence thick enough to hold thumbtacks. I wondered what I was doing here, how I had gotten myself into this, what had ever possessed me to enter into a criminal conspiracy to hunt a monster with such an implausible pair as a goofball hermit with ESP and a macho nonlesbian cop with a night-stick up her ass.

Finally I spoke up. "You know why Zudie needs me?"

She reacted as if I had tried to pull her gun: physically flinched away from me and yelled, "Jesus Christ, don't DO that!"

Her volume frightened me. The car swerved slightly. "Don't do *what,* for fuck's sake?" I yelled back.

She stared hard at me for a while, then visibly relaxed a little and turned away. "I was *just* about to ask you what Zandor needs you for."

I gaped at her for a second . . . and then cracked up.

She didn't join me, so I stopped soon. "Trust me, that was coincidence," I told her. "I'm not telepathic—thank God."

She nodded. "I hadn't thought you were, until just then. Okay, my question stands: why are you even here? Why couldn't Zandor have just come to me directly? What have . . ." She let the last sentence trail away unfinished.

"What have I got that you haven't got?" I hazarded softly. She reddened. "Sorry, that was another lucky hit."

"Look," she said, "I'm not a complete idiot. I understand that he wants to keep his identity and location secret. It's pretty obvious why. If the RCMP knew what he can do, even his power wouldn't be enough to keep them from enslaving him."

"For the fifteen minutes it would take the NSA to come up here from the States and take him away from the horsemen," I agreed. "For all the good it'd do any of the bastards: he'd be dead in a week."

"Okay, so it's smart for him to work through a cutout. But Russell, why *you*?" She shook her head. "No offense, but a doper, class clown, and half an invalid is not what I'd be looking for in a coconspirator." She snuck a glance at me to see how I took it.

I was nodding in agreement. "And that's pretty much what Zudie *was* looking for."

She stared ahead at the road and shook her head. "I don't get it."

We passed the Peterbilt that had nearly creamed us. "It's pretty simple, Nika. He can stand to be near me."

She opened her mouth to answer, and left it open.

After half a klick or so of silence, I said, "Look, all of us who aren't telepaths have at least one folly in common.

We all have an ego, a personality, a viewpoint, and each and every one of us is convinced that our viewpoint is the absolute truth, that we are the one and only reliable observer of reality. We suffer from the delusion that we know what we're talking about. Daniel Dennet says we sell ourselves the delusion that we're conscious. Are you with me?"

"I guess."

"Okay. We each think our viewpoint is truth. The more certain of it we are, the stronger our personality is, the louder our ego broadcast becomes. *A telepath knows better.* He has sampled hundreds of viewpoints and knows perfectly well that they're all full of shit, including his own. In a sense it's the one thing he does know for sure—and every single thing you think at him tries to tell him he's wrong. You in particular, I mean now. You've got a viewpoint so rigid and defended and angle-braced and fail-safed, even at a thousand meters you must seem to Zudie like you're bellowing through a megaphone—trying to obliterate his worldview with your own, to bludgeon him into seeing everything as you do: correctly."

I glanced over to see if I was putting it across, but her face was unreadable.

"Now me, I still can't even make up my mind which Beatle I like best. I'm always open to the heretical opinion, ready to root for the underdog, uncommitted to any party, willing to listen to anyone with manners, prepared to abandon a cherished belief the moment I'm shown persuasive evidence to the contrary. Maybe the Big Bang theory is bullshit. Maybe Lee Oswald acted alone. None of what I said before about driving on pot applies to neophytes, and maybe none of it's true at all: I have no way of knowing if that study was accurate. It was done by government scientists, after all. I've been full of shit so many times it doesn't even embarrass me any more."

"You have no core beliefs?" she asked.

"Sure. A short list, as vague as I can make it, not written down anywhere. Let's see. Kind is better than cruel—I'm sure of that. Loose is better than rigid. Love is better than indifference. So is hate. Laughing is the best. Not laughing will kill you. Alone is okay. Not alone is way better. That's about it . . . and in my life so far there's not a single one of them that's *always* been true."

She was looking thoughtful. "And that's why Zandor is more comfortable around you?"

"Yeah," I said. "Because I may not know much, but at least I know everybody is an asshole."

"Huh?"

"Everybody alive knows, deep down, that they're an asshole. And they are. I defy you to name anyone who ever lived who wasn't an asshole. Being one comes with having one. But nearly everybody is *such* an asshole, they think assholes are a minority. They think they're one of a mere handful of them—so they work like crazy to keep anyone from finding out their secret shame: that they're one of the assholes. I came to terms with being an asshole twenty or thirty years ago. Since then I've been working on being a pleasant one."

Half a klick or so of silence. Then: "I have to say I think you've achieved it."

I had to laugh. I think it was the first thing she ever said to me for that purpose. When you find a cactus, water it. "Thank you."

"You're welcome."

"Anyway, the more you can relax said sphincter, both literally and figuratively, the closer Zudie will be able to approach you without wanting to bang his head on the floor. And pot helps with that."

"I guess we're not going to be meeting face to face, then," she said, and went back to her useless, suspenders-and-belt taping of the wrong side of the road.

About half an hour later, as we were passing through Whistler, she asked, "How did he ever manage to keep people far enough away when you were in college with him?"

"Well, he was a lot less sensitive back then."

"Still."

So I explained about Smelly. Or tried to. It took awhile; she kept asking questions that made me back up two steps and try again. I think I finally succeeded in giving her a pretty good picture of Zudie as I had first known him, and the ways we had worked out to cope with the unique problems he presented. But I failed completely in explaining why I had bothered. She simply could not understand how I could have tolerated something so profoundly offensive as foul odor, and in retrospect I could not really explain it myself.

"I guess," I said finally, "part of it is that until Zudie came along, I was always the weirdest guy in the room. Next to him I looked practically normal. I knew what it was like to be him, at least a little more than other people did. I knew what it was like to be loathed for things you couldn't help—and I could tell his stench was something he just couldn't help, even though I didn't have a clue why not."

She spotted a possible turnoff, and started taping. I

slowed to help. "Back then you never figured out he could read minds?"

I resumed speed. "By the time we went our separate ways I guess I suspected it. But no, I didn't really *know* it until a few days ago when he came crashing back into my life and told me. Because he'd just met the devil himself."

She nodded. "That's about what it would take to get me to open my mouth, if I were Zudie."

"I keep coming back to him in my mind," I admitted. "Allen, I mean. Part of me thinks it's too glib to just write him off as the devil. But I just don't know what else to do with him. What makes a man become so inhuman? Or was he ever human to start with? Do you know anything about serial killers, Nika?"

"A little," she said. "I studied under an expert for a little while. Not long enough, but—"

"Wow—Kim Rossmo?"

"You know him?" I had impressed her.

"Uh, *yeah*. Know of him, at least. He got screwed."

"God damn right he did."

Several years ago, Vancouver had, ever so briefly, a Chief of Police competent and fit to preside over a world-class police force, named Ray Canuel. Unfortunately he didn't get one. Before he left, Chief Canuel promoted the best criminal profiler in North America—Kim Rossmo—the first Canadian police officer with a doctorate in criminology—from constable to detective inspector, and let him set up a criminal profiling unit that won acclaim and awards around the world. Rossmo was so good, the RCMP had to stand in line behind the FBI, CIA and NSA to talk to him. He was so good, in fact, that there began to seem some danger he might actually solve the single greatest disgrace haunting the Vancouver Police Department, and catch the sick bastard who'd been picking off local prostitutes like game birds for the past decade or two. Fortunately, relentless police work managed to turn up a bullshit pretext to fire Detective Inspector Rossmo, just like the chief who'd hired him, before such shame could come to the city's finest. There was no serial killer, the department insisted angrily. Any more than there was a drug supermarket a block from police headquarters. The hooker killer kept working for several more years, burying a total of sixty-one—known—victims on his pig farm in Port Coquitl, before he finally tripped over his own dick and carelessly provided the police too much evidence for even them to ignore.

"Did he give you any kind of handles on someone like Allen? What sort of weaknesses or blind spots he might have?"

She took her time answering. "I don't think so. If what Zudie's told me is true, he doesn't fit *any* of the patterns I'm familiar with. Nobody's genes are that defective, nobody's childhood could be toxic enough to account for him. I don't know any pathology or circumstance or combination of them that would—that could—produce something like him. I don't think Detective Inspector Rossmo does, either. I don't think there's ever *been* one like Allen before."

"Really? Jesus." That was dismaying.

"Except in the movies. Hannibal Lecter. Fu Manchu. That's just what I mean: he's more like an archetype than a real person. A genius ghoul. A brilliant monster. In real life, monsters tend to be morons, brutal goons like the Pig Farm guy or Jeffrey Dahmer."

"Ted Bundy?" I countered.

"Bundy only looks brilliant compared to other serial killers. Trust me, he was an idiot. Just a glib one. But this Allen—the way Zudie tells it, he's a Picasso of pain. Aristotle of agony. A genuine evil genius. I didn't think they existed." She frowned and thought some more. "I'm not saying he's unique, necessarily. But if there are others like him, I suspect they usually tend to gravitate toward jobs like Official Torturer for a tyrant, where they don't get studied."

"Part of the downside of being such a successful species," I said.

"I don't follow you."

"When you have nearly six billion people in the world, it simply stops being possible to say what behavior is and is not human. I mean, if somebody is a one-in-a-million freak . . . that means we have thirty-five just like him right here in Canada. And another three hundred and some odd down in America. A one-in-a-billion freak like Dahmer, there are enough kindred spirits left to form a basketball team."

"There's no telling how many Allens there are in the world right now, is there?" she said.

I gave it some thought, and winced. "No. All we really know for sure is how many have happened to pass within a few hundred meters of Zudie in the last fifty years. And we have no way of knowing whether he's the Einstein of his kind, or just run of the mill."

She literally shuddered.

"What?"

She shook her head and turned away as if to tape a possible turnoff.

"Dammit, Nika, what?"

Slowly she faced forward again. "I just wonder how many of them have found each other on the fucking internet already. Maybe they have a chat group."

I was sorry I'd pressed her. That thought soured the whole rest of the ride back to Vancouver. I kept telling myself, and Nika, that anyone who hated as volcanically as Allen did would hate another Allen most of all, but I never quite convinced either of us. Just about all we knew about Allen, besides his grim hobby, was that he was into computers.

11.

I was willing to drive Nika all the way back into town to the cop-shop parking lot, but she wouldn't hear of it. I admit I didn't struggle much. So instead I stopped at Horseshoe Bay and got in line for the ferry home to Heron Island, and she took the bus from there to downtown Vancouver.

As soon as I was parked in line—a long one; the commuters were going home, now—I used the new cell phone I'd bought that morning to phone my old cell phone. Zudie answered so quickly I knew he'd been waiting for my call. I told him we had plenty of tape for him to look at. "Do you have a VCR out there on Coveney?"

"Of course."

"Compatible with these tapes?"

"Russell, you consulted me before buying the gear, remember?"

"Sorry. It's been a long day of driving."

"I wish you had a boat. I could get started right away."

"I've been thinking about that," I said. "I know a guy who has a place over on the north side of the island, where nobody lives. He's a Buddhist monk and a poet, and this funky hideaway cabin of his is accessible in exactly two ways: by small boat, or by this seriously gnarly woods trail that winds about a mile and a half downhill through leg-breaker country. I'm certain there's nobody within, oh, a kilometer in any direction. And he's in Thailand right now."

"That sounds promising. How do I find it?"

"Well, it's between Apodaca Point and Eagle Cliff Beach, closer to the point than the beach. The cabin's right on the water, tin roof, tall chimney. No others near it. There's a crummy little half-crumbled dock, marked by a big white styrofoam float so you can find it at dusk. Once I get off the ferry at Bug Cove, I could be there in another . . . well, call it forty-five minutes if I don't break an ankle."

"I'll find it," he promised.

And kept his promise. Unfortunately, I didn't. I didn't make it onto the next ferry sailing, and so had to wait another hour. (Part of living on an island is that all ETAs are plus or minus at least one hour.) That made it late enough by the time I started down that trail that it took me nearly twice as long to negotiate as it might have in better light.

But Zudie was there waiting for me when I got to the place, up on the second floor balcony where a quirk of landscape allowed us a view of the setting sun to the west. "Your Buddhist friend is very special," he greeted me. "He's at home in his skin."

"Wow," I said, "you can tell that? Amazing. I don't really

understand how your gift works, I guess. Is it like his thoughts leave echoes, or something?"

He stared at me. "I used my eyes," he said gently.

"Oh." I felt foolish. He was right: one look around told you the man who lived in this stark Zen place needed no distractions from himself, the way the rest of us do.

"How did you and Constable Nika get along in a small enclosed space all day?"

I shrugged. "Not bad, considering."

"Considering?"

"She thinks marijuana is a dangerous drug."

He sighed and nodded. "I found it extremely unpleasant to be within a hundred yards of her."

"We worked it out."

We stood side by side and watched sunset approach. "To be fair," I heard myself say, "she's not really so bad. Considering what she is, and where she comes from, she could be a lot worse."

"Yes," he said. "She could."

"George of Jungle have secret weapon: Dumb Luck."

Another minute of silence. Then: "Do you think she'll really insist on trying to bring him in for kidnapping?"

I thought about it. "I don't know. Will she?"

"I don't know either."

"Why the hell not?"

"Because *she* doesn't know."

"Oh." Great. "Well, if you want my guess, I think she'll come through when it comes to the crunch. I think she'll talk herself into shooting the son of a bitch by the time we have the chance. But I can't be sure."

"I really hope you're right," he said.

"Me too."

"Because there's no way in hell the two of you together can take Allen, if you give him the slightest chance."

"Jesus, Zudie!"

"I'm serious, Russell. Trust me on this, all right? Backshoot him, the second your sights bear, or I promise he will kill you for *days*. Longer days than you can possibly imagine."

Suddenly the sunset wasn't pretty any more. "I've got to go," I said. "My Maglite batteries are nearly shot."

Zudie said, "I'll call you when I spot the place on this tape."

" 'When,' not 'if'?"

"If you shot it, I'll spot it," he said.

We went down to the tiny dock together. He got in his little boat, cast off bow and stern lines, said "Thank you," to a comment I had not made aloud, and went pooting away to the east. My Maglite batteries lasted just long enough, and half an hour later I parked in front of my home and got out.

I was surprised to discover how glad I was to be back home. I stood for a few moments looking at the place before I went inside, seeing it almost as if for the first time. For some time now, it had not really seemed an intrinsically great place to be. But it was, I suddenly realized, it really was—one of the nicer spots on an island so preternaturally beautiful that year in and year out, rich people traveled thousands of miles to stand around and envy us for living there. My house was not large, but adequate to my needs and very sturdy and sound; it didn't let water in or heat out, all its gadgets worked fine, and its layout was agreeable. It was quite a nice house, really, when I thought about it. It was not its fault Susan no longer lived in it. It had done everything it could to keep her alive, just as I had.

And, I realized, if it had been a moldering hulk on a toxic-waste dump site it would have been a more agreeable place to be than the site I had spent the day searching for. From time to time, as we'd explored the mouths of possible access roads, I had allowed my imagination to dwell on what we might actually find at the end of the one we were looking for, once we had identified it. I had let myself picture the site, and the kinds of evidence we might find there—*hoped* to find there, God help us. Now, in this peaceful rustic spot, those images were hard to believe.

I went in the house and made myself one of the five meals I'd had the sense to learn from Susan before she left, I forget which one, and ate it, and put the ingredients away and the dishes in the dishwasher. Then I went out on the sundeck and drank coffee laced with Irish whiskey and listened to a Dianne Reeves CD I'd gotten myself for my last birthday while I watched the stars come out. There is no cruelty in her universe. At least none she can't outsing. While she sang, time hovered. Vehicles went rumbling slowly by a few times, but only one even entered my driveway, and only to turn around; I never got a glimpse of it. Nobody called on the phone. I couldn't remember what shows were on TV tonight, and didn't give a shit.

All the shows I liked, I suddenly realized, were basically cartoon versions of the battle between good and evil. They palled now that I was involved in the real thing.

I found it amazing, as I sat there, how little I doubted

that I was. Allen was a cartoon monster villain if ever there was one, and absolutely the only proof I had that he was any more real than Freddy or Jason was the word of a known whackadoo who claimed he could read minds. Sure, he'd produced proofs . . . but so has every carny huckster who ever worked that line. It's not hard. I had spent my life refusing to believe in anything that couldn't be proven with a double-blind test—did I even have a theory for how telepathy could possibly work, let alone a way to test it? And even if Zudie was a telepath, where was it written that telepaths couldn't be mistaken? How could I be certain whether what he'd seen in Allen's mind was real, or a vivid fantasy racing through the mind of some nerd who thought he was dying, a porn version of Bierce's "Occurrence at Owl Creek Bridge"?

I *was* certain. And not because a tough-minded cop was convinced too, either. I just was. Because Zudie said he was. I *knew* he was a telepath. I'd known it thirty years ago.

As I mused, Fraidy stuck her head out from under the stairs at the far end of the sundeck, and cased the world.

I've already mentioned my cat Horsefeathers, but actually I have one and a half cats. Fraidy is the half. She was there when Susan and I came. She's a feral cat, and terribly damaged. The most obvious symptom is her useless, milk-white right eye. Think what it must be like to be a predator and lack depth perception, to be uncertain whether objects are approaching or receding.

But if you watch her a while you can see Fraidy has even more profound problems. Her sense of smell is poor, for one thing: I've seen her have to hunt for the food dish if it's been moved, and she has to get close to

Horsefeathers before she positively identifies him and stands down from battle stations. But what's actually remarkable is that she's able to place him at all. I've been feeding her daily for many years, now, and she has never once let me come closer than three meters, despite numerous attempts and endless patience. Even Susan only managed to touch her once, for no more than a few gentle strokes, and Susan could charm a baby away from a glass of beer.

I don't think Fraidy remembers who any human is, from one day to the next. I don't think she has any long-term memory storage at all, except possibly for other cats. I think from her point of view, every night she identifies a chink in my defenses, boldly sneaks past my perimeter, robs me of a whole dish full of catfood that happens to be sitting there next to my own cat's, and then makes good her daring escape while my attention is diverted. I can't prove it, but that's the way she behaves.

(I'm only guessing about gender, actually: I've never gotten close enough to check. I'm pretty sure: every so often she makes determined, increasingly irritated attempts to persuade poor neutered Horsefeathers to mount her. But with brain damage so profound, who knows?)

You *cannot* get her to stay indoors five seconds longer than it takes to empty that dish, no matter how cold or rainy or snowy it may be outside: Fraidy would *rather* be alone out in the elements than in a warm dry place occupied only by people who've never so much as frowned at her. Try and keep her in—if you feel like scrubbing shit out of the rug.

Such determined paranoia is a little awe-inspiring. I

confess that a few times over the years I've succumbed to the absurdity of becoming offended by it. I've been feeding you for years—what do I have to *do* to earn your trust, you ungrateful little flea bus? But of course it isn't insulting at all, it's heartbreaking.

Now, for instance. I said, "Hi, Fraidy lady," very softly, and instantly her head swiveled to bring her one good eye to bear. Very slowly, I leaned forward and set my mostly empty coffee mug on the deck. Then with equal slowness and care I stood and backed away. Fraidy likes anything with cream in it, and I'd used that technique before. Normally there was a pretty good chance she'd go for it, as long as you stood well clear and didn't move. This time she looked at the mug, looked at me, looked at the mug—looked quickly round at the world in general for traps or ambushes—and then *galloped* in the other direction and straight up a tree, reaching the peak in seconds. This was more impressive than it may sound: the tree stood well over thirty meters tall—call it a hundred feet. I had to resist two opposing temptations: to be offended, and to burst out laughing. I sat down and finished the cold coffee myself.

Thanks, Fraidy, I thought. *You managed to brighten my mood. No matter how scary life may be, it isn't as scary as you think it is.*

After a while it got too cool to sit outdoors, so I went inside and made another mug of coffee.

My trusty Jura Scala Vario coffee maker is, as I've indicated, a noble machine. Some would say it is the peak of human technology, the ultimate culmination of generations of genius, the finest flower of the tool-making impulse, and among those some would be me. But there is no denying that it is a *noisy* son of a bitch, at least the extremely used model I own. Its grinder is noisy, its dumper is noisy, its boiler is noisy and all its pumps are noisy. Susan had once likened the sound of its operational cycle to a bitter quarrel between two orcs. I stood beside it for the minute or so it took, idly scanning the *TV Guide* to see if there was anything on that night I wanted to bother to watch. There wasn't, of course; we were deep into rerun season by then. Nowadays that seems to affect even cable networks. You'd think one would be smart enough to counterprogram, but no. The wisdom is, in summer everyone is far too busy to stay home and watch television. Nobody in the industry has heard of the VCR, yet. I put the *Guide* down in disgust and decided to watch a DVD. I own very few, but one of them was perfect for my mood, just the right antidote for the kind of bleak, ugly thoughts I'd been thinking all day: *The Concert for George*, the tribute Eric Clapton organized at the Albert Hall one year after George Harrison died. A little "Beware of Darkness" would go down real well now.

As I made that decision, the Jura finished its labors with one last bronchial, "RRR-RRRRRR-RRRR-*thop!*" and I turned to get the cream from the fridge and, ridiculous as I know it sounds, literally *jumped* at least a foot in the air. My reaction was so violent and uncoordinated I somehow swept the sugar bowl off the stovetop and across the kitchen.

And that was before I saw the handgun he was holding.

I don't remember it taking me even the tiniest sliver of a second to get it. There seemed to be zero processing time involved. The physicists are wrong: the words "simultaneous" and "instantaneous" do have meaning. My eyes saw him standing in the kitchen doorway and *simultaneously* I knew who he was and why he was there, even though I could not conceive of any way he could possibly be there. All hope left me *instantaneously*.

That's the only excuse I can offer. There are few things in life I hate more than appearing stupid in retrospect. And it cannot be denied that what left my mouth the moment I saw him was unquestionably the very stupidest thing I could possibly have said, if I'd thought about it for a week.

The first two words, "Jesus *fuck*—" weren't so bad. Just conversational filler, harmless. What they were, really, was a golden two-heartbeat window of opportunity to stifle myself. Instead, I followed them with, "—*Allen!*"

His eyes narrowed.

Flashback:
1968

Grand Central Station
or possibly
Pennsylvania Station
New York, New York
USA

1.

I know more than a little about pain.

In fact, I have it on good authority that I probably know more about it than you do.

It was the end of summer, in New York City. Not a great time to be in pain, any year. But that year was an outstandingly ugly one, and the summer had been its nadir.

In April, some racist coward (if that isn't redundant) had murdered Rev. Dr. Martin Luther King, Jr., from ambush, and pinned it on an obvious patsy named James Earl Ray. The frame held—chiefly because the FBI put its fingers in its ears, held its breath, and ignored anybody who said otherwise. They busted him in June . . . shortly after a genuine lunatic assassin blew Robert F. Kennedy's brains out. The only bright spot in the year so far had been Lyndon Baines Johnson's stunning announcement in March that he would neither seek nor accept his party's nomination for President in the coming election—

and even that proved to be a cursing in disguise.

A week earlier, I had accompanied Bill Doane in his orange VW bug to Chicago, to attend a hippie music festival which we vaguely understood was somehow associated with the Democratic National Convention. Bill had, with his usual panache, somehow contrived to score a couple of hits of genuine Sandoz Laboratories 100% pure lysergic acid diethylamide-25, and we planned to take it there. We never did; lost it, in fact, and didn't miss it.

I've heard people say of that riot that anybody who hurls a bag of shit at an armed man deserves whatever he gets. Hard to argue. But I was there, and I say those uniformed thugs were breaking heads and other bones long before we were reduced to hurling our excrement back at them. I saw a cop deliberately maim a girl: destroy every single facial feature with his club. She was his daughter's age. He had a big happy smile and a hard-on. Toward the end of the second day, as we huddled together inside a dumpster in Griffith Park, Bill said to me, in that gentle voice of his, "I think it's time to go home, Russell."

"You think?" I said, rubbing futilely at the knot on my skull.

"If we don't," he said calmly, "I'm going to fill the Bug up with all the gasoline drums I can buy, and drive it into the center of the biggest bunch of cops I can find. And I don't think I should do that. So we'd better go."

I had once seen Bill take a pretty good beating from a drunk half his size, because, he said, he didn't need to fight back. Twenty minutes later, we were on the road. And that November, Richard Milhous Nixon would become First Crook, and make LBJ look like Gandhi.

But at the end of August, we didn't yet know that. And the lump on the left rear portion of my skullbone I left the Windy City with is by no means the pain I'm talking about. Not even close.

Susan was coming into town by train, from her real father's place up in Toronto, for a week's visit. The idea was for her to meet my parents. There was some little pressure involved, as I had not yet told them she was carrying our child. We *did* plan to marry before the kid turned three (and in fact, did marry on Jesse's third birthday), but I didn't expect that to mollify them much.

So I was more agitated than somewhat, when I went to pick her up. Either I was supposed to meet her at Grand Central Station, and went to Penn Station instead, or the other way round—I can't remember anymore, and it doesn't matter. The point is, I reached the right station one minute *after* her train had arrived, begged directions from a porter, tore through the place at a dead run, and was halfway down the stairs to the right platform—just spotting Susan, forlorn and visibly pregnant and surrounded with luggage down at the far end—when I felt my right lung collapse.

I'll never forget the rapid evolution her face went through as she saw me approach, like an actress's whole career at super-fast forward. *Gee I wish he'd/oh*, there *he/I love him so m/oh my God, what's* wrong *with him?*

"Welcome . . . New York," I said, and gestured at my chest. "Get me . . . hospital. Sorry."

Her eyes widened, she took in a deep breath—and that was all the time she needed. "Officer," she called out, spotting a cop at the other end of the platform, "my husband's lung has collapsed—we need to get him to a hospital!"

New York's finest slowly craned his head around, beheld two hippies in full regalia, one pregnant, and did his duty as he saw it. "Cab's upstairs, lady," he said, and returned to contemplation of the ads on the other side of the tracks.

It took her two trips to get both me and the luggage up the stairs. It would have taken three trips, but she took me first, and by the time she got back for the bags there were fewer of them.

The nearest cabstand was a long way off, to a man with a fist of steel crushing half his chest, breathing in small, terrified sips. For the first fifty yards or so she kept shouting, "Will someone help us, please?" but she soon wised up.

"Take us to the nearest hospital," she told the cabbie, a Sikh. He nodded, said, "Bellevue, sure, sure," and peeled out. He was on his second pass around Central Park before I could find enough breath to tell Susan the words she had to say, and convince her that she had to say all of them. Loudly. "You cocksucker, quit jerking me off or I will have your fucking medallion and your fucking green card." Seven minutes later he was tossing her luggage out of his trunk at Bellevue Emergency Entrance.

There must have been the usual admissions nonsense. I remember none of it. I remember fear. I knew what was coming. To allow a collapsed lung to reinflate, you must remove the fluids that rushed to fill the empty space when it went down. You do this by poking a plastic tube into the patient's chest. Half the times this had been done to me, it had been done with no anesthesia or numbing

of any kind, and it had felt exactly like you think it would
feel to have someone knife you in the ribs and then ram a
tube in there.

God bless Bellevue Emergency. I felt only the horrid
pressure.

Another long wait, holding hands with Susan. My next
clear recollection is a surgeon asking me if I wanted them
to do the operation that would stop my lungs from collapsing.

"The what?" I asked.

"The operation that will stop your lungs from collapsing."

"Um . . . Doc, this is my, let me see, fifth pneumothorax. Why has nobody ever mentioned this operation
to me before?"

Shrug. "Beats me. It's the standard treatment for your
condition. First line in the textbook under 'therapy.' "

"Really." Pause. "What's it involve?"

"You don't want to know."

"Well . . . what are my chances?"

"Ten to twelve percent chance you'll die, probably on
the table."

"And if I live, my lungs won't collapse anymore?"

"Right."

"Do it," I said.

And they did.

That's all they told me about the operation beforehand,
and although afterwards I was given more details, they
were quite right: you don't want to know them. Terrible
things were done to my insides, and when it was over I
had many sawn-through ribs, a scar from my right nipple

almost to my spine, and a right arm that didn't work very well because they'd damaged a major nerve trunk on the way in.

But here's the part you must understand: I did not know—nobody told me, then or ever—I only happened to find out by chance, over twenty-five years later, that the operation I had endured, a thoracotomy, is rated one of the most painful surgical procedures a human can survive. Nobody ever thought to tell me.

I'm grateful I wasn't told going in, or I'd never have let them do it—and believe me, I'm glad they did. Since then, I have had a few very minor lung collapses, but only of the other lung, and only when I was stupid enough to do something silly like try and change a tire: they no longer just happen for no good reason. And when they come, instead of costing a two- or three-month layup each time, they rarely put me in bed for more than a day or two.

But I do wish, I do, that at least after the fact, somebody had thought to tell me about what an extraordinarily painful procedure it is. Instead, I spent the next quarter of a century believing that *all* operations hurt that much, and I was simply an outstanding coward.

Because it took a good three or four months right out of my life, flat on my back, after which I tottered around like a little old man for at least another six months. It was a year before my right arm was back up to snuff—and it would be another decade before I could bear to be touched, however gently, anywhere near the scar.

No, let me go back further, to give you some idea of the kind of pain I'm talking about. Immediately after the operation, they had me on morphine. I hurt so bad I was sure the bastards were cutting it—until they cut me off, dropped me back to lesser narcotics. Those made no perceptible dent at all in the agony that was my every breath. By the time they sent me home to my parents' place, I had not slept since my last morphine shot, a week earlier.

And I did not sleep for the next two weeks. Not for one minute. It hurt too much. It was necessary to remain absolutely still, propped halfway up in bed on a mountain of pillows, every second, all day and all night. If I began to drift off, some part of my body would move—a foot would flex, say, or a few fingers might twitch, or my head sag sideways on the pillow. It didn't matter: every part of my body was directly mechanically connected to the incision. Any possible movement would produce enough pain to jolt me back awake, moaning. The pain sliced right through Demerol, Percodan, Seconal, and anything else I could get a prescription for.

Have you ever been awake for anything *approaching* three weeks? That in itself was mind-shattering, never mind the pain that caused it. If Susan had not been there, I'm pretty sure I would have literally gone insane. God knows I came close enough.

Susan's meeting with my mother, by the way, had been somewhat less than auspicious at first: they met over my semiconscious body, in a ward at Bellevue. Even though I was semiconscious, I remember it. It was like watching two strange cats meet, over a piece of meat. Mom instantly took in Susan's condition, and her eyes widened slightly; Susan instantly took that in, and her ears flattened slightly. "Let's go for a walk, dear," Mom said pleasantly. "Good idea," Susan agreed cheerfully. And they left me there and went off to settle my life. I spent a ghastly hour or so praying—when I could spare a prayer from pleas for anodyne—that I would not, on top of everything else, be forced to choose between the two most important women in my life in my hour of greatest need.

Finally I drifted into an uneasy nap—this was before the surgery—and woke to find my mother bending over me. She was smiling gently, about Mona Lisa wattage. She looked me square in the eyes, made sure she had my full attention, and said, very softly, "Keep this one."

It was one of only two really happy moments in the whole experience—the other being when, a week after they sent me home, Susan proved to me that it is possible both to have and even to enjoy an orgasm while in great pain.

It was perhaps the least of her contributions. I had until then been a committed hardheaded materialist, like most recovering Catholics: if it couldn't be measured, I didn't want to hear about it. Susan taught me about Buddhism, and thus about spirituality in general. She never succeeded in converting me to Soto Zen—which was okay, she wasn't trying—but the meditational techniques they use were of enormous help to me in enduring the endless onslaught of pain. Not enough—but more than the drugs. That, and her own relentless selfless love, helped me to open my heart, for the first time since I'd left the seminary, to spirituality, which changed my life forever, for the better. I won't say I was exactly having visions, there at the end. But I will say I saw some stuff most people haven't—and that just won't fit into words.

It wasn't enough, though. Even with her help and counsel, by the end of the third week I was so squirrely from fatigue and pain and pain-fatigue, I was starting to become seriously suicidal. Serious enough not to mention it to Susan. Curiously, what finally ended up saving my life was not her. It was the Marx Brothers—and Mom.

One of my lifelines during that dreadful time was the portable TV Dad had set up in my sickroom (his old office), and tricked up with a remote control box on a long cable. (All it would do was change channels—among the existing thirteen. For volume control or on/off, you called for help.) As my marathon of awakeness was entering its fourth week, and I was beginning to amass a lethal stockpile of Seconals, one night a rare Marx Brothers movie I had never seen before came on WPIX Channel 11. It was called *The Marx Brothers Go West,* and it's not surprising I'd never seen it; it had to be the worst piece of shit they ever tried to foist on an unsuspecting public. It isn't just that a good third of the jokes were racist Indian-baiting: *all* the jokes were as lame as a one-legged horse, even by Marx Brothers standards. The big finish was a railroad race which the boys won by feeding the entire train into its boiler furnace, maybe only the twentieth time that gag had ever been filmed. There was not one quotable line that I can recall, or one humorous situation that wasn't stolen from a better film—not even a single memorable bit from Harpo.

I didn't give a damn. In my condition, it was a special broken-glass-deep-inside pain to laugh. I didn't give a damn about that either. I was just . . . *in the mood.* From about two minutes in, every second of that movie that I didn't spend laughing, I spent desperately sucking in enough air to resume laughing again. I roared. I howled. I whooped. I wept. With my functional left arm I managed to bang my thigh so hard I could feel it through the sheet. I probably frightened Susan, but I was transported with laughter—just as it had been with the morphine, I was still perfectly aware of the pain, I just didn't give a shit anymore. It moved one crucial degree out of phase from me, and no longer mattered so much.

As the credits were rolling I literally laughed myself unconscious.

According to Susan, that changed almost immediately— in less than a minute, she says, I went from merely out cold to asleep. Deeply, soundly, profoundly asleep. Huge honking snores, shallow but juicy. She had to flee the room at first, lest her tears of relief wake me. She told my Mom, and they wept together. Then she crept back in and sat with me for hours, giving thanks to all Buddhas, before she finally went and passed out in the guest room upstairs, my old bedroom.

The strain had been nearly as hard on her as on me— really, truly, and unmistakably. I had almost ceased to really believe in the existence of love, at the vast age of eighteen, but she clearly met the definition: there was no doubting that my welfare had become essential to her own. I knew I could be fooling myself that I loved her, I'd done that before in my life—but I could *not* have been fooling myself that she loved me, because I simply wasn't that good a fooler.

Anyway, that's why she was so exhausted, she slept through the distant sounds of the last part of the cure.

I awoke in total darkness, total disorientation, total confusion . . . aware only that something was horribly, horribly wrong, and in danger of getting infinitely worse. It seemed to take hours to grasp my situation, but it couldn't possibly have been more than seconds; I just wasn't strong enough.

In my sleep, I slowly understood, I had managed to topple off that mound of pillows and fall out of bed. No, worse. I had fallen halfway out of bed. The only thing preventing me from falling all the way out of bed—*and landing on the incision*—was my right arm. The one that didn't work, so weakened it was a hard-won triumph to lift a Dixie cup half full of water to my lips. There was no hope of slipping a pillow beneath my side before it hit the floor; my left hand was clutching the bedsheet like grim death to help my right arm . . . and slowly pulling the sheet off the mattress. Any second now its elastic corner was going to let go, and *slam* me to the floor.

I screamed, at the top of my lungs. *"Help!"*

That's what happened inside my mind. That's what I wanted to do, and that's what I heard. But almost certainly, out there in the real world, what I actually produced was a sound much more like the bleat of a newborn kitten.

No matter.

In the next room slept my mother and father. Dad's a reasonably heavy sleeper, as humans go. But Mom was like me: a hopeless zombie, fully capable of sleeping through any alarm clock and all but the most relentless and cruel prodding, useless until the second cup of coffee. But she heard her wounded boy bleat.

What I heard, from my point of view, was an inarticulate moan which I later learned was meant to be, "I'm coming, sweetheart," but was hampered by her dry mouth's inability to form consonants, and then an astonishing sequence of cartoon sound effects, ranging from shattering glass to toppling night table to something I couldn't parse that went wump-CRASH, wump-CRASH, wump-CRASH, getting louder.

The door to my sickroom burst open. One final wump-CRASH!! and silence. The lightweight curtains billowed, briefly letting in enough moonlight to reveal my mother. She was in her pink pajamas, both eyes glued shut, chin thrust forward, one foot hopelessly jammed in her bedside wastebasket, the other bare. As I watched, she managed to pry open her right eye—and discover that she had, by chance, stopped about an inch short of impaling it on the TV antenna. The curtains closed—parted again—she refocused past the antenna and saw me, saw me see her—they closed again; opened one last time—we looked at each other across the room for one more second—

—and we both literally fell down laughing.

By sheer animal instinct I managed to land on my shoulder and my fist instead of on the incision, and we lay there together, a few feet apart, helpless with laughter, for a long time. When we had the strength, we began the long crawl into each other's arms, and were rocking back and forth together there on the floor, gasping and meowing and shuddering with mirth, when Dad and Susan burst in demanding to know what the *hell* was going on. It was a long time before we even tried to explain, and I'm not sure Dad ever did get it.

But when he put me back on the bed—horizontal, now, without the pillow-pile prop—it was no longer terrifying to have that much of the weight of my torso resting on my wound. I was asleep again almost at once, and I slept without pause for the next thirty hours straight, and from then on I was getting better.

*   *   *

I tell you all this to support my original statement. By that evening in the summer of 2003—my God, thirty-five years later—just a few months short of my fifty-fifth birthday—I had, sad to say, met a few people who I felt knew as much about pain as I did. But I did not expect ever to meet anyone who knew more.

Then I did.

Allen had been creating pain worse than anything I knew about, for his amusement, and studying it rigorously, for his edification, at least once a week since—well, that's the most ironic part. He was born ten years after me, in 1960, and took his first victim the summer he turned eight.

Flashforward:
2003

Trembling-on-the-Verge
Heron Island, British Columbia
Canada

1.

"**Y**ou know my name," he said. "That's very interesting."

I came very close to peeing in my pants.

I managed not to, but it wasn't easy; I was full of coffee. My other big accomplishment was forcing my diaphragm to take in and expel a cup or so of air at intervals. I couldn't think why I was bothering—wouldn't this be a wonderful time to faint? But I couldn't help it any more than I could control my bladder.

All this was down to his eyes. They were not all I could see, but for the longest time they were all I could look at. Moist, bright, cloudy, utterly cold, like frozen marbles in hot moonlight. Reptile eyes. One of the arguments against evolution is the eye: not only is it insanely complex to have formed by chance, but there is no structure *halfway to an eye*: it must occur fully developed or not at all. These might have been the original eyeballs, passed down over the millennia from one coldblooded killer to the next, squid to shark to snake to saurian to scorpion, the eyes of entropy, watching all in their view become rot and dust, and helping whenever convenient.

If he'd been wearing sunglasses or had his eyes closed, what I would have seen was a man who looked rather like the character who runs the comic book store in the cartoon series *The Simpsons*. A born Trekkie, round and sweaty, bald on top with a long ponytail, wearing a beard that fought a close third with Yassar Arafat and Ringo Starr for world's ugliest. He was actually wearing a black Lord of the Rings T-shirt, tucked in—for the first of the Peter Jackson films, I believe, though the third was nearly out then—with a pale green vest over it, and baggy khaki pants, and a cell phone on his belt that was actually made to look like Captain Kirk's communicator. If I haven't already succeeded in conveying to you how preternaturally, mind-meltingly frightened I was, maybe it will help if I mention that nothing about his appearance struck me as even a tiny bit amusing, even in theory.

Because by the time I saw any of that, his eyes had annihilated the concept of funny in my universe.

There was plenty of fun in *his* universe. He was about to have lots of it, and he planned to enjoy it hugely. His eyes told me that. He was already smirking in anticipation. But for me nothing was ever going to be funny again—not even in a bitter, ironical sense. Against the horror he represented, irony had no power, no significance, no purchase. It was a human response, like heartbreak or defiance or despair, irrelevant now. He was like 9/11 on two legs, and it didn't matter, it just didn't matter at all, whether or not you got the joke.

What I did then did not come from my mammalian

forebrain, but from somewhere way back in the reptile-remnant core it's grafted onto. Those eyes aside, he did not look physically intimidating. He looked like the kind of clumsy, uncoordinated, cowardly nerd even someone as frail as me might well be able to take, given my New York combat experience and a little luck. And my subconscious mind was so dumb, it still believed survival was possible. To my amazement, I found myself charging him. I had no great hope of succeeding, but it wasn't even worth suppressing the attempt—what difference could it make?

By the time I reached him, he hadn't lifted his hands, or even so much as taken a defensive stance. He stood flat-footed, as if he knew he had nothing to fear, and he was right. I tagged him, with everything I had, right where I wanted to hit him, on the shelf of his jaw. I don't think I even rattled him. He snorted contemptuously.

He reached up with his left hand, put a finger lightly on my collarbone, slid along it an inch to the left and settled the fingertip into a little hollow pocket he found there. Then he pressed. If you pressed that hard on the button of a telephone, it might not be enough to register. It would barely have triggered the repeat-character function on a computer keyboard.

It was like being electrocuted. I screamed at the top of my lungs, and this time I did piss my pants.

"Ah," he said, interested. He lifted his finger, paused— I began to cry.

How did he know? Something about my body language? Something in my eyes? Please God don't let it have been anything resembling telepathy, or I'll have to spend the rest of my life washing my mind out with soap. All I can tell you is, the very next thing he did was move that goddam fingertip directly down to the scar that circles my torso. I felt him detect it, through my shirt. A few seconds to inspect it, without taking his eyes from mine, and he again located a spot he liked. It never even occurred to me to lift a hand to stop him, though I desperately wished someone would.

Even before he started pressing, I was screaming at the top of my lungs, this time. Then he stepped slightly to one side, and pressed *hard*. I vomited on the spot he'd just been standing on, without ceasing to scream. The world dissolved to black and I felt my knees hit the kitchen floor.

"There, I think we've got you more or less empty, now," I heard him say over my screams. "Now, we can get started."

I could feel myself toppling forward, and some vagrant part of my brain knew I was probably going to land face-first in my own puke. But it didn't matter; I was out before I hit.

I believe nobody is ever unconscious.

A friend of mine was once involved in an auto accident while driving south, just after she had entered the state of Tennessee. She was in a coma for eight days. I was there when she awoke, and I had to tell her that she was speaking in a soft Tennessee drawl, quite foreign to her, but identical to that of her nurses. Those whole eight days, *someone* was awake in there, listening, noting how they spoke here. I suspect that entity was simply incapable of laying down long-term memories.

So in a sense I probably experienced chest surgery, all those years ago, and in the same sense I was probably in some sense aware during the next twenty minutes or so of my life as Allen's prisoner. But in both cases, the memories, if they even exist, are buried so deep I doubt hypnosis could bring them to the surface. Thank all gods.

So I got no useful thinking done during those twenty minutes, not even subconsciously. My memory insists I was on my knees in the kitchen, closed my eyes, fell forward, and opened them again to find myself sitting upright in one of my living room chairs, the one that swiveled, with broad wooden arms that curved forward and down like upside down sled runners. The amount of time that I'd lost while my eyes had been closed could be inferred, at least roughly, from the changes in my situation. But it took me a surprising amount of time to get that far, because as my eyes opened the very first thing they saw was Allen, a few meters away, sitting in the chair that reclined, staring contemplatively at my favorite photo of Susan. He had found it in my bedroom. He was only the third person ever to have seen it.

That anybody was looking at it was horrible. That *he* was looking at it meant I had failed as a man, failed in my duty to my wife—failed utterly, irrevocably, unforgivably—and the fact that she was ashes long since was no consolation at all. Even death could not sufficiently insulate a pure soul like her from an Allen. Now he knew she had once existed, she was slimed retroactively; now he knew her body's intimacies, she was raped from beyond the grave. No matter what might happen next, that could never be repaired, and it really was worse than dying.

Many things are.

You'd think I'd have woken up groggy. I would have

expected to. But when you *want* your brain to stop working, that's just when it goes into overdrive, every time. When my eyes opened and I saw him studying Susan's picture, I hit the ground running.

I understood at once, for instance, that my first priority should be taking inventory of my situation—and that I would have very little time for it, because the act of waking up would already have altered my breathing enough to alert him; I had maybe one respiration's grace before he would finish his thought and turn his attention to me.

Unfortunately, inventory was dismayingly simple. I was sitting down in damp clammy trousers. He'd wiped my face off. It didn't much matter just where I was in the room, because my ankles were fastened tightly together somehow. There was no point in wondering what potential weapons might lay within reach, because *nothing* was within reach except the smooth wooden arms of the chair, to which my wrists were firmly secured with duct tape. There was nothing useful to think about. There was really only one interesting aspect of my whole fix, and I didn't *want* to think about it. If you were going to tape an unconscious man's hands to the arms of a chair, the natural way to do it would be palms down, right? Allen had taped mine palms up. Maybe he just wanted to prevent me from using even the feeble leverage of my fingers to help me strain against the tape. But I had darker suspicions. Imagination can be a terrible thing.

The only other detail I had time to note was that I smelled awful. Hard to feel strong when you smell like pee.

And then he lowered Susan's photo and switched his gaze to me, and I stopped being aware of anything but his Aztec idol eyes, and his little wet pouting mouth.

He said, "I've rarely been so conflicted."

One of the people I'd known in a previous life—the one with occasional raisins of hope in its oatmeal—had been a guy named Russell Walker. He would have found that opening line hilarious, would have devised at least a dozen snarky comebacks . . . would have stolen some from Leslie Charteris, if he had to.

Allen said, "Intellectually, the choice is quite clear. You have information I want very badly. I can extract it with 100% certainty—effortlessly, in any desired degree of depth, and with perfect reliability—simply by using a combination of certain drugs in a certain sequence." He frowned, and his lower lip pushed out slightly. "But by the time I finished, the you I'm speaking to now would no longer exist. You'd be a much simpler, and I think I can guarantee, infinitely happier animal, for as long as the state or some misplaced charity chose to keep you alive." His frown darkened. "I don't like you *near* that well."

If you strain hard enough against duct tape, there is a noise in your ears like thunder, like a distant, just-barely-subsonic jet engine.

He said, "Information obtained by torture, on the other hand, is somewhat less reliable, and its acquisition takes *much* longer." His frown vanished. He beamed at me. "But you have seriously vexed me. I *prefer* to use pain, and can afford to indulge myself. I am in no hurry at all."

Well, neither was I. I decided to engage him in conversation. There was some stuff I really wanted to know, and once the torture part started, I probably wouldn't care anymore. Perhaps if I impressed him with clever enough repartée, he'd sense a kindred spirit, and mercifully decide to dissolve my brain with drugs after all.

"How—how—how—ow—ow—wow—"

Maybe it was too late for that.

He smile broadened. "Let me see if I can express your thought for you, in human speech. You would like to know how I found out you were after me."

I decided a nod was better than an attempt at speech. Way less to go wrong. Sure enough, I failed to establish a rhythm: my head simply bobbed spastically.

He said, "Wonderful. We have the basis of a bargain, then. I will tell you how I learned you were after me . . . after you tell me *why* you were."

I sat there behind a pathetic imitation of my poker face, trying to construct a little mental video of myself explaining to him that I was after him because my friend Smelly the mind reader had told me about his hobby.

The *worst*-case scenario was that I'd convince him somehow. He could probably kill Zudie just by rowing three times around Coveney Island. If he ever got closer than that, it wouldn't surprise me much if he could make Zudie's skull explode, like in Cronenberg's film *Scanners*.

Or I might get lucky: Allen might refuse to swallow such a preposterous story and kill me on the spot for lying.

Did I have any other assets whatsoever that he didn't know about? Any kind of edge at all? Well—one . . . though I could not see any possible way to make use of it.

He had not finished talking. "And who your girlfriend is. I'm particularly curious about her."

There now, that *was* a useful secret. The reason he was satanically enraged with me was that I had frightened him, though he would never have admitted it. If I timed it right—baited him, attacked his ego, got him agitated, and only *then* let him know that his other amateur antagonist was an off-duty Vancouver police officer—maybe I could scare him *so* badly, I could goad him into cutting my throat. Good to remember.

His voice . . . are you old enough to have ever fooled around with imitating the speaking voices of the Beatles? Do George—then keep the adenoidal glottal stop, but lose the Liverpool accent, change it to American West Coast Generic, and raise the pitch a full tone. The net effect is a man wearing a necktie pulled way too tight. That was Allen's voice. For some reason I pictured a boy being strangled by his father, and wondered if the image actually had anything to do with his life, or was just my frantic brain clutching at straws. I still do.

When you're desperate, and have nothing at all to bargain with, make extravagant promises. Why not? They cost nothing, and fill time with not-pain.

I looked him square in the eye, reached deep into memory, and pulled out the face I had first used back in 1970 to solemnly assure the Dean of Men I didn't have the faintest idea where to go to obtain marijuana, on or off campus. After five minutes' exposure to it, the Dean had blinked, shaken his head, and said, with sneaking respect, "You know, if I didn't *know for a fact* that you're lying . . . I'd believe you. You're good." It had been my earliest evidence that I might have the makings of a journalist, or writer, or lawyer, or some other kind of bullshit artist. I knew there was no chance of it lasting five minutes with this Allen. But I hoped for two.

I told him, "In the hope of establishing good will and mutual respect as the basis of our relationship from the very outset, I am absolutely willing to tell you anything you want to know whatsoever, without reservation, fully and in detail, if you'll just tell me one thing."

"How I backtracked you."

"Jesus, you're fast," I said, hoping the real dismay in my voice would make the flattery sound sincere.

I wish I could say he burst out laughing. He burst into giggles. "Jesus, you're lame."

I glanced down at my unenviable condition. "Well, obviously." To my horror, I giggled.

He studied me, measuring something. Finally he decided the effect of a few more minutes of despairing suspense would be beneficial. Or perhaps only interesting. Or maybe just fun.

"When I was a kid, reading books," he said, "I always hated the part where the evil genius has Simon Templar tied up with a gun to his head . . . and then he stops to explain how smart he is, for just long enough for the Saint to slip his bonds or be rescued. What kind of genius blows everything for the sake of his ego? What's the point of impressing meat?"

That last sentence was so awful I had to say something, anything. "How else is the writer supposed to fill in the holes in the plot?" I asked.

When a human being holds up one fingertip like that, it means, *now, you'll have your turn.* When he did it it meant, *if you interrupt me again I will touch you with this.* I made a determined effort to pressure-weld my teeth together.

"Once I started to experience such situations in life rather than in fiction, however," he went on, confident of the floor now, "I began to understand the appeal. It's like the old joke about the priest God hated so much, he gave him a hole-in-one on a Sunday—*who can he tell?* I've done it literally dozens of times, now, whenever I felt my victim was intelligent enough to appreciate good irony, and I can report that so far, not *once* has it worked out badly for me. It *was* reasonably clever of me to have tracked you to your lair so quickly, and it was reasonably stupid of you not to have foreseen it, and who else will I ever be able to boast to, or rub it in on? Certainly no one who'd appreciate the irony as sharply as you will."

Brilliant. He was on a roll. Poker face—

"Furthermore, I know a secret: *there is no risk.* In real life, as opposed to fiction, nobody ever slips his bonds, or has a knife strapped to his forearm, or gets the villain to light his exploding cigarette for him. Nobody escapes, and there are no rescues. Ever. The cavalry never comes, SWAT never rolls. Not once, not even at the last possible moment. I've watched hundreds of people beg mercy, of every god there ever was, including me. Doesn't happen. When you're fucked, you're fucked. And you're fucked.

"So I have no problem playing Rayt Marius to your Simon Templar. Sadly, it will be a disappointingly short digression. It did not take anything like a Rayt Marius to outsmart you. 'I know the Saint, Senator, and you're no Saint . . . ' "

The *most* infuriating damn thing: I actually figured out the answer myself, about two and a half seconds before he explained it to me! Swear to God. I just didn't dare interrupt.

"All that time you were trying to case the area around the mouth of my private driveway with that ridiculous consumer vidcam of yours . . . did it ever occur to you that someone might be observing *you*, with infinitely better equipment? Did you think I would leave my rural hideaway unguarded? Did you think video security systems were at all expensive, or in some way difficult to set up, conceal, or monitor? You *do* know how I've made my living, right? I find it curiously difficult to pin down the precise magnitude and scope of your ignorance; your stupidity masks it."

My heart was already in my stomach, and my stomach was in my shoes. Now the whole mess dropped into the basement crawl space, where a trillion spiders lived. I wasn't just doomed, I was so God damned dumb I deserved to be. I think I mentioned, I have a particular horror of looking stupid in retrospect. This was undoubtedly my masterpiece.

I saw the thing whole, in an instant. But my bloodstream probably contained every drop of adrenaline in my body. I'll lay it out for you step by step, as best I can:

In the city, even in the suburbs, electronic surveillance would surely have occurred to me, later if not sooner. What had made me assume that it became impossible, or even particularly difficult, in a remote rural setting?

I keep tripping over my age, thinking in terms of technological limits that were overcome long ago. In my wildest dreams, I may have imagined that somewhere down at the far *end* of the dirt road I was looking for, there might be some sort of alarm system, on the order of trip wires or an electric eye. If I *had* bestirred myself to contemplate a rural video surveillance setup right alongside the Sea to Sky Highway, I would probably have pictured a little grey box the size of a pound of butter, on a tripod in some sort of sheltered blind, and wires somehow waterproofed and camouflaged over hundreds of yards, leading to a moisture-sealed VCR whose tape had to be changed every six hours, labeled, and stored—and dismissed the idea as way too much trouble, the sort of thing an army base or an embassy might use, but not a private individual.

In fact, a good color camera and wireless transmitter, motion-activated or heat-activated or sound-activated or any combination thereof, could nowadays probably be tucked into something the size of a pinecone without straining—no reason for it not to look like one as well. Its destination hard drive might be solar-powered, look like an empty can of mixed nuts, and hold a year's worth of false alarms, instantly searchable, before it had to start writing over the oldest ones. If you were a wealthy technophile psycho, you'd probably knew several competing brands, which was the good one, and where to get the best price.

So you could afford to use very broad parameters for what constituted a suspicious event, give free rein to your paranoia. It didn't have to be anything as drastic as a personal incursion, as specific as a moving heat source within a certain distance. A car going by significantly slower than the rest of the traffic might be enough to start the camera rolling. Hell, for all I know, maybe if you were a clever enough computer guy, you could program your pinecone camera to recognize another camera lens looking back at it.

Maybe, if you were paranoid enough, and smart enough, you could program the fucking thing to e-mail you video every time it was awakened, wherever you happened to be on the planet at the time.

And if you placed it close enough to the highway, you would have not just the face of, but at minimum the make, model and plate number of the car driven by whoever was annoying you. With luck and the right lighting you might even get a look at any companions he happened to have as well.

If you were even a moderately competent hacker, car and license number gave you . . . shit, everything. Legal name. Correct current address. Marital status. Citizenship. Color head shot photo. Vehicular history, which is the skeleton of life history. Registration leads you to financial history. Insurance leads you to driving record and medical history. I'm no celebrity or anything, but I Google up pretty good. I'm a columnist, so I piss people off, so they have to tell each other how odious I am, so more than a little of my past, including the parts I tend to stress least when recounting my life story to a woman in a bar, can be found on the internet by any amateur with a laptop and a browser. Somebody like Allen . . . it was a safe bet he now knew my blood type, bank balance, taste in porn, every password or PIN number I'd ever used including the ones I'd forgotten, and the total contents of the file that the CSIS keeps doggedly insisting it is not maintaining on me. For all I knew he could write my DNA sequence out longhand.

Whereas the most he could conceivably know about Nika for certain was that she was close to my height and blonde.

Was that of any imaginable help to me? Suppose I could remake myself in an instant, find moral strength in my last hour, compress my courage to diamond hardness— suppose I reversed my whole life and became the kind of brave son of a bitch who could stand up under torture. Suppose, purely as a thought experiment, I could keep Allen from prying one single bit of information about Nika out of me for, say, an hour. Or even indefinitely.

What the fuck good would it do me?

Sooner or later Nika was going to call me, and then he would have her. No matter what message she left, her phone number in the call display would be enough to end her life too. I already knew Allen well enough, on short acquaintance, to know that it was probably not going to alarm him unduly when he did learn she was a cop. It was probably going to excite him. She would not be the first law officer he'd killed . . . but she might be his first female. He would be *so* disappointed when he learned she wasn't a lesbian.

It was going to be much the same for Zandor Zudenigo. Similar, anyway.

Sooner or later, he would call me to discuss his analysis of the tape. Within the first ten or fifteen seconds of his message he would say enough to seal his fate. He would have no warning; telepathy doesn't work over the phone. A normal human or even a cop would not be able to trace him back to Coveney Island from a cell-phone call, but I believed Allen would find it at worst an invigorating challenge.

It probably didn't even matter: the simple possibility that he might track him down was as good as the deed. Once Zudie knew that Allen was aware of his existence, and disapproved, his best option was to cut his own throat. Or whatever it took; beat himself to death with a rock if necessary. There was no way he could hide from a man like Allen, no chance he could fight him, no hope he could outrun him, and just about any death would be kinder than what Allen would give him. His very existence—the nature of the talent he could not help having—would enrage Allen to incandescence, if not Cherenkov glow. The concept of another human being able to see into his private skull would, for him, be God's most unforgivable insult yet, a kind of cheating—violating a rule even Satan himself respected. The only thing that might make it remotely bearable for him would be the unmistakable agony it caused Zudie. At last, a knowledgable audience!

In a sudden horrid flash, I intuited what Allen might find a suitable punishment for someone who invaded his castle. Pull up the drawbridge. Make him stay. Rub his face in horror and depravity until he suicides.

No, by God, it was even worse. I wasn't thinking it through. If it had been in Zudie to kill himself, he'd have done so decades ago. He just couldn't, the way some people just *can't* bring themselves to stick a finger down their throat even though they know it would make them feel better.

So all Allen had to do for ultimate revenge was put Zudie on a twenty-meter leash. It would always be taut. And it would never be long enough.

I pictured Allen, fascinated in a cold intellectual way by the absorbing technical question of which was ultimately more painful for Zudie to endure: the remorseless thoughts of Allen, or the despairing thoughts of his victims? Was it possible to construct a good double-blind experiment to settle the matter? Or was the phenomenon necessarily subjective? Perspiring minds want to know.

My God. I'd had it just backwards. Allen wouldn't kill Zudie. Allen would *love* Zudie, cherish him, keep him alive as long as possible. If you want your victims to suffer as much as possible, you just can't beat total knowledge of all their deepest secrets and private thoughts. Allen obviously had an instinctive gift for intuiting such things . . . but Zudie could read them like print.

Allen would love the fact that he couldn't help it.

Yes, that was the way of it. I hadn't just given the Beast three more victims, or even three unusually tasty ones. Clever me: I had handed him a prize greater than any he had ever thought to possess, a more interesting toy than the Marquis de Sade had ever dreamed of, a sadist's ideal applause-meter. Someone you could hurt merely by approaching. He was going to treat Zudie like a freshman treats his first sports car: run him flat out until he ruined him, throw horror after horror at him just to determine scientifically the precise point at which it caused his mind to melt.

He would be glad, for instance, to finally have empirical confirmation of something he'd always wondered and theorized about: exactly how long, after a heart stopped beating and lungs stopped pumping, did an entity persist that was still capable of suffering. *Did* anguish end with brain-death? *Did* the soul find oblivion, and if so did that occur before, when, or at some point after the last neuron fired? Had he been missing a bet all these years, by ceasing to torment his victims merely because they were dead?

Oh yeah, no question, in the end, Allen was going to love me. I had brought him the best gift since his mother.

The trouble was, I was pretty sure I was in for a long period of horrid pain before I'd have a hope in hell of making him believe that. God, he'd probably double-think me, waste at least half an hour in the firm belief that I was trying to run a particularly stubborn would-I-stick-with-such-a-crazy-story-if-it-weren't-true? con on him.

"Oh, that *is* a sad face. Bleak. Even given your situation, I mean, and its being your own stupid fault."

I tried to sigh, but could not take in enough air. "In years to come," I said hoarsely, "you will remember me with great fondness. You're going to bless the day you met me."

"So?" His little cupid mouth smiled slightly, like a puckering anus. "That *is* sad. How awful for you."

"Thank you."

"I was applauding. How exactly will you thus exhilarate me?"

"That's the hell of it," I told him. "I may not live to see your eyes light up."

The anus irised open slightly, revealing brilliant white teeth. "I wouldn't worry about that, Russell, old fossil. I'm going to tell you something now that will make you twice as frightened as you are already. Do you believe I can do that?"

I thought it over. "I know I'll probably regret saying this, but I honestly doubt it."

He nodded. "Listen. Here is how badly you have annoyed me. I have half a mind not to kill you."

Hitchcock was truly amazing. When all the blood drains from your head at once, you really do hear something very like the shrieking violins from the shower scene in *Psycho*.

There was also a faint, repeated plosive sound, like spaced shots from a silenced handgun in the next room. Gradually I realized it was my own voice, trying doggedly but unsuccessfully to marshall enough air to start the word "Please."

His lips were now dilated so far his entire overbite emerged, like a prolapsing white hemorrhoid. "Oh, what the hell. I'm not vindictive. I will allow you an opportunity to beg for your death. But I doubt you'll succeed."

Why wasn't I fainting again? Or at least dry-heaving? I found that I wished I could.

He made a little moist bubbling sound, as if he wanted to giggle but was too mature. "Don't bother trying to pass out." I followed his fat pointing finger to my coffee table, where I saw an empty hypodermic needle. "You can't. That door is closed to you." Another liquid snort. "And I know you're nauseous, but I'm afraid you can't barf. And it wouldn't make you any less nauseous if you did." The giggle escaped. It was even worse than I'd expected. "In just a few more minutes, you'll start to notice that things hurt more than they should. Only about twice as much. We're just starting."

I started to cry.

"Now tell me why I'm going to be glad I met you instead of annoyed. If I believe you, I promise to kill you."

All sentience was gone. Words fell out of my mouth without intention. "You will anyway. You have no idea how fragile I am."

"Yes, I do. I've read your Bellevue records, Russell. I've seen X-rays of your chest."

Jesus. I didn't shake my head, but my head was shaking. "Doesn't matter. Truth is so fuckin' crazy, you'll have to half kill me before you believe it—and half killin' me will kill me." No: the room was spinning, that was what it was. "And I'm pret' sure you'll be sorry you killed me. Pret' sure? *Shit* sure. I am your goddam *triumph*, nome sane? Most *ashamed* son of a bitch you're ever going to meet. All my fault, see? Death *way* too kind. Keep me round, see what I did. Round f'rever, on ice, like Sylvester—"

Give me a challenge, go on. Tell *me* I can't lose consciousness. Maybe I can't, motherfucker—but I can damn well *outrun* it for a while, even if I'm only running in circles inside my head.

Random images from my past flashed by as I ran. One of them had just reminded me of the only human being I had ever known who'd been as utterly helpless, as perfectly bankrupt, as I felt now. Sylvester . . .

Flashback:
1968

Postoperative ICU Ward
Bellevue Hospital
New York, New York
USA

I awoke from surgery—let's use that term for a process that took a day or two to complete—to find myself in a large ward, sixteen beds. That's how big an island Bellevue Hospital is: despite outstanding competence, just about every day its dozens and dozens of operations produce at least that many people who are in unusually crappy condition. Circle the drain there, and you'll have enough company to form a softball team in Hell.

Even though I was loaded with morphine, I was well aware of how badly I was damaged, and had at least a glimmering of how badly it was going to hurt sometime soon. I wanted, rather badly, to feel sorry for myself. My position in the room, purely a matter of random chance, made it quite impossible.

Not because of Reenie McGee (I think that's how he spelled it), whose bed lay across the aisle from mine and one over to the left, although God knows his affliction was the most striking in my field of vision. He had offended the NYPD—not just by leading them in a high-speed chase with a stolen Excalibur, but by doing so with such unexpected skill that two black and whites were completely destroyed and four officers injured, one seriously, before they boxed him in. They had expressed their displeasure with nightsticks, heavy shoes, and the butt of a gun. Reenie's face looked exactly like a Picasso, and would for many painful years to come. No two features were located in the correct relationship to each other. But that was tomorrow's problem: it was the internal injuries whose repairs had nearly killed him.

But God bless him, even in extremis, Reenie was charged with manic energy, his rap full of defiance and bravado. Because he was an unadjudicated prisoner accused of serious felonies, a cop sat beside him 24/7, and one of his wrists was kept chained to his bed. When he wanted to hobble to the head, the cop would cuff his hands in front of him and bring him there and back. It was always the same two cops, alternating shifts. Reenie harrassed them both relentlessly. He demanded they play cards with him, beat them consistently, and broke their balls about it. He kept up a running monologue, explaining to anyone within earshot how his police brutality lawsuit was going to make him rich enough to *buy* a freakin' Excalibur. Both cops, burnt out old bulls, utterly ignored him.

No, what ruined a perfectly good orgy of self-pity for me was not Reenie. It was Sylvester, across the way and one bed to the *right*.

He too was an unwilling guest of the City of New York. But unlike Reenie, Sylvester had a different cop companion nearly every day. Nobody could take it. Even cops one step from a pension weren't numb enough.

I asked Sylvester his last name more than once; he never answered. He had been a reasonably happy, upwardly mobile heroin dealer in West Harlem, until the day the Great Shit Lottery had yielded up his number. It began as a routine business reversal: Sylvester and his two roommates were taken off for their product by some upstart Cam*bodian* mothafuckas, who left them all tied up with lamp cord in their own apartment, a fourth-floor walkup. On the way downstairs one of the Cambos, out of sheer exuberance, had popped a cap through somebody's apartment wall, and because it winged a child, that somebody had been indignant enough to call the police. That was something Sylvester and his friends would never have done in a million years, and did not imagine anyone else in their building might do.

So when, after long and noisy struggle, Sylvester managed to free himself from his bonds, his only thought was to arm himself heavily, take off after those punk-ass gooks, and restore the natural order of the universe. He was too angry even to pause to untie his partners. He never dreamed that as he reached the top of the stairwell and started down, the cops would be entering it from below.

And when he did hear their unmistakable big feet, he thought only that his evening was now ruined. He would have to spend half the night dealing with these assholes, let them waste hours trying to bluff him into believing it was a crime to *not* be holding drugs, just because it was easier than chasing the slant-eyes. The cops had to know the perps were long gone; they'd clearly timed their response to be sure of it. He uncocked his gun disgustedly. Sylvester didn't see a pitch-dark stairwell that reeked of piss, blood, and ancient fear as a particularly scary place. It was what he was used to.

For the cops it must have seemed a no-brainer. You respond to an armed robbery narco/squawk in Hell, you enter a black hole, you hear creaking stairs overhead and a pistol action sound, you empty your weapon. Then you pull your throwdown and squeeze off everything but the one essential shot from that, too. Then you reload your duty piece. And then you say, "Freeze. Police."

At least one slug, way too big to be regulation, had actually entered Sylvester's spinal column from below, coring out maybe the bottom third of it—as he put it, like a big final fingerfuck from God. Other bullets struck here and there, but so what? He would never feel anything below the collarbone, good or bad, again.

All that had happened nearly three years before. Sylvester had been quadriplegic ever since, and would be until the day he died. What had brought him to that room was skin grafts—for bedsores the size of dinner plates. In 1968, skin graft technology sucked big rocks if you were a rich white guy. A black prisoner was disadvantaged . . . and the ocean is damp compared to other things.

For three years, the bogus felony charges the cops had filed against Sylvester, to explain why they'd shot him, and the gazillion-dollar lawsuit Sylvester's lawyers had filed against the Department, to explain why they shouldn't have, had been circling each other warily like wounded bulls, each furious but reluctant to close and end the matter. The cops knew their case was pure bullshit. The shysters who'd taken Sylvester's case on spec knew that didn't matter: bullshit or not, the best they'd get for a black drug dealer with no dependents was a lowball payoff so why not wait and hope he died first? Okay with the cops. Haste was good for neither side, and nothing was good for Sylvester.

Therefore Sylvester's legal status remained unresolved; therefore he was a felony suspect—like all suspects, presumed guilty until he proved otherwise. And rules, as they say, are rules. It wouldn't do to be seen treating one prisoner differently from another, especially not an Irishman and a nigger only a bed apart from one another.

So just like Reenie, Sylvester spent his hours—each and every one of them—handcuffed by his wrist to his hospital bed. Guarded by an armed man, a member of the gang that had put him there, for being home when they called.

You try feeling sorry for yourself in the same room with him.

Flashforward:
2003

Trembling-on-the-Verge
Heron Island, British Columbia
Canada

1.

" . . . Whom I used to think was the unluckiest bastard possible. Until tonight."

The dizziness and slurred speech went away as quickly as they had come, and I realized they had been a transient effect of some one of Allen's home-brewed drugs coming on.

It was true. For the first time in my life, I found myself envying Sylvester. All he had fucked up was himself. I had wrecked three lives as thoroughly as he had wrecked his one. And in about the same way: I had gone blindly into the dark without checking carefully enough for monsters. All he'd had to do was lay there in a stultifying absence of physical sensation for a hundred million years of boredom and despair, and never ever do anything fun again. Just then, I'd have given anything for that kind of luck.

Without warning, every molecule of my body *except* my brain and every single nerve fiber that could carry pain to it suddenly encountered an equal mass of anti-matter and was annihilated in a stupendous explosion. All the atoms of my brain except those involved in its pain center were blown to the far corners of the cosmos. The effect was to slow time, so that ultimate pain lasted for infinity, and dying was an eternal state.

He had slapped me. Not even particularly hard.

"An amazing drug, isn't it?"

At the sound of his voice my personality recongealed at lightspeed. I tried very hard to say yes. No—I promised myself I'd be baldly honest in this account: what I tried very hard to say was yes, sir. No matter: all I produced was a hoarse, wheezing "—*heh*—" sound. I knew what I needed to end the word, even knew it was called a sibilant, but could not remember how to produce one.

"I see you agree. And imagine if I had done something a little more intrinsically painful than a slap."

That suggestion seemed to magically accelerate the rebooting of my mind. I was nodding so hard and fast I could actually feel my brain sloshing back and forth in there. "Yes sir, I'm sure that would be very bad, it's *so* great that we don't delve further into that area just yet becau—"

He shook his head and pursed those obscene lips, and I shut up in midword. "You keep saying you're going to make me extremely happy. You're not very good at it, and I don't need any help. Watch."

I craned my head, got a look at what he was fiddling with, and began to panic. "Hey, no. That's not necessary, man. Really—"

"Amateurs fiddle around with ornate leather harnesses, elaborate dungeon hardware, intricate ritual gear, medieval contraptions—what I call toy torture. The serious practitioner needs nothing more difficult to obtain or incriminating to possess than the items commonly found in almost any home in Canada, in two little drawers, both in the kitchen: the silverware drawer, and the junk drawer."

"Listen to me: this is not necessary!"

"Listen to me: it doesn't have to be." He began poking around among the items he had selected, looking for just the right one. "I enjoy it for its own sake."

Corkscrew. Chopstick. Cheese slicer/grater. Circuit tester, with a wicked alligator clip. Curtain hooks. Thank God, something that didn't start with C: a box of yellow plastic pushpins. A bottle cap remover so old it had a triangular fitting on the other end to punch drinking holes into cans. For many years I had stubbornly turned poptop cans upside down and used that tool to open them. Then the bastards had started rounding the lip off the bottoms of the cans, so I couldn't get a purchase.

I finally managed to get my brain running—time to do something with it. I forced myself to remember the fundamentals of a con. Figure out what the mark wants to hear, that was one of the big ones. Try to think like him.

Yech.

"Wouldn't it be more artistic *not* to hurt me?"

He paused in his efforts. "I beg your pardon? Did you say artistic?"

"Sure. You're an artist, right?"

His mouth made a little rosebud. "I would not be so pretentious," he protested too much.

"A doloric artist. Wouldn't that be the word?"

"A student, perhaps," he conceded modestly. "And no,

'doloric' would not be the word, though that's a common misconception. 'Dolenic' or 'dolescent' would be the word."

I frowned. I was overjoyed. Whenever I'm being tortured, I love a lecture. "Are you sure?"

"Quite sure. 'Dolor' refers particularly to disappointment, remorse, rather mild stuff. 'Dolens' has to do with *caused* pain, sharp pain, physical or mental. Actually, 'condolescent' would be better: that connotes severe, acute, longterm suffering."

"Oh my God," I said. "George Bush's National Security Adviser. Condolescent Ruse. I know some Afghanis and Iraqis who'd agree with that definition."

"And some Americans," he said, "who happen to be Muslim."

Awesome, I thought. Even a human being and a reptile monster from Hell can find common ground in revulsion for a *real* asshole. If you looked at it from a purely statistical standpoint, even if he worked hard at his hobby for a long lifetime, Allen's body count was unlikely to ever reach higher than five figures, and the low five figures at that. Four kills a week every week for fifty years is a mere ten thousand rotting bodies, and that would be a killing pace for even a gifted private citizen to maintain without government funding.

"How about 'mordeic art'?" I suggested.

He raised an eyebrow, but only slightly. "Mmm. 'Biting' or 'stinging' pain. Not bad."

"Aren't you impressed that I know Latin at all?"

He shook his head decisively. "Back in your day it wasn't rare, for Catholics anyway. And I saw your year in the seminary in your record."

"Still, that was a long time ago. Oh wow."

"Yes?"

"I just remembered a good one. Hadn't thought of it since the seminary. 'Adflictational.' "

That rated another little rosebud mouth of pleasure, and a glitter in his eyes. "Oh, lovely. Specifically connotes torture. A student of the adflictational arts. Yes, I like it."

I had to try. "Can you explain the kick to a mundane? I'm sorry, I guess it's like golf: I just don't get why that would be fun."

He shrugged. "Can you explain altruism?"

"Beg pardon?"

"Can you tell me in rational terms why, for you, it is *fun* to be kind? Why it gives you pleasure to give someone else pleasure, with no payback? Why you would enjoy, say, rescuing a child from a fire, or giving food to a starving man, or working hard to give a particularly pleasurable orgasm to a casual partner, or introducing a friend to a perfect mate, or getting some poor brown bastard out of Guantanamo?"

"Well . . . I guess—"

"Can we not agree that whatever is going on there, at a fundamental level it comes down like everything else to a matter of brain chemicals? You perform certain actions, evidence certain behaviors, make certain choices, and because they have been evolutionarily successful over the long term, brain chemistry rewards you. Serotonin balance and so on. Like most people, you're wired so that by default, unless made angry or otherwise afraid, you'd generally rather be nice to people than hurt them, yes?"

"Well, yeah."

He shrugged. "Every once in a long while, one leaves the factory wired up just backward."

"Jesus. That simple?"

"What, you mean, nothing to do with how my mother treated me, or where my third foster father put his hand, or what were the socioeconomic circumstances of my early socialization? Yeah. Just that simple. I had a childhood as boring as anybody could possibly hope for. Then I learned how to make it interesting."

"A couple of wires got crossed."

"A sign got reversed in the programming. Whatever analogy you like. You're tuned so that if you see a little girl in the second story window of a burning building, it would give you great pleasure to persuade her to jump, catch her, bring her to safety, and then run inside and rescue her sleeping parents. I'm tuned so it would give me great pleasure to bring her parents out, make them watch her roast, then throw Daddy back inside, bring Mommy home and party. Different strokes."

If there is an appropriate response to that remark, I still haven't thought of it.

"Have you figured out yet that dragging this out makes it much *worse* for you?" he asked me.

I nodded.

"But you just can't help it, can you?"

I shook my head.

He made one of those little pucker-smiles. Fun. "Okay, then, let's try it this way: you tell me everything I want to know, every scrap of information you possess that I want to possess, without any torture at all. Exactly what you know about me. How you learned it. Who else knows it, and where I'll find them. What you intended to do about it until you got killed. What they will intend to do about it until I kill them. All that stuff. You have a sense of what I want to know, and you'll get better at it as we go. What do you say, let's do it like that: you crack like a junkie snitch, and tell me what I want to know *right now without any more stalling*, and I won't have to to hurt you at all. Then afterwards, I'll hurt you anyway, a lot, more than you can probably imagine, and it will be even more fun for me because it will be undeserved . . . but you see, that will be *later*. If you force me to jump to that part first, it will be *sooner*."

I was nodding vigorously to show my understanding. "What a fine plan. I like this plan. I'm very happy with this plan."

"Then *talk!*"

I looked him in the eyes. "I'm going to give you the best Christmas present you ever got—that's exactly my problem: it'll sound too good to be true, like something a con man would dream up. Please, *please* don't jump to that conclusion, just because it's the most likely one. What I have for you *is* too good to be true . . . and it really is true. I promise."

"If this is a stall, I promise you *so* much regret—"

"I believe you," I assured him. "Just don't kill me out of hand for insulting your intelligence, give me a few minutes, and I think that very intelligence will show you that whether my story is too good to be true or not, it's *the only story that explains how I could possibly know a goddam thing about you*, let alone all the shit I know."

He stared at me for a long time. I smelled his breath and wished I didn't. I smelled me and wished I didn't. I didn't smell Susan's perfume, which I have smelled from time to time for absolutely no reason at all since she died, and wished I did.

"Go on."

There was nothing for it but to start at the beginning and tell him the absolute truth. I simply had nothing else. He was too smart to lie to clumsily . . . and I had nothing prepared. Maybe I should have been creative enough to make up, from whole cloth, from a standing start, on horseback, some kind of convincing explanation of how a civilian female friend and I had happened to stumble across the oddly proscribed little bundle of facts we had. You try it. I didn't even have time to tinker with the story. The bald truth was the only thing I could tell convincingly without being tripped up. And I would be lucky to get him to buy *that*—in the limited sense remaining in which that word could possibly apply to me.

I was trying to decide where would be the best place to begin the story—open with Zudie's unexpected arrival a few days ago, or go straight to flashback—when suddenly it became necessary to turn to stone.

Only utter immobility would do. If I allowed any muscles I owned to so much as twitch, then some would surely move on my face, despite my best efforts, and that would be enough to tip Allen, and he would turn his head and look out the big window down at the far end of the room. That would not be good. If he were to do that, he would see the same thing I did.

About a hundred meters from the house, barely visible by the faint glow of one of the little green toadstool lamps that line my driveway and every other driveway on Heron Island: Zudie. Leaning out from behind a big Douglas fir, waving to me.

2.

That changed everything.

But *how*, exactly?

—No time! No time! Allen had said "Go on," whole seconds ago—

I launched into the story.

I told it as simply and straightforwardly and truthfully—and as *slowly*—as I could, so that while I told it I would have some attention to spare for clandestine thought. The point of entry I'd hesitated over picked itself: the first moment in time at which things had started to go wrong for Allen . . . a moment which there was no way I could possibly know about. I described to him the brush with death he'd had in his airplane, the week before, over Coveney Island, start to finish. *From his point of view.*

His eyes kept widening so much at what I was saying, he failed to watch me closely. As I spoke, beneath the surface I timeshared, and he missed it.

It didn't *matter* how Zudie had figured out I was in trouble, or even if he had. He knew now: he was here, and he hadn't knocked. And wouldn't: coming within a hundred meters of the house had been all the warning he'd needed, if he'd needed any.

He couldn't come any closer. In fact, it must be unimaginable hell for him to be even this close to a mind like Allen's. It had to be as far away as he could get, and still read *me*.

If Zudie knew I was in trouble, Nika would know I was in trouble. Soon, if not already. Zudie had a cell phone, and her number.

How fast could she get here? And how would she come? Alone and unofficially—or with backup and warrants and a trained hostage negotiator to soothe Allen into the crosshairs? But either way, how soon?

The fastest possible would be to phone ahead to the Heron Island RCMP detachment, and persuade Constable McKenzie to get out of bed and come check things out. I hoped she wouldn't do that. Killing that sweet old man couldn't possibly take Allen more than five or ten minutes—and then he'd know the heat was on, would probably know everything useful McKenzie had known in fact, and would take me somewhere else to work on me at his leisure without interruption.

I snuck a glance at the clock display on the face of the living room VCR, and tried to work out the timing.

Say Zudie had motored straight home after we parted, and five minutes later saw something on the tape to clue him that all hell was about to break loose. Say he instantly phoned Nika and shared whatever his news was. If she had bolted right out the door, and had good luck with traffic, she might have been able to catch the last ferry to Heron Island.

If that were so, and the skipper made his very best time, and she were the first car off the boat, and she duplicated my record best time from Bug Cove up through the hills to my place . . . my best guess was that if all those conditions were obtained, I might possibly hope to hear the distant sound of her approaching car in as little as another forty minutes.

If she had missed the last ferry, and if she had then managed to line up a fast charter ride of some kind instantly, she could conceivably arrive in as little as half an hour. If so, she'd be afoot, probably with minimal firepower and no backup.

Whether she'd caught the ferry or not, if she had phoned ahead to the West Van cops and told them some story that would get *them* on the ferry in force, then probably what I would hear in forty minutes would be approaching sirens and voices trying to be soothing over bullhorns. The expression "death by cop" doesn't always refer to suicide. I hoped she'd been smarter than that. Allen would be a *lot* better off if they found him standing over my warm corpse than he would be if I lived to tell what I knew about him.

Think it through, Russell! Assume Nika is not going to arrive in time to help—because if she is, you've got no problems. In that case, Zudie tells her exactly what's going on in here, just how quickly Allen could open your throat or otherwise end you, and she creeps up to the window, shoots him through the head, and yells "Freeze!" Cut to commercial. Think about what if you're *not* that lucky.

And hurry up, you're nearly to the end of your prologue.

I need Nika. Without her I'm screwed. I have to stall like crazy.

But he isn't going to let me get away with stalling for another minute, much less forty—

Without Nika, Zudie is my only asset. And my responsibility. At all costs I need to tell Allen as little as possible about Zudie, and most but not all of what I do say about him should be lies.

But Allen's built-in bullshit detector is dismayingly good—

True. But he's never met a liar like me before.

Out of time!

I had used up every scrap I could remember of what Zudie had told me, run out of things to recount about what had gone on inside Allen's head, during those moments he'd thought would be his last. I'm pretty sure what convinced him I wasn't pulling some sort of carny mentalist con on him was the specific details I knew about what he'd planned to do to his family of four in Point Grey. They weren't the kinds of things I could ever in a million years have thought up myself, and maybe that showed on my face, distracted as I was. But now I was fresh out of things to say, out of digressions too, had no way to forestall him from asking the bloody obvious question. So he asked it.

"How do you know all this?"

Careful, now. "Think back. As you were going down, remember off to your left, toward the sunset, some kind of small boat?"

"Yeah." No he didn't. But now he *thought* he did. "So?"

"The guy on it was a telepath."

His reaction astonished and dismayed me. I had confidently expected that statement to generate at *least* five minutes of wasted air, digressionary and circular argument, at the end of which he would finally concede the point only after the third time I'd asked him, *All right then, wiseguy, how* do *I know all this stuff if I didn't get it from a mind reader?* I had forgotten that computer nerds read science fiction. Telepathy doesn't boggle their minds at all.

Instead, the bastard said, "I *knew* it. Nothing else made sense. What's his name?"

Shit. Don't give this guy hot serves; his return is murder.

Rather than hesitate even a microsecond, I just said the first words that came into my head. "How the hell should I know?"

It was only after the words left my mouth that I realized I'd accidentally said something smart.

Because he was nodding, as though that made sense. And by God, it did. The lie wrote itself.

"Of course," he said. "Forgive me. The last thing a telepath would want to do is let anybody find out who he is—*especially* a newsman. If you let the cat out of the bag, he gets to spend the last few days of his life as a free man trying to outrun the NSA, CIA, FBI, CSIS, RCMP, and for all I know the KGB."

I nodded, careful not to overdo it. "Yeah, that's what I figured was going on."

"My God. A genuine telepath. Oh, how splendid."

"I told you you were going to like it," I said grimly.

"Oh yes. Oh *my*, yes."

"I'd actually rather the NSA had him."

He raised one eyebrow. "How did he ever manage to convince you he wasn't just a lunatic—over the phone?"

Tell as much of the truth as possible. "The same way I just did. He told me things about myself he couldn't possibly have known any other way."

The eyebrow lowered. "Yes, I see. So you bought his story."

"Yeah. I didn't have much choice."

He was frowning. "Then I don't understand."

"What? Why a telepath took the risk?"

"No. Why you didn't simply pass his information on to your police contacts, and set a task force onto me. What the hell were you doing poking a camcorder out your own car window? Are you really the sort of egotistical moron who wants a *scoop*?"

I had snorted at the term *police contacts*. *Scoop* made me grimace. "You've made the same mistake he did. You're both civilians. To you a columnist and a newsman must seem like the same thing."

"They're not?"

"Not even close. Au contraire. Just backwards."

"Enlighten me."

"Newsmen dig up facts, confirm them, and sell them to you. No, excuse me, the second step has been dropped in recent years. But even so, they are at least supposed to sell facts. Not me. Any alleged facts in one of my columns, I got 'em secondhand at best. What I sell is *opinions*."

"Ah."

"Furthermore, international and national opinions,

rarely local ones. Remember, I work for *The Globe and Mail*—Toronto, not Vancouver. When you do that, you don't build up a network of local police contacts. Or any other servants of the public. The only ones who know your name are the ones that are pissed off by one or more of your opinions."

He was nodding. "Yes, I see. So you and your girlfriend decided to try and gather enough evidence to bring to the police without having to mention mind readers. Noble of you. What's her name?"

I just looked at him.

"Let me explain how this works," he said patiently. "If you tell me her name and how to find her, when I leave you I will go and kill her at once. If you do not tell me her name and how to find her, I will be forced to waste as much as an hour and a half to learn that information. If that happens I will be so angry, I will *not* kill her at once. So far the longest I've been able to keep anyone dying was twenty-two days. But I learn more each time. I'm shooting for a whole lunar month, and you know, your girlfriend looked *strong*."

Zudie, I understand how you could find touching this mind naked unendurable. Just listening to the noises it makes here outside the skull is nauseating.

"How do I know you'll keep your word?" I temporized.

He shrugged. "How do I know you'll tell me the truth?"

I hesitated as long as I could, hamming it up as much as I dared. This was supposed to be a devastating decision: necessary or not, I was giving up someone I cared about to certain death. I was wishing I'd studied acting long enough to get to the class about crying on cue . . . when I startled myself by bursting genuinely into tears. I must be under stress or something.

Run with it: I looked him square in the face and said, "Her name is Wilma McCarthy. She's a physiotherapist. She lives in Kits, a block up from the beach; the address is in my book and you have that."

Damn. Halfway through the spiel I knew he wasn't buying it. *Zudie, run. Back off a hundred meters, and come back slow. I'm going to have to take one for the team—*

I don't know if he had enough warning. Allen held up a paper clip. He unfolded it into a straight line with a short folded handle, like a pot smoker improvising a pipe cleaner. Then he held my right hand flat against the arm of the chair with his free hand, put the tip of the paper clip beneath my thumbnail, and rammed it up under the nail, nearly halfway to the quick.

Scientists now speak of something called a hypernova, that makes ordinary supernovae look like flashbulbs. Anything you ever want to know about one, just come ask me.

When I could form coherent thoughts again, his face was in front of mine. His eyes glistened moistly. His nostrils were wide with suppressed excitement.

"A paper clip," he said softly, and puckered his lips into that hideous little smirk again. "Imagine what I can do with a pair of pliers."

It still hurt like crazy. But . . . this will sound stupid. I tried as hard as I could *not to mind* the pain. Not to be upset by it. Because if I didn't find some way to reduce my own torment, Zudie would not be able to get back close enough to be of use again. It may be the most twisted backass reason for bravery I ever heard of.

But it worked. Kind of, anyway. Feeling that much pain

was appalling; the idea of inflicting it on someone else, just because I couldn't get hold of myself, was offensive to me. Somehow I was able to recapture from deep memory some of the perspective that comes with a large shot of morphine: the feeling that the pain, while still there, is of far less importance.

"H-h-h-h-h-c-h-h—" I said, swallowed blood, and tried again. Must have bitten my tongue. "How did you know I was lying?"

"Russell, Russell. Think it through. People lie to me a *lot*. But in the end I *always* find out what the truth is, so then I know for sure what the lies were. After awhile it becomes instinctive."

I sighed.

"There must be a real Wilma, if I was supposed to find her address in your book," he mused. "Who is she?"

"A former landlady," I admitted. "First female name I thought of I could spare."

He liked that. A lot. For the first time I got a smile that showed lots of teeth. It was clear why he didn't smile that way often. "You know," he said, "I think I'm going to take her out. The idea appeals to me. I like it when people die for ridiculous reasons."

Shit. I would never have imagined I could possibly end up wanting to apologize to Mrs. McCarthy for anything. But even she didn't deserve Allen. I wasn't positive the late Pol Pot would have, or Idi Amin.

His smile vanished. "So now you have *that* on your conscience, and we're barely started. Why don't you tell me your girlfriend's real name and address, before this gets ugly?"

While all this was going on, deep below the surface a

kernel of my mind was busy plotting, stealing time between processor cycles if you like mind/computer analogies.

Once I answered his question, and possibly one or two brief follow-ups, we were basically done. At that point he had no further interest in me as a source of information, and could and would proceed directly to the torturing me to death part.

But in the best of all possible worlds, Nika had to still be at least . . .

Unexpected happy side-effect of having my hands restrained palm up: I could sneak a look at my watch without being caught at it.

. . . at least fifteen or twenty minutes away.

Shit. How could I stall for five minutes, much less twenty?

Only one thought came to me. Suppose Zudie threw a rock through the living room window, and ran like hell?

Could Zudie outrun a homicidal psychopath, for five minutes?

Well, let's think about that. It was by now pitch dark out there. Zudie and Allen were both big guys, both overweight, both out of shape, both extremely smart, both known to have lived in the woods long enough to presumably know how to move through them in the dark with some confidence. How were the two men different?

Zudie would know exactly where Allen was in the dark at all times, and could not be fooled.

Zudie would have *worse* than the hounds of Hell at his heels to motivate him as he ran; the closer Allen got, the more of a goad he became.

Both useful advantages.

On the other side of the scale, like a ton of lead, was the cold knowledge that chases through a forest were from time immemorial usually decided by superior ferocity, savagery, and combat experience. I was certain Zudie had never so much as punched another kid in the nose; it would have hurt too much. Zudie was a sensitive lamb, Allen was a tiger's worst nightmare. And unlike an animal predator, Allen would *never* decide this particular hunk of protein was a bad bargain energy-wise, and break off the chase.

Also—shit!—Allen would have my Maglite to help him pierce the darkness.

Wait! There was at least one other powerful advantage Zudie would have, that I was overlooking.

Allen was not only in the dark, he was on totally unfamiliar turf. The Maglite would show him only things he'd never seen before. As I thought back over it, I decided he must have entered my house almost immediately after the sound of his car had frightened Fraidy the Cat—there was a good chance he knew *nothing* about the way the land lay around here, not which way downhill was, or where the sudden unexpected drop-offs were, or where territory that looked passable would suddenly turn out to be Thorn City, or where and how wide the stream was, or anything.

Whereas Zudie knew *everything* I knew about the property after having lived there for years.

Would that be enough to keep him alive for ten minutes in the dark with the genuine no-shit boogeyman?

I tried to plan him a route; to work out a path which would continually lead Allen into jams that Zudie would see coming, without ever involving a long straight stretch without cover, where a Maglite beam might pick him out.

I just couldn't do it. It was too much mental gymnastics for me to pull off while carrying on a convincing conversation on the surface. I kept losing my place while I was thinking of things to say to Allen.

I had to settle for just thinking about my land, all of it, picturing it in as much detail as I could manage, doing so a piece at a time and praying he could reassemble them into a three-dimensional whole—and then use it to plan out a useful course. Good spots to break a leg. Good spots to hide. Spots where only Zudie would know it was safe to run flat-out. Spots where only he'd know it was not.

I'm sorry to have to admit I wasted a fair amount of time at first, thinking of potential weapons I had lying around the place, and trying to think of places where Zudie might be able to set up an ambush, and surprise Allen with an axe across the back of the neck or the like. Stupid, stupid. Long before Allen reached the ambush point, he'd hear Zudie screaming. Then he'd take Zudie's axe away and make him quieter.

When I finally realized that, I switched all my thought from ways to fight, to ways to run. In my mind, I left my home in each of the four compass directions, and continued each until that course had brought me to someplace where Zudie would find other people. Then I did the same with northwest, southwest, and so on.

By the time Allen suggested to me that we didn't want this to become ugly, I had run out.

So that was when the rock came through the living room window.

◦   ◦   ◦

It was a fairly large rock, one of the ones that stretch between the green toadstool lights to define my driveway. He must have lobbed it underhanded. It pulverized the window, sending shards of glass flying all around the room, and smashed the coffee table on landing.

I thought it a poor choice. A smaller rock could have been thrown from much farther away, would have given him much more lead time.

Fortunately he hadn't consulted me. If he'd just broken the window, Allen would have looked up at once and seen him, would have marked his silhouette and last known direction at minimum. Because he *demolished* the window, Allen must have thought of SWAT bursting in. Instinctively he dove away from the window and scrambled for cover without stopping to take inventory. By the time he realized his mistake, recovered, figured out that the assailant out there was armed with nothing worse than rocks, and broke for the door, I couldn't see Zudie out there anywhere.

So I'd have been reasonably happy watching Allen go out the door, feeling at least pretty good about the way things were going, if he hadn't stopped at the doorway, picked up a backpack I had failed to notice on the floor there, and taken out a huge six-battery flashlight and a small handgun before running out into the night.

Run like a motherfucker, Zudenigo!

3.

Forget the big picture. Forget the small picture. Think about one tiny step at a time.

Fold injured thumb over, toward palm.

Trap folded end of paper clip between pressed-together ring finger and fuck finger.

Yank thumb violently away, pulling paper clip out from under thumbnail.

Go ahead, scream; no reason not to.

Manipulate paper clip around until it can be grasped firmly between fingers and thumb.

Discover how much thumb still hurts. Throbs. Strobes. Scream some more but don't drop paper clip.

And don't stop working; we have a bit of a time problem.

Use sharp, bloody tip of paper clip to score duct tape securing wrist, at edge.

Fail to reach far enough.

Unbend last fold of paper clip, for maximum length.

Success this time. Rub; continue until—

—tape parts at edge, a small but definite rip.

Strain at tape with whole upper body until vision starts to grey out.

Fail to part tape, or even noticeably widen the small rip at its edge.

Try to lengthen rip with paper clip.

No luck. More than a half inch or so from the edge, there are just too many layers of tape to cut through with a paper clip, without better leverage.

Keep trying, harder.

Drop paper clip.

Suppress moaning sound.

Try a convulsive whole-body spasm.

No good.

Bellow hideous obscenities.

No help.

Scream appalling blasphemies.

No help.

Try to bend over and *bite* through fucking tape.

Fail.

Shriek bloodcurdling maledictions.

Shut the fuck up and think.

Have rush of brains to head: your ankles are secured to each other . . . but *not* to the chair. (Don't even think about why he wanted it that way.) Therefore it is possible to use them to shift your ass *way* over sideways in your chair, halfway out of the seat—

—so far that now, you *can* bend over enough to bring your teeth to bear on that fucking tape!

Bite me, tape. No wait, I'll bite *you* . . .

Chew a third of the way through the tape.

Tear hand free with a punching motion, accompanied by a wordless roar of triumph.

Endure fresh burst of agony from damaged thumb.

Is nail clipper still in usual place, right front pants pocket, in special compartment up at top? Yes.

Use nail clipper to cut through tape at *left* wrist, half an inch at a time, ignoring an unbelievable amount of pain from damaged thumb.

Leap triumphantly to feet, run to door.

Pick self off floor, ignoring an unbelievable amount of pain from damaged face.

How long is goddam pain-enhancing drug going to keep working?

Untie ankles.

Scream. Moron.

Untie ankles again, using left hand this time.

Too fucking long, that's how long.

Survey room; inventory weapons.

Of several choices, choose wood stove's heavy, pointed andiron, good for whacking, stabbing, throwing, or—ideally—rectal insertion.

Sprint for door.

As I reached the doorway I wondered if I should stop and call the police.

But no. A step later, I realized what a dead end that would be. All I could do was dial 911. That would raise a 911 operator somewhere on the mainland. Assuming I could coherently communicate my location, situation and needs in something under ten minutes, the best she could do would be to pass the word to the relevant agency with jurisdiction: Corporal McKenzie. It would be his call whether to contact mainland RCMP for backup, and he wouldn't. I could call them myself directly, if I took the time to find the number in the Greater Vancouver phone book—but at this time of night, I would raise only an answering machine, advising me that if my call was urgent I should consider phoning 911.

(Think that's inadequate coverage? Then you must live someplace where crimes occur routinely. Like Vancouver.)

I summoned up the mental map of my property that I had sent Zudie a square at a time, and—now that I had time for it—tried to work out the best possible escape route for a man on foot. That would probably be what Zudie had picked: he was at least as smart as me, and would be using my opinions about the territory.

The trouble was, he'd been well on his way before he had learned—if he had ever learned, if he hadn't already gotten out of range of me by the time *I* found out—that Allen had a gun.

That changed things. If I'm running away from a man with a gun, then all other things being equal, I'd prefer to run uphill; I've read again and again that firing uphill sucks. If I'm running away from a man armed only with his admittedly deadly hands, I'd rather run downhill for the speed that's in it.

I decided to assume the worst. (That way all surprises are pleasant ones.) He had started downhill before he knew Allen was armed, did not know he was in a footrace with bullets.

So: west. I ran flat-out. There was a little moonlight. Past the garden—the place that had been a garden while

Susan was alive. Past the previous owner's collapsed goat shed and never-finished barn. Beyond that point there was a rough rocky trail that wound back and forth downhill through the woods, crossed a stream, and eventually struck the road. I dove down it as fast as I dared in the dark.

Zudie would certainly have reached the road well ahead of Allen—he knew where the rocky parts of the trail were and where it was safe to open up, and the stream would not come as a nasty surprise to him. But if he didn't know Allen had a gun, he might well feel the flat road surface was an irresistible speed advantage, and—

Gunshot ahead.

Shit.

I wanted to speed up. I had to slow down.

The good news was, I was going the right way. Dumb luck.

The bad news was, my chest was starting to hurt.

I hadn't run this hard or far in over thirty years—since the day I'd raced to meet Susan at Grand Central. Or Penn. So my chest began to ache. And the goddam drug saw to it that it ached a *lot*. Maybe there's some sensation that scares you more, but that's what it's like inside my own personal worst nightmare. I found that I was making a little whimpering sound, and cut it out.

I knew the gunshot would be no help to me. I don't have many neighbors, and two of those I do have believe the myth that a lone puma still survives on Heron Island, and occasionally pop away at shadows in the woods. Besides, even unexplained gunshots will only cause alarm in places where they have crime.

As I came to the stream I had an idea. I crossed it, left

the path and headed south along its bank, paralleling the road perhaps fifty meters from it. I tried to make as little noise as possible, and listen as hard as I could for sounds from the road.

I didn't need to listen that hard. Zudie's moan of pain was a good two hundred meters ahead of me when I first heard it, but it carried clearly. So did Allen's answering giggle.

I slowed even further, tried to gain control of my breathing, placed my feet with care.

Zudie made a long, drawn out, inarticulate sound of utter heartbreak and despair. Allen chuckled. It was obvious from the chuckle that he understood simple proximity to his foul thoughts was killing Zudie, and he just loved that. The thing he had so feared, telepathy, undoing itself. The chuckle went on and on. So did the wail.

I used the masking effect of both sounds to cover distance quickly. I was close when I had to slow down again.

Zudie drew in his breath in a great gasp of horror. Not loud enough for good cover. I believe he intended to expel it in a scream. But Allen must have thought something truly horrendous at him: he guffawed outright—and Zudie must have fainted: the air left his lungs without engaging the vocal cords.

I was so close now that when he hit the pavement I spotted the movement to my right. By random chance, there was a break in the trees big enough to give me a view. Allen's flashlight provided the necessary light.

It looked to me as if Zudie had frozen like a deer at the gunshot, and then as Allen approached, had first gone down to a sitting position, and then into a fetal curl, hammered flat by a cresting wave of mental filth. He was lying on his side, breathing noisily, but I saw no blood anywhere on or under him, so I was pretty sure he hadn't caught a bullet.

I checked the time, nearly swearing aloud when I forgot not to push the light button on my watch with my thumb. Damn. At best, Nika was still ten minutes away; at worst . . . well, at worst she was taking in a movie somewhere on the mainland with her cell and pager switched off, and wouldn't check her messages for hours.

Allen came into view, through the gap in the brush. I'd been warned by the changing angle of his approaching flashlight, but I still had to suppress a small animal sound of terror when I actually saw him. He moved close to Zudie, stood with his back to me. I made myself begin creeping forward, placing my feet with great care. The flashlight had not been enough to ruin my night vision.

"Can't take it, eh?" He prodded Zudie with a shoe tip. "Pussy." He poked him somewhere with the same foot, then stepped on something and rocked back and forth on it, and finally kicked him in the head. It was that last one that finally did it for me.

I don't know exactly what the current record is for the fifty-meter dash, but it's something on the order of six seconds. I had cut the distance from fifty to perhaps thirty meters by the time I heard Allen's foot impact the side of Zudie's skull. It was at that point that I raised my andiron high and began to run. So round off all the fractions and say that Allen had a maximum of something like three and a half seconds' warning of my arrival.

He probably wasted at least a second believing it was some animal that was coming his way. As far as he knew I was still way back up the hill, safely secured to my arm-chair, waiting for the torture to resume. But he had the instincts of a wild animal himself: when I kept coming he decided whatever I was I needed a bullet in me, and fired. He missed widely. He got off one more shot, but he was a hair *too* fast: he fired just before I burst from cover to give him a target. The slug tugged hard at the hair at the top of my head as it went past; with the drug assist, it felt as though it had taken a piece of my scalp with it.

I didn't care. He was not going to have time for another shot before I caved his head in. I was already into my swing—

Zudie screamed and convulsed. A literal convulsion: one second he was out cold and the next he was up on his shoulder blades and heels, spine arched, beating the backs of his hands against the pavement, like a man dying of cyanide poisoning. It wasn't the noise, the ghastliness, or even the unexpectedness that threw me off, so much as the instant understanding of what was happening to him.

He was receiving my thoughts. Me, the one guy whose thoughts had always been tolerable for him. And what he was receiving from me was really not thoughts at all but feelings—ugly feelings—evil feelings—a tidal wave, unstoppable as nausea, of fear and rage and pain and hatred and bloodlust such as I had never imagined myself capable of.

Proximity to Allen, he could endure, by becoming unconscious. Proximity to both of us was more than even his stupified brain could bear. The moment he spasmed, I understood that my presence was killing my friend Zudie.

For the fraction of a second left to me, I was sorely

tempted to accept that as the new price of killing Allen. But I couldn't. I just couldn't. I slammed on the brakes. Instead of hitting him with the andiron, I threw it—past him, a foot to the left of his head, clear across the road. Then I put my hands up and waited for him to shoot me dead.

Of course he didn't. He just wasn't that nice a guy.

When I understood he wouldn't, I began to back away from him slowly. I knew he wouldn't let me get far, but the further I was from Zudie right now, the better his chances got of maybe waking up someday with his mind intact.

I'd backed off maybe twenty-five meters when Allen said, "My SUV is in your driveway."

"Yeah? So?"

He tossed something at me, and I ducked away. Car keys. "If you're back with it in one minute, I won't shoot your friend through the head. Tempted as I am—he *is* your telepath, isn't he?"

"What the hell do you want your car for?"

"We're all going back to your place to continue the party, and you don't look strong enough to carry him that far, and I have no intention of trying. Now are you going to get the vehicle? Or shall I shoot you in one of *your* legs, and go get it myself to haul the both of you in?"

I picked up the keys and began plodding up the road toward my place.

"One minute," he called after me. "No more."

"I'm going to need at least a minute and a half, asshole," I snapped back.

"One second longer and I'll know you're cheating," he said.

"Yeah, yeah, yeah."

The road ran uphill and around a bend before reaching my land. The moment Allen and Zudie stopped being in sight behind me, I could see the end of my driveway ahead of me. And there was indeed an SUV of some kind visible in it, tail out. But beyond the driveway, just past the mailbox farm, I saw something unexpected at this time of night: a car. No, even more puzzling than that, I saw as I got closer: it was my own car.

If you live in rural British Columbia, you might have to walk as much as a kilometer or two to get your mail— from one of the fifty or sixty padlocked drawers in a huge standardized green metal roadside installation I've always called the mailbox farm, about the size of the box a couple of refrigerators would come in. I happen to have been as lucky as possible in the draw: my own mailbox farm is just next to my driveway. For obvious reasons there's a gravel parking area just past it, and in that parking area now sat my Honda.

Why would Allen have taken the trouble to move my car out of my driveway before pulling into it himself? He'd have had to hotwire it, and then risk me hearing him start it from the house. I couldn't see any sense in a backup getaway car that was inferior to his own, and whose registration would not match his name.

Then suddenly I got it, and began to *run* uphill.

It was *Nika's* Honda past the mailbox farm. She was *here*, a good ten minutes before she could possibly be here. As I saw her, I heard the horn of the arriving ferry in the far distance.

Later I would learn the dumb mistake in my calculations. She had *not*, as I'd assumed was best-case, gotten in line for the last ferry, failed to get a berth, and then lined up a charter boat that would actually be ten minutes or so faster. Instead she'd arrived at Horseshoe Bay in plenty of time for the last ferry—and found that the *next*-to-last ferry was running so late that it was just now about to depart. She waved her cop credentials and drove straight aboard, and the skipper piled on the coals. She must have arrived at my driveway just about the time I came bursting out my door and bolted off into the woods.

Christ knew where she was now, presumably up at the house, inspecting the scraps of duct tape on the arms of my chair and the little collection of mundane household objects nearby. If she wasn't right here in front of me it didn't matter where she was: *there was no time*.

For a start, her car had to disappear. Instantly, and without a sound. Since I drove a nearly identical model I had no trouble at all finding the gearshift or getting it into neutral. Cranking the wheel over without power assist was a little more difficult. Getting the damn car moving was a *lot* more difficult, but adrenalin is a wonderful thing. Soon Nika's car was, if not invisible, at least completely occulted from the direction Allen would be looking.

Rushed as I was, I paused then, spending the time necessary for three deep slow breaths to reassure myself that I still hadn't blown a lung. Then I sprinted to Allen's SUV—I have no idea what kind it was; I'm color-blind in that range—clambered in, fired it up, revved it as loudly as I dared, backed it out of the driveway, and backed it downhill to where Allen and the catatonic Zudie were waiting. I hate SUVs; it was like driving a bus.

But I have to admit it made a passable ambulance.

Even though my chest was throbbing with the unaccustomed strain, I got between Allen and Zudie and somehow managed to manhandle his bulk into the back of the SUV by myself. I don't know how I got away with it without busting a lung. I just found the idea of Allen touching him again more than I could bear. I was aware that he'd picked up on that, and knew he would use it against me as soon as he got the chance.

"What's his name?" he asked me.

I was too tired to lie, and he'd only catch me if I did. "Zandor Zudenigo."

"My. What is that, Polish?"

"Serbian, I think."

He snorted. "Lovely. Let's go."

He sat sideways facing me, the gun pointed in my direction but not quite at me.

I didn't slow for the turn into the driveway, partly to minimize the time he'd be looking toward the mailbox farm in case I'd fucked that up, and partly so I'd make noise skidding on the gravel. When he made no objection to cowboy driving, I gunned it the rest of the way up the driveway, putting that alleged cross-country suspension to a test that for my money it failed. By the time we pulled up behind my Honda—really mine, this time—I was certain Nika had heard us coming. She was not in sight, and I could detect no signs that anyone had been here. No lights on that had been left off, or the like. The door I'd left standing open behind me when I left was still open.

Okay. If Nika was here, she knew this was Allen with me. What she might not know—

"You want to watch where you point that fucking gun,

Sundance?" I snapped as I got down from the driver's eyrie.

"Shut up. Where are you going?"

"Give me a second." Just beside the house, in the tool shed, was an item I'd never gotten around to disposing of, had done my best to forget existed. Susan's wheelchair, from the final days of end game. The best we could afford. It made it possible to get Zudie inside without accepting assistance from Allen.

I parked it by the stereo and vinyl/tape/CD collection at the far end of the living room. The nearest place to sit was more than five meters away, and the nearest comfortable place was even further. It was the best I could do.

Where the hell was Nika? I had to know where she was hiding if I was going to sucker Allen into turning his back on her. Was she in the house? Outside?

I couldn't find anything to suggest she'd ever been in here. Allen's backpack was right by the door where he'd left it, apparently untouched.

"How's your thumb, Russell?"

Until then I'd forgotten. "It hurts like you."

"Like me?"

"Like a son of a bitch."

"I'm so glad. Thanks for sharing." He was inspecting the scraps of duct tape I'd left. "What did you do, bite through it?"

"After I started it with the paper clip."

"Really? You're not entirely as stupid as you act."

I sat down in the same chair as before, by the broken window, the one that swiveled. "You want to tape me up again?"

He came over and sat in his old chair, the one that

reclined, his back to Zudie and the room. "Why? It didn't work the last time. I'm thinking it would be simpler to blow your kneecap off."

I couldn't help flinching and grimacing and shuddering. His painhelper drug was still in me, and I knew a broken kneecap was way up there on the agony scale to start with. "What if I bleed out? You won't learn my girlfriend's name until you read it on the warrant."

"Shoot your foot off, then."

"Have you shot many people?"

"To be honest, no. Have you?"

"No, but when I was a kid I worked in a hospital in New York, pushing a mop. I saw a lot of GSWs. I saw guys survive six in the chest, and I saw guys bleed out from a toe wound. I'm six-one and I weigh less than sixty-six kilos. Suit yourself—I'm done running for tonight."

He thought about it. "Very well. Then by all means let's get right to it. Tell me her name and address and particulars, at once." Kissy-smile. "Then I can shoot you with a serene mind, whenever the mood strikes me." He set his gun down on the coffee table beside his chair, hopelessly out of my reach.

It was suddenly time. "Her—"

"Excuse me one moment. Thank you. Have we established to your satisfaction that I can tell when you lie to me?"

I closed my eyes. "Yes, we have," I agreed hoarsely.

"Very well. Let me just say that if you are tedious enough to try, I have a drug in my pack over there which will make it physically impossible for your oversensitive friend Zandor Zagadanuga-naga over there to stay unconscious. How soon I go get it is entirely up to you."

Again I flinched violently, and bowed my head in submission and despair. "Please. I'm cooperating."

"Then go on. Who is she, where is she, what does she do? Speak up!"

I kept my face down, and answered loudly but very slowly, each word dragged out of me with maximum reluctance. "She's not really my girlfriend. I hardly know her, actually. Her name is Nika. Nika Mandiç. I don't even know her home address. She's a cop. That's right. A constable in the Vancouver Police Department. And if I'm timing it right, she should have a gun to the back of your abominable head about . . . now." I looked up. "Yep. I nailed it."

He made his pouty smile of amusement. "Did you see that work in a movie, or something? I turn around to look now, and you disable me with a hardcover book or something?"

Nika said: "I am Constable Nika Mandiç, Vancouver Police. You are under arrest for attempted murder, assault with a deadly weapon and kidnapping. It is my duty to inform you that you have the right to retain and instruct counsel without delay."

A champion tiptoer, that woman.

4.

I was so buzzed I remember thinking how ironic it was that when a cop used the simple, elegant command, *freeze!*, nobody ever froze—and here was Allen, frozen solid as a mammoth by this verbose stream of ritual absurdities.

But by the end of her third sentence, he had managed to thaw at least one limb and his neck. He turned his head to the right and up to get a look at her, moving slowly and carefully to dissuade her from shooting him. As he turned, his right hand quite naturally slid back along the arm of his chair to give him leverage to torque his neck that far.

And then suddenly it darted around *behind* the chair. I couldn't say for sure just what it did back there. Nika drew her breath in with a horrid gasping rasp, a death-rattle sound, and found she could not release it, her throat blocked by a scream too large to come out. Her automatic fell from nerveless fingers and hit the carpet with a thump. Her eyes were bulging.

He faced forward, adjusted his hold slightly, rotated his shoulder and—I don't know, did whatever he was doing back there *very hard.*

The scream tore its way out. Her face went white as a sheet and she went down. Her knees hit the carpet with a bad sound.

He let go, retrieved his own gun from the coffee table, stood, turned around and beamed down at her. "I do hope you brought your own handcuffs, Constable. Ah, excellent."

She was in civilian clothes. Old running shoes. Dark blue jeans. Light grey cotton turtleneck. Brown light-weight waist-length nearly-leather jacket with big lapels. The shade of brown clashed with her empty shoulder holster. She knelt there helpless as a stunned cow, moaning softly, while he hooked her wrists up behind her. He had a very professional way with handcuffs. I think it must have been her first experience with really monstrous pain. It's nothing like ordinary pain, not something you can resist.

He straightened up. "Go sit on the couch," he told her.

She gaped up at him, clearly trying to work out how you communicate the concept *I lack the power to stand* here on Planet Pain.

He nodded understandingly and reached under her armpit with two fingers.

She shrieked, *leaped* to her feet like a spastic marionette, Chaplin-walked to the couch at my left, and sat heavily on it, banging her head against the wall hard enough to make her groan. He got a pair of his own cuffs from his backpack, and hobbled her ankles with them while she was still groggy.

He stood over her and looked down at her for a long time, thinking, now and then thinking out loud. " . . . of *course* you haven't told the department anything; what could you possibly tell them?" Then: " . . . you live alone, obviously . . ." And: " . . . you're straight! Sure, you are . . ." And finally: " . . . recovering already . . . wonderfully, wonderfully strong, like a racehorse!"

"Pisam ti u krvotok, Pickica Drkadzijo," she snarled at him.

He backed away five or six paces, bent and retrieved her gun. He looked it over, made it safe, and tucked it into the right-hand pocket of his baggy slacks. Then he resumed his seat, pointed his gun at a point midway between me and Nika, and beamed at me.

"Russell," he said, "I think I love you."

I cried out, an inarticulate sound of disgust and revulsion.

"Really. You've made me very happy. Happier than anyone since . . . well, in a long time."

"You haven't even tried my coffee, yet," I mumbled.

"A telepath *and* a female cop, delivered into my hands on the same night, with no way in the world to connect me to the disappearance of either one of them? Not to mention this wonderful little place, on this wonderful island. I had no idea places so isolated could be found this close to town. This is *much* more convenient than my Fortress of Solitude up in the country." He shivered with pleasure. "Really, Russell—I had been planning to simply put you quickly out of your misery, like some dog or homeless person. But you've given me such special pleasure, gone so far out of your way to bring me treasures I never dreamed of, that now instead I just feel it incumbent on me to dream up an extra special excruciation of some kind for you. One of my worst deaths ever. Something truly . . . startling, just for you, as a token of my extreme gratitude. I'd like, if I can, to make you as unhappy as you've made me happy. And I freely admit it will be a challenge."

There wasn't much left of me. Emotionally, physically and intellectually, I was running on fumes. I'd have fainted long since if his damn drug had let me. I understood that what he was saying was truly horrible, but the awareness evoked hardly any emotional response. My hopes had bungeed too violently too many times in too short a space of time. I was pretty much out of all the emotional neurochemicals, except a few remaining cc's of despaireum and regrettol. My chest ached. My calves throbbed. My thumb pulsed. My head pounded. Plan-wise, I had nothing. I no longer believed in plans. I no longer believed in anything but unfairness and pain. Come to think of it, I'd believed in them since Susan died. *Okay, motherfucker: bring it.*

Since he seemed to want me to say something, I said the first thing that came into my head. "You really think you're some kind of genius, don't you? On a level with de Sade—"

He laughed out loud. Nothing like the giggles and chuckles I'd heard from him before; this was a guffaw. "Oh, you're wonderful—so *perfectly* wrong!" He shook his head admiringly. "Russell, de Sade was merely the Homer of Cruelty. I am its Aristotle. Its Newton. Its Tesla. I'm not just a fucking artist, I'm a *scientist*." He stood up, walked around behind his chair and rested his hands on its back, still keeping the helpless Nika covered with his gun just in case she decided to fling herself bodily across the room at him and try to chew through his Achilles' tendon. She looked mad enough to try. "But I admit," he said to me, "that I'm as proud of the uglinesses I've invented and catalogued as any human artist could be of the beauties he creates. Like Leonardo, I want my work to live, for the ages. I like the idea that five hundred years after my death, my name will be enough to make strong men pale and children weep."

I had just enough forebrain left to see a logic problem. "But how can you poss—" And then all at once I got it, and shut my eyes so tight I saw neon paisley. "Oh, no. Dear God, no, don't say that. No—"

Twinkling eyes. Puckering anus smile. Bashful nod. "It's true. I have a website."

I heard myself giggle. "Of course. Of course you do."

"Not on the worldwide web, of course. You can't Google me. But I get hits."

I nodded. "No doubt."

"The knowledge I've acquired has been perpetuated, and is being studied. Eventually it will form a book. I plan to call it, *Very Bad Deaths*. Do you like it?"

"Catchy."

"There may well have been other scientists before me, but I'm the first ever to be granted a foolproof way to publish, in perfect safety."

"Information wants to be free," I agreed.

Closing my eyes had made the whole visual world go away. I wondered, if I closed my ears, would the auditory world go away? Then all I'd have to do was figure out what to close to do away with the worlds of smell, taste, and touch—very important that last, don't neglect touch—and I'd be dead. Worth a try.

Allen cocked his gun and said, "Oh, are you fucking *kidding* me?"

Not to my knowledge. Oh God, was Nika trying something suicidally brave and stupid? I lifted my head and opened my eyes to witness her final moments, wishing I'd thought of it first.

Nika was still on the couch, eyes wide, staring.

Allen was standing with his back to me, staring.

At Zudie.

On his feet, and coming.

He looked like a no-shit zombie, a barely animated corpse of no great freshness. His eyes were wild, and his face was twisted up beyond recognition. His knees trembled violently at every slow step.

He kept coming.

"Okay," Allen said. "You asked for it. *Here*—"

Zudie screamed. Whatever Allen hurled at him struck with the force of a firehose to the chest.

And that was exactly how he treated it: leaned into it and kept on coming.

"Yeah? Try *this*—"

This time I could almost *see* the beam of concentrated evil he leveled at Zudie, soiling the air between them. If the last had been a firehose, this was a water cannon. Zudie was beaten back a pace, and then another. One knee started to quiver dangerously.

Nika's bellow was so loud, Allen and I both started violently. "GO, ZANDOR, GO!"

Zudie planted his feet.

I turned my entire brain into a giant bullhorn, that

brayed: *You can do it, Zudie. I have no idea what the fuck you're doing but I know you can do it. You're stronger than you think, Zudie. You always were, Zudie.*

Zandor Zudenigo looked into the face of his ultimate nightmare—everyone's worst nightmare, but his worst of all. He stared into the furnace of Allen's mind and did not blink. He squared his shoulders. Lowered his head. Moved forward.

You can do it, old friend. Whatever it is, I know you can do it.

"Guess again!" Allen cried happily, and with the special thrill cheating gave him, he lifted his gun, took his wrist in his left hand to steady it—

Zudie made a sweeping gesture, quick and crisp as a slap. The gun tore from Allen's grip and flew across the room, ricocheting off the metal chimney with a *crash* and landing on the tile around the wood stove with a *crack*.

"No!" He groped in his pants pocket for the gun he'd taken from Nika.

"Take him now, Zandor!"

I'm sorry, Zudie. You have to.

"Damn you," Zudie told him sadly.

He took the last few steps. Closed the gap. Stood in front of Allen. Locked eyes with him. Rested both his hands gently on Allen's shoulders.

"Jebem ti prvi red na sahrani," he said. Nika told me later what it meant. What I knew right then was, for the first time in my memory there was absolutely no trace of forgiveness anywhere in Zandor Zudenigo's eyes.

Allen gave up on the gun—took his hand from his pocket—reached up like a striking snake—located a spot below Zudie's ribs—pressed *hard*—

Zudie didn't seem to notice.

Allen leaned into it, used his body weight.

No effect.

Zudie took a long slow deep breath. Held it. Closed his unforgiving eyes.

"*Jebem te u mozak*," he murmured.

—Allen stiffened—filled his lungs as deeply as he could—*shrieked* for as long as possible, a sound that went on and on and horridly on—trailed off in a wet gurgle—fell down dead.

There was no question in my mind. He fell strings-cut, landed boneless, failed to inhale, began to bleed from the nose and ears but stopped almost at once. His open eyes looked dry, like marbles. As I watched they seemed to acquire dust.

Zudie opened his eyes. Sighed heavily. Stepped over the corpse and headed for the door.

"Zudie! Wait!"

To my surprise, he stopped and turned. His eyes met mine. They were his eyes once again: they forgave me for stopping him. I didn't ask the question aloud but still he answered it—or tried his best, anyway. "I made his selves disbelieve in himself."

What does that mean? You tell me. I still wonder. All I can tell you is, the way he said it made it sound like the most obscene thing a person could do. Maybe it is.

I was crying. "You had to. God damn it, you had to."

He shrugged. "Sure." He turned again to go.

"Zandor—" Nika began.

"I know, Nika," he said wearily, and trudged on. "Don't worry. I'll handle it. Yes, really. I know someone. Send me his full name, address, and e-mail address: that'll be enough."

In the doorway he stopped and turned. "For forty years," he said to us, "twice every day of my life for the last forty years, morning and night, I've sworn a solemn oath to myself, that I would never, *ever* do that to another human being again, no matter what. No matter what." He smiled with infinite sadness. "Now it's twice." He walked out.

But the fat bastard deserved it, I sent after him.

He stuck his head back in the door. "*Everybody* deserves to die, Russell," he said gently. "God obviously thinks so."

Then he was gone. I didn't see him again for a very long time.

I hated having to touch Allen, even dead, maybe especially dead, but the keys to both sets of cuffs were in his pocket. I turned Nika loose, and made us both strong Irish coffees, and we sat beside the body and discussed things until we had each had and gotten over the shivers, and our cups were empty. Then we slapped a hasty cardboard patch over the hole in the living room window, and closed all the shades and blinds, and I showed Nika the guest room, but when I got to my room she was still right behind me, so we lay down together and held each other and slept like the dead until well after dawn. Then we had coffee and talked some more.

We poked around together until we found a spot we both liked down by the stream. Between us we managed to drag Allen's body down there on a kind of sled we made of an old piece of plywood. We dug a hole with shovel and mattock—Nika did nearly all the digging, I did a little root cutting—and we rolled him into it and filled it back up and tossed the extra dirt into the stream. Then I pissed on him, and we went back up the hill for more Irish coffee.

She really really hated doing it. Erasing him. It went against all her training and most of her beliefs. Some of mine, too. We knew for certain that Allen had had many many victims, most of whose loved ones had no faintest clue what had ever happened to them. Now, because of us, no one would ever speak for all those dead, none of those stories would ever be told, no one could ever bring even that much solace to all those broken hearts yearning for some sort of ending to the story.

But she had heard that last speech of his just as clearly as I had. Any kind of official involvement whatsoever, and the media would have fallen on the story with squeals of glee, playing it up even bigger than the Pig Farm guy, Bakker the Beater, the I-5 Killer and Ted Bundy rolled into one . . . which was if anything a monstrous under-statement. He'd have ended up as immortal as he'd wanted to be, his posthumous website swamped with hits, his inhuman insights pored over by sweaty creeps the world over. I was quite surprised to find that, for the first time in my life, I now believed there *are* some things man is not meant to know.

In the end it was more personal animosity than social conscience that decided us. Retroactive anonymity was the cruelest sentence we could possibly pass on the son of a bitch, and we knew it. And it was about time someone was cruel to *him* for a change. We tumbled him into a hole and covered him with mud and rocks. We made no attempt to mark the spot, and neither of us will ever go there again.

Let the Pickton Pig Farm remain British Columbia's most infamous mass murder site. Whistler doesn't need the business. The Sea to Sky Highway doesn't need any part of its sky darkened, its sea tainted. Almost everything I've told you about the location of Allen's abattoir was wrong.

We learned his full name just before we planted him. It had never once occurred to me to ask him. Not for a moment in that whole endless night of horror had I imagined I might ever get a chance to make any use of the information. His last name turned out to be Campbell. That made me smile sourly. In Canada it's the same as Smith or Jones in America: a name so ubiquitous as to sound vaguely phony.

We copied down that and the address on his driver's license and all his credit card numbers and expiry dates from his wallet before we tossed it into the hole after him. Then I found a laptop in his SUV and got his e-mail address out of that, and e-mailed all the information to Zudie. I never doubted for a moment that a math genius at Zudie's level would know at least one really good hacker, and that in due time every single bit Allen Campbell had ever uploaded to the internet would eventually be located and obliterated beyond recovery.

Little could be done, of course, about any copies that might have already been downloaded by people competent enough to protect their identities. There you go. "Almost perfect" is about as good as you can hope for in this world, and don't look to see *that* often.

5.

Nika and I parted with four-hand, deep-eye-contact handshakes, declarations of mutual respect and life-long friendship, assurances we'd always be there for each other, and firm agreement to get together for a drink just as soon as we'd had time to clean out our heads a little, sort things out just a bit. In the movies, we'd have become best friends. On TV we'd have begun a quirky sexual flirtation that ran the rest of the year and reached boiling point just in time for the season closer.

We spoke on the phone a week later for perhaps twenty minutes, and that was the last time we communicated with each other in any fashion for over a year. It wasn't quite long enough.

What we'd been through together didn't need, or even want, sharing. And what else was there, really, for us to talk about? Our personalities and outlooks on life were so totally dissimilar, about the only thing we had in common was the nightmare we'd both survived—one we'd both entered unwillingly in the first place. There was no real basis for any kind of lasting relationship, much less a friendship. I wished there was. I felt like there ought to be. But I couldn't think of one. I did try, from time to time.

The story did have one last lovely little ironic coda. A little more than a month after we buried Allen by my stream, Constable Nika Mandiç happened to walk into a 7-Eleven on West 10th Avenue to get a bottle of water just as three nitwits were trying to rob the place. Their combined armament totaled a toy pistol and a medium-size wrench. The arrest was largely a matter of remaining in the doorway, blocking the only exit. Nonetheless, Constable Mandiç won a commendation, just as if she'd done something difficult or dangerous like facing a homocidal serial monster without backup, and to her immense gratification she was transferred out of the Police Community Services Trailer detail and onto the streets. Her career began an upward climb that continued for a while.

Right up until the *next* time we found ourselves working together.

I tried to stay in touch with Zudie.

I tried hard for a week. Repeatedly, anyway. But he wouldn't answer my cell phone, no matter when I called or how many times I let it ring. He wouldn't answer my e-mails no matter how eloquent. After a week, both phone number and e-mail address began to list as nulls.

I rented a small boat with a noisy motor from someone who should have taken one look at me and known better, late one afternoon, and managed to make my way to Coveney Island without enraging *too* many other boaters. There was one tricky bit: I was startled to learn that, for some reason, barges don't have any sort of braking system at all. But eventually I got there, and circled the island counterclockwise as close as I dared for an hour or so, while thinking as loudly as I could (if that means anything).

At first I thought things like *Come show me where to land, Zudie, I can't find a place.* Then it was *Damn it, Smelly, I'm liable to rip the bottom out of this fucking boat if you don't help me.* A little while later: *Zandor, I'm sorry, okay? You shouldn't have had to do that. You came to me and I let you down. I know. Let me make it up to you.*

And then finally, all in a tumbling flood: *This isn't fair. You can't leave me under this much obligation. You can't leave yourself under this much obligation. God damn it, you saved me from clinical depression, now you have to at least give me a chance to try and help you. Zandor, none of this is your fault. It isn't your fault you can do what you did. It isn't your fault you had to do it. It isn't your fault you did it. Because you did it, I am alive. Because of you, Nika is alive. Because of you, the Aristotle of Cruelty is dead. Because of you, dozens if not hundreds of innocent people will not have to die very bad deaths.*

No response. Nothing moved on the little island except branches.

Zudie, it couldn't have taken more than thirty seconds from the first moment Allen realized he was in deep shit to the last moment of his life. I don't know what the fuck it means to die of disbelief in yourself, but okay, I can certainly imagine it must be horrible stuff. Okay, I know it is: I heard that scream. I saw his face as it happened. But no matter how horrible it was, it was over in thirty seconds. By Allen's own standards, that wouldn't even qualify as one of the bad deaths. Read my memories of Susan's dying, Zudie, and believe me: nothing that is over in thirty seconds is one of the bad deaths. You showed that bastard way more mercy than he deserved.

Nothing.

He knew all that stuff already, and it didn't help.

Or didn't help enough.

Zudie, you've seen my thoughts. You know what I saw in your eyes, the moment I met you. Forgiveness. You're the world's best forgiver. You taught me most of what I know about forgiving. You've seen all the darkest corners of this swamp I call a mind, and you forgave me—over and over. More than anything else left to me on earth, I want to help you forgive yourself. Please let me. Please let me at least try. Please!

I waited. Thirty seconds. A minute. Nothing.

Coveney Island was in sight off to my right. The sun was low in the sky. No point in another circuit. He probably wasn't even on the damn island. I steered right and gave it the gun—

—so I couldn't have really heard it. Not with my ears. That obnoxious little motor was way too loud. With something *between* my ears, then, I heard, as clear as the proverbial bell and as loud as a shout at arm's length, the words *GIVE ME TIME, SLIM.*

I exhaled so hard with relief, I actually made a little moaning sound, like someone expending effort in a dream.

As long as you need, I thought back. *I'm in the book.*

And I booted it for home, and made it nearly all the way there before running out of gas. An hour of jocular humiliation later I was drinking my own coffee.

Only Zudie knew how much time he needed to heal, how much penance he needed to do. He knew where to find me.

And me?

Did I, as a good protagonist should, experience some kind of arc of character development by surviving all that insanity? Did I grow? Have I found redemption?

Ha.

Well, maybe. Of a kind. To an extent. In a sense.

I still live alone. I'm still poor company. My son still hates my guts. My dead wife still hasn't spoken to me. Allen visits me in nightmares from time to time, though less often as the months pass. Fraidy the Cat is still afraid of me.

But I regard these all as ongoing, manageable problems. I won't let my relationship with Jesse slide for much longer. I'm no longer in any hurry to rejoin Susan. She'll wait for me if it can be done. Instead of being a bitter suicidal misanthropic hermit, nowadays I'm just a solitary cynic who happens to have been granted the kind of peace and isolation it takes to complete a first novel. One of these days maybe I will. Meanwhile—

Last Thursday night, while I was sitting on the porch steps, scratching Horsefeathers behind the ears with my left hand, Fraidy came edging up, a hesitant step at a time, and for a few glorious seconds allowed me to scratch *her* behind the ears with my right hand. I did it slowly, with infinite gentleness and care, using my sharpest nails and everything I've learned about cat-pleasuring. She tolerated it for perhaps ten strokes, then gave me a one-eyed look that said, *sorry, I just don't get the attraction,* and left us. But she left walking, rather than scurrying in fright. I have hopes she might let me try again one day.

And over across the water, in Point Grey, an upscale neighborhood just east of the UBC campus, a family of four I've never met and never will are sleeping soundly tonight. Oblivious.

That's enough redemption for now, I guess. It'll do.

The following is an excerpt from:

HELL'S GATE

by
David Weber
&
Linda Evans

available from Baen Books
November 2006
hardcover

Chapter One

The tall noncom could have stepped straight out of a recruiting poster. His fair hair and height were a legacy from his North Shalhoman ancestors, but he was far, far away—a universe away—from their steep cliffs and icy fjords. His jungle camo fatigues were starched and ironed to razor-sharp creases as he stood on the crude, muddy landing ground with his back to the looming hole of the portal. His immaculate uniform looked almost as bizarrely out of place against the backdrop of the hacked-out jungle clearing as the autumn-kissed red and gold of the forest giants beyond the portal, and he seemed impervious to the swamp-spawned insects zinging about his ears. He wore the shoulder patch of the Second Andaran Temporal Scouts, and the traces of gray at his temples went perfectly with the experience lines etched into his hard, bronzed face.

He gazed up into the painfully bright afternoon sky,

blue-gray eyes slitted against the westering sun, with his helmet tucked into the crook of his left elbow and his right thumb hooked into the leather sling of the dragoon arbalest slung over his shoulder. He'd been standing there in the blistering heat for the better part of half an hour, yet he seemed unaware of it. In fact, he didn't even seem to be perspiring, although that had to be an illusion.

He also seemed prepared to stand there for the next week or so, if that was what it took. But then, finally, a black dot appeared against the cloudless blue, and his nostrils flared as he inhaled in satisfaction.

He watched the dot sweep steadily closer, losing altitude as it came, then lifted his helmet and settled it onto his head. He bent his neck, shielding his eyes with his left hand as the dragon back-winged in to a landing. Bits of debris flew on the sudden wind generated by the mighty beast's iridescent-scaled wings, and the noncom waited until the last twigs had pattered back to the ground before he lowered his hand and straightened once more.

The dragon's arrival was a sign of just how inaccessible this forward post actually was. In fact, it was just over seven hundred and twenty miles from the coastal base, in what would have been the swamps of the Kingdom of Farshal in northeastern Hilmar back home. Those were some pretty inhospitable miles, and the mud here was just as gluey as the genuine Hilmaran article, so aerial transport was the only real practical way in at the moment. The noncom himself had arrived back at the post via the regular transport dragon flight less than forty-eight hours earlier, and as he'd surveyed the much below, he'd been struck by just how miserable it would have been to slog through it on foot. How anyone was going to properly exploit a portal in the middle of this godforsaken swamp was more than he could say, but he didn't doubt that the Union Trans-Temporal Transit Authority would find a way. The UTTTA had the best engineers in the universe—in *several* universes, for that matter—and plenty of experience with portals in terrain even less prepossessing than this.

Probably less prepossessing, anyway.

The dragon went obediently to its knees at the urging of its pilot, and a single passenger swung down the boarding harness strapped about the beast's shoulders. The newcomer was dark-haired, dark-eyed, and even taller than the noncom, although much younger, and each point of his collar bore the single silver shield of a commander of one hundred. Like the noncom, he wore the shoulder flash of the 2nd ATS, and the name "Olderhan, Jasak" was stenciled above his breast pocket. He said something to the dragon's pilot, then strode quickly across the mucky ground towards the waiting one-man welcoming committee.

"Sir!" The noncom snapped to attention and saluted sharply. "Welcome back to this shithole, *Sir!*" he barked.

"Why, thank you, Chief Sword Threbuch," the officer said amiably, tossing off a far more casual salute in response. Then he extended his right hand and gripped th. older man's hand firmly. "I trust the Powers That Be have a suitable reason for dragging me back here, Otwal," he said dryly, and the noncom smiled.

"I wish they hadn't—dragged you back, that is, Sir— but I think you may forgive them in the end," he said. "I'm sort of surprised they managed to catch you, though. I figured you'd be well on your way back to Garth Showma by now."

"So did I," Hundred Olderhan replied wryly. He shook his head. "Unfortunately, Hundred Thalmayr seems to've gotten himself delayed in transit somewhere along the way, and Magister Halathyn was quick enough off the mark to catch me before he got here. If the Magister had only waited another couple of days for Thalmayr to get here to relieve me, I'd have been aboard ship and far enough out to sea to get away clean."

"Sorry about that, Sir." The chief sword grinned. "I hope you'll tell the Five Thousand I *tried* to get you home for your birthday."

"Oh, Father will forgive you, Otwal," Jasak assured him. "*Mother*, now . . . "

"Please, Sir!" The chief sword shivered dramatically. "I still remember what your lady mother had to say to me when I got the Five Thousand home late for their anniversary."

"According to Father, you did well to get him home at all," the hundred said, and the chief sword shrugged.

"The Five Thousand was too tough for any jaguar to eat, Sir. All I did was stop the bleeding."

"Most he could have expected out of you after he was stupid enough to step right on top of it." The chief sword gave the younger man a sharp look, and the hundred chuckled. "That's the way *Father* describes it, Otwal. I promise you I'm not being guilty of filial disrespect."

"As the Hundred says," the chief sword agreed.

"But since our lords and masters appear to have seen fit to make me miss my birthday, suppose you tell me exactly what we have here, Chief Sword." The hundred's voice was much crisper, his brown eyes intent, and the chief sword came back to a position midway between stand easy and parade rest.

"Sir, I'm afraid you'll need to ask Magister Halathyn for the details. All I know is that he says the potential tests on this portal's field strength indicate that there's at least one more in close proximity. A big one."

"How big?" Jasak asked, his eyes narrowing.

"I don't really know, Sir," Threbuch replied. "I don't think Magister Halathyn does yet, for that matter. But he was muttering something about a class eight."

Sir Jasak Olderhan's eyebrows rose, and he whistled silently. The largest trans-temporal portal so far charted was the Selkara Portal, and it was only a class seven. If Magister Halathyn had, indeed, detected a class *eight*, then this muddy, swampy hunk of jungle was about to become very valuable real estate.

"In that case, Chief Sword," he said mildly after a moment, "I suppose you'd better get me to Magister Halathyn."

Halathyn vos Dulainah was very erect, very dark-skinned, and very silver-haired, with a wiry build which was finally beginning to verge on frail. Jasak wasn't certain, but he strongly suspected that the old man was well past the age at which Authority regs mandated the retirement of the Gifted from active fieldwork. Not that anyone was likely to tell Magister Halathyn that. He'd been a law unto himself for decades and the UTTTA's crown jewel ever since he'd left the Mythal Falls Academy twenty years before, and he took an undisguised, almost child-like delight in telling his nominal superiors where they could stuff their regulations.

He hadn't told Jasak exactly why he was out here in the middle of this mud and bug-infested swamp, nor why

Magister Gadrial Kelbryan, his second-in-command at the Garth Showma Institute, had followed him out here. He'd insisted with a bland-faced innocence which could not have been bettered by a twelve-year-old caught with his hand actually in the cookie jar, that he was "on vacation." He certainly had to the clout within the UTTTA to commandeer transportation for his own amusement at that was what he really wanted, but Jasak suspected he was actually engaged in some sort of undisclosed research. Not that Magister Halathyn was going to admit it. He was too delighted by the opportunity to be mysterious to waste it.

He was also, as his complexion and the "vos" in front of his surname proclaimed, both a Mythalan and a member of the *shakira* caste. As a rule, Jasak Olderhan was less than fond of Mythalans . . . and considerably less fond than that of the *shakira*. But Magister Halathyn was the exception to that rule as he was to so many others.

The magister looked up as Chief Sword Threbuch followed Jasak into his tent, the heels of their boots loud on its raised wooden flooring. He tapped his stylus on the crystal display in front of him, freezing his notes and the calculations he'd been performing, and smiled at the hundred over the glassy sphere.

"And how is my second-favorite crude barbarian?" he inquired in genial Andaran.

"As unlettered and impatient as ever, Sir," Jasak replied, in Mythalan, with an answering smile. The old magister chuckled appreciatively and extended his hand for a welcoming shake. Then he cocked his canvas camp chair back at a comfortable, teetering angle and waved for Jasak to seat himself in the matching chair on the far side of his worktable.

"Seriously, Jasak," he said as the younger man obeyed the unspoken command, "I apologize for yanking you back here. I know how hard it was for you to get leave for your birthday in the first place, and I know your parents must have been looking forward to seeing you. But I thought you'd want to be here for this one. And, frankly, with all due respect to Hundred Thalmayr, I'm not sorry he was delayed. All things being equal, I'd prefer to have *you* in charge just a little longer."

Jasak stopped his grimace before it ever reached his expression, but it wasn't the easiest thing he'd ever done. Although he genuinely had been looking forward to spending his birthday at home in Garth Showma for the first time in over six years, he *hadn't* been looking forward to handing "his" company over to Hadrign Thalmayr, even temporarily. Partly because of his jealously possessive pride in Charlie Company, but also because Thalmayr— who was senior to him—had only transferred into the Scouts seventeen months ago. From his record, he was a perfectly competent infantry officer, but Jasak hadn't been impressed with the older man's mental flexibility the few times they'd met before Jasak himself had been forward-deployed. And it was pretty clear his previous line infantry experience had left him firmly imbued with the sort of by-the-book mentality the Temporal Scouts worked very hard to eradicate.

Which wasn't something he could discuss with a civilian, even one he respected as deeply as he did Magister Halathyn.

"The Chief Sword said something about a class eight," he said instead, his tone making the statement a question, and Magister Halathyn nodded soberly.

"Unless Gadrial and I are badly mistaken," he said, waving a hand at the letters and esoteric formulae glittering in the water-clear heart of his crystal, "it's *at least* a class eight. Actually, I suspect it may be even larger."

Jasak sat back in his chair, regarding the old man's lined face intently. Had it been anyone else, he would have been inclined to dismiss the preposterous claim as pure, rampant speculation. But Magister Halathyn wasn't given to speculation.

"If you're right about that, Sir," the hundred said after a moment, "this entire transit chain may just have become a lot more important to the Authority."

"It may," Magister Halathyn agreed. "Then again, it may not." He grimaced. "Whatever size this portal may be—" he tapped the crystal containing his notes "—*that* portal—" he pointed out through the open fly of his tent at the peculiar hole in the universe which loomed enormously beyond the muddy clearing's western perimeter "—is only a class three. That's going to bottleneck anything coming through from our putative class eight. Not to mention the fact that we're at the end of a ridiculously inconvenient chain at the moment."

"I suppose that depends in part on how far your new portal is from the other side of this one," Jasak pointed out. "The terrain between here and the coast may suck, but it's only seven hundred miles."

"Seven hundred and nineteen-point-three miles," Magister Halathyn corrected with a crooked smile.

"All right, Sir." Jasak accepted the correction with a smile of his own. "That's still a ridiculously short haul compared to most of the portal connections I can think of. And if this new portal of yours is within relatively close proximity to our class three, we're talking about a twofer."

"That really is a remarkably uncouth way to describe a spatially congruent trans-temporal transfer zone," Halathyn said severely.

"I'm just a naturally uncouth sort of fellow, Sir," Jasak agreed cheerfully. "But however you slice it, it's still a two-for-one."

"Yes, it is," Halathyn acknowledged. "Assuming our calculations are sound, of course. In fact, if this new portal is as large as I think it is, and as closely associated with our portal here, I think it's entirely possible that we're looking at a cluster."

Despite all of the magister's many years of discipline, his eyes gleamed, and he couldn't quite keep the excitement out of his voice. Not that Jasak blamed him for that. A portal cluster . . . In the better part of two centuries of exploration, UTTTA's survey teams had located only one true cluster, the Zholhara Cluster. Doubletons were the rule—indeed, only sixteen triples had ever been found, which was a rate of less than one in ten. But a cluster like Zholhara was of literally incalculable value.

This far out—they were at the very end of the Lamia Chain, well over three months' travel from Arcana, even for someone who could claim transport dragon priority for the entire trip—even a cluster would take years to fully develop. Lamia, with over twenty portals, was already a huge prize. But if Magister Halathyn was correct, the entire transit chain was about to become even more valuable . . . and receive the highest development priority UTTTA could assign.

"Of course," Magister Halathyn continued in the tone of a man forcing himself to keep his enthusiasm in check, "we don't know where this supposed portal of mine connects. It could be the middle of the Great Ransaran Desert. Or an island in the middle of the Western Ocean, like Rycarh Outbound. Or the exact center of the polar ice cap."

"Or it could be a couple of thousand feet up in thin air, which would make for something of a nasty first step," Jasak agreed. "But I suppose we'd better go find it if we really want to know, shouldn't we?"

"My sentiments exactly," the magister agreed, and the hundred looked at the chief sword.

"How soon can we move out on the Magister's heading, Chief Sword?"

"I'm afraid the Hundred would have to ask Fifty Garlath about that," Threbuch replied with absolutely no inflection, and this time Jasak did grimace. The tonelessness of the chief sword's voice shouted his opinion (among other things) of Commander of Fifty Shevan Garlath as an officer of the Union of Arcana. Unfortunately, Sir Jasak Olderhan's opinion exactly matched that of his company's senior non-commissioned officer.

"If the Hundred will recall," the chief sword continued even more tonelessly, "his last decision before his own departure was to authorize Third Platoon's R&R. That leaves Fifty Garlath as the SO here at the base camp."

Jasak winced internally as Threbuch tactfully (sort of) reminded him that leaving Garlath out here at the ass-end of nowhere had been his own idea. Which had seemed like a good one at the time, even if it had been a little petty of him. No, more than a little petty. Quite a bit more, if he wanted to be honest. Chief Sword Threbuch hadn't exactly protested at the time, but his expression had suggested his opinion of the decision. Not because he disagreed that Fifty Therman Ulthar and his men had earned their R&R, but because Shevan Garlath was arguably the most incompetent platoon commander in the entire brigade. Leaving him in charge of anything more complicated than a hot cider stand was not, in the chief sword's considered opinion, a Good Idea.

"We'd have to recall Fifty Ulthar's platoon from the coast, if you want to use him, Sir," the chief sword added, driving home the implied reprimand with exquisite tact.

Jasak was tempted to point out that Magister Halathyn had already dragged *him* back from the company's main CP at the coastal enclave, so there was really no reason *he* shouldn't recall Fifty Ulthar. Except, of course, that he couldn't. First, because doing so would require him to acknowledge to the man who'd been his father's first squad lance that he'd made a mistake. Both of them might *know* he had, but he was damned if he was going to *admit* it.

But second, and far more important, was the patronage system which permeated the Arcanan Army, because patronage was the only thing that kept Garlath in uniform. Not even that had been enough to get him promoted, but it was more than enough to ensure that his sponsors would ask pointed questions if Jasak went that far out of his way to invite another fifty to replace him on what promised to be quite possibly the most important portal exploration on record. If Magister Halathyn's estimates were remotely near correct, this was the sort of operation that got an officer noticed.

Which, in Jasak's opinion, was an even stronger argument in favor of handing it to a competent junior officer who didn't have any patrons . . . and whose probable promotion would actually have a beneficial effect on the Army. But—

"All right, Chief Sword," he sighed. "My respects to Fifty Garlath, and I want his platoon ready to move out at first light tomorrow."

The weather was much cooler on the other side of the base portal. Although it was only one hour earlier in the local day, it had been mid-afternoon—despite Jasak's best efforts—before Commander of Fifty Garlath's First Platoon had been ready to leave base camp and step through the immaterial interface between Hilmaran swamp and subarctic Andara in a single stride. The portal's outbound side was located smack on top of the Great Andaran Lakes, five thousand miles north of their departure portal, in what should have been the Kingdom of Lokan. In fact, it was on the narrow neck of land which separated Hammerfell Lake and White Mist Lake from Queen Kalthra's Lake. It might be only one hour east of the base camp, but the difference in latitude meant that single step had moved them from sweltering early summer heat into the crispness of autumn.

Jasak had been raised on his family's estates on New Arcana, less than eighty miles from the very spot at which they emerged, but New Arcana had been settled for the better part of two centuries. The bones of the Earth were the same, and the cool, leaf-painted air of a northern fall was a familiar and welcome relief from the base camp's smothering humidity, but the towering giants of the primordial forest verged on the overpowering even for him.

For Fifty Garlath, who had been raised on the endless

grasslands of Yanko, the restricted sightlines and dense forest canopy were far worse than that. Hundred Olderhan, CO of Charlie Company, First Battalion, First Regiment, Second Andaran Temporal Scouts, couldn't very well take one of his platoon commanders to task in front of his subordinates for being an old woman, but Sir Jasak Olderhan felt an almost overpowering urge to kick Garlath in the ass.

He mastered the temptation sternly, but it wasn't easy, even for someone as disciplined as he was. Garlath was *supposed* to be a temporal scout, after all. That meant he was supposed to take the abrupt changes in climate trans-temporal travel imposed in stride. It also meant he was supposed to be confident in the face of the unknown, well versed in movement under all sorts of conditions and in all sorts of terrain. He was *not* supposed to be so obvi-ously intimidated by endless square miles of trees.

Jasak turned away from his troopers to distract him-self (and his mounting frustration) while Garlath tried to get his command squared away. He stood with his back to the brisk, northern autumn and gazed back through the portal at the humid swamp they had left behind. It was the sort of sight with which anyone who spent as much time wandering about between universes as the Second Andarans did became intimately familiar, but no one ever learned to take it for granted.

Magister Halathyn's tone had been dismissive when he described the portal as "only a class three." But while the classification was accurate, and there were undeni-ably much larger portals, even a "mere" class three was the better part of four miles across. A four-mile disk sliced out of the universe . . . and pasted onto another one.

It was far more than merely uncanny, and unless someone had seen it for himself, it was almost impossible to describe properly.

Jasak himself had only the most rudimentary understanding of current portal theory, but he found the portals themselves endlessly fascinating. A portal appeared to have only two dimensions—height, and width. No one had yet succeeded in measuring one's depth. As far as anyone could tell, it *had* no depth; its threshold was simply a line, visible to the eye but impossible to measure, where one universe stopped . . . and another one began.

Even more fascinating, it was as if each of the universes it connected were *inside* the other one. Standing on the eastern side of a portal in Universe A and looking west, one saw a section of Universe B stretching away from one. One might or might not be looking west in that universe, since portals' orientation in one universe had no discernible effect on their orientation in the other universe to which they connected. If one stepped through the portal into Universe B and looked back in the direction from which one had come, one saw exactly what one would have expected to see—the spot from which one had left Universe A. But, if one returned to Universe A and walked *around* the portal to its western aspect and looked *east*, one saw Universe B stretching away in a direction exactly 180° reversed from what he'd seen from the portal's eastern side in Universe A. And if one then stepped through into Universe B, one found the portal once again at one's back . . . but this time looking west, not east, into Universe A.

The theoreticians referred to the effect as "counterintuitive." Most temporal scouts, like Jasak, referred to it as the "can't get there" effect, since it was impossible to move from one side to the other of a portal in the same universe without circling all the way around it. And, since that held true for any portal in any universe, no one could simply step through a portal one direction, then step back through it to emerge on its far side in the same universe. In order to reach the far side of the portal at the other end of the link, one had to walk all the way around *it*, as well.

Frankly, every time someone tried to explain the theory of how it all worked to Jasak, his brain hurt, but the engineers responsible for designing portal infrastructure took advantage of that effect on a routine basis. It always took some getting used to when one first saw it, of course. For example, it wasn't at all uncommon to see two lines of slider cars charging into a portal on exactly opposite headings—one from the east and the other from the west—at the exact same moment on what appeared to be exactly the same track. No matter how carefully it had all been explained before a man saw it for the first time with his own eyes, he *knew* those two sliders had to be colliding in the universe on the other side of that portal. But, of course, they weren't. Viewed from the side in that other universe, both sliders were exploding out of the same space simultaneously. . . but headed in exactly opposite directions.

From a military perspective, the . . . idiosyncrasies of trans-temporal travel could be more than a little maddening, although the Union of Arcana hadn't fought a true war in over two centuries.

At the moment, Jasak stood roughly at the center of the portal through which he had just stepped, looking back across it at the forward base camp and the swamp they'd left behind. The sunlight on the far side fell from a noticeably different angle, creating shadows whose shape and direction clashed weirdly with those of the cool, northern forest in which he stood. Swamp insects bumbled busily towards the immaterial threshold between worlds, then veered away as they hit the chill breeze blowing back across it.

This particular portal was relatively young. The theorists were still arguing about exactly how and why portals formed in the first place, but it had been obvious for better than a hundred and eighty years that new ones were constantly, if not exactly frequently, being formed. This one had formed long enough ago that the scores of gigantic trees which had been sliced in half vertically by its creation had become dead, well dried hulks, but almost a dozen of them still stood, like gaunt, maimed chimneys. It wouldn't be long before the bitter northern winters toppled them, as well, yet the fact that it hadn't happened yet suggested that they'd been dead for no more than a few years.

Which, Jasak told himself acidly, was not so very much longer than it appeared to be taking Fifty Garlath to get his platoon sorted out.

Eventually, however, even Garlath had his troopers shaken down into movement formation. Sort of. His single point man was too far from the main body, and he'd spread his flank scouts far too wide, but Jasak clamped his teeth firmly against a blistering reprimand . . . for now. He'd already intended to have a few words with Garlath about the totally unacceptable delay in getting started, but he'd decided he'd wait until they bivouacked and he could "counsel" his subordinate in private. With Charlie Company detached from the Battalion as the only organized force at this end of the transit chain, it was particularly important not to undermine the chain of command by giving the troops cause to think that he considered their platoon CO an idiot.

Especially when he did.

So instead of ripping Garlath a new one at the fresh proof of his incompetence, he limited himself to one speaking glance at Chief Sword Threbuch, then followed along behind Garlath with Threbuch and Magister Kelbryan.

Although Jasak had enjoyed the privilege of serving with Magister Halathyn twice before, this was the first time he'd actually met Kelbryan. She and Halathyn had worked together for at least twenty years—indeed, she was one of the main reasons the UTTTA had acquired the exclusive use of Halathyn's services in the first place—but she normally stayed home, holding down the fort at the institute at Garth Showma on New Arcana which Halathyn had created from the ground up for the Authority. Jasak had always assumed, in a casual sort of way, that that was because she preferred civilization to the frontier. Or, at least, that she would have been unsuited to hoofing it through rugged terrain with the Andaran Scouts.

He still didn't know her very well. In fact, he didn't know her at all. She'd only reached their base camp three weeks earlier, and she seemed to be a very private person in a lot of ways. But he'd already discovered that his assumptions had been badly off base. Kelbryan was a couple of years older than he was, and her Ransaran ancestry showed in her almond eyes, sandalwood complexion, and dark, brown-black hair. At five-eight, she was tall for a Ransaran . . . which meant she was only eight inches shorter than he was. But delicate as she seemed to him, she was obviously fit, and she'd taken the crudity of the facilities available at the sharp end of the Authority's exploration in stride, without turning a hair.

She was also very, very good at her job—as was only to be expected, given that Magister Halathyn must have had his choice of any second-in-command he wanted. Indeed, Jasak had come to realize that the true reasons she'd normally stayed home owed far less to any "delicacy" on her part than to the fact that she was probably the only person Magister Halathyn fully trusted to run "his" shop in his absence. Her academic and research credentials were impressive proof of her native brilliance, and despite the differences in their cultural heritages, she and her boss were clearly devoted to one another.

It had been obvious Magister Halathyn longed to accompany them this morning, but there were limits in all things. Jasak was prepared to go along with the fiction that vos Dulainah wasn't far past mandatory retirement age as long as the old man stayed safely in base camp; he was not about to risk someone that valuable, or of whom he was so fond, in an initial probe. Magister Kelbryan had supported him with firm tactfulness when the old man turned those longing, puppy-dog eyes in her direction, and Magister Halathyn had submitted to the inevitable with no more than the odd, heartfelt sigh of mournful regret when he was sure one of them was listening.

Now the hundred watched the team's junior magister moving through the deep drifts of leaves almost as silently as his own troopers. Despite—or possibly even because of—the fact that he'd never worked with Kelbryan before, he was impressed. And, he admitted, attracted.

She opened a leather equipment case on her belt and withdrew one of the esoteric devices of her profession. Jasak was technically Gifted himself, although his own trace of the talent was so minute that he was often astonished the testing process had been able to detect it at all. Now, as often, he felt a vague, indefinable stirring sensation as someone who was very powerfully Gifted indeed brought her Gift to bear. She gazed down into the crystal display, and her lips moved silently as she powered it up.

Jasak saw the display flicker to life and moved a little closer to look over her shoulder. She sensed his presence and looked up. For an instant, he thought she was going to be annoyed with him for crowding her, but then she smiled and tilted her wrist so that he could see the display more clearly.

—end excerpt—

from *Hell's Gate*
available in hardcover,
November 2006, from Baen Books

IF YOU LIKE...
YOU SHOULD TRY...

DAVID DRAKE
David Weber

DAVID WEBER
John Ringo

JOHN RINGO
Michael Z. Williamson
Tom Kratman

ANNE MCCAFFREY
Mercedes Lackey

MERCEDES LACKEY
Wen Spencer, Andre Norton
Andre Norton
James H. Schmitz

LARRY NIVEN
James P. Hogan
Travis S. Taylor

ROBERT A. HEINLEIN
Jerry Pournelle
Lois McMaster Bujold
Michael Z. Williamson

HEINLEIN'S "JUVENILES"
Rats, Bats & Vats series by Eric Flint & Dave Freer
Cosmic Tales I & II, ed. by T.K.F. Weisskopf

HORATIO HORNBLOWER OR PATRICK O'BRIAN
David Weber's Honor Harrington series
David Drake's RCN series

HARRY POTTER
Mercedes Lackey's Urban Fantasy series

THE LORD OF THE RINGS
Elizabeth Moon's *The Deed of Paksenarrion*

H.P. LOVECRAFT
Princess of Wands by John Ringo

GEORGETTE HEYER
Lois McMaster Bujold
Catherine Asaro

GREEK MYTHOLOGY
Bull God and *Thrice Bound* by Roberta Gellis
Pyramid Scheme by Eric Flint & Dave Freer
Forge of the Titans by Steve White
Blood of the Heroes by Steve White

NORSE MYTHOLOGY
Northworld Trilogy by David Drake
A Mankind Witch by Dave Freer

ARTHURIAN LEGEND
Steve White's "Legacy" series
For King and Country by Robert Asprin
& Linda Evans
The Dragon Lord by David Drake

SCA/HISTORICAL REENACTMENT
John Ringo's "After the Fall" series
Harald by David D. Friedman

SCIENCE FACT
Borderlands of Science by Charles Sheffield
Kicking the Sacred Cow by James P. Hogan

CATS
Larry Niven's Man-Kzin Wars series

PUNS
Rick Cook
Spider Robinson
Wm. Mark Simmons

VAMPIRES
Tomorrow Sucks ed. by Cox & Weisskopf
Fred Saberhagen's Vlad Tapes series
Nigel Bennett & P.N. Elrod
Wm. Mark Simmons

Robert A. Heinlein

"Robert A. Heinlein wears imagination as though it were his private suit of clothes. What makes his work so rich is that he combines his lively, creative sense with an approach that is at once literate, informed, and exciting."
—*New York Times*

Wen Spencer's Tinker:
A Heck of a Gal In a Whole
Lot of Trouble

❧❦❧

TINKER
0-7434-9871-2 • $6.99

Move over, Buffy! Tinker not only kicks supernatural elven butt—she's a techie genius, too! Armed with an intelligence the size of a planet, steel-toed boots, and a junkyard dog attitude, Tinker is ready for anything—except her first kiss. "Wit and intelligence inform this off-beat, tongue-in-cheek fantasy . . . Furious action . . . good characterization . . . Buffy fans should find a lot to like in the book's resourceful heroine."—*Publishers Weekly*

WOLF WHO RULES
1-4165-2055-4 • $25.00 • HC

Tinker and her noble elven lover, Wolf Who Rules, find themselves stranded in the land of the elves—and half of human Pittsburgh with them. Wolf struggles to keep the peace between humans, oni dragons, the tengu trying to escape oni enslavement, and a horde of others, including his own elven brethren. For her part, Tinker strives to solve the mystery of the growing discontinuity that could unstabilize everybody's world—all the while trying to figure out just what being married means to an elven lord with a past hundreds of years long. . . .

❧❦❧

Desire

"Feel the heat. Be consumed in passion. Read a Desire."
—*New York Times* and *USA TODAY*
Bestselling Author Brenda Jackson

Look for all six
Special 30th Anniversary Collectors' Editions
from some of our most popular authors.

TEMPTED BY HER INNOCENT KISS
by Maya Banks
with "Never Too Late" by Brenda Jackson

BEHIND BOARDROOM DOORS
by Jennifer Lewis
with "The Royal Cousin's Revenge"
by Catherine Mann

THE PATERNITY PROPOSITION
by Merline Lovelace
with "The Sheik's Virgin" by Susan Mallery

A TOUCH OF PERSUASION
by Janice Maynard
with "A Lover's Touch" by Brenda Jackson

A FORBIDDEN AFFAIR
by Yvonne Lindsay
with "For Love or Money" by Elizabeth Bevarly

CAUGHT IN THE SPOTLIGHT
by Jules Bennett
with "Billionaire's Baby" by Leanne Banks

* * *

Find Harlequin Desire on Facebook,
www.facebook.com/HarlequinDesire,
or on Twitter, @desireeditors!

Dear Reader,

Happy 30th anniversary, Desire!

It is hard to believe that Desire is thirty years old. Time sure flies when you're having fun reading the hottest books in the publishing world. I can remember when I picked up my very first Desire and read it on my lunch break at work. I thought the same thing about it then that I do now. "Wow, this little red book is hot!"

Little did I know that thirty years later I would be one of those authors writing those "hot" stories. Doing so has been both an honor and a privilege. And I remain in the ranks of readers who often say, "There's nothing like a Desire."

I have written more than twenty stories for Desire, and I am honored to be sharing one of my short stories with you. "A Lover's Touch" is a very special story that takes place in one of my favorite places, Fernandina Beach, Florida. I hope you enjoy reading about Kendra Redding and Slate Landis and how lovers torn apart can find their way back to each other. The way isn't easy, and the path takes difficult turns at times, but True Love is at the end of the road.

Congratulations, Desire! Happy 30th anniversary! And may you have many, many more!

Brenda Jackson

JANICE MAYNARD

A TOUCH OF PERSUASION

ISBN-13: 978-0-373-73159-6

A TOUCH OF PERSUASION

Copyright © 2012 by Harlequin Books S.A.

The publisher acknowledges the copyright holders of the individual works as follows:

A TOUCH OF PERSUASION
Copyright © 2012 by Janice Maynard

A LOVER'S TOUCH
Copyright © 2002 by Harlequin Enterprises Limited
Brenda Jackson is acknowledged as the author of this work.

Recycling programs for this product may not exist in your area.

CONTENTS

Books by Janice Maynard

Harlequin Desire

The Billionaire's Borrowed Baby #2109
**Into His Private Domain* #2135
**A Touch of Persuasion* #2146

Silhouette Desire

The Secret Child & the Cowboy CEO #2040

*The Men of Wolff Mountain

Other titles by this author available in ebook format.

JANICE MAYNARD

came to writing early in life. When her short story *The Princess and the Robbers* won a red ribbon in her third-grade school arts fair, Janice was hooked. She holds a B.A. from Emory and Henry College and an M.A. from East Tennessee State University. In 2002 Janice left a fifteen-year career as an elementary teacher to pursue writing full-time. Her first love is creating sexy, character-driven, contemporary romance. She has written for Kensington and NAL, and now is so very happy to also be part of the Harlequin family—a lifelong dream, by the way!

Janice and her husband live in beautiful east Tennessee in the shadow of the Great Smoky Mountains. She loves to travel and enjoys using those experiences as settings for books.

Hearing from readers is one of the best perks of the job! Visit her website at www.janicemaynard.com or email her at JESM13@aol.com. And of course, don't forget Facebook (www.facebook.com/JaniceMaynardReaderPage). Find her on Twitter at www.twitter.com/JaniceMaynard and visit all the men of Wolff Mountain at www.wolffmountain.com.

Dear Reader,

I read my very first Harlequin Romance book in seventh grade, and I've been hooked ever since! What a delight it is to be part of celebrating Desire's 30th anniversary. The men and women you meet in series romance every month reflect all that is heartwarming and breathtaking about romantic commitment.

I hope you had a chance to meet part of the Wolff family in my January release, *Into His Private Domain*. Writing this series about The Men of Wolff Mountain has been the most fun I've ever had with a group of interesting, sometimes arrogant, but always fascinating siblings and their cousins!

Each hero is different, because each hero has his own demons to conquer. In *A Touch of Persuasion,* Kieran Wolff finds that his past has caught up with him. He must make difficult decisions, and all in the context of a family and home that he has run from for most of his adult life. I hope you enjoy his story—one of secrets, lost love and divided loyalties.

Don't forget to visit www.WolffMountain.com for bonus content about all things Wolff.

See you on the mountain!

Janice Maynard

For Deener

Your energy, enthusiasm and *joie de vivre*
challenge the rest of us to embrace life more fully.
I'm glad you are my friend!

* * *

THE MEN OF WOLFF MOUNTAIN:
Wealthy, mysterious and sexy…
they'll do anything for the women they love.

For an inside look at the wealthy, reclusive Wolff family,
visit WolffMountain.com! Bios, sneak peeks,
contests and more… See you on the mountain!

A TOUCH OF PERSUASION

Janice Maynard

One

Kieran stood on the front porch of the small, daffodil-yellow house and fisted his hands at his hips. In the distance, the sounds of a lawn mower mingled with childish shouts and laughter. The Santa Monica neighborhood where he had finally tracked down Olivia's address was firmly, pleasantly middle class.

He told himself not to jump to conclusions.

The article he'd clipped from one of his father's newspapers crackled in his pocket like the warning rattle of a venomous snake. He didn't need to take it out for a second read. The words were emblazoned in his brain.

Oscar winners Javier and Lolita Delgado threw a lavish party for their only grandchild's fifth birthday. The power couple, two of the few remaining MGM "Hollywood royals," commanded an A-list crowd that included a who's who of movie magic. Little "Cammie," the star of the show, enjoyed pony rides, inflatables and a lavish afternoon buffet that stopped just short of caviar. The child's mother, Olivia Delgado, stayed out of the limelight as is her custom, but was seen occasionally in the company of rising film star Jeremy Vargas.

Like a dog worrying a bone, his brain circled back to the stunning possibility. The timing was right. But that didn't mean he and Olivia had produced a child.

Anger, searing and unexpected, filled his chest, choking him with confusion and inexplicable remorse. He'd done his best to eradicate memories of Olivia. Their time together had been brief but spectacular. He'd loved her with a young man's reckless passion.

It couldn't be true, could it?

Though it wasn't his style to postpone confrontation, he extracted the damning blurb one more time and studied the grainy black-and-white photo. The child's face was in shadow, but he knew her family all too well.

Did Kieran have a daughter?

His hands trembled. He'd been home from the Far East less than seventy-two hours. Jet lag threatened to drag him under. Things hadn't ended well with Olivia, but surely she wouldn't have kept such a thing from him.

The shocking discovery in his father's office set all of Kieran's plans awry. Instead of enjoying a long overdue reunion with his extended family on their remote mountaintop in the Virginia Blue Ridge, he had said hello and goodbye with dizzying speed and hopped on another plane, this time to California.

Though he'd be loath to admit it, he was jittery and panicked. With a muttered curse, he reached out and jabbed the bell.

When the door swung open, he squared his shoulders and smiled grimly. "Hello, Olivia."

The woman facing him could have been a movie star

herself. She was quietly beautiful; a sweeter, gentler version of her mother's exotic, Latin looks. Warm, sun-kissed skin. A fall of mahogany hair. And huge brown eyes that at the moment were staring at him aghast.

He probably should be ashamed that he felt a jolt of satisfaction when she went white. The urge to hurt her was unsettling. "May I come in?"

She wet her lips with her tongue, a pulse throbbing visibly at the side of her neck. "Why are you here?" Her voice cracked, though she was clearly trying hard to appear unconcerned.

"I thought we could catch up…for old times' sake. Six years is a long span."

She didn't give an inch. Her hand clenched the edge of the door, and her body language shouted a resounding *no*. "I'm working," she said stiffly. "Now's not a good time."

He might have been amused by her futile attempt at resistance if he hadn't been so tightly wound. Her generous breasts filled out the front of a white scooped-neck top. It was almost impossible not to stare. Any healthy man between the ages of sixteen and seventy would be drawn to the lush sexuality of a body that, if anything, was more pulse-stopping than ever.

He pushed his way in, inexorably but gently. "Perhaps not for you. I happen to think it's a damn good time."

She stepped back instinctively as he moved past her into a neat, pleasantly furnished living room. Though it was warm and charming, not an item was out of place. No toys, no puzzles, no evidence of a child.

On the far wall, built-in bookcases housed a plethora of volumes ranging from popular fiction to history and art appreciation. Olivia had been a phenomenally intelligent student, an overachiever who possessed the unusual combination of creativity and solid business sense.

A single framed picture caught his eye. As he crossed the room for a closer look, he recognized the background. Olivia had written her graduate thesis about the life and work of famed children's author and illustrator Beatrix Potter. On one memorable weekend, Olivia had dragged Kieran with her to England's Lake District. After touring the house and grounds where the beloved character Peter Rabbit was born, Kieran had booked a room at a charming, romantic B and B.

Remembering the incredible, erotic days and nights he and Olivia had shared on a fluffy, down-filled mattress tightened his gut and made his sex stir. Had he ever felt that way since?

He'd tried so damned hard to forget her, to fulfill his duty as a Wolff son. A million times he had questioned the decisions he made back then. Leaving her without a word. Ending an affair that was too new…too fragile.

But he had ached for her. God, he had ached. For Olivia…elegant, funny, beautiful Olivia…with a body that could make a man weep for joy or pray that time stood still.

He shoved aside the arousing memory. There was a strong chance that this woman had perpetrated an unforgivable deception. He refused to let his good sense be impaired by nostalgia. And let's face it…this meeting should be taking place on neutral ground. Because without witnesses, there was a good chance he was going to wring Olivia's neck.

Again, he studied the photo. Olivia stood, smiling for the camera, holding the hand of a young child. Kieran's world shifted on its axis. He lost the ability to breathe. My God. The kid was a Wolff. No one could doubt it. The wide-spaced eyes, the wary expression, the uptilted chin.

He whirled to face his betrayer. "Where is she?" he asked hoarsely. "Where's my daughter?"

Two

Olivia called upon every parentally bestowed dramatic gene she possessed to appear mildly confused. "Your daughter?"

The man facing her scowled. "Don't screw with me, Olivia. I'm not in the mood." She saw his throat work. "I want to see her. Now."

Without waiting for an invitation, he bounded up the nearby stairs, Olivia scurrying in his wake with her heart pounding. She'd known on some level that this day would come. But in her mind, she'd always thought that *she* would be the one orchestrating the reunion.

Kieran Wolff had been her first and only lover. Back then she'd been a shy, lonely, bookish girl with her head in the clouds. He had shown her a world of intimate pleasures. And then he had disappeared.

Any guilt she was feeling about the current situation evaporated in a rush of remembered confusion and pain.

On the landing he paused, then strode through the open door of what was unmistakably a little girl's bedroom. A Disney princess canopy bed…huge movie posters from a variety of animated children's films…a pair of ballet slippers dangling from a hook on the door.

For a moment, Olivia was reluctantly moved by the anguish on his face, but she firmed her resolve. "I repeat the question. What are you doing here, *Kevin?*"

A dull flush of color rose from the neck of his open-collared shirt. Short-cropped hair a shade darker than hers feathered to a halt at his nape. He was dressed like a contemporary Indiana Jones, looking as if he might be ready to take off on his next adventure. Which was exactly why, among other reasons, she had never contacted him.

He faced her, his gaze an impossible-to-decipher mélange of emotions. "So you know who I am." It was more of a statement than a question.

She shrugged. "I do now. A few years ago I hired a private investigator to find out the truth about Kevin Wade. Imagine my surprise when I learned that no such man existed. At least not the one I knew."

"There were reasons, Olivia."

"I'm sure there were. But those reasons mean less than nothing to me at this point. I need you to leave my house before I call the police."

Her futile threat rolled off him unnoticed. He was intensely masculine, in control, his tall lanky frame lean and muscular without an ounce of fat. Amber eyes narrowed. "Maybe *I'll* call the police and discuss charges of kidnapping."

"Don't do this," she whispered, her throat tight and her eyes burning. "Not after all this time. Please." The entreaty was forced between numb lips. She owed him nothing. But he could destroy her life.

"Where is the child?" His unequivocal tone brooked no opposition.

"She's traveling with her grandparents in Europe." Not for anything would Olivia reveal the fact that Cammie's flight wasn't departing LAX for several hours.

"Tell me she's mine. Admit it." He grasped her shoulders and shook her, his hands warm, but firm. "No lies, Olivia."

She was close enough to smell him, to remember with painful clarity the warm scent of his skin after lovemaking. Her stomach quivered. At one time she had believed she would wake up beside this man for the rest of her life. Now, in retrospect, she winced for the naive, foolish innocent she had been.

In high heels she could have met him eye to eye, but barefoot, wearing nothing but shorts and a casual top, she was at a distinct disadvantage. She pushed hard against his broad chest. "Let me go, you Neanderthal. You have no right to come here and push me around."

He released her abruptly. "I want the truth, damn it. Tell me."

"You wouldn't know the truth if it bit you in the ass. Go home, *Kevin Wade*."

Her deliberate taunt increased the fury bracketing his mouth with lines of stress. "We need to talk," he said as he glanced at his watch. "I have a conference call I can't miss in thirty minutes, so you have a choice. Tonight at my hotel. Or tomorrow in a room with two lawyers. Your call. But the way I'm feeling, a public forum might be the best option."

The sinking sensation in her belly told her that he would not give up easily. "I don't have anything to say to you," she said, her bravado forced at best.

He stared her down, his piercing golden eyes seeming to probe right through her to get at the truth. "Then I'll do all the talking."

Olivia watched, stunned, while he departed as quickly as he had come. She trailed after him, ready to slam the front door at the earliest opportunity, forcefully closing the door to the past. He paused on the porch. "I'll send a driver for you at six," he said bluntly. "Don't be late."

When he drove away, her legs gave out beneath her. She sank into a chair, her whole body shaking. Dear God. What was she going to do? She was a terrible liar, but she dared not tell him the truth. Kieran Wolff—she still had trouble thinking of him by that name—was not the laughing young man she remembered from their graduate days at Oxford.

His skin was deeply tanned, and sun lines at the corners of his eyes gave testament to the hours he now spent outdoors. He was as lethal and predatory as the sleek cats that inhabited the jungles he frequented. The man who helped dig wells in remote villages and who built and rebuilt bridges and buildings in war-torn countries was hard as glass.

She shuddered, remembering the implacable demand in his gaze. Would she be able to withstand his interrogation?

But there were more immediate details to address. Picking up the phone, she dialed the mother of Cammie's favorite playmate. The two families' backyards adjoined, and Cammie was spending part of the afternoon with her friend. Olivia had been terrified that Cammie would come home while Kieran was in the house.

Twenty minutes later, Olivia watched her daughter labor over a thank-you picture for her grandparents. Despite Olivia's reservations about the recent birthday party, the worst that had happened to her precocious offspring was the almost inevitable spilled punch on a five-hundred-dollar party dress...and a sunburned nose.

The dress had been a gift from Lolita. Olivia warned her mother that the exquisite frock was highly inappropriate for a child's birthday party. But as always, Lolo, as she liked to be called by her granddaughter, ignored Olivia's wishes and bought the dress, anyway.

Cammie frowned at a smudge in the corner of the drawing. "I need some more paper," she said, close to pouting. "This one's all messed up."

"It's fine, sweetheart. You've done a great job." At five, Cammie was already a perfectionist. Olivia worried about her intensity.

"I have to start over."

Sensing a full-blown tantrum in the offing, Olivia sighed and produced another sheet of clean white paper. Sometimes it was easier to avoid confrontation, especially over something so minor. Did all single mothers worry that they were ruining their children forever?

If Cammie had a father in her life, would she be less highly strung? More able to take things in stride?

Olivia's stomach pitched. She wouldn't think of Kieran right now. Not until Cammie was safely away.

She would miss her baby while Cammie was gone. The hours of reading storybooks. The fun baking experiments. The leisurely walks around the neighborhood in the evenings. The silly bathtub bubble fights. They were a family of two. A completely normal family.

Was she trying to convince herself or someone else?

She desperately wanted for Cammie the emotional security Olivia had never known as a child. The simple pleasure of hugs and homework. Of kisses and kites.

Olivia had been raised for the most part by a series of well-meaning nannies and tutors. She had learned early on that expensive Parisian dolls were supposed to make up for long absences during which her parents ignored her. The stereotypical poor little rich kid. With a closet full of expensive and often inappropriate toys, and a bruised heart.

Olivia remembered her own childish tantrums when her parents didn't bring presents she wanted. Thinking back on her egocentric younger self made her wince. Thank heavens she had outgrown that phase.

Maturity and a sense of perspective enabled her to be glad that her parents were far more invested in Cammie's life than they had ever been in their own daughter's. Perhaps grandparenthood had changed them.

Olivia's determination to live a solidly middle class life baffled Lolita and Javier, and they did their best to thwart her at every turn, genuinely convinced that money was meant to be spent.

The weekend party was an example of the lifestyle Olivia had tried so hard to escape. It wasn't good for a child to understand that she could have anything she wanted. Even if Olivia died penniless—and that wasn't likely—Cammie stood to inherit millions of dollars from her grandparents.

Money spoiled people. Olivia knew that firsthand. Growing up in Hollywood was a lesson in overindulgence and narcissism.

Cammie finally smiled, satisfied with her second attempt. "I wish Lolo had a refrigerator. My friend Aya, at preschool, says her nana hangs stuff on the front of the refrigerator."

Olivia smiled at her daughter's bent head. *Lolo* owned several refrigerators, all in different kitchens spread from L.A. to New York to Paris. But it was doubtful she ever opened one, much less decorated any of them with Cammie's artwork. Lolita Delgado had "people" to deal with that. In fact, she had an entourage to handle every detail of her tempestuous life.

"Lolo will love your drawing, Cammie, and so will Jojo." Olivia's father, Javier, wasn't crazy about his nickname, but he doted on his granddaughter, probably—in addition to the ties of blood—because she gave him what he craved the most. Unrestrained adoration.

Cammie bounced to her feet. "I'm gonna get my backpack. They'll be here in a minute."

"Slow down, baby…." But it was too late. Cammie ran at her usual pace up the stairs, determined to be ready and waiting by the door when the limo arrived. Olivia's parents were taking Cammie to Euro Disney for a few days in conjunction with a film award they were both receiving in Florence.

Olivia had argued that the trip was too much on the heels of the over-the-top birthday party, but in the end she had been unable to hold out against Cammie's beseeching eyes and tight hugs. The two adults and one child, when teamed against Olivia, made a formidable opponent.

Cammie reappeared, backpack in hand. Olivia had her suitcase ready. "Promise me you'll be good for your grandparents."

Cammie rolled her eyes in a manner far too advanced for her years. "You always say that."

"And I always mean it."

The doorbell rang. Cammie's screech nearly peeled the paint from the walls. "Bye, Mommy."

Olivia followed her out to the car. In the flurry of activity over getting one excited five-year-old settled in the vehicle, Lolita and Javier managed to appear both pleased and sophisticated as they absorbed their granddaughter's enthusiasm.

Olivia gave her mother a hug, careful not to rumple her vintage Chanel suit. "Please don't spoil her." For one fleeting second, Olivia wanted to share the truth about Kieran with her parents. To beg for guidance. She had never divulged a single detail about her daughter's parentage to anyone.

But the moment passed when Javier bussed his daughter's cheek with a wide grin. "It's what we do best, Olivia."

The house was silent in the aftermath of the exodus. Without the distraction of Cammie, the evening with Kieran loomed menacingly. Olivia wandered from room to room, too restless to work. Cammie would be going to kindergarten very soon. Olivia had mixed emotions about the prospect. She knew that her highly intelligent daughter would thrive in an academic environment and that the socialization skills she acquired with children her own age would be very important.

But it had been just the two of them for so long.

And now Kieran seemed poised to upset the apple cart.

When Olivia felt her eyes sting, she made a concerted effort to shake off the maudlin mood. Life was good. Her days were filled with family, a job she adored and a cadre of close, trusted friends. Kieran wasn't part of the package. And she was glad. She had made the right choice in protecting Cammie from his selfishness.

And she would continue to do so.

The remainder of the day was a total loss. She had a series of watercolors due for her book publisher in less than two weeks, but putting the finishing touches on the last picture in the set was more than she could handle today. She loved her work as a children's illustrator, and it gave her flexibility to spend lots of time with Cammie.

But the concentration required for her best efforts was beyond her right now. Instead, she prowled her small house, unable to stem the tide of memories.

They had met as expatriate grad students at a traditional English country house party hosted by mutual friends. With only six weeks of the term left, each knew the relationship had a preordained end. But in Olivia's case, with stars in her eyes and a heart that was head-over-heels in lust with the handsome, charismatic Kevin Wade, she'd spun fairy tales of continuing their affair back in the U.S.

It hadn't quite turned out that way. During the final days of exam week, "Kevin" had simply disappeared with nothing more than a brief note to say goodbye. Thinking about that terrible time made Olivia's stomach churn with nausea. Her fledgling love had morphed into hate, and she'd done her best to turn her back on any memory of the boy who broke her heart. And fathered her child.

After a quick shower, she stared at her reflection in the mirror. Even if Olivia wanted to follow in her mother's footsteps, she would never have stood a chance in Hollywood. She was twenty pounds too heavy, and though today's pool of actresses was more diverse, many directors still preferred willowy blondes. Olivia was neither.

By the time the limo pulled up in front of her house, Olivia was a wreck. But since birth, she'd been taught "the show must go on" mantra, and to the world, Olivia Delgado was unflappable. For six years, she had spun lies to protect her daughter, to make a life so unexceptionable that the tabloids had long since left her alone.

An unwed mother in Hollywood was boring news. As long as no one discovered the father was a Wolff.

Tonight Olivia would be no less discreet.

She had dressed to play a part. Confident and chic were the qualities she planned to convey with her taupe linen tank dress and coral sandals. Though she had not inherited an iota of her parents' love for acting, she had inevitably learned from them along the way what it meant to present a serene face to the world, no matter if your life was in ruins.

Kieran Wolff's hotel was tucked away in a quiet back street of Santa Monica. Exclusive, discreet and no doubt wildly expensive, it catered to those whose utmost wish was privacy. The manager, himself, actually escorted Olivia to the fifth floor suite.

After that, she was left to stand alone at the door. Instead of knocking, she took a few seconds to contemplate fleeing the country. Cammie was everything to her, and the prospect of losing her child was impossible to imagine.

But such thoughts were defeatist. Though she might not be able to go toe-to-toe with the Wolff empire when it came to bank accounts, Olivia did have considerable financial means at her disposal. In a legal battle, she could hold her own. And judges often sided with a mother, particularly in this situation.

She had no notion of what awaited her on the other side of the door, but she wouldn't go down without a fight. Kieran Wolff didn't deserve to be a father. And if it came to that, she would tell him so.

Deliberately taking a moment to shore up her nerve, she rapped sharply at the door and took a deep breath.

Kieran had worn a trail in the carpet by the time his reluctant guest arrived. When he yanked open the door and saw her standing in the vestibule, his gut pitched and tightened. God, she was gorgeous. Every male hormone he possessed stood up and saluted. A man would have to be almost dead not to respond to her inherent sexuality.

Like the pin-up girls of the 1940s, with legs that went on forever, breasts that were real and plenty of feminine curves right where they should be, Olivia Delgado was a vivid, honey-skinned fantasy.

But today wasn't about appeasing the hunger in his gut, even if he *had* been celibate during a recent, hellacious foray into the wilds of Thailand. Bugs, abysmal weather and local politics had complicated his life enormously. He'd been more than ready to return to central Virginia and reconnect with his family. Not that he ever stayed very long, but still…that closely guarded mountain in the Blue Ridge was the only place he called home.

With an effort, he recalled his wayward thoughts. "Come in, Olivia. I've ordered dinner. It should be delivered any moment now."

She slipped past him in a cloud of Chanel No. 5, making him wonder if she had worn the evocative scent on purpose. In the old days, she had often come to his bed wearing nothing but a long strand of pearls and that same perfume.

He waited for her to be seated on the love seat and then took an armchair for himself a few feet away. In the intervening hours, he'd rehearsed how this would go. Having her here, on somewhat public turf, seemed like a good idea. He was determined to keep his cool, no matter the provocation.

They faced off in silence for at least a minute. When he realized she wasn't going to crack, he sighed. "Surely you can't deny it, Olivia. You were a virgin when we met. I can do the math. Your daughter is mine."

Her eyes flashed. "My daughter is none of your business. You may have introduced me to sex, but there have been plenty of men since."

"Liar. Name one."

Her jaw dropped. "Um…"

He chuckled, feeling the first hint of amusement he'd had since he saw the article about the party. Olivia might look like a woman of immense sophistication and experience, but he'd bet his last dime that she was still the sweet, down-to-earth girl he'd known back at university, completely unaware of her stunning beauty.

"Show me her birth certificate."

Her chin lifted. "Don't be ridiculous. I don't carry it around in my purse."

"But you probably have it at the house, right? In order to register her for kindergarten?"

She nibbled her bottom lip. "Well, I…"

Thank God she was a lousy liar. "Whose name is on the birth certificate, Olivia? You might as well tell me. You know I can find out."

Suddenly she looked neither sweet nor innocent. "Kevin Wade. Is that what you wanted to hear?"

The sharp pain in his chest took his breath away. "Kevin Wade…"

"Exactly. So you can see that no judge would think you have any rights in this instance at all." Her eyes were cold, and even that realization was painful. The Olivia he had known smiled constantly, her joie de vivre captivating and so very seductive.

Now her demeanor was icy.

"You put my name on her birth certificate," he croaked. It kept coming back to that. Kevin Wade was a father. Kieran had a daughter.

"Correction," she said with a flat intonation that disguised any emotion. "In the hospital, when I gave birth to my daughter, I listed a fictional name for her father. It had nothing to do with you."

He clamped down on his frustration, acknowledging that he was getting nowhere with this approach. Unable to sit any longer, he sprang to his feet and paced, pausing at the windows to look out at the ocean in the far distance. One summer he had lived for six weeks on a houseboat in Bali. It was the freest he had ever felt, the most relaxed.

Too bad life wasn't always so easy.

Olivia continued to sit in stubborn silence, so he kept his back to her. "When you hired an investigator, what did you find out about me?"

After several seconds of silence, she spoke. "That your

real name is Kieran Wolff. You lost your mother and aunt to a violent abduction and shooting when you were small. Your father and uncle raised you and your siblings and cousins in seclusion, because they were afraid of another kidnapping attempt."

He faced her, brooding. "Will you listen to my side of the story?" he asked quietly.

Olivia's hands were clenched together in her lap, her posture so rigid she seemed in danger of shattering into a million pieces. Though she hid it well, he could sense her agitation. At one time he had been attuned to her every thought and desire.

He swallowed, painfully aware that a king-size bed lay just on the other side of the door. The intensity of the desire he felt for her was shocking. As was the need for her to understand and forgive him. He was culpable for his sins in the past, no doubt about it. But that didn't excuse Olivia for hiding the existence of his child, his blood.

"Will you listen?" he asked again.

She nodded slowly, eyes downcast.

With a prayer for patience, he crossed the expanse of expensive carpet to sit beside her, hip to hip. She froze, inching back into her corner.

"Look at me, Olivia." He took her chin in his hand with a gentle grasp, lifting it until her gaze met his. "I'm not the enemy," he swore. "All I need is for you to be honest with me. And I'll try my damnedest to do the same."

Her chocolate-brown eyes were shiny with tears, but she blinked them back, giving him a second terse nod. He tucked a stray strand of hair behind her ear and forced himself to release her. Touching her was a luxury he couldn't afford at the moment.

"Okay, then." He was more a man of action than of words. But if he was fighting for his daughter, he would use any means necessary, even if that meant revealing truths he'd rather not expose.

He leaned forward, elbows on his knees, and dropped his head in his hands. "You were important to me, Olivia."

A slight *humph* was her only response. Was that skepticism or denial or maybe both?

"It's true," he insisted. "I'd been with a lot of girls before I met you, but you were different."

Dead silence.

"You made me laugh even when I wanted you so badly, I ached. I never meant to hurt you. But I had made a vow to my father."

"Of course you had."

She could give lessons in sarcasm.

"Sneer if you like, but the vow was real. My brothers and cousins and I swore to my father and my uncle that if they would let us go off to college without bodyguards, we would use assumed names and never tell *anyone* who we really were."

"So it was okay to sleep with me, but you couldn't share with me something as simple as the truth about your real name. Charming."

This time it was Olivia who jumped to her feet and paced. He sat back and stared at her, tracking the gentle sway of her hips as she crisscrossed the room. "I was going to tell you," he insisted. "But I had to get my father's permission. And before I could do that, he had a heart attack. That's when I left England so suddenly."

She wrapped her arms around her waist. "Leaving behind a lovely eight-word note. *Dear Olivia, I have to go home. Sorry.*"

He winced. "I was in a hurry."

"Do you have any clue at all how humiliated I was when I went to the Dean's office to beg for information about you and was told that Kevin Wade was no longer enrolled? And they were not allowed to give out any information as to your whereabouts because of privacy rules? God, I was embarrassed. And then I was mad at myself for being such a credulous fool."

"You weren't a fool," he said automatically, mentally replaying her words and for the first time realizing what he had put her through. "I'm sorry."

She kicked the leg of the coffee table, revealing a hint of her mother's flamboyant temper. "Sorry doesn't explain why suddenly neither your cell phone nor your email address worked when I tried to reach you."

"They were school accounts. My exams were over. I knew I wasn't coming back, so I let them go inactive, because I thought it was the easiest way to make a clean break."

"If you're trying to make a case for yourself, you're failing miserably."

"I never wanted to hurt you," he insisted.

"They call them clichés for a reason." The careful veil she'd kept over her emotions had shredded, and now he was privy to the pure, clean burn of her anger.

"Things were crazy at home," he said wearily. "I stayed at the hospital round-the-clock for a week. Then when Dad was released, he was extremely depressed. My brother Jacob and I had to entertain him, read to him, listen to music with him. I barely had a thought to myself."

She nodded slowly. "I get it, Kieran." He watched her frown as she rolled the last word on her tongue. "I was a temporary girlfriend. Too bad I was so naive. I didn't realize for a few weeks that I had been dumped. I kept making excuses for you, believing—despite the evidence to the contrary— that we shared something special."

"We did, damn it."

"But not special enough for you to pick up the phone and make a call. And you had to know I was back home in California. Yet you didn't even bother. I should thank you, really. That experience taught me a lot. I grew up fast. You were a horny young man. I was easy pickings. So if that's all, I'm out of here. I absolve you of any guilt."

Fortunately for Kieran, the arrival of dinner halted Olivia's headlong progress to the door. She was forced to cool her heels while the waiter rolled a small table in front of the picture window and smiled as Kieran tipped him generously. When the man departed, the amazing smells wafting from the collection of covered dishes won Olivia over, despite Kieran's botched attempts to deal with their past.

Neither of them spoke a word for fifteen minutes as they devoured grilled swordfish with mango salsa and spinach salad.

Kieran realized he'd gotten off track. They were supposed to be talking about why Olivia had hidden the existence of his daughter. Instead, Kieran had ended up in a defensive position. Time for a new game plan.

He ate a couple of bites of melon sorbet, wiped his mouth with a snowy linen napkin and leaned back in his chair. "I may have been a jerk," he said bluntly, "but that doesn't explain why you never told me I had a daughter. Your turn in the hot seat, Olivia."

Three

Olivia choked on a sliced almond and had to wash it down with a long gulp of water. The Wolff family was far more powerful than even Olivia's world-famous parents. If the truth came out, she knew the Wolff patriarchs might help Kieran take Cammie. And she couldn't allow that. "You don't have a daughter," she said calmly, her voice hoarse from coughing. Hearing Kieran's explanation of why he had left England so suddenly had done nothing to alleviate her fears. "I do."

Kieran scowled. Any attempts he might have made to appease her were derailed by his obvious dislike of having his wishes thwarted. "I'll lock you in here with me if I have to," he said, daring her to challenge his ability to do so.

"And how would that solve anything?"

Suddenly her cell phone rang. With a wince for the unfortunate timing, she stood up. "Excuse me. I need to take this."

Kieran made no move to give her privacy, so she turned her back on him and moved to the far side of the room. Tapping the screen of her phone to answer, she smiled. "Hey, sweetheart. Are you in New York?"

The brief conversation ended with Olivia's mother on the other end promising to make Cammie sleep on the flight over to Paris. Olivia's daughter had flown internationally several times, but she wasn't so blasé about jet travel that she would simply nod off. Olivia had packed several of the child's bedtime books in her carry-on, hoping that a semi-familiar routine would do the trick.

When Olivia hung up and turned around, Kieran was scowling. "I thought you said she was in Europe."

She shrugged. "That's their ultimate destination."

"So this morning when I came to your house, where was she?"

"At the neighbor's."

"Damn you, Olivia."

It was her turn to frown in exasperation. "What would you have done if I had told you, Kieran? Made a dramatic run through the yard calling her name? My daughter is now traveling with her grandparents. That's all you need to know."

"When will they be back?"

"A week…ten days… My mother isn't crazy about abiding by schedules."

His scowl blackened. "Tell me she's my daughter."

Her stomach flipped once, hard, but she held on to her composure by a thread. "Go to hell."

Abruptly he shoved back his chair and went to the mini bar to pour himself a Scotch, downing the contents with one quick toss of his head. His throat was tanned like the rest of him, and the tantalizing glimpse of his chest at the opening of his shirt struck Olivia as unbearably erotic.

Sensing her own foray into the quicksand of nostalgia, she attacked. "If you want to have children someday, you should probably work on those alcoholic tendencies."

"I'm not an alcoholic, though God knows you could drive a man to drink." He ran a hand through his hair, rumpling it into disarray. She saw for the first time that he was exhausted, probably running on nothing but adrenaline.

"You don't even own a house," she blurted out.

Confusion etched his face. "Excuse me?"

"A house," she reiterated. "Most people who want a family start with a house and a white picket fence. All you do is travel the globe. What are you afraid of? Getting stuck in one place for too long?"

Her random shot hit its mark.

"Maybe," he muttered, his expression bleak. "My brothers have been begging me to come home for a long time now. But I'm not sure I know how."

"Then I think you should leave," she said calmly. "Get back on a plane and go save the world. No one needs you here."

"You didn't used to be so callous." His expression was sober. Regretful. And his cat eyes watched her every move as if he were stalking prey.

"I'm simply being realistic. Even if I *had* given birth to a child that was yours, what makes you think you have what it takes to be a father? Parenting is about being *present*. That's not really your forte, now is it?"

She heard the cruel words tumbling from her lips and couldn't stop them. If she could drive him away in anger, he would go and leave Olivia to raise her daughter in peace.

"I'm here now," he said quietly, his control making her ashamed of her outburst. "Cammie is my daughter, I want to get to know her."

Olivia's heart stopped. Hearing him say her daughter's

name did something odd to her heart. "How exactly do you mean that?"

"Let me stay here with you for a little while."

"Absolutely not." She shivered, imagining his big body in her guest bed...a few feet down the hall from hers.

"Then I want the two of you to come to Wolff Mountain with me for the summer and meet my family. This afternoon I talked to the CEO of my foundation, Bridge to the Future. He's lining up people to take my place until early September."

"Thank you for the invitation," she said politely. "But we can't. Perhaps some other time." *When hell freezes over.* If she let Cammie go anywhere near the Wolff family compound, Olivia stood a chance of never seeing her daughter again. Kieran's relatives made up a tight familial unit, and if they got wind that another wolf had been born into the pack, Olivia feared that her status as Cammie's mother would carry little weight.

He shoved his hands in his pockets. "At the risk of sounding like one of your father's action hero characters, I'm warning you. We can do this the easy way or the hard way. I can get a court order for a DNA sample."

Olivia shivered inwardly as she felt her options narrowing. She could buy some time by stonewalling, but ultimately, the Wolff would prevail. "My daughter and I have lives, Kieran. It's unrealistic of you to expect us to visit strangers for no other reason than your sudden odd conviction that you are a daddy."

"Your work is portable. Cammie doesn't start school until the fall. I'll make a deal with you. I won't claim her as mine.... I won't even tell my family what I know to be true. But in exchange, you agree to let me see her as much as possible in the next few weeks."

"She's not yours." The words were beginning to sound weak, even to her ears.

He came toward her. The silent intensity of his stare was hypnotic. When they were almost touching, chest to chest, he put his hands on her shoulders, the warmth of his touch searing her skin even through a layer of fabric. "Don't be afraid of me, Olivia."

His mouth moved over hers, light as a whisper, teasing, coaxing. The fact that her knees lost their starch should have made her angry, but there was no room for negative emotion in that moment. For no other reason than pleasure, her lips moved under his. Seeking. Responding.

He made an inarticulate murmur that encompassed surprise and masculine satisfaction. Then the kiss deepened.

His leg moved between her thighs as he drew her closer. "You haven't changed," he said roughly. "I've dreamed about you over the years. On nights when I couldn't sleep. And remembered you just like this. God, you're sweet."

She felt the press of his heavy erection against her belly, and everything inside her went liquid with drugged delight. How long had it been? How long? No longer a responsible mother, she was once again a giddy young woman, desperate for her lover's touch.

Unbidden, the memories came flooding back….

"You're a virgin?"

Kevin's shock worried her. Surely he wouldn't abandon her now. Not when they were naked and tangled in her bed. "Does it matter? I want this, Kevin. I really do. I want you."

He sat up beside her, magnificently nude, his expression troubled. "I haven't ever done it with a virgin. You're twenty-two, Olivia. For God's sake. I had no idea."

With a confidence that surprised her, she laid a hand on his hard, hairy thigh, her fingertips almost brushing his thick penis. "I told you I had led a sheltered life. Why do you think I wanted to cross an ocean to finish my school-ing? I'm tired of living in a cocoon. Make love to me, Kevin. Please."

His hunger, coupled with her entreaty, defeated him. Groaning like a man tormented on a rack, he moved between her legs once more, his erect shaft nudging eagerly at her entrance. Braced on his forearms, he leaned down to kiss her...hard. "I know I'll hurt you. I'm sorry."

"No apology needed," she whispered, sensing the momentous turning point in her life. "I need this. I need you."

He pushed forward an inch, and she braced instinctively against the sharp sting of pain.

"Easy," he whispered, his beautiful eyes alight with tenderness. "Relax, Olivia."

She tried to do as he asked, but he was fully aroused, and she was so tight. His whole big body trembled violently, and she wanted to cry at the beauty of it. Another inch. Another gasped cry to be swallowed up in his wild kiss.

She felt torn asunder, violated, but in the best possible way. Never again would her body be hers. Kevin claimed it, claimed her.

When he was fully seated, tears rolled silently down her cheeks, wetting her hair, sliding into her ears.

He rested his forehead on hers. "Was it that bad?" he asked, clearly striving for humor, but unable to hide his distress over what had transpired.

"Try moving," she said breathlessly. "I think I can handle it."

"Holy hell." His discomfiture almost elicited a giggle, but when he followed her naive suggestion, humor fled. Slowly, inexorably, her untried body learned his rhythm. Deep inside her a tiny flame flickered to life.

She moaned, arching her back and driving him deeper on a down thrust. It was easier now, and far more exciting.

Her long legs wrapped around his waist. Skin damp with exertion, they devoured each other, desperately trying to get closer still.

Kevin went rigid and cursed, closing his eyes and groaning as he climaxed inside her. She was taking the pill, and he had been tested recently, so no condom came between them.

As he slumped on top of her, she wrinkled her nose in disappointment. She had been so close to something spectacular. But the feeling faded. Taking its place was a warmth and satisfaction that she had been able to give him pleasure.

He rolled to his side. "Did you come?"

She nibbled her lip. Would it hurt to lie? It wasn't a habit she wanted to start. "Not exactly. But I know it takes practice. Don't worry about it...really."

He chuckled, yawning and stretching. "For a novice, you're pretty damned wonderful. Hold still, baby, and let's finish this."

Without ceremony, he put his hand between her legs and touched her. She flinched, still not quite comfortable with this level of intimacy, and also feeling tender and sore. His fingers were gentle, finding a certain spot and rubbing lightly. Her hips came off the bed.

"Um, Kevin?"

"What, honey?"

"You don't have to do this. To tell you the truth, I'm feeling sort of embarrassed."

"Why?" The strum of his fingers picked up tempo.

"Well, you're...um...finished, and it's a little weird now." *Her voice caught in her throat. "That's enough. I feel good. Really."*

He entered her with two fingers and bit the side of her neck. "How about now?"

Her shriek could have peeled paint off the walls, but she

*was too far gone to care. The attention she gave herself now
and again when the lights were out barely held a candle to
this maelstrom. Kevin gave no quarter, stroking her firmly
until her orgasm crested, exploded and winnowed away,
leaving her spent in his arms.*

She cried again.

He made fun of her with gentle humor.

*Then they turned out the lights and spent their first night
together, wrapped in each other's arms.*

Kieran cupped her breast with his hand, and just like
that, Olivia was fully in the present. What shocked her back
to reality was the incredible realization that she was a hairs-
breadth away from letting him have her again. No protest.
No discussion. Simply mindless pleasure.

And while that may have been okay six years ago, now
she had a daughter to think about. Sexual reminiscing with
Kieran Wolff was not only self-destructive and stupid, but
also detrimental to her role as a parent.

"Enough," she said hoarsely, tearing herself from his
embrace and warding him off with a hand when he would
have dragged her back for another kiss. "I mean it," she said.
"We're not doing this. You can't seduce me into agreeing to
your terms."

"Give us both more credit than that, Olivia. What happened just now proves that we've always had chemistry...
and still do."

"If you're expecting to pick up where we left off, you're
destined for disappointment."

"Is that so? From what I could tell, what just happened
was a two-way street."

"It's late," she said abruptly. "I have to go."

He crossed his arms over his chest and leaned a hip
against the back of the sofa, his eyes narrowed. From the
look of him, no one would guess that sixty seconds ago he'd

been kissing her senseless. "You can't run from me, Olivia. Closing your eyes and thinking about Kansas is a child's game. I want some answers."

Her phone chimed to signal a text, and she pulled it from her pocket, glancing at it automatically. Her mother's words chilled her blood.

Kieran touched her shoulder as she sank to a seat. "What is it? What's wrong?"

"The flight was delayed. My mother has a stalker fan, and he showed up at the airport."

He squatted beside her, his mere presence lending comfort. "What happened?"

"When he tried to burst through a checkpoint, calling her name, TSA arrested him."

He frowned. "I don't like the thought of Cammie being exposed to something like that."

"First of all, my parents take security very seriously, and second of all, this is none of your business. I'm her mother. It's up to me to keep her safe."

From his vantage point crouched at her side, their gazes collided. "You don't have to do this alone anymore," he said quietly, the words like a vow. "Any child with my blood running in her veins has the protection of the entire Wolff clan at her back."

She swallowed hard, near tears, missing her daughter and feeling out of her depth. "A child is not a belonging. She's her own person. Even if she *is* only five."

"You think I don't know that? I was a year younger than she is now when my mother was killed." He sprang to his feet, pacing once more. "My brother Gareth was the only one of us really old enough to understand and remember the details, but I lived it, and those terrible days are buried somewhere in my psyche…the confusion, the loneliness, the knowledge that my world was never going to be the same.

No child should lose a parent, Olivia, even if she thinks she has only one."

Guilt reached inside her chest and squeezed hard. Kieran Wolff had hurt her badly. Did she have the right to make her daughter vulnerable to his undeniable charm? Conversely, was she wrong to deny her child a father, even an absentee one? The same questions had haunted her for half a decade.

Her head ached. "We'll visit for a long weekend," she said, her voice tight. "As soon as Cammie gets back from Europe. But that's all it will be. All it will ever be. And if you break your word to me, I'll take her away and never speak to you again."

His lips quirked in a half smile. "Mama Bear protecting her cub. I like seeing you in this maternal role, Olivia. It suits you."

She gathered her purse and the light sweater she'd brought with her. "No one and nothing in this world means more to me than Cammie. And you'd do well to remember that. Good night, Kieran. Pleasant dreams."

He followed her to the door, having the temerity to press another hard kiss to her lips before allowing her to leave. "I'll dream," he said, brushing her cheek with the back of a hand. "But I have a feeling that pleasant won't be the right word for it."

Four

Kieran had never liked waiting. The ten days that elapsed between his confrontation with Olivia and her arrival at Wolff Mountain were interminable. Every moment of every day he imagined a dozen excuses she could make to keep from showing up.

As an adolescent he'd imagined the walls of the monstrous house closing in on him, as if he were trapped in a castle dungeon. Even now, his homecoming was tainted with confusion. Mostly he felt the agitation of being stuck in one place. He liked the freedom of the open road.

But if he were honest with himself, he had to admit that Wolff Mountain drew him home time and again despite his conflicted feelings about its past…his past.

Having his brothers close went a long way toward passing the time. They shared meals at the "big house," and Kieran was introduced to Gracie, Gareth's new wife.

Kieran's older brother was happier than Kieran had seen him in years, and it was clear that he adored his bride.

In the mornings, Kieran hiked the mountain trails with Gareth, and after lunch every day, he helped Jacob add on a new room to the doc's already state-of-the-art clinic. Kieran welcomed the physical exertion. Only by pushing himself to the point of exhaustion was he able to sleep at night. And even then he dreamed... God, he dreamed.

Olivia...in his bed, beneath him, her fabulous mane of hair spread across the pillows like a river of molten chocolate shot with gold. Her honey smooth skin bare-ass naked, waiting for him to touch every inch of it with his lips, his tongue, his ragged breath...

He'd dreamed of her before... At least in the beginning. When he first lost her. But the pain of doing so had ultimately led him to pretend she didn't exist. It was the only way he had survived.

But now, knowing that he and Olivia would soon be sharing a roof, the chains he'd used to bind up his memories shattered. He'd taken more cold showers in the past week than he had as a hormone-driven teen. And in the darkest hours of the night, he wondered with no small amount of guilt if he was using his own daughter as leverage to spend more time with the woman he'd never been able to forget.

Olivia wasn't coming here to be his lover. She'd made that crystal clear. Her single concession was to allow Cammie a visit. And that was only because Kieran threatened court proceedings.

He still felt bad about that, but Olivia's stubbornness infuriated him. Why couldn't she just admit that in the short time they were together, they created a life? He knew the truth in his gut, but he needed Olivia to be honest...to tell him face-to-face. Until he heard her say the words out loud, he wouldn't be satisfied.

With Cammie as his child, everything changed. It meant that when he was laboring in some godforsaken corner of the world, he could dream about returning home to someone who was his, a child who would love him and hug his neck.

Kieran's family loved him, but coming home to Wolff Mountain was painful. So painful, in fact, that he made it back to the States only a couple of times a year. No matter how hard he tried, the memories of his mother, though vague and indistinct, permeated the air here. And those same memories reminded him of how helpless he had felt when she died.

Seeing his father and uncle and brothers and cousins crying had left an indelible mark on an impressionable four-year-old. Until then, he'd believed that men never cried, especially not his big, gruff daddy. Kieran had been confused, and fearful, and so desperate to make everything better.

The day of the funeral he pretended to take a nap while the adults were gone. While the nanny was on the phone with her boyfriend, Kieran slipped into his mother's bedroom and ransacked the large walk-in closet that housed her clothes. He tugged at the hems of blouses and dresses and evening gowns, ripping them from the hangers and piling them up haphazardly until he had a small mountain.

The fabrics smelled like her. With tears streaming down his face, he climbed atop his makeshift bed, curled into a ball of misery and fell asleep, his thumb tucked in his mouth.

Kieran inhaled sharply, realizing that he had allowed himself the bittersweet, two-edged sword of memory. That's why he came home so seldom. In another hemisphere he could pretend that his life was normal. That it had always been normal.

Returning to Wolff Mountain always pulled the Band-Aid off a wound that had never healed cleanly. He remembered being discovered on that terrible funeral day and escorted out of his parents' bedroom. No one chastised him. No one took him to task for what he had done. But three days later when he worked up the courage to once again sneak into his mother's closet, every trace of her was gone… as if she had never existed. Even the hangers had been removed.

That day he'd cried again, huddled in a ball in the corner of the bare closet. And this time, there was no comfort to be found. His world had shredded around him, leaving nothing but uncertainty and bleakness. He hated the stomach-hollowing feelings and the sensation of doom.

No child should ever have to feel abandoned, and sadly, Kieran and his brothers had been emotional orphans when their father fell apart in the wake of Laura Wolff's death. It took Victor Wolff literally years to recover, and by then, the damage was done. The boys loved their father, but they had become closed off to softer emotions.

Kieran cursed and kicked at a pile of loose gravel in the driveway. *Was* Cammie his daughter? A tiny shred of doubt remained. He found it almost impossible to believe that Olivia had gone from his bed to another man's so quickly. But he had hurt her badly…and she might have done it out of spite.

The girl in the photograph at Olivia's house looked like a Wolff, though that might be wishful thinking on Kieran's part. And as for the Kevin Wade on the birth certificate, well… Olivia might have done that to preserve her privacy. Using the name of a man who didn't exist to protect her rights as a mother.

But God help him, if Olivia had lied…if she had kept him

from his own flesh and blood, there was going to be hell to pay.

His cell phone beeped with a text from the front gate guard at the foot of the mountain. Olivia's car had arrived.

She had flatly refused Wolff transportation, either the private jet or a ride from the airport. Her independence made a statement that said Kieran was unnecessary. It would be his pleasure to show her how wrong she was.

When a modest rental vehicle pulled into sight, he felt his heart race, not only at the prospect of seeing Olivia, but at the realization that he might be, for the first time, coming face-to-face with his progeny.

The car slid to a halt and Olivia stepped out. Before she could come around and help with the passenger door, it was flung open from the inside, and a small, slender girl hopped into view. She had brown hair pulled back into pigtails and wore a wary expression as she surveyed her surroundings. Though Kieran didn't move, she spotted him immediately. Try as he might, Kieran could see no hint that she resembled his family. She looked like a kid. That's all. A little kid.

She slipped her hand into Olivia's. "It's like Cinderella's castle. Do we get to sleep here?"

"For a few nights."

Kieran wondered if Olivia was intimidated by the size and scope of the house. She had grown up as the only child of famous, wealthy parents, but this structure—part fortress, part fairy tale—was beyond imagination for most people. All it was missing was gargoyles on the parapets. With turrets and battlements and thick, gray stone walls, it should have looked unwelcoming, but somehow, it suited this wild mountaintop.

"Who's that, Mommy?"

Kieran stepped forward, but before he could speak,

Olivia gave Kieran a warning look. "His name is Kieran. He's a friend of mine. But you can call him Mr. Wolff."

"She'd better call me Kieran to avoid confusion, because she's going to be meeting a lot of Mr. Wolffs."

Olivia's lips tightened, but she didn't argue.

Kieran knelt beside Cammie. "We're glad to have you and your mommy here for a visit. Would you like to see the horses?" He took a punch to the chest when he realized the child's eyes were the same color as his own, dark amber with flecks of gold and brown.

He glanced up at Olivia, his heart in his throat. *Tell me,* his gaze signaled furiously.

Olivia didn't give an inch. "I think it would be best if Cammie and I rested for a while. It was a long, tiring flight and we're beat."

"But, Mommy," Cammie wailed. "I love horses."

Kieran straightened. "Surely a quick trip to the stables wouldn't hurt. And after that you'll nap with no argument, right, Cammie?"

The child was smart enough to know when a deal was worth taking. "Okay," she said, the resignation in her voice oddly adult. She slipped her hand into Kieran's. "C'mon, before she changes her mind."

Olivia followed behind the pair of them, realizing with chagrin that she would have been better served letting Kieran stay with them in California. On his turf, already Olivia felt at a disadvantage. And she hadn't missed Kieran's poleaxed look when he saw her daughter's eye color. It was unusual to say the least. And a dead giveaway when it came to parentage.

Behind the massive house stood an immaculate barn with adjoining stables. Inside the latter, the smell of hay mingled not unpleasantly with the odor of warm horseflesh.

Kieran led Cammie past the stalls of mighty stallions to

an enclosure where a pretty brown-and-white pony stood contentedly munching hay. He handed Cammie a few apple chunks from a nearby bin. "Hold out your hand with the fingers flat, like this."

She obeyed instantly, her small face alight with glee as the pony approached cautiously and scooped up the food with a delicate swipe of its lips. "Mommy, look," she cried. "It likes me."

Kieran put a hand on her shoulder. "Her name is Sunshine, and you can ride her as long as you're here."

"Now?" Cammie asked, practically bouncing on her feet. "Please, Mommy."

Over her head, the two adults' gazes met, Olivia's filled with frustration, Kieran's bland. "Later," Olivia said firmly. "We have plenty of time."

She had been afraid that she would have to meet a phalanx of Kieran's relatives while she was still rumpled and road weary, but he led them to a quiet, peaceful wing of the house where the windows were thrown open to embrace the warm, early summer breezes.

"This will be your room, Olivia." Kieran paused to indicate a lovely suite decorated in shades of celadon and pale buttercup. "And through here…" He passed through a connecting door to another room clearly meant for a child. "This is yours, Cammie."

Olivia saw her daughter's eyes grow wide. The furnishings had been made to resemble a tree house, with the sleep space atop a small pedestal accessed by rope netting, which coincidentally made any possibility of falling out of bed harmless.

Cammie kicked off her shoes and scampered up the rope apron like the monkey she was. "Look at me," she cried. "This is awesome. Thank you, Kieran."

Soon she was oblivious to the adults as she explored the

tree trunk bookcase, the two massive toy chests shaped like daisies and the enormous fish tank.

Olivia drew Kieran aside. "Are you insane?" she asked, her low whisper incredulous. "This must have cost a fortune. And for three nights? You can't buy my compliance, Kieran. Nor hers."

"The money isn't an issue," he said quietly, a small smile on his face as he watched Cammie scoot from one wonder to the next. "I wanted my daughter to feel at home here."

"She's not your daughter." The denial was automatic, but lacked conviction.

Kieran barely noticed. "She's smart, isn't she?"

"Oh, yes. Talking in full sentences before she was two. Reading at three and a half. Learning how to use my laptop almost a year ago. I can barely keep up with her."

"A child needs two parents, Olivia." He wasn't looking at her, but the words sounded like a threat.

"You grew up with only one," she shot back. "And you've done all right."

He half turned and she could see the riot of emotions in his eyes. "I wouldn't wish my childhood on anyone," he said. The blunt words were harsh and ragged with grief.

Shame choked her and she laid a hand on his arm. "I'm so sorry, Kieran. I really am."

He took her wrist in his hand, bringing it up to his mouth and brushing a kiss across her knuckles. "Tonight. When she's asleep. We'll talk in my suite. One of the housekeepers can babysit and make sure she's okay." His grip tightened. "This isn't optional, Olivia."

Once again she was thrown by the way he mingled tenderness with masculine authority. Kieran wasn't a man who could be "handled." He expected to be obeyed, and it incensed her. But at the same time, she knew she dared not cross him and risk having him blurt out the truth to

Cammie. That she had a father. A flesh and blood man who wanted to know her and be part of her life. What kind of mother would Olivia be if she stood in the way of that?

What else did Kieran want? Was this weekend visit going to appease him? Would he sue for joint custody? Or perhaps at the urging of his paranoid father, would he insist on full custody and try to lock Cammie up here in the castle until she was old enough to escape?

That's essentially what Kieran and his brothers had experienced. They had been hidden away from the world until they were allowed to go away to school with aliases.

Olivia couldn't live like that. And she certainly didn't want her daughter to endure such isolation. So she had no choice but to convince Kieran that being a father was too much for him to handle.

He left them finally, and Olivia and Cammie fell into an exhausted sleep, both of them in Olivia's bed. For a five-year-old, even with a private playground at her disposal, sometimes the most comfortable place to be was curled up in Mommy's arms.

Shadows filled the room when they awoke. Someone had slid a note under the door indicating that dinner would be at seven. As Olivia and Cammie washed up and changed clothes, a smiling young maid brought by a tray of grapes, cheese and crackers.

Olivia blessed whoever had the foresight to be so thoughtful. When Cammie got hungry, she got cranky, and her resultant attitude could be unpredictable.

Fortunately Cammie was on her best behavior that evening. And it helped that the whole Wolff clan was not in residence. Only Kieran's father, Victor, Kieran's brothers, Gareth and Jacob, and the newest member of the family, Gracie's wife, Gracie, were seated around the large mahogany dining table when Olivia and Cammie walked into the room.

Olivia put a hand on her daughter's thin shoulder. "Sorry if we're late. We took a wrong turn in the third floor hallway."

Victor Wolff, one of the clan's two patriarchs, lumbered to his feet, chuckling at Olivia's lame joke. "Quite understandable. No problem. We're just getting ready for the soup course." His gaze landed on Cammie and stayed there, full of avid interest. "Welcome to the mountain, ladies. Kieran rarely brings such lovely guests."

"Thank you, sir." Olivia took a seat, and settled Cammie beside her, surprised to find that she was nervous as hell. It certainly wasn't the formal dinner that had her baffled. She'd conquered dining etiquette as a child. No, it was the barely veiled speculation in the eyes of everyone at the table when they looked at Olivia and Cammie.

Only Kieran seemed oblivious to the undercurrents in the room. After digging into his pan-fried trout, caught in one of the streams on the property, he waved a fork at his father. "So tell me, Dad…what big projects do you and Uncle Vincent have lined up for the summer?"

He sat to the left of Olivia, and in an aside, he said, "My dad always likes to keep things humming here on the mountain. One year he repainted the entire house. Took the workmen six weeks and untold gallons of paint. Another time he added a bowling alley in the basement."

She smiled, hyperaware of Kieran's warm thigh so close to her own. "I imagine with a place this size there is always something that needs your attention."

Victor nodded. "Indeed. But this time I'm branching out. I've decided to plant a portion of the back of the mountain in Christmas trees."

Cammie's face lit up, her attention momentarily diverted

from her macaroni and cheese. "I *love* Christmas. My mama covers the whole house with decorations."

Victor smiled at her. "How old are you, young lady?"

"Five," she said casually, returning her attention to her meal.

Victor honed in on Olivia then. "My son hasn't told us much about you, Olivia. Have you known each other very long?"

The food she had eaten congealed into a knot in her stomach. She had been dreading just such a line of questioning. It took all she had to answer in a matter-of-fact voice. "We met when Kieran and I were doing graduate work at Oxford. You were taken ill soon after that, and he and I lost touch."

"I see." Olivia was very much afraid that he *did* see.

Her phone buzzed in the pocket of her skirt. Javier and Lolita tended to worry when she and Cammie were out of their reach, and they called often to check in. Since there was a lull before dessert, she smiled at the group in general and said, "Excuse me, please."

When she returned a few moments later, Kieran jumped up to move out her chair. He leaned over as he seated her, whispering in her ear, "What's wrong? You're pale as a ghost."

She wanted to hold on to him for comfort, and that scared her. So she swallowed her dismay and produced a smile. "Everything's fine. That was my mother checking up on us."

Kieran frowned, obviously unconvinced. "Olivia's parents are Javier and Lolita Delgado."

A rippled murmur swept the table. Gareth Wolff lifted an eyebrow. "I remember seeing her in *Fly by Night* when I was sixteen. She's amazing."

Jacob joined in the verbal applause. "And I'll never forget

when your dad played his first big role in *Vigilante Justice*. I thought he was the coolest dude ever."

Hearing Kieran's reserved brothers speak so enthusiastically about her parents made Olivia realize anew how much the older couple was beloved around the world. As their daughter, she saw them in a different light, but she understood the admiration and passion they generated in audiences.

Unfortunately not all of it was positive.

Biting her lip, she decided to share her unease. "My mother has a stalker fan who has been causing some problems. She just told me that he has hacked into her private email account and started sending her weird messages."

All four Wolff males wore matching expressions of ferocity. "Like what?" Kieran demanded, sliding an arm across the back of her chair.

Olivia slanted a worried glance at her daughter, but Cammie was engrossed in playing with a kitten that had wandered into the dining room. Olivia lowered her voice, anyway. "He's threatening violence. To my mother and to the people she holds dear. I could tell my mother is really spooked."

"It's a good thing you're here," Victor boomed, his florid face indignant. "How long are you staying?"

"Just until Monday."

Kieran brushed her arm with his fingertips. "I could only get her to agree to a three-night visit, but I'm hoping to change her mind." In front of God and everyone at the table, he leaned in and kissed her gently on the lips.

Olivia stiffened and turned red with mortification. Kieran's family only grinned.

Victor signaled an end to the dinner by rising unsteadily to his feet. "Well, keep us posted. I'd be happy to help in any way I can."

Gracie moved around the table and gave her brother-in-law a hug. "Nice of you to bring some estrogen to this male enclave." She smiled at Olivia. "I hear you're a children's book illustrator. I'd love to pick your brain about that if you have time. I'm a painter."

"I'd be happy to," Olivia said. "But at the moment, I need to get Cammie ready for bed. When we cross time zones, it's tough to keep her routine intact."

Kieran took her arm as they left the dining room. "Remember," he said. "My suite. Don't make me hunt you down."

She shivered, looking into his eyes for any sign of weakness. But there was none. His gaze was steady, confident, implacable. Her time of reckoning was nigh.

Cammie was irritable and uncooperative, perhaps picking up on Olivia's unsettled mood. It was close to ten o'clock when the child finally went to sleep in her tree house bed.

One of the older housekeepers took a seat in front of the television in Olivia's sitting room and promised to be vigilant in keeping an eye and ear out for Cammie. Olivia knew that her daughter rarely woke up after falling asleep, so she had no real reason to procrastinate any longer.

She slipped into the bathroom and changed out of the dress she had worn to dinner. Instead, she opted for soft, well-worn jeans and a light cashmere pullover sweater in pale mauve. Her mass of hair seemed unruly, so she swept it up in a thick ponytail.

The woman in the mirror had big eyes and a troubled expression. She'd been waiting for six years to face what was coming. But knowing the day had finally arrived made it no easier.

Somehow she had to prevent Kieran from seeing how much she still responded to him sexually. Giving him that

advantage would weaken her, and she couldn't afford that…
not when Cammie's life and well-being were at stake.

Kieran's suite of rooms was across the hall from hers.
Was the arrangement designed to let him see more of his
daughter or to remind Olivia that she could no longer hide
from him?

She wiped damp palms on her jeans and knocked.

Five

Kieran had wondered if she would come. It wouldn't have surprised him if she had used jet lag or some other excuse to postpone this meeting, yet here she was. In casual clothes and with her hair pulled back, she seemed scarcely old enough to be the mother of a five-year-old child. "Come in," he said, feeling his muscles clench as she slipped past him. "Would you like some wine?"

"Yes," she said, her voice husky and low. "White, please."

He handed her a glass of the zinfandel he remember she liked and motioned for her to be seated. His suite, like the one he had chosen for her, included a bedroom, a lavish bath and this sitting room.

Olivia perched primly on a comfy chair, her knees together, ankles and feet aligned. Her curvy ass filled out the jeans she wore in a mouth-drying way. And that sweater. Jesus. Had she dressed this way deliberately to throw him off track?

Kieran remained standing, finishing his drink and setting the glass aside. "Cammie is mine," he said slowly, still stunned by the notion. "Without a doubt. But you told me six years ago that you were taking the pill."

She grimaced. "I was. But one morning I forgot to take it, and I found it lying by the sink when I got ready for bed that night. I swallowed it down right away, but obviously the damage was already done."

"Hmm." He was itchy, nervous, unsettled as hell. Tiptoeing through a minefield, that's what this was. He cleared his throat. "We're done with dancing around this, Olivia. I need to hear you say it. Tell me that Cammie is my daughter."

When she remained stubbornly silent, he sighed. "Do you want to know the real reason I didn't contact you after I left England?"

Shock flashed across her face, and she nodded cautiously, looking at him as if waiting for bad news from a doctor.

He ran both hands through his hair, searching for the right words. "After we had been together for a couple of weeks, you began telling me stories from your childhood... about what it was like to be the daughter of world famous celebrities. How there were always bodyguards and races to avoid paparazzi. You said you hated the isolation and never being able to play at a friend's house. You told me you weren't allowed to go to school, but instead, had private tutors. Do you remember saying all that?"

She nodded, frowning. "Of course."

"Well, what I couldn't tell you was that your story mirrored my own in many ways. We both suffered growing up, and I understood completely your feelings of being trapped, of wanting to fly the coop. You said on more than one occasion that all you wanted out of life was to be normal. To raise any children you might have like regular people."

Grimacing, she took a sip of wine. "You really listened."

"I did. And that's why I never called. It's not ego talking when I say that I knew you were falling in love with me. I felt the same way. You weren't like any girl I had ever dated, and I wanted you so badly I couldn't think straight half the time."

"You never said anything."

"I thought you'd be able to tell how I felt when we were making love. And I didn't want to bare my soul when you knew me as Kevin Wade. If I told you I loved you, I wanted you to know I was Kieran."

"And when your father had his heart attack?"

"It shook me. The night before I had called him and asked permission to tell you the truth. He was terribly upset, and the next morning I got the call that he'd been taken to the hospital. It felt like I had caused the heart attack, and maybe I did."

"So you decided before you ever left England that we were over?"

"If I'm being honest…yes. I knew I could never give you what you needed, and I didn't want to hurt you. My family is not normal. So it seemed kinder in the long run to end things before we both got in too deep. No matter how far I try to run from it, I'll always be a Wolff, and the money will always make me and those I love a target. You have this dream of being a PTA mom and having a white picket fence. There's not a place for me in that scenario."

He thought his explanation would make her feel better. Instead, she looked furious.

"What gives you the right to make decisions for me, to map out my life?" she said angrily. "I had nothing but lies to go on, Kevin Wade. You're an arrogant ass." Her eyes flashed fire at him and her chest heaved.

How the hell did he become the bad guy, when he was

only trying to protect her from hurt? "Tell me that Cammie is mine," he demanded through clenched teeth.

Her lustrous eyes were wounded, her lips pale where she had pressed them together so hard. "Your sperm may have generated her life, but Cammie is *my* daughter."

His heart caught in his throat and he sank onto the sofa, not for the world willing to admit that his knees had gone weak. "So you're admitting we made a baby?"

Olivia's face softened, and she came to sit beside him. Not touching but close. "Of course we did. Have you *looked* at her?"

Fury built in his belly. "How could you keep her from me for five long years? Damn it, Olivia. Do you have any idea what I've missed?" He vaulted to his feet, unable to bear her presence so close. He didn't know whether to kiss her in gratitude for giving him a child or to strangle her for her deception.

He was shaking all over, and the weakness and turmoil he experienced infuriated him. Grief for the time he would never recoup mingled with wonder that a part of him lay asleep in a nearby room.

"When can we tell her?"

Olivia went white. "It's not the kind of thing you blurt out. Maybe you should get to know her first."

"In three days?" He was incredulous that she didn't understand his urgency. "Guess again. I'm keeping her here this summer."

"You can't."

"Oh, yes," he said in dead earnest. "I can and I will. Both of you will move in here for the duration."

"You can't order me," she whispered, anguish marking her face.

He shrugged. "I'm not being unreasonable. Your work

can be done anywhere. She's not in school yet. If you don't agree, I'll take you to court. I know plenty of judges who frown on parents who kidnap their own kids."

"I didn't kidnap her. That's a terrible thing to say."

"You kept her existence a secret from her father. Semantics, Olivia. I'm calling the shots now."

"You're bluffing."

He felt a tingle of sympathy for her distress, but only that. She'd do well to understand that he fought for what was his. "It wouldn't be such a terrible thing, would it? To spend time here on the mountain?"

Clearly unconvinced, she frowned stubbornly as she stood up and crossed the room to stand nose to nose with him. "I can't turn my life upside down overnight. You're a bully."

He grinned, feeling suddenly lighthearted and free. A daddy. He was a daddy.

Olivia cocked her head. "What's so funny?"

"You. Me. Life in general."

"I don't see any humor in this situation at all," she huffed.

He scooped her up, lifting her until his belt buckle pressed into her stomach. Her arms went around his neck. "Thank you, Olivia, for giving me Cammie." He kissed her nose.

"She's not a *thing* to give. But you're welcome."

He slid his lips across hers, tasting the flavors of the coffee and lemon pie she had consumed earlier. "One summer," he coaxed.

"One weekend," she countered.

He palmed her ass, pulling her into his thrusting erection. The clothes separating them were a frustration. So he set her on her feet and began undressing her.

Olivia went beet-red and batted at his hands. "What do

you think you're doing?" she sputtered. "Sex won't make me change my mind."

"The decision's already made." He groaned aloud as he peeled away her sweater and revealed a mauve demi-bra barely concealing its bounty. "Sweet heaven. Please don't stop me, Olivia. I need you more than my next breath." His body was one huge ache that concentrated in his hard erection.

Her eyelids fluttered shut as her shoulders rose and fell in a deep sigh. He removed the remainder of her clothing posthaste. The well-washed jeans, the socks and shoes, the scanty bra and, finally, the lacy thong.

Was it possible that he had forgotten how gorgeous she was? Full breasts with light brown centers topped a narrow waist and hourglass hips. He must have been insane six years ago. How had he left her?

He weighed both her breasts in his hands. "Look at me, Olivia."

She opened her eyes and what he saw there humbled him. Sadness, resignation, need. "This won't solve anything, Kieran."

He nodded, refusing to let the future taint the moment. "Then don't think. Just let me make you feel."

A bleak smile lifted the corners of her lips. "Do you think you're that irresistible? You have a bad habit of wanting to run the show."

"I'll work on my failings," he promised, ready to agree to anything as long as she stayed in this room with him for the next half hour.

"What makes you think I'll be lured into your bed given our history?"

"It's *because* of our history that I believe it. We could never keep our hands off each other, and you know it."

"I won't have Cammie be hurt or confused by any relationship we might initiate."

"Of course not. This is no one's business but ours."

"Someone might come in," she said, nibbling her bottom lip.

"I locked the door, I swear."

"And the housekeeper?"

"I told her you'd be back no later than eleven-thirty."

Her face flamed again. "Oh, my God, Kieran. Don't you think she knows we're across the hall having sex?"

"We're *not* having sex," he pointed out ruefully.

"You know what I mean."

His hands moved to her waist, petting her, soothing her. "She thinks we went for a walk in the moonlight. And she's a romantic soul. Quit worrying."

For one interminable heartbeat he thought Olivia would refuse him. But finally she nodded as if coming to some unknown decision. Her hands went to his belt buckle. "If we have a curfew, I suppose we'd better not waste any time."

"I agree," he said fervently, batting her hands away and ripping off his clothing in two quick swipes as he toed off his shoes.

Her eyes rounded in a gratifying way as she took stock of his considerably aroused state. "I seem to have forgotten a few things about you," she said, cupping him in her hands.

He sucked in a breath between clenched teeth. "I'm on a hair trigger, Olivia. It's been a while. Maybe you shouldn't touch me."

"There you go again, bossing me around." She dropped to her knees on the plush carpet and licked him daintily.

The shock of it ricocheted through his body like streaks of fire. He cursed, gripping her head, and with one snap of his wrist breaking the band that held her ponytail in place.

That fabulous hair tumbled across her cheeks, around his straining penis. The eroticism of the image sent him over the edge, and he came with a ragged shout.

They collapsed to the floor and Olivia lay beside him, a small, pensive smile on her face.

He rubbed his eyes with the heels of his hands. "Was that meant to prove something?"

"Maybe. I'm not a kid anymore, Kieran. I'm a woman, and I've been running my life for six years without your help."

"But you have to admit that when we do things together, the results are pretty spectacular."

"Is that a sexual reference?"

"Could be, but in this case I was talking about Cammie."

She curled into him, hooking one long, slender leg over his thigh. "I can't argue with that."

He stroked her hair. "We don't have to be adversaries."

"As long as you understand that you can't ride roughshod over my feelings and opinions. And we don't have to be a couple."

"Fair enough."

She touched him intimately. "If you're trying to manipulate me with sex, it won't work."

His erection flexed and thickened. "Understood."

"Then I think we're on the same page."

He stood and pulled her to her feet. "Bed this time," he grunted, reduced to one syllable words. He lifted her into his arms and deposited her in the center of his large mattress. The old Olivia would have pulled a sheet over herself immediately, but this more mature version lifted one knee, propped her head on her hand and smiled.

It was the smile of a woman learning her own power. Kieran was not immune. He sprawled beside her and entertained himself by relearning every curve and dip of her feminine body.

Olivia melted for him, her soft gasps and tiny cries filling him with determination to pleasure her as she had never been pleasured before. He brought her to the brink with his hands and then moved between her legs. At the last moment he remembered the need for a condom. He wasn't taking any chances this time.

Not that he considered Cammie a mistake, but because he needed to learn how to be a father. One child was enough for the moment.

He sheathed himself in the latex and positioned the head of his penis against Olivia's warm, moist flesh. She was pink and perfect, her sex swollen where he had teased her.

Her eyes were shut. "Look at me," he insisted. When she obeyed, he drove into her, eliciting groans from both of them. Her body squeezed him, begged him not to leave. Panting, he withdrew and surged deep again. "We're good this way," he muttered. "So damn good."

The truth of the statement tormented him.

He was not a family man. After a lifetime of living caged up, he needed the freedom he found in anonymous villages on the other side of the world. Olivia was important to him, and Cammie was part of him, flesh and blood.

But what did it matter when he was condemned to be alone? Loving meant loss, and he'd had his share of that.

Olivia's sultry smile was drowsy. "Does it have to end?"

Even the question was enough to send heat streaking down his spine, sparking into his balls and rushing through the part of him that longed for release. His jaw clenched, the muscles in his neck corded and he shouted half in relief, half in awe when his body shuddered in the throes of a climax that left him weak.

Dimly he was aware that Olivia joined him at the end.

Panting, half addled from the scalding deluge of release, he rolled to his back, dragging her on top of him, their bodies still joined.

"Stay the night." The words were muffled as he buried his face in her cleavage.

"I can't," she said, disentangling their limbs and rolling to sit on the side of the bed.

"I could come to your room."

Her body stilled, her back to him. "No."

As he watched, only momentarily sated, she dressed rapidly and finger-combed her hair. He frowned, already missing the feel of her in his arms. "Dismiss the housekeeper and come back. We could set an alarm so you'll be in your room by morning."

"I have responsibilities," she said, not meeting his gaze.

"And that precludes meeting your needs as a woman?"

She stopped at the door and faced him across the room. In her eyes he saw regret and resolution. "I can't afford to get involved with you again. Sharing a daughter will be hard enough. Let's view tonight as one for Auld Lang Syne and put it behind us."

"I'm not a fan of that plan. It wouldn't hurt for Cammie to see us getting along."

"We can be civil without starting something we can't finish. I'm here for a very short time. And unlike you, I don't happen to see recreational sex as an appropriate lifestyle."

Now he was pissed. "Who said anything about recreational sex?"

He strode to where she stood backed up against the door and got in her face. "I'm attracted to you, Olivia Delgado. I like you. And as of today, I know we share a child. Any intimacies we indulge in are far from casual."

She licked her lips, her eyes huge. "You're bullying me again," she whispered.

Damn it. He was hard. And hungry. And mad as hell that she seemed to see him as some kind of a lowlife. He backed up two feet and crossed his arms over his chest. "You have more power than you think. But I won't be pushed away."

She reached behind her for the knob and opened the door. Since he was buck naked, and knowing that one of the housekeepers sat just across the hall, he didn't have a prayer of stopping her.

But his chest was tight when he closed the door and banged his forehead against the unforgiving wood. She was making him crazy. Two steps forward…one step back. Perhaps it was time for a change of plan. He would get to know his daughter, and in the meantime, maybe Olivia would acknowledge the fire that burned between them and return to his bed on her own.

Six

A strange house. Odd night sounds. And dreams that were riddled with images of Kieran Wolff. No wonder Olivia slept poorly. She had no more defenses against him now than she had as a naive university student. All he had to do was crook his little finger and she fell into his arms without protest.

It was infuriating and humbling and, if she were honest, exciting. Her days since Cammie was born had been pleasant. And the white-picket-fence life she had so deliberately created was good. Really good. But what woman—still two years shy of thirty—should be willing to settle for that?

Kieran's recent intrusion into her life was a jolt of adrenaline. Now she was scared and aroused and worried and challenged, but she wasn't bored.

Finally, at 4:00 a.m., she fell into a deep sleep, only to be awakened at the crack of dawn when Cammie crawled into bed with her. Crossing three time zones was not an easy adjustment for a child.

Olivia yawned. "Good morning, sweetheart."

"What are we going to do today?" Cammie snuggled close, her small, warm body a comfort Olivia never tired of.

"I think Kieran wants to hang out with us. Is that okay?"

In the semidark, her daughter's face was hard to read. "Yep. I like him."

That was it. Four short words. But hearing her daughter's vote of confidence relieved at least some of Olivia's concern.

Olivia dozed off again. When she woke, Cammie was gone, and light streamed into the room. Good Lord. She was a sweet kid, but mischievous at times. Olivia stumbled from her bed and rushed through the connecting passageway to Cammie's whimsical bedroom. She stopped short when she realized that Cammie was sprawled on the floor on her stomach alongside Kieran, who was aligned in a similar position.

Both of them were playing with an expensive model train set. A small black engine *choo-chooed* its way around a figure-eight track. Seeing the two of them side by side wrenched something inside her chest and brought hot tears to her eyes. She blinked them back, refusing to dwell on what might have been.

Kieran looked up, his gaze raking her from head to toe, taking in the flimsy silk nightie that ended above her knees, her thinly covered breasts, her tousled hair. "Rough night, Olivia?"

His bland intonation was meant to bait.

"Slept like a baby," she said, glaring at him when she thought her daughter wouldn't see. Kieran looked delicious…clear-eyed and dressed casually in jeans and an old faded yellow oxford shirt with the sleeves rolled up. His big masculine feet were bare, and Olivia discovered that there was no part of him that didn't make her heart beat faster.

He motioned to a nearby tray. "Cook sent up fresh scones and homemade blackberry jam. And there's a carafe of coffee."

Cammie had barely acknowledged her mother's presence, too caught up in the new entertainment. Olivia shifted her feet, reluctant to parade in front of her host to get a much-needed cup of caffeine. The awkward silence grew.

Kieran took pity on her. "Go take a shower if you want to. I'll pour you some coffee and set it on the nightstand. Okay?"

"Thanks," she muttered, escaping to the privacy of her room. In twenty minutes she had showered and changed into trim khakis and a turquoise peasant shirt that left one shoulder bare. She hadn't needed to wash her hair this morning, so she brushed it vigorously and left one swathe to lie over the exposed skin.

The coffee awaited as promised. She drank it rapidly and went in search of a second cup. What she saw stunned her. Cammie, often shy around strangers, sat in Kieran's lap in a sunshine-yellow rocker as he read to her from an Eric Carle book.

The two of them looked up with identical expressions of inquiry. Cammie's typical smile danced across her face. "You look pretty, Mommy. Kieran's going to take us to the attic."

Olivia glanced down ruefully at her fairly expensive outfit. "Do I need to change?"

Kieran laid the book aside and shook his head. "The Wolff attic is more of a carefully maintained museum than a dusty hiding place. You'll be fine."

While Cammie took another turn with the train, Kieran spoke, sotto voce to Olivia. "She's right. You look lovely."

He brushed a kiss across her cheek. "I wanted you when I woke up this morning."

The gravelly statement sent goose bumps up and down her arms. She glanced at Cammie, but the child was oblivious to the adult's tension. "You shouldn't say things like that. Not here. Not now."

He shrugged, unrepentant, and suddenly she saw the source of Cammie's mischievous grin. Circling Olivia's waist with one arm, he pulled her close and whispered in her ear, his hot breath tickling sensitive skin. "If you had stayed in my bed last night, neither of us would have gotten any rest. Remember the evening after the Coldplay concert? We didn't sleep that night at all."

His naughty reminiscence was deliberate. In a hotel room high above the streets of London, they had fallen onto the luxurious bed, drunk on each other and the evening of evocative music. Again and again he had taken her, until she was sore and finally had to beg off.

The resultant apology and intimate sponge bath had almost broken his control and hers.

"Stop it," she hissed. "That was a lifetime ago. We're different people."

"Perhaps. But I don't think so." He bit gently at her earlobe, half turned so Cammie couldn't see his naughty caress. "You make me ache, Olivia. Tell me you feel the same."

She broke free of his embrace. "Cammie, are you ready for the attic?"

Kieran grimaced inwardly, realizing that he had already strayed from his plan. As long as he pushed, Olivia would run. Only time would tell if another tack would woo her in the right direction.

As they climbed the attic stairs, Cammie slipped her little hand into his with a natural trust that cut him off at the knees. Frankly it scared him spitless. What did he know about raising a kid? He'd been too young when his mother died to have many memories of her. And when his father imploded into a near breakdown, the only familial support Kieran had known was from his uncle, his two brothers and his cousins, all of whom were grieving as much or more than he was.

He halted Cammie at the top of the stairs. "Hold on, poppet. Let me get the switch." It had been years since he had been up here, but the cavernous space hadn't changed much. Polished hardwood floors, elegant enough for any ballroom, were illuminated with old-fashioned wall sconces as well as pure crystalline sunbeams from a central etched glass skylight. Almost thirty years of junk lay heaped in piles across the broad expanse.

Olivia's face lit up. "This is amazing...like a storybook. Oh, Kieran. You were so lucky to grow up here."

Though her comment hit a raw nerve, he realized that she meant it. Seeing the phenomenal house through a new-comer's eyes made him admit, if only to himself, that not all his memories were unpleasant. How many hours had he and Gareth and Jacob and their cousins whiled away up here on rainy days? The adults had left them alone as long as they didn't create a ruckus, and there was many a time when the attic had become Narnia, or a Civil War battle-field, or even a Star Wars landscape.

He cleared his throat. "It's a wonderful place to play," he said quietly, caught up in the web of memory. Across the room he spotted what he'd been looking for—a large red carton. He dragged it into an empty spot and grinned at Cammie. "This was my favorite toy."

"I remember having some of these." Olivia squatted down beside them and soon, the Lincoln Logs were trans-formed into barns and bridges and roads.

Kieran ruffled Cammie's hair. "You're good at building things," he said softly, still struggling to believe that she was his.

"Mommy says I get that from my daddy."

His gut froze. "Your daddy?"

"Uh-huh. He lives on the other side of the world, so we don't get to see him."

Kieran couldn't look at Olivia. He stumbled to his feet. "Be right back," he said hoarsely. He made a beeline for the stairs, loped down them and closed himself in the nearest room, which happened to be the library. His throat was so tight it was painful, and his head pounded. Closing his eyes and fisting his hands at his temples, he fought back the tsunami of emotion that had hit him unawares.

A child's simple statement. *We don't get to see him....* How many times had Olivia talked to Cammie about her absentee father? And how many times had a small child wondered why her daddy didn't care enough to show up?

His stomach churned with nausea. If he had known, things would have been different. Damn Olivia.

As he stood, rigid, holding himself together by sheer will, an unpalatable truth bubbled to the surface. He *did* live on the other side of the world. He'd logged more hours in the air than he'd spent in the States in the past five years. What would he have done if Olivia had found him and told him the truth?

His lies to her in England had been the genesis of an impossible Gordian knot. One bad decision led to another until now Kieran had a daughter he didn't know, Olivia was afraid to trust him and Kieran himself didn't have a clue what to do about the future.

When he thought he could breathe again, he returned to the attic. Cammie had lost interest in the Lincoln Logs, and she and Olivia were now playing with a pile of dress-up clothes. Cammie pirouetted, wearing a magenta tutu that had once belonged to Kieran's cousin Annalise. "Look at me," she insisted, wobbling as she tried to stand up in toe shoes.

Kieran stopped short of the two females, not trusting himself at the moment to behave rationally. "Very nice," he croaked.

Olivia looked at him with a gaze that telegraphed inquiry and concern. "You okay?" she mouthed, studying him in a way that made him want to hide. He didn't need or want her sympathy. She was the one who had stripped him of a father's rights.

He nodded tersely. "I'll leave you two up here to play for a while. I have some business calls to make."

Olivia watched the tall, lean man leave, her heart hurting for him. In hindsight, she wondered if she and Kieran might have had a chance if he hadn't lied about who he was, and if she had been able to get past her anger and righteous indignation long enough to notify him that she was having his baby.

It was all water under the bridge now. The past couldn't be rewritten.

She and Cammie were on their own for most of the afternoon, despite Kieran's insistence that he wanted to get to know his daughter. After lunch and a nap, Olivia took her daughter outside to explore the mountaintop. They found Gareth's woodworking shop, and Cammie made friends with the basset hound, Fenton.

On this beautiful early summer day, Wolff Mountain was twenty degrees cooler than down in the valley, and Olivia fell in love with the peace and tranquility found in towering trees, singing birds and gentle breezes.

She and Cammie ran into Victor Wolff on the way back to the house. He was slightly stoop-shouldered, and his almost bald head glistened with sweat. From what Olivia had gleaned from the private investigator and from a variety of internet sources, Victor had been a decade and a half older than his short-lived bride...which meant he must now be banging on the door of seventy.

The old man stared at Cammie with an expression that made Olivia's heart pound with anxiety. He shot a glance at Olivia. "The child has beautiful eyes. Very unusual."

Olivia held her ground, battling an atavistic need to tuck her baby under her wing. "Yes, she may grow up to be a beauty like my mother."

Cammie had no interest in adult conversation. She started picking flowers and dancing among the swaying fronds of a large weeping willow that cast a broad patch of shade. Victor's eyes followed her wistfully. "I may die before I get to see any grandchildren. Gareth is the only one of my sons who is married, and he and Gracie have decided to wait a bit to start their family."

"Are you ill?" Olivia asked bluntly.

He shook his head, still tracking the child's movements. "A bad heart. If I watch what I eat and remember to exercise, my son, the doc, says I probably have a few thousand more miles under the hood."

"But you don't believe him?"

"None of us knows how many days we have on this earth."

"I'm sorry about your wife, Mr. Wolff. I can't imagine how hard that must have been losing her so young."

He shrugged. "We argued that day. Before she left to go shopping. She wanted to let the boys take piano lessons and I thought it was a sissy endeavor. I told her so in no uncertain terms."

"And then she died."

"Yes." He aged before her eyes. "I've made a lot of mistakes in my life, Olivia."

"We all do, sir."

"Perhaps. But I almost ruined my sons, keeping them locked up like prisoners. My brother, Vincent, was the same. Six children between us, vulnerable little babies. I was terrified, you know. My brother and I both were."

"That's understandable." She began to feel a reluctant sympathy for the frail patriarch.

Suddenly his eyes shot fire at her, and the metamorphosis was so unexpected that Olivia actually took a step backward. "Kieran's a good boy. It's not his fault that the memories here keep him away."

"We all have our own demons to face," Olivia said. "But children shouldn't have to suffer for our mistakes."

"Are you talking about me or about you?"

His candor caught her off guard. "I suppose it could be either," she said slowly. "But know this, Mr. Wolff. I will do anything to protect my daughter."

He actually chuckled, a rusty sound that seemed to surprise him as much as it did her. "I like you, Olivia. Too bad I didn't have a daughter to take after my dear Laura."

Olivia couldn't think of a response to that, so she held her peace, walking beside Kieran's father as the three of them made their way back to the house.

Seven

Kieran saw the three of them approach the house. He was watching from an upstairs window. Part of him resented the fact that his father was sharing time with Olivia and Cammie, something Kieran had intended as the primary focus of the weekend. But anger boiled in his veins, and he was afraid that if he snapped and confronted Olivia in Cammie's presence, the child would be frightened.

Still, it was time for a showdown, and since nothing appeared to mitigate the harshness of the rage that gripped him, Olivia had better beware.

Dinner was an awkward affair with only the four of them. Jacob had been called way unexpectedly, and Gareth and Gracie were still in the honeymoon phase of their marriage, enjoying time together at home alone.

Cammie behaved beautifully at the overly formal table, conversing easily with Kieran and smiling shyly when Victor Wolff addressed her. Olivia was pale and quiet, perhaps sensing that a storm was brewing. The courses passed slowly. At last, Victor pushed back from the table. "I'll leave you young people to it. If you'll excuse an old man, I'm going upstairs to put on my slippers and sit by the fire."

Cammie wrinkled her nose as he left. "A fire? That's silly. It's summertime."

Kieran smiled, loving how bright she was, how aware of her surroundings. "You're right about that, little one. But my father has his eccentricities, and we all adjust."

"X cin…" She gave up trying to replicate the difficult word.

Olivia leaned over to remove crumbs from her daughter's chin with a napkin. "It means that Mr. Wolff has lived a long time and he sometimes does strange things."

"Like when Jojo puts hot sauce on his ice cream."

Olivia grinned. "Something like that."

Kieran saw himself suddenly as if from a distance, sitting at a table with his lover and their child. Anyone peering in the window would see a family, a unit of three. A mundane but extraordinarily wonderful relationship built on love, not lies.

But appearances were deceiving.

So abruptly that Olivia frowned, he stood up and tossed his napkin on the table. "Why don't I tuck Cammie in tonight? Is that okay with you, Olivia?"

He saw the refusal ready to tumble automatically from her lips, but she stopped and inhaled sharply, her hands clenching the edge of the table. "I suppose that would be fine. What do you think, Cammie?"

"Sure. Let's go, Kieran. Do you have any boats to play with in your bathtub?"

After they were gone, the silence resonated. Olivia realized that she was inconveniencing the waitstaff as long as she sat at the table, so she got up, as well. There were so many rooms in the huge house, it was easy to get lost. Not wanting to be too far away from Cammie, she found a staircase that led to the second floor and walked toward her suite. When she could hear laughter and splashing from the bathroom, she paused in the sitting room to call her mother.

Lolita's well-modulated voice answered on the first ring. "Hello, darling. How's the visit with your school friend?"

Olivia might possibly have fudged a bit on the details of her trip. "Going well. But I'm worried about you and Dad. Anything else from your psycho fan?"

"Don't be so cruel, Olivia. Men can't help falling in love with me. It's the characters on the screen, of course, but I play them so well, they seem genuine and warm, especially to someone who has already experienced a disconnect with reality. We should have compassion for the poor soul who is obsessed with me."

Olivia's mother had no problem with self-esteem. But her nonchalance seemed shortsighted. Olivia might have been even more worried were it not for the fact that Javier Delgado took his responsibilities as a husband very seriously. He was narcissistic to a fault, but he did love his tempestuous wife, and he had the bodyguards and manpower to prove it.

"Still, Mom, please be vigilant. Don't let down your guard."

"It's a tempest in a teapot, Olivia. Just a sad man wanting attention. Quit worrying."

"Has he sent more emails?"

"A few. The police are monitoring my computer."

"What did the notes say?"

"More of the same. Threats to me and the people I love. But you and Cammie are in a safe place for now, and your father and I are well taken care of. Everything's fine."

The conversation ended with Olivia feeling no less concerned than she had been earlier. As much as she hated to admit it, her parents would always be targets because of their celebrity and their wealth. Which was exactly why Olivia had struggled so hard to make a home for herself and her daughter away from the limelight that surrounded Lolita and Javier. Even letting Cammie travel with her grandparents was a leap of faith, but Olivia wanted the three of them to be close, so she bit her tongue and prayed when necessary.

The noise of Cammie's bedtime rituals moved from the bathroom to the bedroom. Olivia walked through the door in time to see Kieran tuck his daughter into the raised bed, giving her a kiss in the process. "My turn," she said.

Feeling awkward beneath Kieran's steady gaze, she hugged Cammie and tucked the covers close. "Sweet dreams."

Cammie's eyes were already drooping. "Nite, Mommy. Nite, Kieran." The two adults stepped into the hall. Kieran's expression was brooding, none of the lightheartedness he'd exhibited in Cammie's presence remaining. "Put some other shoes on," he said. "We're going for a walk."

Kieran saw on her face that she recognized the blunt command for what it was.

She frowned. "When you have a child, you can't waltz away whenever you want. She's too small to be left alone."

"I'm not stupid, Olivia." Her patronizing words irritated him. "Jacob returned a little while ago. Cook is fixing him some leftovers. He's bringing a stack of medical journals with him and has promised to sit up here until we get back."

"I don't know why we have to leave the house."

"Because it's a beautiful night and because I don't think you want to risk having our conversation overheard."

That shut her up. He was in a mood to brook no opposition, and the sooner he stated his piece, the better.

About the time Jacob appeared upstairs, Olivia returned wearing athletic shoes as instructed. She had changed into jeans and a long-sleeve shirt in deference to the chill of the late hour. Even in summer, nights on the mountain were cool.

They chatted briefly with Jacob, and then Kieran cocked his head toward the door. "Let's go."

Outside, Olivia stopped short. "You haven't told me where we're going."

"To the top of the mountain."

"I thought we *were* on top."

"The house sits on a saddle of fairly level land, but at either end of the property, the peak splits into two outcroppings. One has been turned into a helipad. We're headed to the other."

She followed him in silence as he strode off into the darkness, deliberately keeping up an ambitious pace. If she ended up exhausted and out of breath, perhaps she wouldn't be able to argue with him.

When the trail angled sharply upward, she called out his name. "Kieran, stop. I need to rest."

He paused there in the woods and looked at her across the space of several feet. Her face was a pale blur in the darkness. The sound of her breathing indicated exertion.

"Can we go now?" He was determined not to show her any consideration tonight. Nothing would dissuade him from his course of judgment.

She nodded.

He spun on his heel and pressed on. They were three miles from the house when the final ascent began. "Take my hand," he said gruffly, not willing to place her in any actual danger.

The touch of her slender fingers in his elicited emotions that were at odds with his general mood of condemnation.

He pushed back the softer feelings and concentrated on his need for retribution.

Clambering over rocks and thick roots, they made their way slowly upward. At last, breaking out of the trees, they were treated to a vista of the heavens that included an unmistakable Milky Way and stars that numbered in the millions.

Despite his black mood, the scene humbled him as it always did. Every trip home he made this pilgrimage at least once. To the right, a single large boulder with a flat top worn down by millennia of wind and rain offered a seat. He drew her to sit with him. Only feet away, just in front them, the mountain plunged into a steep, seemingly endless ravine.

Olivia perched beside him, their hips touching. "Are you planning to throw me off?" she asked, daring to tease him.

"Don't tempt me."

"It's a good thing I'm not afraid of heights."

"We'll come back in the daylight sometime. You can see for miles from up here."

They sat in silence for long minutes. Perhaps this had been a mistake. The wild, secluded beauty of this remote mountain was chipping away at his discontent. Occasionally the breeze teased his nostrils with Olivia's scent. All around them nocturnal creatures went about their business. Barred owls hooted nearby, their mournful sound punctuating the night.

Olivia sat quietly, her arms wrapped around her.

He rested his elbows on his knees, staring out into the inky darkness. "You committed an unpardonable sin against me, Olivia. Robbing me of my daughter—" His voice broke, and he had to take a deep, shuddering breath before he could continue. "Nothing can excuse that…no provocation, no set of circumstances."

"I'm sorry you missed seeing her grow from a baby into a funny, smart girl."

"But that's not really an apology, is it? You'd do the same thing again."

"The father of my child was a liar who abandoned me without warning or explanation. And later, when I did discover the truth, I found out what kind of man you are. An eternal Peter Pan, always searching for Neverland. Never quite able to settle down to reality."

"You think you have me all figured out."

"It's not that hard. All I have to do is look at the stamps on your passport."

"Traveling the world is not a crime."

"No, but it's an inherently selfish lifestyle. I'll admit that your work is important, but those bridges you build have also created unseen walls. You've never had to answer to anyone but yourself. And you like it that way."

The grain of truth in her bald assessment stung. "I might have made different choices had I known about Cammie."

"Doubtful. You were hardly equipped to care for a baby. And by your own admission, you've returned to Wolff Mountain barely a handful of times in six years. You may feel like the wronged party in this situation, Kieran, but from where I'm standing, both of our lives played out as they had to—separate…unrelated."

He couldn't let go of the sick regret twisting his insides with the knowledge that he had never been allowed to hold his infant child. "You call me selfish, Olivia, but you like playing God, controlling all the shots. That hardly makes you an admirable character in this scenario."

"I did what was necessary to survive."

"Lucky for you, your parents had money."

"Yes."

"Because, otherwise, you'd have been forced to come

crawling to me, and that would have eaten away at your pride."

"I would never have come to you for money."

He pounded his fists on his knees. "Damn you. Do you know how arrogant you sound?"

"Me? Arrogant?" Her voice rose. "That's rich. You wrote the book, Kieran. All you do is throw your weight around. I won't apologize for protecting my daughter from an absentee father."

"Military families deal with long absences all the time and their children survive."

"That's true. But those kids suffer. Sometimes they cry themselves to sleep at night wishing with all their hearts that their mommy or daddy was there to tuck them in. It's a tough life."

"But you never gave us a chance to see if we could make it work."

"You had sex with me for six weeks and never told me your real identity. What in God's name makes you think I would have put myself out there to be slapped down again? You hurt me, Kieran…badly. And when I found out a baby was on the way, it was all I could do to hold things together. If you had at least contacted me, who knows what might have happened. But you didn't. So forget the postmortems. What's done is done."

"I want to tell her I'm her father."

"No."

"I have legal rights."

"And you have plane tickets to Timbuktu at the end of the summer. Telling her would be cruel. Can't you see that?"

"She needs me. A girl should have a daddy to spoil her and teach her how to ride a bike."

"And you'll do that via Skype? Is that what you had in mind?"

"God, you're cold."

"What I am is a realist. We're not talking about how much Cammie needs *you*. This is really about you needing *her*, isn't it? And if you'll stop and think about it, the mature thing to do would be to walk away before she gets hurt."

"I want her to stay for the whole summer."

"She would fall in love with you and then be crushed when it was over. Absolutely not."

"We're getting nowhere with this," he groused. "It's a circular argument. I have a proposition. My cousin Annalise is returning tomorrow. She's great with children, and Cammie will love her. I have to make an overnight trip the following morning to New York to meet with a charitable board about the September project. I want you to come with me and we'll see if we can work this thing out."

"There's nothing to work out."

"Let me put it this way…either you agree to go to New York and hash things out on neutral ground, or I tell Cammie the truth when she wakes up in the morning."

"You can't."

"Try and stop me." He was beyond pleasantries, fighting for his life, his future.

Olivia leaped to her feet and he grabbed for her wrist. "Be careful, damn it. You're too close to the edge of the cliff."

She struggled instinctively, and then froze when his words sank in. "Take me back to the house." Unmistakable tears thickened her voice.

He stood up and backed them both from the precipice. "Don't make this so hard, Olivia," he murmured, sliding his hands down her arms. "We're her parents. Together. I don't want to fight with you."

"But you want to torture me."

"Not that, either." Her nearness affected him predictably.

"I want to make love to you, but I don't have a death wish, so I suggest we get off this ledge."

He steered her down the winding, narrow path until they were once again cloaked in the pungent forest of fir and pine. When he halted and slid his hands beneath her hair to tilt her face toward his for a kiss, she didn't protest. But her lips were unmoving.

His thumbs stroked her cheeks, wiping away dampness. "You have to trust me, Olivia." He could feel the tremors in her body as he pulled her closer. "I won't hurt Cammie. I won't hurt you." He said it almost like a vow, but as the words left his lips, he realized the truth of them.

Traditional or not, Olivia and Cammie were his family... as much or more than Gareth, Jacob and Victor. He would protect them with every fiber of his being, to the death if necessary. If he could make Olivia understand how deep his feelings ran, how desperately he wanted to take care of both the women in his life, perhaps she would be more inclined to believe his sincerity and his resolve.

With aching slowness he claimed her mouth, tasting her, nipping at her tongue. At last, her arms circled his neck and her sweet lips dueled with his. There was less tenderness tonight, more unrestrained passion. Frustration and conflict segued into ragged hunger and rough caresses.

He jerked her shirt over her head and fumbled with the bra, dragging it down her arms and tossing it away haphazardly. Red-hot desire hazed his vision, and he trembled as if he had a fever.

Her lush breasts took on gooseflesh in the night air, and her nipples pebbled into small, hard stones. He took them in his mouth, one after the other, and suckled her, dragging on her tender flesh with his mouth and plumping her breasts with worshipful hands.

Olivia moaned, a sound that went straight to his groin

and sent scalding heat to scorch him alive. He ripped at her jeans, shoving them down her hips only enough to touch her between her legs. She was damp and ready for him.

Freeing his own eager sex, he fumbled in his pants pocket for a condom, rolled it on and then lifted her and braced her against the nearest tree. It was animalistic and raw and absolutely necessary.

With a grunt of determination, he thrust up and into her warm, hot passage. The sensation of being caressed by wet silk made him groan aloud. "I can't get enough of you," he said, the words muffled against her neck. "God, you make me burn."

After that, conversation evaporated in the white-hot conflagration of his drive to completion. Olivia's fingernails bit into his shoulders as she clung to him in desperation. He gripped her ass and lifted her high, angling his hips to fill her more deeply.

She cried out and trembled, heart pounding against his as she climaxed wildly, her inner muscles milking him. Her release triggered his. Keeping his hands under her ass to protect her from painful contact with the tree, he thrust recklessly, not caring if his hands suffered in the process. Nothing could have separated him from her in that moment.

She kissed him softly, and the simple caress was his undoing. Shaking, breathing hoarsely, he came with a rapid fire punch of his hips, feeling his strength drain away as he reached the end.

Legs embarrassingly weak, he went down, rolling onto his back in a sea of pine needles, settling Olivia on top of him as they both recovered. "Stay the summer," he begged.

She put her hand on his lips. "Stop. Let it go for now. I'll travel to New York with you. That's two more nights, total. After that, Cammie and I have to go home. I have a project to finish, and she has play dates scheduled with friends. We have a life, Kieran. But I'll consider returning later in the summer for a visit. Don't push me on this."

It was hard to be angry when she laid on top of him, every voluptuous inch of her his for the taking. Lazily he rubbed her firm, generous ass. She was the most intensely *female* woman he had ever known. As though her entire body was created for the purpose of male fantasy.

His erection was already perking up, but he had only brought one condom. Bad mistake. Instead of feeding his own hungry obsession, he reached between them and touched the tiny bud of nerves that made her quiver and pant. Deliberately he brought her to the brink again. She tried to fight him, but her body defeated her.

"Come for me, baby," he urged, relishing the feel of her dew on his fingers. He might ache, unappeased, for hours, but it was worth it to hear her call his name as she spiraled into bliss and then slumped onto his chest.

Eight

Olivia wanted to remain in the dark. Deep in the woods, she could pretend that she wasn't scared of repeating mistakes that should have been far behind her.

She wasn't lying to Kieran when she said she didn't want Cammie falling in love with him only to experience a child's broken heart when he left. But that was only half the truth.

Olivia couldn't, shouldn't, wouldn't fall in love with him again, either, and that's what was bound to happen if she remained on Wolff Mountain for the summer. Though she'd die rather than admit it, Kieran *was* irresistible. Look how she'd tumbled into his arms with barely a protest. Only physical distance could protect her. In New York, she planned to make her position clear.

Neutral ground, Kieran had said. The proposition sounded sensible on the surface. But Olivia had been to

New York several times, and she knew that with the right man, the city would be magical.

She could always make celibacy a condition of the trip, but that would be self-deceptive in the extreme. She *wanted* Kieran...looked forward to spending an uninterrupted night in his arms. And by reminding herself that when it was done, it was done, she could protect her heart.

Maybe in August she and Cammie would make one final quick trip for Kieran to see his daughter. Then he'd fly out across the globe, and she and Cammie could get back to their normal lives.

Why did that thought have to hurt so much?

Olivia had grown up in chaos, being dragged around to movie sets all over the world, hiding in her bedroom when her flamboyant parents indulged in one of their theatrical shouting matches. All she had ever wanted was a peaceful, normal existence to raise her child. And if she looked seriously, surely there was some nice guy out there who would want to marry her and add to the family.

Try as she might, such a picture never came into focus.

Kieran held her hand as they made their way back to the house. Their feet made scarcely a sound as they walked.

Her fingers clung to his, wishing she had the right to be with him like this forever. He was a loving man, and an honorable one, despite his youthful misjudgments. He loved his family, and he was clearly on his way to loving Cammie, as well.

But ultimately he saw Wolff Mountain as a trap, one that had robbed him of his childhood. And though he might visit from time to time, he was never going to settle in one place.

They entered through the back of the house, treading quietly in deference to sleeping servants. When they entered the room where Jacob kept watch, he stood up and stretched. "I was about to give up on you."

Kieran grimaced. "Sorry. The time got away from me. It's a beautiful night."

Jacob's gaze settled on Olivia. He was a quiet, intense man, and his piercing eyes, like the X-ray machines he used, seemed to see right through her. "You need to watch out for my brother," he joked. "We used to call him the 'were-Wolff,' because he loved roaming the woods at night."

She blushed, feeling as if Jacob could see exactly what she and Kieran had been up to. "I enjoyed the walk," she said. Her red cheeks were probably a dead giveaway, but she kept her expression noncommittal.

In the wake of Jacob's departure, an awkward silence bloomed. Kieran's jaw was rigid, and hunger still tightened the planes of his face. "Will you come to my room?" he asked.

She shook her head, backing away. "I need to get some sleep. Cammie will be up early. Good night."

Her retreat was embarrassing to say the least, but she needed distance. His masculinity dragged her in, demanding a response, and for tonight, she needed to regroup and figure out how to protect her vulnerable heart.

Late the following morning Kieran's cousin Annalise arrived. She blew in on a burst of wind and rain, her laughter contagious and her genuine welcome hard to resist.

"So glad to meet you both," she said, squatting in Prada pumps to hug Cammie.

She was tall, dark-headed and gorgeous. And when she looked at Cammie, she was clearly shocked.

Olivia squirmed under her assessing gaze, but refused to be lured into saying something she would regret. "How was the family vacation?"

Annalise hugged her cousins, as well. Kieran and Jacob had showed up to eat lunch with her before going back to their construction project at Jacob's clinic. Gareth had gone home to see Gracie. "Daddy and the boys are still fishing in Wyoming, but I reached my fill of tying lures and fighting mosquitoes. Plus, I had to get home to see Kieran. It's like a sighting of the Loch Ness monster. You don't want to miss it."

"Very funny." Kieran suffered her teasing with an easy grin, slinging an arm around her shoulders as they walked to the dining room. "Admit it, brat. You just had to come home and meet my guests."

She wrinkled her classically beautiful nose. "You got me." She gave Olivia a rueful glance. "It's a well-known failing of mine," she said, patting Cammie's head as she seated herself at the table. "Whenever we were little, the guys tortured me by pretending to have secrets I wasn't privy to. I'd badger them unmercifully, until half the time they admitted that they had made it all up."

"It must have been hard being the only girl."

"You have no idea." She paused, expression concerned. "Where's Uncle Victor?"

"He had a rough night," Jacob said. "But he hopes to be with us for dinner."

Over a lunch of cold salads and fresh fruit, Olivia watched Annalise interact with her family. There were three more males not present, the brothers Annalise spoke of, as well as Vincent Wolff, who was Victor's twin. Clearly Annalise was close to Kieran and Jacob. She teased and kidded them with open affection.

The six young cousins had been raised in isolation in this huge house after the violent deaths of their mothers. It was no wonder they had formed a bond. Tragedy had marked this family and shaped its face.

When the meal was concluded, the men were itching to get back to work. Annalise turned to Olivia, her face alight with enthusiasm. "Why don't we go swim in Gareth and Gracie's pool?"

"A pool?" Olivia looked askance at the window where lightning flashed and water rolled down the panes.

"Indoors, silly." Annalise laughed.

Kieran frowned. "Does Cammie know how to swim?"

"We're from southern California. Of course she does." Olivia noted Kieran's response, as did Annalise. He had reacted with a parent's automatic concern. Olivia wondered how long it would be before someone in Kieran's family came right out and demanded to know if Cammie was a Wolff.

The pool was amazing. Built to resemble a natural tropical lake, it featured a waterfall, twittering parakeets and water that was heated just enough to be luxuriously comfortable.

Cammie loved it. She swam like a fish, and soon she was all over the pool. Gracie joined them soon after they arrived. The small redhead had a quiet smile and a look of contentment about her that Olivia envied.

At one point, Annalise threw back her head and laughed in delight. "I *love* having women here," she exclaimed, beaming in her gold bikini that seemed more suited to sunbathing at a resort on the French Riviera rather than actually getting wet.

Gracie nodded. "Me, too. After our honeymoon, Annalise was gone, and I have to confess that I was lonely sometimes for girl talk."

"How long have you two been married?" Olivia asked.

"Less than two months. I'm still getting used to this amazing house."

Gareth's Western-themed home was spectacular, though not as large as Wolff Castle, of course. And Olivia had glimpsed Jacob's more modern house through the trees. She frowned. "Why has Kieran never built his own place?"

Annalise shrugged. "Doesn't need one. He's here less than a dozen nights during the year. Two days at Christmas if we're lucky. Other than that, he's always on the go. The constraints of our situation were hard on all of us kids growing up, but Kieran chafed at them more than anyone. At the first opportunity, he struck out for freedom and has never really looked back. You can't cage a man who wants to roam."

Was that pity Olivia saw in Annalise's eyes? Olivia hoped not. It was bad enough for Olivia to acknowledge to herself that a future with Kieran was impossible. She didn't want or need anyone's commiseration, no matter how well meant.

When Gracie hopped out of the pool to dry off and get back to her painting, Olivia spoke quietly to Annalise, all the while keeping tabs on Cammie's high energy stunts. "Kieran has asked me to go to New York with him overnight. He thought you wouldn't mind keeping Cammie. Did he volunteer you too freely?"

"Of course not." Annalise straightened one of the flimsy triangles of her bathing suit top. Though she was the complete antithesis of Olivia's mother in looks, she possessed the same star quality. A woman no one, particularly no man, could resist. She smiled. "Cammie is a delight, and I'd be happy to look after her."

Standing next to her, waist deep in silky water, Olivia felt frumpy and large, though Kieran certainly seemed to have no complaints about her less than reed-thin figure. His appreciation for her…assets was flattering.

She signed inwardly. "Just one night, and we won't be late the following day, because Cammie and I will have to catch the red-eye back to the West Coast. That reminds me, I need to shift our tickets one day later."

"Why don't you take the family jet? Did Kieran not offer?"

"He has. Several times. But I prefer to make my own travel arrangements."

"Because you don't want to feel beholden to him?"

"It's not that. I've tried to raise Cammie away from the over-the-top lifestyle my parents enjoy."

"How's that workin' out for you?"

Olivia shook her head ruefully. "Sometimes I think it's a losing battle."

"So you didn't like growing up with all the bells and whistles?"

"I liked the toys and activities as much as the next kid. But I had friends whose parents were what I thought of as *normal*. Nine-to-five jobs, cookouts on the weekend. T-ball games. That wasn't part of my life, and I wanted it for Cammie."

"Sometimes we don't appreciate what's in our own backyard. There's something to be said for not having to worry constantly about money. And there's also the satisfaction that comes from helping people less fortunate. Our family has never wanted for anything, but I like to think we aren't spoiled. Our fathers instilled in us a sense of responsibility, *noblesse oblige,* if you will."

"If I can do as much for Cammie, I'll be happy."

Annalise twisted the ends of her long hair and squeezed out water. "She's a great kid, already. For a single mom, you've done a great job. It can't have been easy."

Here it comes. Olivia braced herself, waiting for Annalise to demand an explanation of Cammie's parentage. But the other woman merely smiled.

"Thank you," Olivia said awkwardly. She followed Annalise out of the pool and began drying off.

"If you ever need a friendly ear, I'm here." For once, the bubbly personality shifted to reveal a deep vein of seriousness. Her eyes, like Jacob's, seemed to see all.

"I appreciate that." For a moment, Olivia was tempted. She wanted to share with another female the fears and heartaches that came with being Kieran's lover, with bearing his child. But Annalise was Kieran's cousin, part of his family. Olivia had not even allowed Kieran to claim his daughter yet, so it would be unethical at the very least to share their secret.

She wrapped a towel around her waist and stretched out on a lounge chair to watch Cammie play. Annalise did the same. From speakers tucked away somewhere in the foliage, pleasant music played. Olivia yawned, ruefully aware that her unsettled sleep had everything to do with Kieran. When she wasn't actually with him, she was dreaming about him. What did that say about her subconscious desires?

Annalise's long legs were tanned and toned, making Olivia realize it had been some time since she herself had hit the gym. It was tough with a child. An older woman in Olivia's neighborhood came most mornings for several hours to watch Cammie so Olivia could work. Cammie still napped in the afternoons, and after that it was time to fix dinner, play games and enjoy bath time.

The routine worked well for them, and Olivia wasn't willing to leave her child with an evening babysitter to go work out. Perhaps after Cammie started kindergarten it would be easier.

Cammie did a handstand in the shallow end, making sure both women were watching. They clapped and cheered her success.

Olivia grinned, pleased that her daughter was enjoying

this visit. "Cammie found one of your old ballet costumes in the attic. I hope it was okay for her to play with it."

"Of course." Annalise yawned, leaning back her head and closing her eyes. "Tomorrow I'll show her my secret trove of Barbie dolls. I had to keep them hidden or the boys would pop off their heads."

"That's terrible." But Olivia chuckled in spite of herself.

Annalise lifted one eyelid, her expression morose. "Don't get me started."

Nine

Olivia and Kieran left for New York at first light. Though Olivia had worried about abandoning Cammie, it was clear the child was having the time of her life. Victor Wolff doted on her. Jacob promised her a tour of his clinic and a lollipop, and Gareth and Gracie had sent up a note inviting Cammie to swim again.

And then there was Annalise. She and Cammie had bonded like long lost sisters. If anything, Cammie was the more sensible of the two. Annalise had planned out a twenty-four-hour agenda of fun that would be impossible to fulfill, but she delighted in making Cammie laugh at her antics.

Kieran and Olivia said their goodbyes and departed via helicopter to a small airstrip near Charlottesville. There, the Wolff family jet sat waiting, its brilliant white fuselage gleaming in the sunlight. Though Olivia was well accustomed to luxury and pampering, the level of wealth enjoyed by Kieran and his clan far surpassed anything she had experienced.

Fortunately she had packed liberally in preparation for her trip to Wolff Mountain. Knowing nothing of Kieran's family or what to expect socially, she had gladly paid for extra bags so her wardrobe and Cammie's would cover all eventualities. Which meant that she had plenty of choices for this impromptu New York trip.

Inside the plane, a handsome male attendant offered Olivia her pick of beverages along with a midmorning snack, in case her breakfast had been inadequate. She declined the fruit parfait with murmured thanks. Her earlier meal had been more than generous. Victor Wolff's current chef had once served in the White House, and with three full-time cooks to assist him, the menu offerings were varied and delicious.

Kieran grabbed a bag of cashews and went forward to chat with the pilot. As Olivia fastened her seat belt in preparation for takeoff, she had time to appreciate her plush seat. It was more of an armchair, really. She stretched her legs and felt a little frisson of excitement wend its way through her veins.

Rarely did she take time all to herself for something as frivolous as a vacation. Tending to a rambunctious child, even when she and Cammie traveled with Lolita and Javier, generally meant little downtime.

Closing her eyes with a smile of contentment, she let her mind drift. It was a shock when she felt a warm hand settle on her shoulder. When she looked up, Kieran grinned at her, his expression more lighthearted than she had seen him at any time since their university days.

He sat down in the seat adjacent to hers and clicked his belt. "Are you a good flier, or one of the white-knuckled types?"

"I love it," she said simply. "How about you?"

"It gets me from A to B quickly, and for someone in my line of work, that's the main thing. But I also love the freedom and the sense of adventure. I've never lost that. Don't guess I ever will."

Olivia's heart sank. This Kieran, chomping at the bit to take off, was the man who circumnavigated the globe. She could see in his body language the expectation, the energy.

The day dimmed suddenly and her anticipation of the trip palled. It was painful to see the evidence of what she had only surmised. Her lover, the father of her child, was a road warrior, an adventurer. He would never be content to live inside Olivia's mythical white picket fence.

Soon, the noise of takeoff overrode the possibility of conversation. Olivia closed her eyes again and pretended to sleep. Her emotions were too close to the surface. She could fall in love with him again so easily. Not with the nostalgic reminiscence of a young woman's rosy fantasy, but in a solid, real way. How could she not? He was caring and honorable. With Cammie, he showed a gentle side that ripped at Olivia's heart.

Kieran loved his daughter, even knowing as little of her as he did. He was committed to being her dad. Only Olivia's fears and reservations stood in the way. That and her determination to protect herself from the pain of losing him again. The devastation six years ago still rippled inside her, waiting to be resurrected. Terrifying in its power.

As Kieran spoke to the attendant, Olivia studied his profile. Classic nose, sculpted chin. Straight teeth that flashed white in a tanned face when he smiled. His body was fit and healthy; his long limbs and broad shoulders were a pleasing package of masculine perfection.

Her mouth dried and her thighs tightened as she remembered last night's lovemaking. When they were together, he made her feel like the most important, most desirable woman in the world. His frank hunger and sensual demands called to the essence of her femininity.

Though she was well capable of taking care of herself, she enjoyed his protectiveness, his innate gentlemanly core of behavior. In a crisis, Kieran Wolff would be a rock.

At one time, being his wife had been her dream. Now she knew that even if he put his name on a piece of paper, the dream would end in pain and frustration. Olivia knew herself. She needed a lover who would be there on the ordinary days and not just in the midst of an emergency.

Kieran could handle the crises. No doubt about that. But Olivia was pretty sure that he would just as soon not have to deal with the mundane aspects of family life.

Taking out the trash, paying bills, mowing the grass. Ordinary husbands and fathers did those things.

Too bad Kieran Wolff was not ordinary. And too bad that *ordinary* was what Olivia had always wanted.

To Olivia's surprise, she actually slept. Kieran woke her in time to peek out the nearest window and see the Statue of Liberty as they flew past. Soon, the landing gear deployed, the pilot set them down with a tiny bump and it was time to go.

A limousine awaited them on the tarmac.

In no time at all, Kieran and Olivia were speeding toward the city amidst a maze of taxicabs. He took her hand, surprising her. As he lifted it to his lips for a kiss, he smiled lazily. "We're going to drop you downtown. Do you mind entertaining yourself for a couple of hours while I get this meeting out of the way?"

"Of course not, but I…"

"What?"

She bit her lip. "I owe you an apology. I thought this *business trip* was only an excuse to get me alone."

They were sitting so close, she could inhale the after-shave he had used that morning. In a severely tailored charcoal-gray suit with a pale blue shirt and matching tie, he looked nothing like the man she had come to know. If he had reminded her of Indiana Jones before, now he looked more like a character from Wall Street. She wasn't sure she liked the transformation.

He tugged her closer, one strong arm encircling her waist as he claimed her mouth with an aggressive kiss. When she was breathless, her heart pounding, he released her and sat back. "Sucking up to the fat cats is a necessary evil for the work I do."

"What do you mean?"

"I'm meeting this morning with the heirs of a wealthy socialite. The dead mother wanted to fund a variety of charitable works around the world. But her charming children thought the ten million she left each of them was an insult, so they went to court. Fortunately the judge couldn't be bought and he upheld the will. Unfortunately for me, the kids sit on the foundation board, so I have to deal with their greedy, petulant demands to get what I need for my next project."

"The one in September?"

He nodded. "We're going to design and build an orphanage in the Sudan. A variety of church agencies will do the staffing and oversee operations."

"Isn't it dangerous there?"

He shrugged. "Have you looked around the Big Apple? You can get killed crossing the street."

Before Olivia could respond, the car pulled up in front of a row of small, and obviously expensive, designer shops. She wrinkled her nose. "I'd really rather go to Macy's, the original on 34th Street. You know…from the movie. Is that too far out of our way?"

"No. But I thought given your Hollywood roots you'd enjoy the upscale shopping."

She shrugged. "I'm really more of a Macy's kind of gal."

"Whatever you say." The ride to midtown didn't take long. When Kieran hopped out to open Olivia's door and escort her to the sidewalk, he tucked a stray hair behind her ear, his gaze filled with something she wanted to believe was more than affection. "Here's my card with all my numbers. Have fun," he said softly, brushing a kiss across her lips.

Her arms wanted to cling, to beg him to stay. She forced herself to back up. "Go to your meeting. I'll be fine."

He winced when a cacophony of horns protested the illegally parked limo. "I'll call you when we're done."

Kieran tolerated the meeting with less than his customary patience. The "awful offspring," as he had nicknamed them in his mind, were no more difficult than usual, but today he was in no frame of mind to placate them. All he could think about was getting Olivia back to a hotel room and spending twenty-four hours in bed.

It was a great fantasy, but, of course, the gentlemanly thing to do would be to show her a good time out on the town first. Even that would be fun with Olivia.

And then there was the issue of Cammie. Once he made his case for claiming his rights as a father, would the mood be ruined? He wasn't sure where Olivia stood at the moment. Sometimes it seemed as if she was ready for him to tell Cammie the truth. But on other occasions, she bowed up, determined that Kieran was not father material.

To further strain his mood, the meeting ran long. At twelve-thirty, he finally stood and excused himself. The major business had been completed. All that was left was the minutiae that didn't require his presence.

He called downstairs, and the limo was waiting when he strode out into the sunshine. Unfortunately the lunch hour rush had traffic backed up in all directions. When they finally reached Macy's, after sending Olivia a text that they were on the way, Kieran's head was pounding from hunger and tension.

Olivia jumped in quickly, all smiles. A lot of women would be bitching about his late arrival. Instead, she seemed happy to see him. Kieran reacted to her greeting automatically, but inside, he dealt with a stunning realization. He had become addicted to her smile. In fact, he couldn't imagine going a day without seeing that look on her face.

The knowledge shook him. Since the death of his mother and his father's involuntary emotional abandonment, Kieran had never really allowed himself to *need* anyone. He prided himself on being self-sufficient, a lone Wolff.

He took Olivia's hand in his, clearing his throat to speak. "I know several great restaurants where we can have lunch. Do you have a preference?"

She patted the large shopping bag at her feet. "When your meeting ran late, I picked up several things at the gourmet shop around the corner. I thought we could have a picnic in Central Park. What do you think?"

Suddenly the irritations of the past several hours rolled away. "Sounds perfect." He gave the driver a few directions, and soon they were hopping out in front of the Metropolitan Museum of Art. As they crossed Fifth Avenue and entered the park, he took Olivia's heavy bag. "Good Lord. What all did you buy?"

She laughed, shoving her hair out of her face as the wind whipped it carelessly. Her beautiful creamy skin glowed in the sunlight, revealing not a flaw or an imperfection. He suspected that Olivia, growing up as she had in the shadow of her outrageous mother, had no clue that she was equally stunning. It would be his job and his pleasure to convince her.

With no blanket to stretch on the grass, they instead sat on a bench overlooking the lake, in a patch of shade that lent dappled shadows to their alfresco feast. Olivia wore a white sundress scattered with yellow-and-orange sunflowers. When she took off her small sweater, Kieran's food stuck in his throat.

Her body was like a centerfold's, curvaceous, even voluptuous. With her sienna hair and chocolate eyes, she reminded him of a young Sophia Loren. The dress was not particularly immodest, but the crisscrossed vee of the neckline was hard-pressed to contain her full breasts. He imagined licking his way from her collarbone down each rich slope, and his body hardened painfully, visualizing what it would be like to peel back the cloth and reveal pert nipples.

Nestled against the cleavage was a yellow diamond pendant that he remembered from their university days. Her parents had given it to her for her twenty-first birthday. Olivia had been loath to wear the expensive bauble on a daily basis, but he had lobbied for enjoying the gift and not worrying about losing it.

He tore his gaze from her charms and guzzled his Perrier, wishing fervently that they had dined in a more private locale. All around them life ebbed and flowed…the dog walkers, the teenage lovers, the nannies pushing expensive strollers. Seeing the babies made him frown.

How *would* he have reacted if Olivia had let him know she was pregnant? Back then, he'd been full of piss and vinegar, chomping at the bit to make a name for himself in the world, especially a world that had nothing to do with the Wolff empire. Parenthood wasn't even on his radar.

As soon as Victor recovered from the heart attack that had brought Kieran home from Oxford, Kieran had hit the road, determined to explore the globe despite his father's concerns about safety. Where Kieran went, no one knew or cared who he was. He waded through rice paddies, canoed down rivers of sludge in mosquito-infested jungles, hiked soaring peaks where the air was so thin a man gasped to breathe.

And every mile took him farther and farther away from the mountain that had been his prison, albeit a luxurious one. He'd kept in touch via the occasional email and phone call, learning that Gareth and Jacob were acting out their own rebellions. As far as the civilized world knew, Kieran Wolff had ceased to exist.

Gradually his nomadic existence with no purpose began to pall. His first project had come about almost by accident. He'd been in Bangladesh during a monsoon, and the resultant water damage had left a huge cleanup effort. Kieran had pitched in to rebuild bridges that connected remote villages to the help they so desperately needed.

After that, he'd found his architectural skills in demand from place to place. He used to joke that he was a cross between Johnny Appleseed and Frank Lloyd Wright. His work gave him a sense of peace and fulfillment, something he'd never been able to find at home.

But what if he had known about Cammie?

The question buzzed in his brain like an annoying gadfly.

Olivia brushed bread crumbs off her skirt and stretched out her legs, crossing them at the ankles. Her toenails were painted a deep coral that matched her dress. Kieran wanted desperately to kiss each delicately arched, perfect foot.

God knows he'd never been a fetishist, but somehow, Olivia was turning everything he thought he knew about himself on its ear. She made him ache and sweat and laugh all in the space of a single conversation. How had he ever made the decision to leave her six years ago?

The answer was easy. For once in his life, he'd done the mature thing. When Olivia talked back then, he had listened. Hearing about how much she hated the unsettled childhood she had experienced and how badly she wanted to settle down and be *normal* made him realize he had to give her up before either of them got in too deep.

The Wolffs were not a normal family.

But his altruistic decision had, in the end, caused Olivia even more pain. She believed he didn't want her. Surely she couldn't doubt that now. He needed the summer to prove to her that he had wanted her back then and he wanted her still.

Cammie's existence changed everything. Kieran and Olivia *were* involved. Only time would tell how deeply.

He sighed inwardly, wondering if such a thing as salvation existed. He was more than happy to pay atonement, but Olivia had to accept his offering. "What now?" he asked abruptly. "A Broadway matinee? A harbor tour? More shopping?"

Olivia half turned to face him, her face shadowed with worry. "We can't ignore the elephant in the room. You brought me here to hash out our situation. We might as well deal with that, and maybe then I'll be able to enjoy the rest of the day."

He shrugged, stretching his arms along the back of the bench and staring out across the water. "You know my position. I want you to stay for the entire summer, and I want to tell Cammie that I'm her dad."

Olivia nibbled her bottom lip, hands twisting in her lap. "I have work to finish, Kieran. I need to get back to my studio."

"Tell me about that," he said, wanting to know everything concerning her life, what made her tick. He'd been impressed with her talent for whimsical watercolors when they first met, and he'd recognized an ambition and drive for perfection that mirrored his own.

"I illustrate children's stories for two publishers here in New York. It's a flexible job, which means I can be there for Cammie when she needs me. One of my last books was nominated for an award."

"You've done well, then."

She nodded. "I never wanted to live off my parents. I like my independence and the security of knowing I'm providing for my daughter."

"So why can't you work on the mountain?"

"It's not as easy as that, Kieran. I have paints and papers and supplies. And besides…"

"Yes?" He had a feeling he wasn't going to like this one.

"I haven't changed my mind about what your leaving would do to Cammie. She sees you as a buddy now, but it would be so much worse if you were her father. I haven't told you this, because I didn't want to cause you pain, but she has always begged me for a daddy, ever since she was old enough to know that she was supposed to have two parents and not just me. If we told her the truth, she would jump to the conclusion that you were going to come back to California and live with us."

The image of his baby daughter begging for a daddy haunted him. Regret sat like a boulder on his chest. "So that's your final word?"

She stared at him, solemn, wary. "Are you going to take me to court?"

He stood up and turned away from her, afraid of what she might see on his face. "Oh, hell. Of course not." Impotence and rage tore at him, but what made it worse was that he had no target for his anger.

Olivia joined him, wrapping an arm around his waist and laying her head on his shoulder. "Don't be mad…please. I'm trying to do what's best. Maybe not for you or for me, but for Cammie."

He tugged her close with his left arm, still staring at boaters on the lake that sparkled like diamonds in the sun. "I'm not mad," he said gruffly.

"Let me go home tomorrow," she said. "I'll finish my project. Cammie and I have some fun summer activities planned. Then in August we'll come back for another visit before you have to leave for the Sudan."

He thought of all the long, lonely weeks that stretched between now and then. "Will you promise to think about letting me tell her who I really am?"

Her body stiffened in his embrace and finally relaxed. "I'll think about it," she said softly.

"That's all I ask." He wanted more…so much more. But for now he would bide his time.

Ten

Olivia felt terrible. Kieran was being firm, but reasonable, and she was the one refusing to compromise. But how could she? Nothing Kieran suggested had any basis in reality.

At least they had solved the question of whether or not she and Cammie would go home. Olivia badly needed physical distance to recoup her equilibrium. If she stayed with Kieran much longer, she would end up agreeing to anything solely to see his smile and to feel his body wrapped around hers.

He had shed his suit jacket in the limo earlier, and had rolled up his shirtsleeves. To the casual observer he was a big city businessman taking a lunch break in the midst of a busy day. But Olivia knew better. Like a chameleon, he had assumed the camouflage that enabled him to get what he wanted.

Kieran Wolff might appear civilized at the moment, but in reality, he was a man's man—steel-cored, physically honed, mentally sharp. Olivia had no doubt that he could accomplish anything he put his mind to...which didn't bode well for her ability to hold out against his wishes in the long run. He might very well be planning to wear down her resistance by any means necessary...including intimacy.

She had little defense against him, though she'd tried to keep her distance. Men could have sex for the sake of sex. Why couldn't women? If Olivia kept her head, she could enjoy the time with Kieran but not let her good sense be swayed by his magnetism.

Two choices, both risky. Leave and take Cammie away, provoking Kieran's anger and possible vengeance. Or stay, and keep her heart intact by regarding any sexual relationship as temporary and recreational.

She gulped inwardly. There was no doubt that she and Kieran were going to end up in bed together before the day was out. Not because he was going to lure her there, but because she wanted him desperately. One more day. Surely she could keep her messy emotions at bay for one more day. And then a brief visit in August. After that, Kieran would be safely on the other side of the world, and there would be no chance of Olivia doing something embarrassing like going down on her knees and begging him to stay and love her *and* her daughter.

He released her and gathered up their lunch debris, tossing it in a nearby receptacle. "Have you ever taken a carriage ride in the park?" he asked.

"No. But I'd rather do that at night, I think."

"Okay. Then what shall we do now? Anything you want. I'm at your disposal."

"How about we check into our hotel and not waste any more time?"

Her boldness shocked him. Heck, she shocked herself. It was almost amusing to see the slack-jawed surprise on

Kieran's face. Almost, but not quite. Limbs trembling and stomach doing flips, she awaited his answer.

Kieran stood there in the sunlight, gorgeous as a big jungle cat, and equally dangerous. "Are you serious?"

She approached him slowly, her feet having a hard time making the steps. "Completely. I want to be with you for as much time as we have. I want to sleep in your bed and wake up beside you. I want it all."

All constituted a heck of a lot in her book, surely more than he was willing or able to give. But he would think she was referring to sex, and that was okay. No reason for him to know that she was so much in love with him that the thought of returning to California was an actual pain in her chest.

He took her wrist and reeled her in, snaking an arm behind her waist and pulling her against his chest. "You're going to get me arrested," he muttered, his mouth moving over hers with sensual intent. "I'm not sure I can resist taking you here…now." He dragged her off the path near a clump of trees. Privacy was still not an option, but at least they weren't smack in the middle of the walkway.

His erection thrust between them, full, hard, seeking.

Her knees went weak, and if he hadn't been supporting her, she might have melted to the ground in a puddle of need. No one was paying any attention to them. But this game was dangerous. "Isn't the hotel close?" she panted.

"Not close enough." He bit her bottom lip and pulled it into his mouth, sucking until she shuddered. She wanted to climb inside his clothes, rip them from his body.

"Call the car," she begged.

He smelled of starched cotton and warm male skin. His hands cupped her ass. "I could tell the driver to circle the city…over and over and over. Have you ever made love in a limo, Olivia?"

Dizzy, needing oxygen, she leaned into him. "No. Have you?"

"Never had the pleasure. But damned if I couldn't be persuaded right about now."

She whimpered when he pulled away and barked an order into his cell phone. The planes of his face were taut, his eyes glittering with arousal. "C'mon. He's picking us up in five minutes."

Hand in hand, they walked rapidly. His breathing was audible and as choppy as her own.

Unfortunately the car ride from the edge of the park to the Carlyle was long enough for only one heated kiss. Suddenly a uniformed gentleman was opening Olivia's door and they were engulfed in the bustle of check-in. Twenty minutes later, in a luxurious suite that was blessedly quiet and totally private, Kieran faced her, arms folded across his chest. "Take off your dress."

The blunt command, combined with the intensity of his regard made her thighs quiver and her sex dampen. Never contemplating refusal, she shed the tiny shrug sweater and reached behind her for the zipper. When she stepped out of the dress and tossed it on a chair, she saw his eyes widen and his Adam's apple bob up and down.

The dress didn't require a bra, so she stood facing him in nothing but a lacy red thong and high heels. Her generous breasts were firm and high. The urge to cover them with her hands was there, but she resisted, wanting to please him.

His whispered curse was barely audible. She saw his fists clench at his hips. "Walk toward me."

The distance between her and the door where he stood was considerable, more so because she was naked and he was eyeing her like a condemned man who hadn't seen a woman in months.

When she was halfway across the room, he held out a hand. "Stop. Turn around. Take down your hair."

She had tucked it up in a loose chignon during lunch when the heat of the day made the weight of her long hair uncomfortable. Now she reached for the pins and removed them, dropping them into a cut glass dish on the coffee table. Deliberately she ran a hand through the masses of heavy, silky strands and shook her head.

When she was done, she looked at him over her shoulder through lowered lashes. "Does this meet with your approval, Mr. Wolff?"

His jaw firmed. "Are you sassing me, Olivia?"

"Would I do that?" Her eyes widened dramatically.

"Face me. Touch your breasts."

They were playing a game of chicken, and Kieran had just upped the stakes. Olivia felt her throat and cheeks flush, but she reversed her position and hesitantly placed her hands on her chest. Her voice was gone, locked down by the giant lump in her throat.

"I said *touch* them. Put your fingers on your nipples."

Good Lord. She licked her lips, dizzy and desperate for his touch. Feeling awkward but aroused, she did as he demanded, feeling her sensitive flesh bud and tighten as she stroked herself. The sensation was incredible, pleasuring herself as Kieran watched with a hooded gaze.

"Beautiful." He breathed the word like a prayer, the three syllables almost inaudible.

When her skin became too sensitive to continue, her hands dropped to her sides.

Kieran didn't move. How did he do it? She was so hungry for him, her whole body trembled.

But he wasn't finished. His gaze blazing with his heat, he narrowed his eyes. "Go to the bedroom. Don't look back. Lie down on the bed on your stomach."

She flinched in momentary fear. But it was a gut reaction. Kieran would never hurt her or make her uncomfortable. This was all about pleasure. His and hers.

Turning away from him was difficult. She knew he watched her, hawklike, as she walked slowly toward the doorway that led into the rest of the suite. Once, she stumbled, but she finally made it into the bedroom. For a moment, she stood in indecision. Was she supposed to turn back the covers?

The bedding was expensive and ornate. Making a rapid decision, she folded back the top layers and lay, facedown, on the smooth crisp sheet. Her heartbeat sounded loud and irregular in her ears. Her arms were by her sides. Ten seconds passed. She raised her arms over her head.

What did he want? What were his plans?

Moments later she heard the sound of his footsteps on the carpet. Nearby a rustle and then the rasp of a zipper. A soft clink when the belt buckle slid free. The sounds of a man undressing.

An activity that was at once commonplace and yet deeply erotic, particularly when the woman in his bed was not allowed to witness the disrobing. She imagined his long, muscular limbs, narrow hips, jutting arousal.

The bed shuddered when he put a knee beside her hip and joined her on the mattress. Without warning, he took her two wrists and bound them together with what felt like his necktie. She struggled instinctively. He paid her no mind.

The silk fabric tightened, and then she felt him lean down as he whispered in her ear. "You're at my mercy now. Everything I ask of you, you'll do, and in exchange, I'll make you burn."

"Kieran…" The word ended on a cry as he ran his tongue around the shell of her ear and winnowed his fingers through her hair. With a slow, steady touch, he massaged her scalp. His fingertips skated to her nape, the back of her ear. Her whole body craved his attention, but he was set on a course that was drugging, slow and steady.

Gradually, almost imperceptibly, he moved south, digging his thumbs into the tense muscles of her neck and shoulders. Her spine caught his focus. He ran his tongue the length of it and then rubbed gently on either side.

At her ass, he made a sound, a cross between a groan and a curse. Quivering, helpless, she felt him plump the cheeks, trace the cleft, reach beneath her and brush the part of her that ached the most.

When she spread her legs, begging wordlessly, he chuckled and abandoned the ground he had barely conquered. "Patience, Olivia."

She felt his hands beneath her hips, lifting her, turning her. Now she could see him, and the sight took her breath and shredded it. His broad chest was tanned and rippled with muscle. An arrow of fine, dark hair traced the midline, all the way down to where his shaft reared proudly against his abdomen.

His erection was thick and long, and a drop of moisture glistened on the tip. "Please," she begged without pride. "Please don't make us wait."

"Waiting is half the fun. I want you crazed when I finally take you, so lost to reason that nothing exists but you and me and this bed."

It was as if he were a hypnotist. Her body responded to his words atavistically, ceding control without a qualm. But by the look on his face, *his* control was more fragile than he was willing to admit. His jaw was tight. The dark flush of color staining his cheeks made him look wild and uncivilized…a man close to the edge.

He bent over her, no part of his body touching hers except

his lips. "I love your mouth," he said, tracing the soft flesh with his tongue and sliding through to taste her.

She tried to link her bound wrists over his head to trap him close, but he moved away, using one big hand to pin hers to the mattress. "Naughty, naughty," he teased.

Suddenly very serious, he kept his gaze locked on hers as he slid his free hand down her stomach and between her thighs. Two large fingers entered her, testing her readiness. Her hips came off the bed, her heartbeat racing as sweat beaded her forehead.

He never looked away and neither could she. All the secrets of a man's desires were there in his eyes if she could only translate them. Was this all he wanted from her? Dare she hope he needed more?

Stroking lazily, he turned interrogator. "Tell me about the men in your life, Olivia. Who has benefitted from what I taught you back in England?"

His finger brushed her clitoris and she gasped. "None of your damned business, Wolff man. I haven't quizzed you about your women in every port."

Back and forth. Back and forth. That brazen fingertip brought her closer and closer to the edge. "There haven't been that many," he said slowly, looking at his hand's mischief and not her face. "I work long hours when I'm overseas. Not much time for play."

"But a man like you can't go without sex for long. Back in university you wanted it twice a day, three times if we were lucky."

"That's because I was obsessed with you."

The blunt confession gave wings to her heart. But she reined in her excitement. The pertinent word in that sentence was in the past tense. *Was.* Kieran had been a horny young adult male. And Olivia had fallen into his bed like the proverbial ripe peach.

As a fully mature man, he was no less sexually primed, but he'd had any number of women since he left England so suddenly. And even now, being with Olivia was probably more about expedience and availability than any deep-seated obsession.

Kieran's early experiences in life had clearly stunted his ability to express deep emotion. He was a passionate man, but she doubted whether he was capable of true romantic love. That would mean putting a female first in his life, and she had seen no sign of such willingness in his behavior.

He clearly *wanted* her, but for Olivia, that would never be enough.

His hand moved, and she gave up analyzing the situation. Today was about physical pleasure. Her heart was safely locked away.

Kieran released her wrists. Sliding far down in the bed, he used his hands to widen the vee of her legs. When she felt his hot breath on her thighs, she tensed in panic. They had never explored this kind of intimacy when she was younger. "No, wait…" she blurted out. "I don't like this."

"How do you know?" he asked, a lazy smile tilting the corners of his mouth.

"Seriously, Kieran." She pushed at his shoulder. "I mean it. Stop."

He reared up, all humor erased from his face. "I'll stop. If you insist. But it would give me great pleasure to do this with you."

She nibbled her lower lip, caught between unease and cautious interest. "What if I can't come, because I'm too self-conscious?" Blurting out what she was thinking wasn't something she planned, but he might as well know the truth.

"Relax, Olivia. It's not an exam you have to study for. I want to make you happy. That's all. You don't have to do a thing."

Her hand fell to the sheet. "Well, I…"

Anticipating her consent, he resumed his earlier position. She felt the softness of his hair on her leg, jerked briefly as his hot breath feathered over her belly. "You're beautiful," he murmured.

She closed her eyes, arching her back at the first gentle pass of his tongue. When she moaned, helpless in the grip of shivering sensation that spread in warm ripples throughout her lower body, he repeated the motion. The sensation was indescribable. Like a warm, electric shock that built and built until she called out his name in a frenzy of need. "Kieran. Oh, God. Kieran."

His muffled response was neither decipherable nor important. She was lost, caught up in a whirlwind that slammed into her, dragged her over the edge of a perfect climax and dropped her helpless into his embrace.

When she recovered, he had moved up beside her and was leaning on an elbow watching her with a totally masculine satisfaction. "Still don't like it?" he asked drolly. One eyebrow lifted in a questioning stance.

She tried to corral her ragged breathing. "Don't brag."

He placed his hand, palm opened flat, on her belly. "Watching you come like that ranks as the highlight of my year."

"The year's only halfway done," she quipped, trying not to let him see how completely undone she was. "Too early to tell." She put her hand on top of his and laced their fingers together.

"Don't be so modest. I'm sure they heard you in Brooklyn."

"Kieran!" Mortification washed over her and she rolled to her side, bending her knee and resting her leg across his hairy thighs. They were hard and corded with muscle. His deep tan extended everywhere except for a narrow band of white at his hips and the tops of his thighs.

She imagined him, laboring out beneath a blazing tropical sun, shirtless, wearing only cargo shorts and boots. Did he ever get lonely always living among strangers? The question hovered on her lips, but she knew it was self-serving. Obviously his lifestyle suited him. Otherwise, he would have come home long ago.

He lifted her without warning and settled her astride his hips. His hunger unappeased, he flexed and grew at least another centimeter beneath her fascinated gaze. She put both hands on him, measuring the length and breadth.

Hard steel pulsed beneath his velvet skin. Even if she had been with a dozen lovers in the interim, she couldn't imagine that any of them would have been as beautiful in body and spirit as Kieran Wolff. Perhaps such a virile man might balk at the feminine adjective, but Olivia chose not to retract it, even in her own private discourse.

Kieran's body was perfect. Even the smattering of scars that were part and parcel of the hard physical labor he performed only served to make his physique more interesting.

She saw him reach for a condom, and her heartbeat accelerated.

Extending his hand, he challenged her. "Will you do the honors?"

Eleven

Kieran waited, amused and impatient, as Olivia fumbled
with the condom. The earnest intent on her face filled him
with tenderness and another feeling not so easy to diagnose.
He brushed aside the unfamiliar emotion and concentrated
on the physical.

While she labored, he played with her breasts displayed
so temptingly in front of his face. He tweaked a nipple, noticing with interest that his gentle pinch washed her face
with color. A similar firm caress on the other breast deepened the crimson.

Olivia finished her task, her face damp with perspira-
tion. "There. All set."

He tested the fit and nodded. "Good thing I brought a
dozen."

"A dozen?"

The strangled squeak in her voice made him chuckle despite the fact that the skin on his penis was tight enough to

cause every vein to bulge. He'd been in this state, in varying degrees, for over an hour now. In fact, he might set some kind of damned record for extended foreplay.

Not that he hadn't enjoyed himself immensely. God, she was sweet. And hot as a firecracker. Though she probably didn't see it in herself, she was one of the most innately sensual women he had ever met.

With his hand, he positioned himself. "You ready, honey?"

Her eyelids were at half-mast, her lips swollen from his kisses. The skin at her throat bore the marks of his passion, and her nipples puckered as if begging for his kisses. He leaned up and obliged, just as he thrust as hard as he could manage into her welcoming heat.

Their foreheads actually bumped together.

"Hell," he said ruefully, the pain giving him a moment's respite from total insanity. "Rub my head." His hands were clenched on her curvy ass, and he had no plans to let go.

She kissed his forehead. "Poor baby."

Her innocent motion seated him more deeply. "Hold still," he said through clenched teeth. "Damn it, I'm about to come."

"Isn't that the object of this exercise?"

He groaned, caught between incredulous laughter and the imminent explosion in his loins. Had any woman ever made him experience both in such measure? His heart caught, and he buried his face in her neck, panting, trying to stay the course. "You're killing me."

Reaching behind her, she found his sac and delicately played with him. It was like being hit by a lightning bolt. He lost control of himself, of her, of the entire flippin' situation.

Pumping his hips wildly, he thrust upward again and again, deaf, blind, mute...except for the caveman grunts that were all he could manage. Olivia clung to his shoulders as he fell to his back. Her breasts glided across his face, sweet-smelling, soft and warm.

God, he never wanted to stop. He wanted to mark her as his, to stake a claim. She found his lips and kissed him. That was all it took. He shot so hard that his balls pulled up, a vise tightened around his forehead and he saw nothing but blackness and yellow sparks for long, agonizing seconds.

At last, he lay spent, Olivia draped over him like a weary nymph.

"Good God in heaven."

She nodded, her breasts smashed against his heaving chest, her cheek resting atop his thundering heart. "I hope you're in good shape. I'd hate to have to call the concierge for the number of the closest cardiac center."

He stroked her ass, deciding he might never move. "You're something else, Olivia Delgado."

One eyelid lifted and then fluttered shut. "Mmm…"

"Don't go to sleep on me."

"Is that literally or metaphorically?"

Given her current posture, it was a fair question. "Either, I suppose." He yawned and stretched. "Any idea what time it is?"

"Do we care?"

"I may not have been entirely truthful." When she stiffened in his arms, he could have kicked himself for his unfortunate phraseology. "I promised we could do this for twenty-four hours, but I think I'm going to need sustenance."

"Room service?"

He patted her butt. "I was thinking of something a bit more upscale. After all, we *are* in the greatest city in the world. We should go somewhere incredibly expensive and over-the-top."

"And you know such a spot?" She slid off him, sat up and clutched the sheet to her chest.

Her sudden modesty was baffling. But then again, he never claimed to understand women. "I've heard Jacob talk about a place he likes."

"Jacob, the strong silent doctor? Somehow I thought he was above us mere mortals who need to eat."

"Jacob has his weaknesses. New York style cheesecake, for one. He's usually here in the city for medical conferences every year or so. In fact, he did a consult at Lenox Hill Hospital last Christmas."

"He's scary smart, isn't he?"

Kieran grinned. "Oh, yeah. Perfect score on the SATs. Four years of college in two and a half." He paused, and cocked his head. "Do we have to talk about my brother any longer, or can I interest you in a shower?"

"I'll race you."

He was treated to a delicious view of Olivia's backside as she dropped her only covering and darted into the bathroom. When he followed her, she was already hidden from view, water running. "Room for two?" he asked, stepping in without an invitation.

When Olivia sputtered with maidenly affront, he grinned. "I'll take that as a yes."

Olivia discovered that even a man who slept in grass huts and swallowed the occasional disgusting, edible bug could drum up romance if he put his mind to it, starting with a tuxedo that appeared as if by magic, delivered by a uniformed bellman.

When Kieran strode out of the bedroom clad in crisp black and white, fumbling with a bow tie, her breathing hitched. He was gorgeous. No other word to describe him.

"Help me with this damned thing," he said. "They're a necessary evil, but I'm out of practice."

She stood behind him and wrapped her arms around his neck, deftly folding the fabric into the desired configuration. "Out of practice?" She nipped his earlobe with her teeth. "I don't think so."

He turned and scooped her off her feet, twirling her in a circle before setting her back down. "I love reviews from satisfied customers."

"Customer? Good grief. Am I going to get a bill for services rendered?"

"I haven't decided yet. This afternoon was only my warm-up. I'll have to let you know."

He slid his hands beneath her hair and steadied her head while he dove deep for a hungry, forceful kiss.

On tiptoe, Olivia clung to his forearms and tried not to get the vapors. Kieran Wolff was like hundred-proof whiskey: guaranteed to go straight to a woman's head.

The night was clear and relatively cool so they decided to walk. The restaurant Kieran had chosen was only a couple of blocks away on a side street around the corner from East 76th.

He didn't hold her hand. But he did wrap an arm around her shoulders and tuck her close to his side. She felt warm and cherished, and for the span of an evening's stroll, she allowed herself to knit cobwebby dreams about happily ever afters.

When they arrived, Olivia paused on the sidewalk. "Do you mind if I call Cammie? She'll be in bed by the time we finish dinner."

"Of course not."

Olivia took her cell phone from her purse and punched in the contact info she'd saved for the Wolff house. An employee answered, and seconds later, Cammie's excited voice came on the line.

"Hi, Mommy. Me and Annalise are dressing up for dinner."

"Oh?" She grinned at her daughter's enthusiasm.

"We're going to be…" A muffled conversation ensued to the side and then Cammie said loudly, "…flappers."

"That sounds fun. Will you ask Annalise to take a picture for me?"

"Yes, ma'am. May I speak to Kieran now?"

Olivia hesitated, taken aback. Usually Cammie chattered away forever on such a phone call. "Sure," she said, handing her cell toward Kieran. "She wants to talk to you."

He blinked, and then smiled, barely masking his pleased surprise. But he hit the button for speakerphone, a thoughtful gesture that made Olivia ashamed of her odd jealousy. "Hey there, ladybug. What's happenin'?"

"I got to play with your wooden submarine today," Cammie said. "It's way cool, and Annalise tried to torpedo me a bunch of times, but I got out of the way."

Kieran laughed out loud. "Tomorrow morning, ask her to show you the secret tunnel. It's a little spooky, but a brave girl like you will like it."

Suddenly the line went silent, but in the background they could hear Cammie's excited squeal.

Annalise picked up the call. "How are you lovebirds getting along in New York?"

Kieran's lips quirked. He gave Olivia a rueful smile. "Behave, brat," he told his cousin firmly. "We're fine. Should be home by lunch tomorrow. I'll bring you a dozen bagels if you're nice to me."

"Oooh…bagels. Big spender."

Olivia giggled. "I can do better than that, Annalise.

Thanks again for keeping Cammie. Give her a kiss and hug for me."

They all said their goodbyes, and Kieran took Olivia's arm. "Ready to eat?"

She nodded, relieved to know that Cammie was happy and content. "I'm starving."

Patrice's was delightful, with snowy linen tablecloths, fresh bouquets of Dutch iris and freesias, and a modest string ensemble tucked away in a far corner. Even the lighting was perfect.

Olivia sank onto a velvet-covered banquette and leaned back with a sigh of appreciation. "Order for me," she said. "I'm in the mood to be surprised."

Kieran wondered how surprised Olivia would be if he were honest about his intentions. After dinner, he planned to hustle her back to the room and hold her captive there until they were forced to check out the following morning. He'd let her sleep…occasionally. But the sand in his hourglass was running out rapidly, so he didn't plan to waste a minute.

As they'd entered the restaurant earlier, practically every head had turned, the women's faces reflecting envy, and the men's expressions frankly lustful. Olivia was oblivious. How could she not recognize the impact she made? He'd never met a woman more genuinely modest and unselfconscious, especially not one with Olivia's stunning beauty.

The dress she wore tonight was deceptively simple…a slender column of deep burgundy with a halter neck and a back that plunged to the base of her spine. Her hair was pinned on top of her head in one of those messy knots women managed to create. The only accessory she had chosen to wear was a pair of dangling earrings comprised of tiny ruby and jet beads.

He knew her body intimately, and he was pretty certain she was wearing nothing beneath the sinuous fabric that clung to her body like a second skin.

A waiter interrupted Kieran's musings. By the time their order was placed, the sommelier appeared to offer a wine selection. Kieran perused the extensive list. "We'll have champagne," he said. "To celebrate." He indicated a choice near the top of the price list.

Olivia propped her chin on one hand and gazed at him curiously. "What are we celebrating?"

"How amazing you look in that dress."

His sincere compliment flustered her. She straightened and fidgeted, looking at their fellow diners. "Thank you."

"I mean it," he said. "You outshine your mother any day."

"Oh, please," she huffed. "I could stand to lose a few pounds, my mouth is too wide and my chest is too big."

He burst out laughing.

"What?" she cried.

"You really have no clue, do you?"

"I'm not sure what you mean." She played with her silverware, refusing to meet his gaze.

"First of all, my naive chick, as far as a man is concerned, there's no such thing as a chest that's too big. God in his infinite wisdom created breasts in all shapes and sizes, and yours are a work of art."

Her head snapped up at that, a small frown between her brows. But she didn't speak.

"Second of all," he continued, "just because your mother is petite and thin doesn't make her more beautiful than you. The camera may love the way she looks, but you are fabulous just the way you are. You're incredibly feminine and knock-'em-dead gorgeous. Every man in this room wishes he were sitting in my chair."

Her cheeks went pink. "You're a tall-tale raconteur, but thank you. That's very sweet."

He threw up his hands. "I give up. But know this, Olivia Delgado. I wouldn't change a thing about you." As the words left his mouth, he understood just how true they were. She was his ideal woman. And if he were in the market for a wife, he'd have to look no farther.

But he wasn't…in the market, that is. He was a man destined to travel alone. Despite that reality, he hoped to forge a bond with Cammie this summer that could withstand the long separations. He might not be the best dad in the world, but he would ensure that his daughter knew her father loved her.

Over a meal of stuffed quail and apple-chestnut dressing, they conversed lazily. Though he drank guardedly, the wine went to his head, and all he could think about was getting Olivia naked again. She, on the other hand, seemed content to enjoy the formal, drawn-out dinner.

Finally the final bite of dessert was consumed, the last cup of coffee sipped. Kieran summoned the waiter, asked for their check and waited, fingers drumming on the tablecloth, for Olivia to return from a trip to the ladies' room.

As he watched her make her way between the carefully orchestrated maze of tables, someone reached out a hand to stop her. Olivia's face lit up, and the next thing Kieran knew, his lover was being kissed enthusiastically on the mouth by a tall, handsome man in a dark suit.

Feeling his temper rise, Kieran got to his feet. Olivia didn't even look his way. Now she was hugging the mystery guy and patting his cheek. The waiter had the temerity to block Kieran's field of view for a few seconds as he provided the bill. Kieran scribbled his name with leashed impatience on the credit card slip and started toward the couple on the far side of the room.

"Olivia?"

She stayed where she was, only now the fellow had his arm around her waist. By the look of things, Olivia's admirer was dining alone. And in the meantime, trolling for other men's girlfriends?

Kieran tamped down his annoyance. "Am I missing the party?" he asked, not managing entirely to squelch his pique.

She reached for his hand. "Come meet someone, Kieran. This is my dear friend, Jeremy Vargas. We've known each other forever. We used to be in school together on the MGM lot. He's here in New York rehearsing for a stint in a Broadway play…during a brief lull between shooting a string of great movies. Jeremy, this is Kieran Wolff, my…" She stumbled, licked her lips and trailed off.

"Olivia and I are seeing each other." Kieran shook the man's hand, taking in the firm grip and easy smile that said Jeremy Vargas was confident and in no way threatened by Kieran's glower. "Nice to meet you," Kieran said, lying through his teeth.

Vargas might be a stage name, because Jeremy didn't appear to have a drop of Latino blood. He was the quintessential Hollywood golden boy, blond hair, blue eyes and a killer smile.

Olivia recovered and beamed her approval back and forth between the two of them.

Jeremy continued to embrace Olivia. "It's a pleasure, Kieran. You've snagged a great girl."

"A great *woman*." Was he the only one who noticed the note of over-familiarity in Jeremy's voice? And did Jeremy know about Cammie?

Olivia finally freed herself from the other man's proprietary hold and stood beside Kieran. "I wish we'd known you were here. We could have shared a meal."

Like hell. Kieran suddenly remembered where he had heard Vargas's name. He was mentioned in the article about Cammie's birthday party…as Olivia's date.

Intellectually Kieran knew that Olivia hadn't been a nun for the past five years. She was a passionate, gloriously beautiful woman. But seeing with his own eyes that other men weren't blind to her beauty put a sour taste in Kieran's mouth.

One day soon, when Olivia was ready to expand her white picket fence, perhaps with a second baby on the way, she wouldn't have any trouble finding men to line up for the role of husband and father.

Kieran brooded on the way back to the hotel. Damn Jeremy and his inopportune arrival. "Have you and Vargas dated?" he asked abruptly, tormented by the fact that she had an entire life apart from him.

"He's like a brother." The blunt response shut him up. After that, Olivia was mostly silent. Kieran wasn't sure if she was sleepy from too much champagne or if she was remembering all the reasons she wanted to keep him at arm's length.

In their hotel room, he paced, stripping off his jacket and tie, and swallowing a glass of ice water, hoping it would cool him down. Olivia removed her earrings. When that innocent tableau turned his sex to stone, he knew he was in trouble.

He cleared his throat. "Are you ready for bed?"

Twelve

Olivia dropped the earrings on the table. "For bed or for sex?" She met his gaze squarely, no pretense, no games. Her big brown eyes were rich and dark, masking her secrets.

"I want to make love to you." The words ripped his throat raw. He'd never said them to any woman.

Her face softened as if she read his inner turmoil. "I don't expect you to change for me, Kieran. You are who you are. I am who I am. We're two people who met at the wrong time and the wrong place. But we created a child and we have to put her first."

When he stood rigid, torn between honesty and seduction, she came to him and held out her hand. "Let's have tonight. Tomorrow will take care of itself."

He allowed himself to be persuaded. There was no choice, really. If he didn't have Olivia one more time, he would die, incinerated by the fire of his own reckless passion.

This time, he vowed to give her tenderness. He'd been

rough with her earlier, rough and earthy and carnal. What she deserved was a man who would worship at her feet.

He dropped to his knees, heart in his throat. Encircling her hips with his arms, he laid his head against her belly. She had carried his child, her lovely body rounded and large with the fruit of their desire. God, how he wished he had been with her, had been able to see her flesh expand and grow in lush, fertile beauty.

Her swollen breasts had nursed their baby. If life had played out differently, Kieran would have been there to watch. To be a part of something wonderful and new.

Regret was a futile emotion, one he'd learned a long time ago to push down into a dark, unacknowledged corner of his gut. The only important thing was the here and now. He lived for the moment...*in* the moment.

Olivia trembled in his embrace.

She stroked his hair. The light caress covered his skin in gooseflesh. What he felt for her hurt, reminding him of a dimly remembered anguish from his childhood. Women were soft and warm and wonderful. But loving them meant vulnerability. A man could not afford to let down his guard.

Without speaking, he snuggled her navel with his tongue, wetting the fabric of her dress. Carefully he bunched the cloth in his hands and lifted the long, slim skirt until he could see what had tantalized him all evening. A wispy pair of black lace panties, a thong, which explained why he'd thought she might be naked.

Despite his vow of gentleness, he gripped the thin bands at either side of her ass and ripped the fragile undergarment. It fell away, exposing her intimate feminine flesh.

Her smooth, honey-skinned thighs were scented with the distinctive perfume he'd come to recognize as her favorite.

Olivia tugged at his hair. "You're embarrassing me," she whispered. "Quit staring."

He stood abruptly and scooped her into his arms. "Whatever the lady wants." As he strode with her into the bedroom, Olivia nestled her head against his shoulder. The trust implicit in her posture dinged his conscience. He had failed her once before. This time he had to do what was right. He wanted the world to know he was Cammie's father, but if Olivia truly believed that was a mistake, Kieran might be forced to humble his pride and step back.

Retreat had never been his style. But for Olivia, he would try.

Beside the bed he stood her on her feet and, without ceremony, removed her dress. She stepped out of her shoes and put her cheek to his chest, hands on his shoulders. "Thank you for bringing me to New York," she whispered. "I think we needed this…for closure. I didn't want bad feelings between us."

He ignored her comments that intimated a swift and unwelcome end to their physical relationship. "Let me love you," he said hoarsely, the "L" word rolling more easily from his lips this time. "Lie down, Olivia."

Stripping off his clothes, he joined her on the bed. When she held up her arms, he couldn't decide if the smile on her face was a lover's welcome or the erotic coaxing of a siren, luring a man to doom.

Foreplay wasn't even an option. That had gone up in smoke during a four-course dinner with Olivia sitting across from him wearing a dress designed to turn a man's brain to mush. He found a condom, rolled it on and moved between her legs.

Their eyes met. As he entered her slowly, her lashes widened. Her breath caught. Her throat and upper chest flushed with color. He put his forehead to hers, filled with a maelstrom of inexplicable urges.

Half a millennium ago, he would have slain dragons for

her, might even have used his travels to bring home chests of gold and jewels. But Olivia didn't want the knight on the white charger. She was looking for a more stable fellow, perhaps the village miller or the town carpenter.

If Kieran truly wanted to make her happy, he would head out on his next crusade and leave her to build a life between the castle walls. Without him.

The room was silent save for their mingled breathing. He moved in her so slowly that her body seemed to clasp him and squeeze on every stroke. It was heaven and hell. Giving a man what he hadn't known he needed and in the next breath reminding him that the gift had an expiration date.

He braced most of his weight on his arms, but his hips pressed against hers, pinning her to the mattress. Her hair, fanned across the pillows, made an erotic picture that seared into his brain, never to be forgotten.

As he picked up the tempo, her legs came around his waist. Lifting up into his strokes, she arched her back and took what she wanted. Sensual and sweet, she looked like the girl he had first met on a rainy Saturday in the English countryside. She'd been alone, away from the hustle and bustle of an overcrowded house party, standing in the lane beneath a giant black umbrella, fumbling with a map and muttering mild imprecations beneath her breath.

Why hadn't he recognized what had landed in the palm of his hand for one brief spring? The vibrant, fragile butterfly that had been his relationship with Olivia….

How had he been so foolish as to crush those wings by his abrupt departure?

She touched his forehead, rubbing at the unconscious frown that had gathered between his brows. "You'll always be my first love," she said, gasping as he thrust deep. "No matter what happens next."

First love. Was that his only role? That and sperm provider?

Gentleness fled, chased away by frustration and self-directed anger. Damn the past. What about the future?

His body betrayed him then, slamming into hers with a violence that shook the bed. Olivia cried out as she climaxed, her eyes closed, her hands fisted in the sheets.

He felt his own orgasm breathing hot flames down his neck and tried to battle it back. But it was too late. Molten lava turned him inside out, gave birth to a shout of exultation laced with surrender, and trailed away, leaving a dark, inexplicable confusion.

Easing onto his back, he tried to corral his breathing. Olivia lay unmoving beside him, her chest rising and falling rapidly.

"We should get married," he said, the words coming from out of nowhere and surprising him as much as they apparently did Olivia.

Her body jerked, and she stiffened. "What? Why?"

Because I love you madly and can't imagine living my life without you. Any version of that response would have been acceptable to Olivia. But Kieran hadn't read the same script.

He ran a hand over his face and sighed. "It would be good for Cammie, I think. Assuming you're eventually going to tell her that I'm her father. If you and I were married, all the times I'm gone, she would have the security of knowing that we're a family."

"That won't make her miss you less."

"Maybe not. But she would know that I'm coming home to her eventually."

Eventually. Olivia hated that word. And she hated the fact that her stupid heart threw her under the bus again and again. Kieran wasn't in love with her. He felt *something* for her…affection, maybe…and a sense of duty. But that was never going to be enough. Not when Olivia wanted to give him every bit of her passion and devotion.

Kieran didn't need her. They weren't a couple.

"I don't like the idea," she said flatly. "I deserve to have a man in my life who loves me and can't live without me. What you're describing would be dishonest. Children are more intuitive than you realize. She would know the truth. I promised to think about you and Cammie. Give me time. Let me go home. In August I'll give you your answer."

He didn't respond, and to her chagrin, she realized that he had fallen asleep. Disheartened, she turned her back to him, and did the same.

When she woke up, Kieran wasn't in the bed beside her. A whiff of aftershave lingered in the air, so she surmised that he had risen early to shower. Perhaps after their awkward conversation the night before, he'd had no inclination to initiate any early-morning fooling around.

She leaned up on an elbow to look at the clock. Still plenty of time before their scheduled flight. The jet would be on standby, ready to go at their convenience. But Kieran had promised Annalise that he and Olivia would be back by lunchtime, so Olivia needed to get dressed.

When she appeared in the sitting room thirty minutes later, Kieran stood in front of the window, hands behind his back, looking down at the quiet street below.

He turned to face her, his expression grave. "Where's your cell phone?" he asked.

She grimaced. "I forgot to charge it last night. The battery's probably dead."

"Sit down, Olivia." He came to join her on the sofa, taking her hands in his and studying her face, his eyes filled with compassion. "Your parents have been trying to reach you. They finally called the house to relay a message, and Father contacted me."

Her heart thudded with fear. "What's wrong?"

"I need you to be brave," he said. "We'll get through this."

"Oh, my God…was there an accident?" Her blood turned to ice in her veins.

"Not that. They're fine."

"Then what?"

She actually saw on his face the struggle to choose a correct phrase. And Kieran's loss of words scared her more than anything had in a long, long time. "Just tell me," she croaked. "I can take it."

His thumbs rubbed absently over the backs of her hands, the repetitive motion not at all soothing given that his expression was torn and troubled. "Your mother's psycho stalker fire-bombed your house last night. It burned to the ground. Everything is gone."

She saw his lips moving, but the roaring in her ears drowned it out. Her eyes closed as hysteria welled in her chest. "No. You're wrong," she said, batting his hands away when he tried to hold her. "That's not possible. Cammie's baby album is there…and my paintings. All her toys…" Agony clogged her throat, exacerbated by the way Kieran looked at her. It couldn't be true.

"Take me there," she said. "Take me now. I want to see it." She was shaking all over, and the last words came out on a cry of pain.

Kieran took her shoulders and dragged her close, ignoring her wildly flailing fists, stroking her hair. "Hush, baby," he said. "I'm right here. It's going to be okay."

She cried in broken, gasping, wretched sobs that hurt her chest. A great, yawning chasm opened up at her feet, and she was terrified that she was going to fall into the depths and never claw her way back to the top. Again and again she repeated his words in her head. *Everything is gone.*

It seemed impossible and at the same time terrifyingly real.

She clung to Kieran, unashamed. Nothing else made sense. Time lost all meaning.

When the tears ran out, she lay limp in his embrace, her breathing ragged. "Did they catch him?" For some reason, that was the first question that popped into her brain.

"Not yet. But they will. He knew you weren't at home. The police profiler doesn't think he really wants to hurt anyone. This was a bid for attention."

"What about my parents?"

"They're surrounded by a twenty-four-hour security detail. The authorities think you and Cammie need to stay where you are until the man is in custody."

The irony didn't escape her. Kieran was getting exactly what he wanted. More time with his daughter.

She jerked out of his arms, wiping her cheeks with the heels of her hands. "I have to see my house. If you won't take me, I'll go on my own."

"Of course I'll take you," he said, frustration replacing his solicitous tone. "But I think it's a bad idea. There's nothing there. You don't want to see it, believe me."

"I don't *want* to," she said bleakly. "I have to."

Kieran didn't know it was possible to hurt so badly for another human being. Standing beside Olivia a few hours later, giving her all the support he was able to in light of her mercurial mood, he watched as she surveyed what was left of her property. They'd made the trip via jet in record time, though sadly, there was no reason to hurry.

Yellow police tape cordoned off the area. Curious neighbors gawked, but kept a respectful distance. Olivia had already been questioned by police personnel as well as the chief fire marshal.

The house had literally burned to the ground, leaving nothing but a smoldering mass of debris. On a bright, sunny California afternoon, the evidence marking a violent act seemed even worse.

Olivia wrapped her arms around her waist, face paper-white, eyes haunted. "At least we weren't at home," she said.

"They think the man was watching the house…that he knew when you packed up and left."

Her bottom lip trembled. "Cammie was supposed to grow up here. I always felt so safe," she whispered. "Our little haven away from the world. But there's no hiding, is there?" She gasped on a hiccupping sob.

Kieran didn't bother to answer the rhetorical question. The difficult truth was one he'd learned at the tender age of four, a painful, vivid lesson that had marked the course of his subsequent life.

Rage filled him at the senseless destruction. Rage and an impotent guilt. A man was supposed to protect his family. Now, more than ever, he understood his father's actions. Though occasionally misguided, Victor Wolff and his brother, Vincent, had taken the necessary steps to protect what was theirs, to make sure their children were safe.

Losing their wives, having them murdered in cold blood, had been the catalyst for founding a sanctuary at Wolff Mountain. And now, thank God, Kieran would be able to keep Olivia and Cammie there, cocooned from further danger, until the dangerous fire-bomber was apprehended.

The thought that the man might track Olivia and Cammie to the mountain made Kieran's blood run cold.

Unexpectedly a uniformed investigator approached them, gingerly holding a small item that was apparently hot to the touch. He tipped his hat briefly in a polite salute and extended his hand toward Olivia. "I found this…thought you might want it. Be careful. It's still warm."

He ducked back under the tape and quickly returned to his job, perhaps not comfortable with tears. Kieran didn't think Olivia even realized she was crying. But slow, wet trickles made tracks down her cheeks.

She looked down at the silver object in her hand, and the shaking she'd finally brought under control began anew.

Kieran put his arm around her, holding her close.

When Olivia looked up at him, her wet lashes were spiky. "It's the baby rattle I bought for her when she was born. I had it engraved."

He glanced at the spot where she had rubbed away the soot to reveal a shiny patch. *To Cammie with love from Mommy and Daddy.* Throat tight, he shot her a questioning glance.

"I didn't want her to think that her father didn't care."

He should have been angry, faced anew with the proof that Olivia had hidden his existence. But he couldn't drum up any negative emotion, not with the mother of his child looking as if she might shatter into a million tiny pieces.

Not only that, but he ached from the certainty that his own mistakes had brought them to this tragic point. "Let's go," he said gruffly. "We need to get home to Cammie."

Even with the convenience of a private jet, crossing from the East Coast to the West Coast and back in one day was no easy feat. Jacob had called a pharmacy in Olivia's neighborhood and ordered a light sedative. Once on the plane, Kieran insisted she swallow it with a glass of milk and a handful of saltines.

So far he hadn't managed to persuade her to eat a morsel of food. Olivia was operating on nothing more than adrenaline and sheer will. He settled her in a seat and reclined it to the sleeping position. The steward furnished a pillow and blankets. Olivia was asleep before the wheels left the tarmac.

After takeoff, Kieran unfastened his seat belt and crouched beside her, brushing the hair from her face with a gentle touch. One of her hands was tucked under her cheek. Her eyelashes fanned in crescents over the dark smudges beneath her eyes.

As he watched the almost imperceptible rise and fall of her breasts, he felt a painful pressure in his own chest. *He loved her.* Body and soul. What he had tried to cut off at the root half a dozen years ago had regenerated in the warmth and sunshine of Olivia's return to his life.

And the knowledge that they shared a daughter....

He stood abruptly and strode up to the cockpit, unable to deal with the rush of emotion. It made him dizzy and sick and terrified. What if he lost one of them...or both? It didn't have to be some tragic circumstance. Olivia might simply take Cammie and walk away. After all, she had turned down his marriage proposal without so much a blink.

Kieran stepped through the curtain, legs weak. "Captain, how's the weather looking up ahead?" Idle chitchat wouldn't distract him for long from his dark thoughts, but sitting beside Olivia was torture.

Olivia fought the nightmares. At long last, her heart pounding and her skin clammy with sweat, she surfaced from a drugged sleep. It took several interminable seconds for her to identify her surroundings...and then to remember why she was on a plane.

A shaky sob worked its way up her throat, but she choked it back, sitting up to rub her eyes. Thousands of people around the world had lost their homes this year alone, during floods and tornados and hurricanes. Olivia had been knocked down. But the crying was over. She had Cammie. She had her health. And she had financial resources.

She would be fine. But in truth, the prospect of starting over was daunting.

Kieran appeared suddenly from the front of the plane. His shirt was rumpled. He hadn't shaved. And there were deep grooves etched into his forehead and at the sides of his mouth. Lines she could swear weren't there yesterday.

Exhaustion shrouded him, decimating his usual energy. Seeing Kieran made her wonder how bad she must look. He didn't give her the opportunity to find out. He took his seat and fastened the belt. "We're landing shortly."

She raised her seat and folded the blankets, handing them and the pillow to the steward with a murmured thanks. "How long was I out?"

He shrugged. "You slept across five states, give or take a few. But don't worry…you didn't miss much. It was mostly clouds."

For a wry attempt at humor, it wasn't bad, especially given the circumstances. She summoned a weak smile, her face aching with the effort. "Thank you, Kieran." She reached across the small space dividing them and took his hand in hers. "Thank you for going with me."

The sound of the flaps being deployed and the whine of the engines powering down made conversation difficult. Kieran stared down at their linked fingers. "You going to be okay?" He played with the small cameo ring on her right hand.

She nodded, unable to speak. Clinging to him and never letting go was very appealing. Either that or asking the pilot to fly them to Antarctica.

Thinking about what lay ahead scared her. How do you tell a five-year-old that the only home she has ever known is gone?

Kieran's grasp tightened on her hand. "What is it?" he asked. "What are you thinking?"

"Cammie," she said simply. "How am I ever going to tell Cammie?"

Thirteen

In the end, they did it together. Annalise had bathed Cammie and fed her and tucked her into clean pajamas. They were reading a book when Olivia and Kieran finally made their way upstairs to the bedroom that Kieran had so carefully picked out for his daughter.

The child's face lit up when she saw them. "Mommy! Kieran! I missed you. Did you bring me a present?"

Annalise excused herself quietly, pausing only to give Olivia a quick hug as she left the room. The gentle gesture of compassion tested Olivia's tear-free resolve.

Kieran scooped Cammie up in his arms and held her tight. On his face, Olivia saw her own sadness and thankfulness. Things could have been so much worse.

The three of them sat together on a cushioned window seat overlooking the mountainside in the gathering dusk. Kieran gazed at Olivia over the five-year-old's head, telegraphing a question. *You ready?*

She shook her head, putting her fist to her mouth. *You do it,* she signaled. If she tried to explain, she might burst into tears, and she didn't want to scare her child.

Kieran rested his chin on Cammie's head for a long moment, and then pulled back when she wiggled. "Something bad has happened, sweetheart. I need you to be brave when I tell you this."

Every ounce of childish glee melted away to be replaced by an oddly adult expression of anxiety. "What is it?"

Olivia saw the muscles in his throat work, and knew how unfair she was being to make him do her dirty work. He had to know the impending news would hurt their daughter. But like parents wincing in empathy for an uncomprehending infant about to get vaccinations, she and Kieran had no choice but to tell Cammie the awful truth.

"There was a fire at your house in California," he said slowly, choosing his words with care.

Cammie's eyes rounded. "Did Mommy leave the iron on?"

In spite of everything, Olivia wanted to giggle. "No, baby."

Kieran's sober expression softened. "A bad man made a fire and it got out of control."

"Is Princess Boots okay?"

At Kieran's baffled look, Olivia jumped in. "Kitty is still with Mrs. Capella. Remember?"

"Oh, yeah." She frowned, scrunching up her nose and eyes in concentration. "So we have to stay here for a while?"

Kieran nodded slowly. "If that's okay with your mom."

Olivia nodded, her eyes wet. Clearly Cammie didn't understand the import of what had happened…at least not yet. She was only five. Time enough for upsetting revelations as she asked questions in the coming weeks.

Cammie wiggled off Kieran's knee. "I'm glad Bun-Bun

was here with me." Bun-Bun was the much-loved stuffed animal without which Cammie couldn't sleep. Perhaps in Cammie's eyes, that was enough.

Kieran ruffled her hair. "I'm glad, too. Time for bed, big girl. Your mommy and I have been flying all day, and we're beat."

As they tucked her in, Cammie yawned and surveyed them sleepily. She studied Kieran's face. "Are you my mommy's boyfriend?"

Olivia choked. "Where did you hear about boyfriends?"

"Mrs. Capella says that her daughter is getting a dee-vors because she has a boyfriend *and* a husband. You don't have a husband, so I thought Kieran might be your boyfriend."

The two adults held back their laughter with heroic effort. Kieran's face was red when he said, "Your mommy and I are friends. And we both love you very much. Now go to sleep, and tomorrow, we'll all do something fun together."

Outside in the hall, they collapsed against the wall, laughing uncontrollably until at last they both wheezed and gasped and braced their hands against the Chinese silk wallpaper. Olivia knew the moment of hilarity was a cleansing response to the day's tragedy.

Trust a child to restore a sense of balance to life.

Olivia wiped her eyes. "Thank you," she said. "For telling her. You were perfect."

He put the back of his hand to her hot cheek. "Far from perfect. But I love that little girl."

What happened next was inevitable. In shared grief and exhaustion, they came together, heart to heart, breath mingling with breath. Kieran held her as if she might break, his embrace gentle, his body warm and solid and comforting.

They kissed carefully, as if for the first time. She came so close to blurting out her love, laying it at his feet in gratitude. It would be unfair to burden him with her feelings when he had done so much for her already.

Gradually tenderness heated to passion. She felt him tremble as her hands roved his back.

He sighed, hugging her so tightly her ribs protested. "I need to stay with you tonight, Olivia. To make sure you're okay. Please."

How could she deny what she wanted so badly? "Yes."

He kissed her again, covering her face with light, almost-not-there brushes of his lips. "But first I'm going to feed you."

Food? Her awakening arousal protested. She wrapped her arms around his neck and pressed closer. Sex offered oblivion. Forgetfulness. That was all she wanted and needed right now.

He broke free and stepped back, breathing heavily. "Go get cleaned up. Put on a nightgown. I'll consult with the chef and bring up a tray."

"I'm not hungry," she grumbled. The thought of food made nausea churn in her stomach.

"Doesn't matter." His mien was more drill sergeant than lover. "You have to eat."

She followed his initial direction and stepped into the shower. Beneath the hot, pelting spray, she had to admit that Kieran was right. The water was cleansing in more ways than one. If a few more tears were shed amidst the soapy rivulets swirling down the drain, no one was the wiser.

Though her body ached, her breasts felt heavy and full as she washed them. Imagining Kieran's hands on her sensitive flesh brought a different kind of healing. And she trembled anew with fear for the future. Not for lack of housing. That was minor in the grand scheme of things.

Saying goodbye to Kieran when she went home to start over would make today's events mere shadows of pain. How would she live without him in her life? She had been doing it for six long years. Cammie had filled her days with joy and purpose.

But now Olivia wanted more. She wanted and needed the man she'd fallen in love with during an idyllic semester in Oxford, England.

After drying off and dressing in her favorite silk peignoir of coffee satin and cream lace, she checked on Cammie. Her little girl was sleeping peacefully, but a forbidden thumb was in her mouth, a habit Olivia thought they had defeated a long time ago.

Was the childish comfort technique a sign that Cammie was more affected by the news of the fire than she had seemed?

Olivia removed the thumb without waking her and re-arranged the covers. "I love you," she whispered, kissing Cammie's cheek and inhaling the wonderful combined scents of shampoo and graham crackers from her bedtime snack.

When she returned to her bedroom via the connecting door, Kieran was already there...and in the process of setting a large silver tray on a low table in front of the settee. His eyes warmed as he turned and saw her. With heated regard he swept his gaze from her bare toes, up her body to her freshly washed hair. She'd shampooed it three times, convinced that the smell of smoke still lingered.

He held out a hand. "Come. Eat with me."

The massive fireplace normally sat empty in the summertime, hidden behind a large arrangement of fresh flowers. Kieran had removed the vase and stacked logs and kindling, which were now burning brightly.

She cocked her head, her gaze drawn to the warmth of the crackling blaze. "Isn't this extravagant?"

He shrugged, looking like a mischievous boy. "I had to

crank down the AC ten degrees, but I like the ambience. You deserve extravagance after the day you've had."

"The food looks amazing." She joined him on the small sofa, feeling oddly shy considering the activities they'd indulged in the past couple of days. Her stomach rumbled loudly. "I could get used to having a chef on call."

Kieran uncovered a silver salver. "Nothing too heavy... roasted chicken, lemon-infused rice and fresh kale from the garden." He waved at a smaller dish. "And a surprise for dessert if you clean your plate."

They ate in companionable silence, both of them starved. With the warmth from the fire and a full tummy, Olivia's lids grew heavy. At last she sat back, unable to eat another bite. "That was delicious," she said. "And I'm not just raving because I was so hungry."

Kieran poured two cups of fragrant coffee, handing her one. "I'm glad you enjoyed it." Leaning forward, he removed the top of the mystery dish and uncovered a bowl of sugared dates. "Now for your treat." He picked up one piece of fruit and held it to her lips. "Try this."

As she opened her mouth automatically, Kieran tucked the sugary sweet between her lips. She bit off a piece and without thinking, licked the crystals that clung to his fingertips. He froze, his eyes heating with arousal and his breathing growing harsh. "Have another."

The room was heavy with unspoken desire, hers... his. The fire played a mesmerizing symphony of pop and crackle. Three times he fed her, and three times she sucked his fingertips into her mouth to clean them.

Kieran cracked first. He stood up and strode to the window, throwing up the sash and letting in a rush of cool night air. "Bloody stupid idea having a fire," he muttered. He took off his shirt, exposing a chest that made Olivia's toes curl.

He was all hard planes and rippling muscle.

"I like it," she protested, removing the negligee that topped her barely there gown.

His eyes grew wide. "I am not going to have sex with you tonight. You don't need that."

"Don't tell me what I need."

She lowered the tiny straps of the satin garment and let it slither over her hips and fall to the carpet. "*You* haven't had dessert," she pointed out.

The front of his trousers lifted noticeably. His torso gleamed damp in the soft lamplight. Hooded eyes tracked her every movement. "I wanted to comfort you tonight…to hold you in case you had bad dreams."

"Perhaps if you *entertain* me, my dreams won't be bad at all."

He shoved his hands in the pockets of his pants, frowning. "I think you may still be in shock. You should get a good night's sleep."

Though his mouth spoke prosaic words, his body told a different story. His entire frame was rigid, the cloth of his trousers barely containing his thrusting shaft.

She walked right up to him, buck naked, her toes curling in the soft, luxurious carpet beneath their feet. Now the tips of her breasts brushed his bare rib cage.

"Stop." He inhaled sharply, groaning as she laid her cheek against his shoulder.

"We're just getting started," she murmured. Insinuating one of her thighs between his legs, she rubbed up against him like a cat.

Kieran was a strong man, but he was only a man. How in the hell could he cosset her when she was hell-bent on seducing him? He gave up the fight, because losing was better than anything he had planned. Cupping her firm butt in his palms, he pulled her closer still. "Did anyone ever tell you you're stubborn?"

She went up on tiptoe to kiss his chin. "All the time."

"The door?"

"I locked it. We'll hear her if she stirs...but she won't."

"I'll leave before morning." He wouldn't confuse Cammie, not with so much at stake.

"That's a whole seven hours from now," Olivia said, her nimble fingers attacking his belt buckle. "I can think of a few ways to fill the time."

The ornate mantel clock marked off the minutes and hours as Kieran devoted himself to entertaining Olivia. She tried rushing the game, but he was on to her tricks. With one hand, he manacled her wrists over her head, and at the same time trapped her legs with his thigh.

Her chest heaved, eyes flashing in annoyance. "I want to touch you."

The agitation of her breathing made her breasts quiver. The sight of those magnificent heaving bosoms mesmerized him for a split second. He cleared his throat. "Not yet."

"When?"

"After I've finished with you."

Eyes rounded, she gazed up at him. "That sounds ominous."

"I promise you'll enjoy every second."

Her eyes fluttered shut. A tiny sigh of anticipation slipped from her pursed lips and filled him with purpose. Tonight was for Olivia alone.

Flipping her to her stomach and sitting astride her thighs, he reached for a bottle of lotion on the nightstand and squeezed a generous amount into his hand. Warming the thick liquid between his palms, he gazed down at her. Those narrow shoulders had carried a heavy burden for the past six years, a burden that he should have been sharing.

The knowledge was a sharp pang in his belly. Deliberately he placed his hands on her upper back and began a deep massage. Olivia moaned and settled more deeply into the mattress, her body boneless and limp.

In his younger, wilder days, he'd once had the good fortune to spend a three-day vacation with a sexy Indonesian masseuse. She'd taught Kieran a thing or two about the human body and how to relax. Dredging up those pleasant memories, he applied himself to making Olivia feel pampered, hopefully draining away the stresses of their long, emotionally fraught day.

Touching her was a penance. If his hands shook, surely she didn't notice. He was tormented by the notion that Olivia and Cammie might have been in the house when it went up in a ball of flame. Nothing he could have done would have saved them if he had been on the other side of the world. Olivia could have died, and Kieran would not have known for weeks, months.

He'd been living without her for a long time. How was it that the possibility of her death, and his daughter's, as well, turned his stomach to stone?

He finished at last and brushed her cheek with a fingertip. "Olivia?" Though *her* muscles were warm and loose, he was strung tightly enough to snap. "Olivia?"

A gentle snore was his only answer.

Incredulous, frustrated, but oddly proud that he had lulled her into slumber, he slid down into the bed beside her, condemned to a painful night. Her nude body snuggled into his even in sleep, her bottom coming to rest against his rock-hard erection. He contemplated giving himself relief, but he didn't want to wake her.

He closed his eyes. The covers suffocated him. Willing himself to breathe slowly, he used the deep inhale and exhale technique he knew would eventually coax sleep.

Arms tight around Olivia, he yawned and pressed his cheek to her back.

As the moments passed, he gained control and a sense of perspective. Contentment washed over him with the unexpected advent of a gentle summer rain. This house had held nothing for him in the past but pain and duty. He'd never known real happiness here. All he ever wanted to do in the midst of his rare visits was to escape.

Even spending time with his family had not blunted the hurtful memories that in his mind hung over the massive house as a shroud.

Gareth had built a home here, as had Jacob. Why were they able to get past the tragedy when Kieran couldn't? Was he weaker than his brothers? Kieran and Annalise were the youngest of all six of the cousins when they lost their mothers. Did that make a difference? Annalise hadn't settled down on the mountain, either.

But unlike Kieran, she was filled with light and a happiness that was almost palpable. Her soul wasn't scarred by what had happened.

He allowed himself for one wary second to reach for the memories of his mother. A scent. A fleeting visual. The sound of her gentle laugh. She danced in his memory, hand in hand with her little son, twirling him around in a dizzying circle. Then the image faded. It was all he had…all he would ever have.

This was the point at which he usually surrendered to the urge to flee, a knee-jerk reaction to pain so strong it brought a toughened man to the brink of despair.

As he lay there in the darkness, dry-eyed, he realized with stunned certainty that the pain was gone. Obliterated. In the depth of the night, he heard his mother's whisper. *Be happy, Kieran. For me….*

Did she know about Olivia and Cammie? Was she somewhere up there in heaven, grieving because she couldn't meet her granddaughter?

He closed his eyes, throat tight with emotion, grateful that no one was around to see his weakness. Had his mother really counseled him to be happy? Was it even possible? Did he have it in him to let go and simply live again?

Existing from job to job, tent to tent, was the perfect camouflage for a man who was empty inside. He never stopped moving long enough for anyone to realize…to care.

Olivia murmured his name in her sleep. He stroked her hair, curling a mass of it around his hand and holding it in his fist as if by doing so, this unprecedented feeling of peace might last.

She felt perfect in his arms.

But he was an imperfect man.

Could he change for her? For his daughter?

Fourteen

When Olivia awoke, she was alone. The pillow beside hers bore the imprint of Kieran's head, but the bed was empty. She knew he had to leave her…it made sense. But her heart grieved.

Outside her window, dawn had barely arrived; the tree-tops no more than shadowy sentinels, though birdsong filled the early-morning air. She yawned and stretched, wondering how long it would be before Cammie bounded into the room with her usual burst of energy.

It was too soon to call Lolita and Javier. They were on Pacific Time, still the middle of the night in California.

Had the police made an arrest? Was her mother's stalker continuing to lurk in the shadows of their lives?

Itchy and restless, Olivia climbed out of bed, feeling the aches and pains of an old woman. The benefits of Kieran's selfless massage evaporated in a rush of uncertainty that tightened her neck muscles. It had been only a short time since the fire, but already, waiting for an end to the drama was unbearable. She longed to go home, but she had nowhere to call her own anymore.

The truth was ugly and inescapable.

By the time she finished her shower, Cammie was up and demanding breakfast. To Olivia's surprise, Victor awaited them in the formal dining room.

"Good morning, sir," she said, sitting stiffly in a chair and giving Cammie a visual warning to behave. Cammie needed little urging. She was too busy digging into a plateful of small pancakes shaped like bears and fir trees.

The old man had an empty plate in front of him, but it bore the evidence of bacon and eggs. He nursed coffee in a china cup that looked far too fragile for his big hands. Like his sons, he was a large man, but his hair had faded away to little tufts of white over his ears, and his florid skin spoke of unhealthy habits.

His portly figure and piercing eyes were intimidating to say the least.

Olivia ate without speaking, all the while making sure Cammie was not poised to launch into one of her stream of consciousness chattering sessions.

The meal was silent and uncomfortable.

When Olivia had swallowed as many bites as she could manage of an omelet and crisp toast, she shoved her plate aside. "We'll get out of your hair," she said, biting her lip when she realized that Cammie was still finishing up.

Victor Wolff raised one beetling eyebrow. "So soon? I've arranged for the sous chef to make cookies with Cammie so you and I can talk, Olivia. Is that okay with you, little one?"

Cammie looked up, a drizzle of sticky syrup coating one side of her chin. Her mouth was too full for speech, but she nodded enthusiastically.

Unease slithered down Olivia's spine. "Where is Kieran?" she asked, needing reinforcements before a confrontation with her host.

Victor shrugged. "He and Gareth and Jacob took off at first light for Charlottesville, something about buying a new Jeep."

"It takes three men to purchase a vehicle?"

"My boys are close. And they seldom have the opportunity to spend time together as a trio."

A pleasant young woman appeared from the direction of the kitchen, introducing herself as LeeAnn. Olivia watched, helpless, as Cammie's face lit up. She took her new friend's hand, and the two of them disappeared, leaving Olivia to face Victor alone.

He stood up. "We'll go to my study," he said, allowing Olivia no opportunity to refuse.

Trailing in his wake, she pondered his intent. There was little time to formulate a plan of rebuttal for whatever was about to transpire. Victor's private sanctum was on the main floor, as was the kitchen.

The room was like something out of a movie. Heavy hunter-green drapes flanked mullioned windows that sparkled as if they were cleaned every night by an army of elves...and perhaps they were. The thick folds of velvet picked up and accentuated the intricate design in an antique Persian rug that covered a large expanse of the hardwood floor.

Victor motioned to a wing chair opposite his dark mahogany desk. "Have a seat."

Feeling a bit too much like a wayward schoolchild, Olivia sat, hands in lap, and waited. She wasn't intentionally silent, but in truth, she could not think of a single subject, other than the weather, with which to counter Victor's liegelike summons.

He frowned at her. "When are you going to tell me I have a grandchild?"

Nothing like a direct attack to catch the unwary off guard. Olivia bit her lip, stalling for time. "Is that why you asked me to come in here? Did you wait for your son to leave so you could ambush me?"

Guilt landed briefly on his heavy features before disappearing. "You're impertinent."

"I mean no disrespect, but I won't be bullied."

They tiptoed around the subject that couldn't be broached. Not yet. Not without Kieran's participation.

Victor harrumphed and sat back in his chair, swiveling from side to side just enough to make Olivia dizzy. Despite his bluster, or maybe because of it, she suddenly saw that he was afraid. Of what? she wondered.

After tapping an empty pipe on the blotter, he put it to his lips and took a lengthy draw, perhaps using the scent of tobacco long past to satisfy an urge. "Ask him to stay," he commanded. "Ask Kieran to stay. He'll do it for you. I know he will. He's never before brought a woman to Wolff Mountain. You're special to him."

Her heart sank. "Sorry to burst your bubble, Mr. Wolff, but you're wrong."

"Call me Victor. And I'm seldom wrong. What makes you so sure that I am now?"

Time to bury her pride. Taking a deep, painful breath, she gave him the unvarnished truth. "He offered to marry me in order to give Cammie security. A family on paper. But he wasn't offering to stay. That wasn't part of the package. He's leaving for the Sudan in September. Nothing has changed."

Before her eyes, the old man aged a decade, his brown-spotted hands trembling before he gripped the arms of the chair to steady them. "Damn it. This is his home. He needs to settle down…."

His words trailed off in impotence. He wasn't the first parent to rue a son's choices, and he wouldn't be the last.

Olivia sighed. "I've never had any illusions about Kieran. He's a wonderful man, but more than anyone I've ever known, he needs to wander. It's a lifestyle well suited to a single man."

"And if he has a family?"

"If he has a family, it wasn't by choice." Her words were blunt. Said as much to remind herself of the truth as they were to make the truth clear to a desperate father. "He'll continue to come back from time to time if you don't harass him. That's probably the most you can hope for."

Victor glared at her. "In my day women knew how to use sex to get what they wanted from a man."

Olivia's face flamed. Aghast at his gall, she gaped at him. "Are you actually suggesting that I try to manipulate your son with intimacy?"

"Any fool, even an old one, can see the fireworks between you two. Make the boy crazy. Reel him in. Don't worry about being so damned politically correct."

"Forgive me if I don't want a man I have to coerce into loving me."

"Who said anything about love? Once he parks his boots, he'll figure out that you and Cammie are good for him."

"Like prunes and brussels sprouts? No, thank you. I deserve a man who will love me and my child and put us first."

"Then fight for the boy, damn it."

Olivia stood up, beyond finished with the circuitous conversation. "I appreciate your hospitality, Mr. Wolff, but my relationship with Kieran is none of your business. I wish I could give you what you want."

He waved a hand as if dismissing her stilted words. "Any

news about your house…or the stalker? I'm sorry about that, by the way. Must have been a damned shock."

"Nothing yet. I'll call my parents when it gets a little later." His compassion touched her in spite of their adversarial meeting.

"You're always welcome on Wolff Mountain. I give you my word." His rheumy eyes glittered with tears.

Her throat tightened. This magnificent house was part of Cammie's birthright. Whatever transpired between Kieran and Olivia, that relationship would never change. Victor Wolff was Cammie's grandfather.

"Thank you," she said softly. "I'll bring her to visit when I can."

He nodded, a single tear streaking down his leathery cheek. "See that you do, Olivia Delgado. See that you do."

She escaped Victor's study, and after checking on Cammie who was still elbow-deep in cookie dough, Olivia retrieved her cell phone from the bedroom and began making a necessary string of phone calls. The insurance adjuster, of course. And the neighbor to check on the cat.

That second call meant answering a host of questions. Mrs. Capella was a dear, but a notorious gossip. No doubt she'd be preening on the block since she had direct contact with Olivia.

Finally, when it was a decent hour to roust her night-owl parents out of bed, Olivia dialed their number.

Lolita's sleep-thickened voice answered. "You do realize that a woman my age needs her beauty sleep," she complained.

"You're gorgeous, Mother…with or without sleep." The implied request for flattery was received and acknowledged. "Are you and Daddy okay?"

Javier Delgado picked up the conversation. "She went

to make coffee. We're fine, baby. Are you and my grand-daughter staying put?"

"Yes." But not for long. She had another phone call to make that would set things in motion. Unfortunately every minute spent with Kieran made the inevitable parting that much harder. It was time to break free.

"Why didn't you tell us you were flying out here yesterday?"

Her father's pique made her feel guilty. "You said on the phone that Mom had gone to bed with a sedative. I didn't want her to see my house. Not yet. We both know she doesn't handle crises well."

"We'll get the bastard who did this."

Javier often spoke like a movie character. But his vehemence made Olivia smile. "I know. I just called to say I love you and to tell you to be very careful. This man is obsessed with Mother. No one knows what he'll try next."

"Not to worry, my love. The house is surrounded with so much firepower, I feel like we're hiding out at the Alamo."

"That standoff didn't end well, Daddy."

"No. But it was a hell of a role." Javier had played Davy Crockett once upon a time, and could still produce a creditable southern accent.

She wiped her cheek, surprised to realize she was crying. Her parents were eccentric and self-centered and prone to overdramatization in every situation, but she loved them dearly. "I'll call again soon," she promised. "Keep me posted."

When she hung up, she gnawed her lip, worried that her mother wouldn't take the threat seriously, despite the fire. Olivia was sure that a part of Lolita felt flattered that a fan cared enough to be irrational.

The three Wolff men were not back by lunchtime. Cammie pouted, missing Kieran's attentions. Olivia felt much the same, but without the luxury of acting like a five-year-old. For the next several hours, Cammie was fractious and inconsolable. Refusing to nap, she sulked around her wonderful bedroom until Olivia was at her wit's end. Was all this bad behavior a result of last night's news? Would it help if Olivia coaxed her daughter into talking about the fire? Or would that make things worse?

It was far too hot to play outside. Huge thunderclouds built on the western horizon, and the sticky, oppressive heat shimmered in waves, obscuring the usual, far flung vistas.

When Cammie finally succumbed to a fitful sleep, it was after four o'clock. Olivia fell into a chair exhausted. It was always a mistake to let her offspring nap this late in the day. It meant Cammie wouldn't want to go to bed at her normal bedtime, and battle would inevitably ensue.

But the child was clearly in need of rest. Olivia wasn't about to wake her up, even for dinner. They could always raid the kitchen later.

At six-thirty, Olivia dressed in a salmon voile sundress that she had not yet worn. The filmy layers were cool, and the color flattered her skin tones. No bra was required. Her breathing quickened as she pictured Kieran's reaction later when they were alone.

She owed him something for last night. After her insistence that they make love, she had flaked out on him in no time. Had he been terribly disappointed?

No matter. They had time for one last metaphorical dance. Then Olivia would go home. Kieran was who he was. He wouldn't change. And Olivia couldn't bruise her heart any longer hoping for a different outcome. After running a brush through her hair, she clipped it up in a loose chignon. Dangling crystal earrings added a note of formality to her appearance. If she had to play verbal badminton with Victor Wolff again, she needed all the armor she could muster.

Poor Cammie looked like an urchin when Olivia checked on her. She had shed her shorts and top and was wearing an old T-shirt Kieran had given her that said, Girls Rule, Boys Drool.

Grinning wryly, Olivia picked up the monitor and tucked it in the pocket of her full skirt. When Cammie awoke, it would be easy to hear her. The child usually demanded a snack before her eyes were open. More like her grandmother than her mother, she didn't waken easily.

Olivia descended the stairs to the main floor, stopping short when Kieran came striding toward her. Something was different about him, but she couldn't pinpoint it. There was almost a spring in his step.

He gave her a broad grin. "Hello, beautiful. Did you miss me?"

Fifteen

Kieran had thoroughly enjoyed the day with his brothers. Catching up on each others' lives, sharing stupid inside jokes from their adolescent years...all of it had been comfortable and familiar and pretty damned wonderful. There'd been nothing touchy feely or emotionally intrusive. But Gareth and Jacob, by their behavior and conversation, had made it clear how glad they were to have him home.

Even in the midst of a testosterone fest, though, Kieran had missed his girls. He hugged Olivia now, inhaling her scent with a deep, cleansing breath.

She pulled back and smiled at him. "Yes. We missed you. In fact, Cammie was a spoiled brat today. Not having you here to entertain her was not fun."

"Where is she now?"

"Taking a late nap." She pulled the monitor from her pocket. "I'll hear her when she wakes up."

"Do you think she was acting out because of what we told her last night?"

"I thought about that. But she never mentioned the fire."

"What have you heard from California?"

"Nothing much. The man is still on the loose. Mom and Dad are fine...holed up with a phalanx of security guards."

He squeezed her hand. "And how about you?"

"I'm fine."

Her words weren't all that convincing. The shadows smudged beneath her eyes accentuated her pallor. He had a feeling that she was running on nothing more than adrenaline and determination. Olivia was strong, very strong. But losing a home was a blow to anyone.

He put his arm around her as they walked to the dining room. "We'll do whatever needs to be done," he said quietly. "Try not to worry."

Gareth had lingered, and Gracie joined them for dinner. With Jacob and Annalise present, as well, it was a lively meal. Annalise's siblings and father were due back to the mountain in another week.

Surprisingly it was quiet Jacob who pressed Olivia for details. "When they catch the guy, what will you do?"

She took a sip of her wine and winced. "As soon as that happens, Cammie and I will head home.... I mean..."

Kieran's hand tightened on hers beneath the tablecloth.

She took a breath. "Cammie and I will stay with my parents, I suppose, until we decide what to do...whether to rebuild in the same place or closer to my mom and dad. I haven't really had time to think it through."

"Speaking of Cammie, I thought she'd be awake by now," Kieran said. He watched as she pulled the monitor from her pocket, listened a moment and shook it. He frowned. "What's wrong?"

"I think the batteries are dead."

Olivia's look of consternation mirrored his own gut feeling of trouble. "I'll go get her," he said. "Stay and eat your dinner."

But he'd barely had time to stand up when Cammie appeared in the doorway—sucking her thumb, wearing an old T-shirt. Her hair was sleep tousled. Relief flooded him, along with amusement. "Hi, sweetheart. You ready for some dinner?"

She surveyed the assemblage at the table, her small face solemn. "I forgot Bun-Bun. He wants to eat with us." Turning back, she ran out of the room.

"Put your clothes on," Olivia called after her.

Kieran sat back down. "Don't hassle her. As kids we showed up at meals in all varieties of threadbare shirts and jeans."

Victor chuckled. "Not for lack of trying on my part. Vincent and I did our best to impart rules of etiquette, but rarely did they stick. It was a household of hellions back in those days."

"Not me." Annalise's smile was smug. "Somebody had to have some couth around here."

The men hooted. Gareth grinned, his arm stretched out along the back of his wife's chair. "You were a goody two-shoes. But what Dad and Uncle Vincent didn't know was that you came home from playing in the woods just as nasty as the rest of us. Unfortunately you had this feminine knack for turning grubby Cinderella into an infuriating, sanctimonious princess in the blink of an eye. Made us mad as hell."

In the burst of laughter that followed, Kieran leaned toward Olivia. "Should I go get Cammie?"

She shook her head. "Not in the mood she's in. I'll deal with it. Just don't eat my dessert," she added as she went to retrieve her daughter.

Kieran had finished his meal and was having a second

glass of wine when Olivia rushed back into the room, panic written all over her face.

"She's not upstairs. I can't find her. She's gone."

He grabbed her shoulders, easing her into a chair before she fainted on him. Her skin had gone milk-white. "Don't jump to conclusions, honey. She probably got turned around and lost her way down a hall somewhere. You know how this house is."

"Cammie has a perfect sense of direction." Olivia gazed up at him, clutching his sleeve. "She never gets lost. Something's wrong."

Terror ripped at his chest, but he fought it back. There had to be a simple explanation.

Everyone at the table was on their feet in an instant, Victor included.

Kieran sucked in a breath and barked out orders. "Gareth, you and Gracie take the yard and your house. She loves the dog and the pool. Jacob, search this floor with Father. Olivia and I will start with the second floor and work our way up. Annalise, question the staff. When each of you finishes, come back. Does everyone have a cell phone? Call if you locate her."

The next half hour was a nightmare. They tore the house apart, from basement to attic. Cammie was nowhere to be found.

When the search parties met, empty-handed, Olivia broke down finally, sobbing so hard Kieran feared she would make herself ill. Holding her close, he breathed hope into her, shoring her up with only his will. Deep in his gut, her anguish was his own.

She sank onto a sofa, her eyes haunted. "That man has her. I know it. He said he was going to hurt the people my mother loves, and my mother adores Cammie."

Kieran's hands fisted. "How would he even know how to find you here?"

"The police said he's been watching my house. You came there. He must have figured out who you were."

"I was in a rental car."

"But you gave your real name?"

"Yes." Dear God in heaven...

Jacob spoke, his words carefully neutral. "We at least have to consider the possibility."

Olivia bowed her head. "There are no fences," she said dully. "Only the one at the front gate. Anyone could walk in."

Victor shook his head. "It would be a fool's mission. We have four hundred acres."

"Gracie made it up here," Gareth pointed out, his face troubled. His new wife had once upon a time sneaked onto the property to confront Gareth on her father's behalf.

"But Gracie didn't try to get into the main house, kidnap a child and leave again." Kieran's fierce shout cowed no one. In the faces of the people he loved, he saw compassion, concern and his own bubbling fear.

Olivia gathered her composure with a visible, superhuman effort, her chest heaving as tremors threatened to rattle her bones. "Do we call the police?"

A momentary silence fell over the room. The Wolff family had suffered terribly at the hands of the press over the years. Privacy was practically inscribed on the family crest. And for Lolita and Javier, this kind of publicity was not desirable, either. The tabloids would have a field day.

Kieran squatted in front of Olivia. "We'll do whatever you want. You're her mother." He took her hands in his, trying to warm the icy skin. She was close to being in shock, and he was damn glad Jacob was on hand.

"It will take them a long time to get here, won't it?" The words were barely a whisper, spoken through bloodless lips.

Everyone nodded. Victor's breathing was harsh and labored. "The nearest law enforcement is forty-five to fifty minutes away."

Olivia shook free of Kieran's solicitous grasp and stood up. "We'll give it an hour, then…before we make a call."

Gareth spoke up, pacing restlessly. "I scouted the perimeter of the house. No sign of forced entry, no footprints, nothing to indicate an intruder. But that doesn't mean anything. Psychopaths are often brilliant. He would try to cover his tracks."

A blinding flash of lightning lit up the room in which they all stood as a simultaneous crack of thunder roared across the mountaintop and rattled glass in the windows.

Kieran made a decision. "If he has her, he'll use one of the trails. It would be too hard to travel through the underbrush. I'm going to walk the closest sections to look for signs that anyone has passed by recently. I'll start with the north and the east since that portion of the property is nearest a road."

Jacob nodded. "Gareth and I will take the west and south quadrants."

"I'm going with you." Olivia in her dainty, feminine dress held her stance as aggressively as a bulldog.

"It's too dangerous," Kieran said through clenched teeth. "Trust me."

"I do trust you," she said. "But that's my baby out in the storm."

He eyed her low-heeled sandals. They were flimsy at best, but the clock was ticking. She was close to collapse, and the knowledge that he had not been able to protect her or his daughter flailed him like a whip. "Fine," he ground out, his anger self-directed. "Suit yourself. Let's move out."

Olivia stumbled behind Kieran, trying to keep up with his loping stride. She knew he was angry with her, but she couldn't stay inside the house and wait. She couldn't. Not when Cammie was terrified of storms.

Who had her? What was his intent? Ransom? Kieran's mother had been murdered in just such a situation. Was Kieran thinking of Laura Wolff right now? Did fear turn his limbs to jelly as it did Olivia's?

All around them lightning danced. Rain poured from the skies relentlessly, drenching Olivia to the skin and blinding her. Kieran called to Cammie again and again, until his voice was hoarse and exhausted.

There were at least a dozen trails crisscrossing the mountaintop. None of them showed a single sign that anyone had walked them recently. But the rain was rapidly turning everything to mud, so even if there had been shreds of cloth or remnants of footprints, they would soon be eradicated completely.

In a clearing, Kieran stopped abruptly. During a brief flash of illumination, Olivia saw anguish and grief on his face. But when she touched his arm, his expression morphed into determination.

Had she imagined his emotion?

He strode on, giving her no choice but to follow.

When they finally met up with Jacob and Gareth, the four adults looked for signs of hope in each others' faces. Huddled against the wind, they wordlessly acknowledged the truth. If an intruder had taken Cammie out in this storm, the chances of finding her were slim to none.

Stumbling back into the house with the others, Olivia struggled not to collapse in hysteria. Annalise and Gracie had prepared hot coffee. Olivia grasped a warm mug, trying to still the trembling that threatened to drag her under.

Annalise tugged her out of the foyer into a side chamber.

"I brought down dry clothes. You need to change immediately. It won't help Cammie if you make yourself sick."

With clumsy fingers, Olivia tried to do as she was asked. But her coordination was shot. Annalise took over, dealing with zippers and buttons. She stripped Olivia all the way down to her bare skin and then bundled her up quickly in dry underwear, a fleecy sweatshirt and jeans.

When they returned to the front of the house, the men were huddled together, their clothing still dripping onto the marble floor. Gareth turned his eyes to the ceiling, his body rigid with concentration.

Suddenly he swung around and pinned Annalise with a laserlike gaze. "Did you take Cammie to the secret tunnel?"

Annalise nodded. "I showed her where it was, but we didn't go in. The whole thing is probably full of spiders and mice. Ick. No child would want to get in there."

Kieran's expression was bleak. "I did. When I was just her age."

For a moment, the silence was stunned and uncomfortable. Olivia knew he was telling them that the secret tunnel was where he used to hide to grieve his mother.

En masse, they started up the stairs. Second floor, third floor, attic.

Olivia was confused. "But we've searched all this," she cried. "Several times."

"Over here," Kieran said, already crossing the attic to a portion of the wall where a frieze of carved flowers decorated a protruding section that looked like it was concealing ductwork. But it suddenly dawned on Olivia that the vents for the heat and air system were on the opposite side of the room.

Kieran pressed on a rose. Nothing happened. He glanced over his shoulder at Annalise. "Do you remember which one?"

She shrugged unhappily. "I never actually got it to open. All I did was tell Cammie how it worked in theory. I didn't think she paid attention to what I was saying."

Kieran pressed and punched until his knuckles were raw.

Annalise shoved him aside. "For Pete's sake. Move, you big lug."

Delicately, skimming her fingertips over the rough surface as if she were reading Braille, she searched for the mechanism. With a little click and a whir, the wheels engaged and the door swung open. It was only four feet high.

The seven adults gasped in unison. Annalise had not been wrong. The corners of the gaping opening were laced with spiderwebs. And the interior of the space was pitch-black, the single lightbulb long since burned out.

But lying curled up on the floor was Cammie, fast asleep. Her dirty face was streaked where tears had run through layers of dust. Her little fingernails were caked with grime from scratching at the inside of the door.

Kieran crouched and scooped her into his arms. "Wake up, baby. I'm here. Your daddy is here."

Olivia touched her daughter's soft cheek. "Wake up, Cammie. Please."

The child's lashes fluttered and lifted, causing her to blink against the sudden advent of bright light into her dark prison. "I got locked in," she complained, her arms around Kieran's neck. "Annalise never explained how to get out."

The indignant glare she shot Kieran's cousin might have made them all laugh had not each one been choking back emotion.

Olivia smoothed her daughter's rumpled hair, hoping it was spider free. "Why did you hide, sweetheart? We thought you were coming down for dinner, but when you went to get Bun-Bun you never came back."

Cammie's lower lip trembled. "When I woke up and went down to the dining room, I heard you say that when they catch the bad man you're gonna take me back to California. I want to stay here, Mommy. With Kieran. And you, too. I like it here."

"But, honey…"

Victor touched her arm in warning, silently pointing her attention to Kieran's face. Olivia's once incognito lover had nothing to hide now. His love and his pride were laid bare for all to see. He looked down at Cammie in his arms like a man who had finally found the treasure he'd spent a lifetime looking for.

Before Olivia could say another word, Kieran pulled her close, drawing the three of them into a tight hug. Saying a litany of thank-you prayers, she put her head on his shoulder and wept tears of gratitude.

When Cammie finally struggled to get down, demanding food, Olivia realized that the others had crept silently away, leaving this odd family of three to a reunion. Cammie faced off against her parents, arms akimbo. "You said you're my daddy," she accused, pointing at Kieran with an imperious finger. "I heard you."

Olivia saw him struggle for words. She knew he hadn't meant to betray her trust without her consent. The declaration had tumbled out, straight from his heart in the heat of the moment.

"Cammie, I…" He ran his hands through his hair, glancing in desperation at Olivia.

She stepped forward, squatting to look her daughter in the face. "He *is* your daddy, my sweet little jelly bean."

Cammie's eyes rounded. "Why didn't you tell me when we got here?"

It was a fair question. Cammie's hurt and confusion were exactly what Olivia had been hoping to avoid. Speaking slowly, choosing her words carefully, Olivia explained, "Kieran didn't know he was your daddy until I told him. When you were born, I didn't know where he was, because he works on the other side of the world."

"Did you look for him?"

Another zinger.

"I was busy taking care of you. I loved you very much and I was very happy to be your mommy."

Cammie stared at Kieran, Bun-Bun dangling from one fist, dragging the floor. "Do you want to be my daddy?"

Her innocence and vulnerability would have shredded a heart far more hardened than Kieran's. He blinked once. "I *am* your daddy," he said forcefully, crouching beside her. "But even if I weren't, I would want to be. Because I think you are the most special little girl in the whole wide world... and I love you."

Olivia knew the words were torn from his throat. He was not a man to say them lightly. When Cammie threw herself against his chest and his arms closed around her, Kieran's expression was painfully open, his raw and bleeding heart on display.

She had to look away, feeling anew the guilt of her decision to keep father and daughter apart.

The past couldn't be undone. Now all the three of them could do was move forward.

Kieran scooped Cammie up and stood with her, gazing at Olivia with an inscrutable expression. "Let's get our little chick some food," he said quietly.

Without ceremony, they made their way downstairs to Olivia's suite of rooms. One call to the kitchen netted them a child's feast of chicken fingers, peanut butter crackers, cooked apples and chocolate cake for dessert.

Olivia and Kieran sat side by side, not touching, as they watched their daughter devour an astounding amount of food given her small size. When she was satisfied, she wiped her mouth with her hand, yawning.

Suddenly her face brightened. "If our other house is gone, this can be my new bedroom. Forever."

Olivia felt Kieran tense. She gnawed her lip. "Kieran and I are going to talk about that," she said, wishing this conversation had been preceded by some kind of well-thought-out plan.

He had no such qualms. "It's your bedroom forever. Definitely. No matter what happens."

"You can stay here for the rest of the summer," Olivia conceded, knowing she had little choice at this point. "But Lolo and Jojo live in California…and you'll be starting kindergarten soon. We have lots to think about."

Kieran shot her a sharp glance, but didn't interrupt.

Puzzlement etched the features that already bore the stamp of the Wolff clan, emphasizing Cammie's resemblance to Annalise. "What does that mean?"

Kieran stood. "Grown-up stuff, poppet. Let's get you in a bath. You smell like a skunk."

With Cammie giggling in delight, the two of them disappeared into the bathroom, leaving Olivia to sit alone with her troubled thoughts.

Sixteen

Kieran brooded out on the terrace, reluctant to go back inside and face the inquisition from his family about why he'd had a daughter for five years and had never told them about her.

Cammie. His daughter. Even now the words sounded unfamiliar, and yet somehow right.

The storm had passed, and the summer sky was lit with scores of stars. The night was peaceful and serene in the aftermath of the tempest.

His own situation was not so calm. For his entire adult life, he'd had no one to worry about but himself. That thought drew him up short. It wasn't exactly true. He'd worried about his father plenty, especially after the heart attack that had brought Kieran home from university and caused him to leave Olivia behind.

Kieran had spent many a night praying for his father's recovery…wondering bleakly if Olivia had found some cocky English chap to pick up where Kieran had left off.

But as the months passed, once Kieran had made the choice to set out on the open road, he'd been remarkably self-centered. Okay, maybe not selfish exactly. He was kind, and his work was important to the people it benefited. But all in all, nothing had mattered to him but the next dot on the map and how soon he'd be on his way there.

Now, he stood at a new crossroads…one that a GPS couldn't locate on any grid. He had a daughter…and a lover…and a mountain that was calling him home. Normally he'd be chomping at the bit to pack his duffel bag and head out for parts unknown. Usually his passport was in his back pocket, ready for the next stamp.

But now, inexplicably, the thought of leaving at the end of the summer was unbearable.

He strode back into the house, eager to see Olivia, ready to make plans, to map out a course of action.

His father met him in the hallway. "There's a fellow at the front gate by the name of Jeremy Vargas. The guard wants to know whether to send him up or not."

Kieran frowned, wishing he could say no. "Let him in," he said.

Victor put a hand on his arm. "When you're ready, we'd all like to hear about you and Olivia and Cammie." He winced. "Olivia is the one you wanted to tell the truth to… back in Oxford."

It was a statement, not a question. "Yes."

"But I had a heart attack and you left her." His face twisted. "God, I'm sorry, son."

"It wasn't your fault."

"Why did she never let you know you had a daughter?"

"Because she thought my name was Kevin Wade, and when she found out I'd been lying to her…when she learned my true identity, she didn't think I deserved or needed to know."

Victor's head bowed. "Son of a bitch…" The expletive held little heat. The old man was defeated, worn down.

"Don't sweat it, Dad. It's all water under the bridge. We'll get through this."

The front door opened, and in walked Jeremy Vargas. Kieran introduced his father, then Victor excused himself. The two men faced off in the foyer.

"Why are you here?" Kieran asked bluntly, in no mood to play the welcoming host.

A lazy smile lifted the corners of a mouth that had kissed a variety of big name actresses. "Olivia called me after the fire. I'm to escort her home."

"The hell you say." Fury ignited deep in Kieran's belly. Caveman instincts kicked in. No one was leaving this house without his consent.

Olivia descended the stairs at that moment, wearing dark jeans and an emerald-green tank top. Her feet were bare. The smile she sent Jeremy's way was sweet, uncomplicated. Kieran had never received such a smile from her, and that pissed him off.

God, she was beautiful. Already it seemed like years since he had made love to her. He wanted to scoop her up and kiss her senseless. Or maybe kiss some sense into her.

He glared. "You never said anything about Vargas coming."

Her gaze was cool. "I wasn't sure how quickly he could get here. I didn't really expect him until tomorrow."

Jeremy stood in silence, allowing the two of them to duel with words and unspoken innuendo.

"I thought we agreed that you weren't leaving…not until your mother's stalker is in custody."

"Cammie will stay here. The two of you will have the

time you asked for to get to know each other better. I'll be able to deal with all the details about the fire and not have to worry about her."

Kieran ground his teeth. "May I speak with you in private?"

She shook her head. "We've said enough, I think. Once I've had some time to figure out my plans about what to do next, we can talk about custody arrangements."

She was shutting him out. Drawing a line in the sand. To hell with that. If she thought Kieran would agree to let her run the show, she was in for a big surprise.

"And when are you planning to leave?" He folded his arms across his chest.

"In the morning when I'm sure Cammie is okay." She turned to Jeremy. "I'll go check with Kieran's father and see if it's okay for you to spend the night. Thanks for coming, Jeremy."

In the wake of her departure, the silence lengthened. Jeremy stood, hands in his pockets, with an enigmatic smile on his handsome face.

Kieran wanted to punch him hard enough to rearrange those perfect features. He stared at the unwelcome intruder. "What's the deal with you and Olivia?"

Jeremy shrugged. "No comment."

"I don't like you, Vargas. Not one damn bit."

The smile deepened.

"You're in love with her."

Jeremy shrugged. "I *love* her. And I've known her long enough to realize you were the one who screwed over her life. I don't plan to let you do it again."

"Sanctimonious bastard." Kieran simmered, his fists itching for a brawl. But it had been years since he and his brothers had settled their differences with a fight. And

Victor would frown on bloodshed in his foyer. "You have no say in what goes on between Olivia and me."

"We'll see. But I'll be keeping an eye on you, Wolff. So watch your step."

The next morning, Olivia hugged Cammie so tightly the child finally wiggled free with a protest. Olivia brushed her daughter's wispy bangs with a fingertip. "You're sure you want to stay? You don't have to."

Cammie made a face. "I'll miss you, Mommy. Tell Lolo and Jojo I love them." Before Olivia could snag another kiss, Cammie was gone, running off to play with Gareth's dog.

Kieran stared at her, face impassive. She'd heard him knock on her door last night. But she had locked it. She was pretty sure he was going to propose marriage again, and that would have shattered her brittle heart. Everything was out in the open now. Cammie was Kieran's daughter...a Wolff who had been welcomed into the pack with open arms. His family loved her and had a lot of years to make up for.

This would be the longest time Olivia had ever been separated from her daughter. Leaving her this way was agony. But not even for Cammie's sake could Olivia linger. If Kieran continued to press for marriage as a practical solution, she might eventually cave to his persuasions. And that would be disastrous.

Olivia couldn't bear to play the dutiful wife, tucked away on Wolff Mountain like Rapunzel in her tower, waiting for her prince to come home. Not without love.

She handed her carry-on to Jeremy who was loading their belongings into his rental car. Turning back one last time, she went up on tiptoe and kissed Kieran's cheek. "Good-bye," she said quietly. "Look after our girl. I'll be in touch."

As Jeremy headed the car down the mountain, tears

trickled down Olivia's cheeks. He handed her a tissue. "Why don't you put him out of his misery? You love him."

"He doesn't love me. He's attracted to me, and he loves the fact that we share a daughter, but I can't live with that."

"So it's better to live without him?"

"Infinitely. I did it for five years and it wasn't so bad."

"But now you've been in his bed. You've shared things with him you've never shared with anyone else."

"How do you know?"

"Because I know *you,*" he said simply, shooting her a sideways glance. "You've had maybe ten dates in the last five years, and a couple of those were premieres with me, which doesn't really count."

"It's hard being a single mom. A lot of men aren't interested in raising another man's child."

"That's not it. Most guys I know would fall all over themselves to be with you, even if you had a dozen rug rats. You're smart and funny and sweet and flat-out gorgeous."

She sniffled, wiping her nose and sighing loudly. "You're good for my ego, sweet Jeremy."

He waited for the massive front gate to slide open before steering the car through and aiming for the airport. "I call 'em as I see 'em, and I think you should decide what or who you want, and then fight for your future."

"That's funny. Victor Wolff gave me a variation of the same advice."

"Maybe you should take your head out of the sand and listen."

Olivia spent three weeks in California. The first seven days were filled with meetings and planning and insurance questions. Not only that, but she had to finish up her illustrations and overnight them to her publisher, a task that made her feel lighter once it was done. Fortunately she always carried her originals with her in a sturdy folio. Much had been destroyed in the fire, but not her latest work.

Week two brought the arrest of Lolita's stalker, a sad, lonely man with definite mental issues. After that came the really difficult decisions, such as Olivia giving the go-ahead to raze the remnants of her property in order to sell the lot.

Jeremy stood with her the day the bulldozers came. He held her hand, and she cried as the last of her "normal" life was lifted and dumped into rubbish bins.

She stared at the destruction, remembering Cammie's first Christmas…the marks on the kitchen wall that measured her height. The big, fuzzy leopard-print throw that they snuggled beneath together to watch cartoons on Saturday mornings.

"All I ever wanted was to have a regular family."

Jeremy's childhood and adolescence were as tumultuous as hers. He understood exactly what her dreams were and why. Which made the shock all the bigger when he turned on her.

"Quit being such a drama queen," he said, squeezing her shoulders. "Unless you're willing to admit you're more like your mother than you realize. You lost your house, and yeah, that's a bitch. But look what you've gained. A daddy for Cammie. Relatives who love you. And a new home if you're willing to think outside the box."

"Except for my time in school, I've never lived anywhere but California."

"Me, either. But it turns out, I love New York City. And I think you love Wolff Mountain. You've damn sure talked about it nonstop for the last two and a half weeks."

"What about my parents?"

"Your folks are a hell of a long way from needing a nursing home. They have their own life with all its crazy excitement. And we have these things called jets now that fly cross-country. Don't you think it's time for you to have everything you want?"

"I'm scared, Jeremy. He hurt me so badly the last time."

"You were a kid. Now you're a grown woman. And besides, he knows I'll kick his ass if he's mean to you."

They both laughed, arm in arm, feeling the warmth of a southern California sun. It was a long way to the Blue Ridge Mountains of Virginia.

Turning her back on what was but would never be again, Olivia walked back across the street, Jeremy at her side. As they paused, looking at each other over the top of the car, she grinned at him. "We've got to find you a nice woman, Jeremy Vargas."

He chuckled, sliding into the car and turning the ignition. "I like being single," he said. "Let's concentrate on you for now."

Seventeen

Olivia's return to Wolff Mountain was anticlimactic. The big house was virtually empty save for the staff who went about their work so unobtrusively that it seemed as if phantoms ran the place. The head housekeeper welcomed Olivia politely and was able to explain the whereabouts of almost everyone.

Annalise and Victor had taken Cammie to Charlottesville to buy her new clothes for school. Jacob was working in his lab. Gareth and Gracie were repainting a room at their house.

Only Kieran's activities were a mystery. Supposedly he was still on the mountain, but no one had seen him since breakfast.

Olivia freshened up in her suite and changed into casual clothes, glad to be alone for the moment. Her composure was in shreds. She had returned to Wolff Mountain for a brief visit because she missed her daughter terribly, and because she and Kieran needed to talk about custody arrangements. Cammie had been told her mother would stay a week. Olivia was not sure she could hold out that long. Returning to the mountain gave new life to her regrets.

She had pondered Jeremy's advice about fighting for what she wanted. And if she had believed it was possible to win, she would have. But she was a realist. The situation was beyond compromise. She and Kieran were too different. End of story.

All she needed now was closure. It would help if Kieran would go ahead and fly away. Then maybe her heart could finally accept that the two of them were never meant to be.

Olivia grimaced at the state of Cammie's room. Apparently without her mother around, she had forgotten every one of Olivia's lectures about keeping her toys and things tidy.

The housekeeper hovered in the doorway, bringing an armload of fresh towels. "Sorry about the mess, ma'am. But Mr. Kieran said that if I cleaned up after the little one, she'd never learn responsibility."

Surprised and impressed, Olivia nodded. "He's right. I'll have a chat with her at bedtime tonight."

"She's still a baby."

"Yes. But not too young to learn how to be neater."

The older woman smiled and excused herself, leaving Olivia to wander the halls, familiarizing herself once again with the sights and sounds and smells of the "castle." Kieran and his brothers called it that when they wanted to tease their father, but the description wasn't far off.

At last, she gave up on finding anyone to talk to and decided to take a walk. When Cammie came back, there would be little time for quiet reflection. It was a perfect summer afternoon, the moist air heavy with expectation. A day for dreaming…a day when time seemed to stand still.

Passing the turn to Gareth's house, Olivia wandered on, across the back of the property and deeper into the woods where the forest was cool and shady and the wind whispered secrets.

She needed to talk to Kieran about their future as a blended family. And it should be done in private. Which likely meant she'd have to wait until after dinner. Contact between the two of them had been virtually nonexistent since she left. Cammie got on the phone most evenings and Annalise always chatted when Olivia called. But Kieran was mysteriously unavailable whenever Olivia asked about him.

She had no clue as to his state of mind. And no idea what he expected of her.

Thinking about the intimacies they had shared made her face flame, even though she was alone. For three weeks she'd had trouble sleeping, tormented by memories of Kieran's lovemaking. In his arms, she'd felt complete…content.

As if she had conjured him out of thin air, he appeared suddenly, pushing aside a low-hanging branch of maple, ducking beneath it and stopping a few feet away. Hungrily she looked her fill. His shoulders were still as broad, his dark eyes as wary and unreadable as ever. Ripped, faded jeans covered the lower half of his body, but his torso was bare.

A faint sheen of sweat covered his chest.

He leaned against a tree, his indolent pose at odds with the intensity of his gaze. "You're back."

"Yes." She nodded, as if he might not have understood the word.

"Is Vargas with you?"

"Jeremy? No." Frowning, she wondered why he asked. "How are things with Cammie?"

His expression softened, making him look younger, happier. "She's great. We've been fishing, hiking... I taught her how to play checkers."

"Sounds fun."

"You've done a great job with her, Olivia. You should be proud."

His praise made her uncomfortable. "Thank you."

Straightening, he rubbed the back of his arm across his forehead. "I could use a drink. You ready to go back to the house?"

He held out a hand, but she couldn't bring herself to touch him, afraid that she might resort to begging. It was not a pose she wanted to assume.

Kieran's face darkened when she pretended not to notice his gesture. In silence, they made their way back.

He made a beeline for the kitchen, where a pitcher of fresh-squeezed lemonade sat ready on the granite counter-top, the sides of the glass container glistening with moisture.

As she watched, he poured two glasses, handing one to her. Their fingers brushed. A spark of electricity arced between them. Over the rim of his tumbler, his gaze tracked every move she made as she drank.

"I want to show you something," he said abruptly, draining his glass and putting hers in the sink, as well.

Puzzled, she followed him up the stairs all the way to the attic. One corner of the massive room had been partitioned off and a door added. Kieran ushered her inside.

She stopped, her progress halted by awe and amazement. A second enormous skylight had been cut into the roof, permitting rays of pure, brilliant sunlight to shine down on what appeared to be every art supply known to man. Brushes, canvases and easels. A top-of-the-line desk. Towels and turpentine. Palettes and paint.

Turning in a slow circle to take it all in, she said, "What is all this?"

He paced, not looking at her as he spoke. "A studio for you to use…when you're here."

Torn between confusion and despair, she touched him on the shoulder, halting his restless motion. "I don't understand."

They were so close she could see the muscles in his throat work as he swallowed. "I was hoping this could be your new home. Permanently."

Desperately she searched his face for clarification. "That's very kind of you, but I wouldn't want to impose on your family." And she needed distance to survive.

He brushed her cheek with the back of his hand. "Then marry me," he muttered. "And you'll *be* family."

Wincing, she pulled away, backing clumsily into a ladder-back chair that held an artist smock. "We've been through this," she said. "You're Cammie's father now. I've brought papers that give you shared custody. Fifty-fifty. Even if all three of us occasionally share the same roof, it isn't necessary for you and me to be married."

"It's necessary to me," he said quietly.

"I'll bring Cammie often. Every time you come home. You needn't worry that I'll try to keep her from you."

"Olivia," he said abruptly, running both hands through his hair. "For God's sake. You're not listening. I *love* you."

She bit her lip. "You want me," she corrected, not willing to be duped by her own wistful heart.

"Of course I want you. More than my next breath. These last few weeks have been hell. All I can think about is stripping you bare and sinking into you until we both die from pleasure. So yes, I do want you. But what I said was that I *love* you. Till death do us part. For eternity. Am I making myself clear?"

"You're shouting," she said, her teeth chattering with nerves. She wanted so badly for this scene they were playing out to be real, but caution held her back.

Cords stood out on his neck as he squeezed his eyes shut and pinched the bridge of his nose. "You weren't this much trouble at twenty-two."

"And you weren't Kieran Wolff. So I guess we're even." She picked up a small paintbrush and tested the sable bristles on the palm of her hand. "I'm not sure it would work."

"What?" he asked, confusion replacing annoyance.

"A long-distance relationship. Seeing each other only once or twice a year. Annalise told me your pattern. Father's Day, and sometimes Christmas. That's not much for Cammie and me to hang our hats on."

The string of curses he muttered beneath his breath was extraordinary for its variety and complexity. She was pretty sure the imprecations covered five or six languages.

He grabbed her by the shoulders and smashed his mouth to hers in a kiss that was not at all elegant, but that made her knees wobble. She tasted his desperation, her own dawning hope. Wrapping her arms around his neck, she moaned when his fingers plucked roughly at her tight nipples through the thin fabric of her blouse.

She wanted him so badly, she felt faint from need, weak with hunger.

Kieran came up for air at last, his chest heaving. She was pretty sure her fingernails had left scratch marks on his back. He stared down at her, telling her with his eyes the wild and wonderful truth. "I'm not going anywhere," he said.

"Today?" She tried to move back into her safety zone, but he had his hands at her hips, immobilizing her for the moment.

"Ever," he said flatly. "Do you believe me?"

"But what about your job?"

"I'll get someone to sub for me in September. Everything else can be passed off to other architects and engineers."

"What will you do?" This sudden about-face was mind-boggling.

He slid his hands up her waist until they landed beneath her breasts. Weighing each one with a gentle lift, he bent to kiss her again, this time with agonizing gentleness. "First of all," he said, his words slurred as he moved his mouth over the skin of her throat. "I'll build our house…and a swing set…and a corral for the pony…and—"

She put her hands over his lips. "You're serious?" It didn't seem possible. "You think you can give it up cold turkey? No more jetting round the globe? No more frequent flier miles? No more mosquito nets and hard hats?"

He bit her finger, enough to sting. "I have no reason to leave," he said simply. "Everything I want and need is here if you'll stay with me."

Tears stung her eyes. "Don't say it if you don't mean it," she begged. "I couldn't bear it if you changed your mind."

"God, Olivia. I know I kicked the shit out of your ability to trust me, but you have to believe me. If you give me another chance…if you'll make a family with me, you'll never regret it. I'm going to spend the rest of my life making you scream my name, night after night. It will be so loud, the neighbors will complain."

She laughed and hiccupped a sob at the same time. "There are no neighbors," she pointed out, caught by the image of Kieran making her cry out as she climaxed.

He scooped her up in his arms and crossed the room. "Did you notice I had the interior design team include a settee? All great artists have settees."

"Is that so people can pose for me?" She lifted her arms obediently as he undressed her with more urgency than care.

"It's so I can screw you," he panted, now working on his own clothing. His gaze was fixated on her chest. "Lie down."

She didn't have to be told twice. It was either that or melt into a puddle on the floor.

He came down between her legs, shifting her left foot to prop it on the back of their makeshift nest. His thumbs traced the folds of her sex, gathering moisture and spreading it on the head of his erection. The shaft was long and hard and throbbing with eagerness.

Kieran groaned, closing his eyes. "I love you, Olivia." Positioning himself at the mother lode, he plunged deep, wringing a cry from her and filling her so completely, she forgot to breathe. He stilled for a moment, allowing both of them to absorb the shattering pleasure.

Inside her, he flexed. She gripped handfuls of his hair as he bent to taste her breasts, one after the other, licking and suckling them until she sensed her first orgasm in the wings.

His hands moved, sliding under her bottom to lift her into his thrusts. She clung to him, dizzy and panting. "Kieran…" She didn't know what she wanted to say, what she needed him to hear.

"I'm here, honey. Always."

The vow… and the swivel of his hips that ground the base of his erection against her sweet spot sent her over the edge. The climax lasted forever, raking her body with shivers of sensation that rode the edge of pain and ecstasy.

Before she had fully recovered, he went rigid, his back arched in a rictus of release that lasted for long, shuddering seconds.

Minutes later, maybe hours, she recovered the ability to speak. "I love this settee," she muttered, licking a drop of sweat from her upper lip. The sun warmed them like a benediction. Kieran's weight was a delicious burden, his shaft still pulsing with aftershocks.

"Hell," he said, his body shaking with laughter. "I didn't wear a condom. I swear, woman. Around you I take leave of my senses."

She stroked his hair, staring up at a sky so blue it seemed to go on forever. Peace, utter and infinite, filled her heart, her mind, her soul. "I'd like to be pregnant again," she whispered, daring to dream of home and hearth with the man she loved.

Wolff Mountain was a wonderful place to grow up. And now that she'd experienced the fear generated by violence and danger, she decided that being tucked away from the world wasn't altogether a bad thing.

Kieran sat up, rubbing his eyes. "I haven't slept at all since you left. This wedding has to be soon. I want you in my bed. Every night."

"I want that, too." She bent down to rescue her bra and blouse. "Annalise strikes me as someone who would love to plan just such an occasion."

"We can set up a large tent…to keep the paparazzi at bay. Unless, of course, your parents don't mind being photographed."

She laughed. "You never know with them. My mother does love keeping count of how many times her face appears on the tabloids. She thinks they're sleazy gossip rags, but she hates being left out."

They managed to dress, but it was a slow process. Kieran kept interrupting her to nibble her rib cage, caress her bottom, bite her earlobe. Finally, completely clothed except for her shoes, she looked at him. "Do you think anyone is home yet?"

He zipped his fly. "Who knows? Why do you ask?"

She cupped him boldly, her fingers squeezing softly as

she found his sex tucked in the front of his jeans. "I'm still not sure I'm not dreaming. Maybe you could take another shot at convincing me."

By the time they ultimately made their way back downstairs, they were eager to share their news. Kieran used his cell phone to convene an audience for afternoon tea, and soon, in the large, formal living room, the entire clan was gathered, including Annalise's brothers and father.

Cammie spotted her mother and ran across the room, throwing herself into Olivia's arms. "You're back. You're back."

Olivia hugged her, feeling uneasy at being the cynosure of all eyes. "I surely am. Have you been a good girl while I was gone?"

"Yes, ma'am."

Victor stood up, his weathered face beaming. "I think some introductions are in order...and perhaps a formal announcement?" He looked inquiringly at his youngest son.

Kieran moved closer, putting his arms around Cammie and Olivia. "Six years ago, Olivia and I met each other at Oxford. But as you all know, we Wolffs attended college under false names. When I left suddenly to come home in the aftermath of Dad's heart attack, Olivia and I lost touch. But she had my baby."

Olivia wondered if she was the only one who noticed the crack in his voice.

He continued, scanning the room, his gaze landing one by one on the faces of the people who had shared tragedy with him in the past. "My traveling days are over," he said quietly. "Olivia has agreed to marry me. My next design project will be our new house here on Wolff Mountain."

The whoops and hollers that erupted rattled the rafters. Cammie and Olivia and Kieran were engulfed in a barrage of hugs and kisses and congratulations. Olivia enjoyed every moment of it. The Wolffs were not a normal family, but they were *her* family...from now on.

She managed to get their attention, and the room quieted. "Thank you all for welcoming me and for being so sweet to Cammie. This will be pretty close to a shotgun wedding as far as the time frame goes, but if Annalise is willing, I'm going to let her handle all the details."

Gracie piped up, eyes dancing. "I'll help, too. It's about time we had some girly stuff going on up on this mountain."

Everyone laughed.

Victor held out a hand, cradling a champagne flute as two young women passed around matching glasses to the crowd. Cammie's was filled with orange juice.

When everyone was served, Victor cleared his throat to quiet the rambunctious assemblage. "To Kieran...and his bride-to-be and daughter. May you always be as happy as you are today."

Glasses were raised and emptied. Kieran leaned down to kiss Cammie and then Olivia. "To my girls," he said softly. "I love you both."

Hours later, when the clock was about to strike midnight, Kieran and Olivia stood beside their daughter's bed. Olivia held his hand, her head on his shoulder. "You missed so much," she said. "I'll never be able to give that back to you."

He was quiet for long moments, his chest barely moving as he breathed. "We all walk our own road, Olivia. Yours and mine diverged at the worst possible time, but we won't ever have to worry about that again. Side by side. Day by day. We're marking a new path that will be ours alone."

"And you *do* want more children?"

He turned to face her. "Give me a dozen," he said, teeth

flashing white in the semidarkness. "We've got room to grow on this mountain. God willing, there will be plenty of cousins, too."

She went up on tiptoe and kissed him. "I knew the first day I saw you that you were the man I wanted to marry."

He scooped her into his arms, carrying her to the adjoining bedroom where half a dozen candles were lit. As he laid her on the bed, coming down beside her, he grimaced. "If I had handled things better back then, we wouldn't have wasted so much time."

She caressed his face, cupping his cheeks, rubbing her thumbs across his bottom lip. "I tried to convince myself that what we had was a fling, a college romance. But deep in my heart, I've always known you were the one. Which made it pretty difficult to go out with other guys."

"I don't want to hear about the other guys," he muttered. "Not now, anyway." He slid a hand along her thigh from her ankle to the place that readied itself for him with damp heat.

She stopped him, trapping his fingers by placing hers on top. "There were none," she said simply. "Only you."

Silence throbbed. His eyes widened, and something that was a combination of astonishment, relief, joy and humble gratitude flashed in their depths. "You're mine, Olivia. I'm yours."

As Kieran positioned himself for a thrust that would take him home, he heard a faint voice…words that faded as the one who spoke them moved into another realm. *I love you, my son. Be happy*….

Unexpected tears stung the backs of his eyes as he filled Olivia's tight passage with a surge of longing and the length of his passion.

He *was* home…and he was happy.

* * * * *

A LOVER'S TOUCH
Brenda Jackson

One

Kendra Redding inhaled a deep, fortifying breath as she took off jogging down the sandy beach. She kept her gaze focused in front of her as she ran along the shoreline. Already the awakening sun was peeking through the sky. It would be a beautiful June day; a hot one, but beautiful nonetheless.

She loved this time of the morning, when most of the residents of the small beach community where she lived were still sleeping. This was her quiet time. She would be busy soon enough when she opened her optometry office in a few hours. But now, the only sound she heard, other than the seagulls flying overhead, was the steady wash of surf over sand.

As she continued her run, Kendra thought about her father. She regretted he had lived only a few months after she'd joined him at the office last year, before a heart attack had claimed his life. Her mother had died when Kendra was four, and she and her father had been extremely close.

As Kendra's sneakered feet continued to pound into the sand, she suddenly felt a tingling sensation in her midsection and the tips of her breasts became sensitive against her midriff top. She slowed the pace of her jog while scanning the deserted stretch of beach, seeking out anything that would confirm her suspicion…or rather, her body's pronouncement. But she saw no one.

Thinking she must have imagined things, she took a deep breath and increased the pace of her jog. Moments later, she came to a complete halt. Taking another deep breath, she glanced around. This time, she knew her body was not playing games with her. The tingling sensation that had been in her midsection earlier was now a deep throb that had moved lower, settling right smack between her legs, and her breasts were more sensitive than before.

Squinting, she could barely make out the jogger who loomed on the horizon, and although he was still some distance away, she could tell the human form was that of a man. He was jogging at a brisk pace, seemingly as one with the elements surrounding him.

She inhaled sharply when her body reacted once again. There was only one man who had the ability to bring her body to such an aroused state, even from a distance and even after a seven-year absence. He was the man she had fallen in love with at sixteen; the man she had given her virginity to at seventeen; the man her body had craved ever since. And although she didn't want to, she could feel his touch as though it had been just yesterday when his strong hands had stroked her body into a feverish pitch and introduced her to passion of the most profound kind.

Swallowing deeply, she forced the memories away and

accepted that her body's reaction to the person jogging toward her could mean only one thing.

Slate Landis was back in town.

Two

Slate saw the feminine figure slowly jogging toward him and recognized her immediately. It was about time their paths crossed, and what better place than the sandy shores of Fernandina Beach, Florida, where they had first declared their love seven years ago?

He'd tried to keep his return to town quiet since arriving two nights ago. He had been busy unpacking and getting updates on everything and everyone from Marcie Wilkins, an old friend of his deceased grandmother's. He had known that there was a good chance he would run into Kendra this morning. In fact, he'd been counting on it. He had discovered over the years that there were some things in life that a man could not get out of his system, and the woman he had once loved to distraction was one of them.

His mind suddenly went back to the first day he had ever laid eyes on her. He had been twenty, a junior in college, and she had been sixteen. That summer he had come to live with Ms. Marcie, an old family friend, the first year after his parents' death in an auto accident. After getting a job as a lifeguard, he had gone to the optometrist's office in town to undergo the required eye exam. Kendra had been working there, assisting her father, and from the first moment he saw her, he had been drawn to her like a moth to a flame.

Sighing deeply, he tried to compose himself when he finally came to a stop directly in front of her. "Kendra." He greeted her in a low, husky voice that he almost didn't recognize as his own.

"Slate," she said breathlessly, whether from the run or from startled surprise he wasn't sure. She met his intense gaze with one of her own. "You said you'd never come back. Why are you here?"

Her question made his thoughts shift to that ill-fated day seven years ago when he had left town. At the time, she had been a youthful-looking eighteen-year-old. Now she was a gorgeous woman of twenty-five and was everything male fantasies were made of.

His gaze did a slow burn down the length of her body. Her skimpy top and shorts made him very much aware of her bare thighs, long legs, curvy hips and generous cleavage. His eyes then moved upward and zeroed in on her nut-brown face, which was more beautiful than ever. He knew her lips tasted just as good as they looked—full, ripe and with a flavor that was distinctively hers.

Heat pooled low in his belly, and his blood grew hot and heavy in his veins when he remembered the number of times his tongue had stroked those lips.

"Slate?"

He realized he hadn't answered her question, and a part of him suddenly became obsessed with having the woman

he'd walked away from back in his life. Feeling he had nothing to lose and everything to gain, he decided to show her
rather than tell her why he had returned.

Three

Kendra didn't know what had happened. One moment she was staring at Slate, and the next moment she was wrapped firmly in his arms with his mouth devouring hers.

Her body stiffened, then relaxed as any thought of resisting him was destroyed the second his tongue entered her mouth, capturing hers and evoking memories she'd tried to suppress over the years.

His mouth was hot and sweet to the taste. Even the light musky scent of his sweat was intoxicating. Waves of desire uncoiled inside of her as he stroked her tongue, making every emotion she had skate around in her brain. He'd always had this sort of effect on her, even when she'd been too young to understand what sexual chemistry was about.

The sudden feel of his tongue on hers made all-consuming heat ignite between her legs, and she heard herself moaning deep in the back of her throat. He wrapped his fingers in her hair to hold her mouth in place, as if she could possibly think of going anywhere. Although logic ruled that indulging in this kind of kiss with him was crazy, she intended to get her fill now and criticize her foolishness later.

When the distant sound of the horn from a shrimp boat invaded, he slowly lifted his mouth from hers. It was then that she noticed that at some point she had grabbed hold of his shoulders to keep from falling when her knees had weakened.

She slowly lowered her arms to her side and felt him untangle his fingers from her hair. She realized that any attempt to pretend she hadn't been affected by his kiss would be futile, because she had been, and had a feeling he knew it. The one thing they had never been able to hide from each other was desire. When it came to arousing her, he had the process down pat.

"Kendra," he murmured, in a low, sexy drawl, recapturing her attention.

She drew in a steady breath as heat poured through her. He was well over six feet tall, had a nice build and was the color of semisweet chocolate. At twenty-nine, he had aged handsomely and was still the kind of man who women, both young and old, noticed at first glance.

A deep frown came to her face when she remembered how easily he had walked away seven years ago and not looked back, and the pain she had suffered. "Why, Slate? Why did you come back after all this time?"

He reached out and stroked his thumb across her bottom lip, a lip still tingling from their kiss. She hoped he didn't detect the hot, fiery desire that was running rampant inside of her; however, judging by the dark, hot look in his eyes, he did.

"I'd hope after that kiss the reason I'm back would be obvious, Kendra," he said huskily in a deep voice that shook her to the core. "I came back for you."

Four

Slate focused his attention on Kendra and watched how her body stiffened with his words. Marcie Wilkins had been right. Gaining Kendra's forgiveness for leaving the way he had seven years ago would not be easy.

"Aren't you going to say anything, Kendra?"

She finally met his gaze, and when she did, he winced from the pain he saw in her features.

"You came back for me? Do you think you can jog back into my life after seven years and say that?" she asked heatedly. "It's been seven years, Slate. Seven years without a call or a letter. Did you not think I had gotten on with my life?"

He sighed as he continued to meet her gaze. "No, Kendra, I didn't think that."

"Well, what did you think?" she snapped.

Now was not the time to tell her that he had thought, hoped and prayed that, after finally coming to terms with that fateful day that had nearly destroyed him, the two of them could have a future together. He had walked away from her and everyone else because he believed that he was to blame for Susan Conrad's drowning. He'd felt there was something he could have done differently to save the six-year-old who had wandered too far out into the ocean.

Although he and Kendra had been on the beach that day, he hadn't been on duty as a lifeguard when he'd heard Susan's mother's screams. Knowing he was more experienced and could swim a lot faster than the lifeguard who was on duty, he had taken off, charging into the ocean, swimming faster than he'd ever swam before in his life in an attempt to save the little girl. But the undercurrent had been too strong, and by the time he'd reached her it had been too late.

Although everyone had told him he'd done all that he could—including nearly losing his own life in the process—he had never been able to forget the look on that little girl's face as she clung to the hope that he would save her. And the one thing that he had not been able to let go of was the guilt that he had let her down.

It had taken years of soul-searching, counseling and therapy to put the past behind him and to finally let go. But over the past year he'd come to realize that although he had been able to purge the guilt of Susan from his soul, purging Kendra from his heart was not possible.

So he'd made a decision to return to win her back. He knew the odds of doing so were against him. But he had a week to show her just what his heart already knew. She was his life, and there was no way he could continue to survive without her in it.

He finally decided to answer her question as he met her gaze. "What I think is that we need to talk. We owe each other that much."

Five

Once again the sound of Slate's voice evoked heat through Kendra. She forced her gaze away from his, and it came to rest on the waistline of his jogging shorts. She quickly snatched her gaze back to his face. He was the only man she knew who could get that aroused from a kiss. But, then, it had always been that way between them. It was like a domino effect. His arousal would automatically trigger hers, and hers in turn would automatically trigger his.

"We don't owe each other anything, and there's nothing for us to talk about," she finally said. "You made it clear when you left that you never intended to come back."

Slate nodded. "Yes, I know that's what I said, and I meant it at the time. But I had to come back to ask your forgiveness over the way I left."

Kendra sighed. She had always understood his need to leave the beach; his need to be alone for a while to come to terms with Susan Conrad's death. But at no time had she thought he would completely shut her out and turn his back on their love.

But he had.

"I can forgive you for leaving, Slate. I understood what you were going through. But I'm not sure that I can forgive you for giving me not so much as a phone call to let me know you were okay. You didn't even contact Ms. Marcie, and the two of you were close."

"I was going through some rough times, Kendra," he said softly.

"What a shame," she said coolly. "So was I, Slate." She inhaled deeply, wanting that episode of her life to go back to the past where it belonged. "How long will you be in town?" she asked, needing to know how long she had to avoid him.

Slate paused for a few seconds before answering her question. "I'll be here a week."

Kendra nodded. Then he would return to New York. She'd overheard Ms. Marcie tell Mrs. Butternut at church a few months ago that he lived in Harlem and owned a very successful internet sales company that he operated from his home, designing websites and databases for major corporations.

"Are you staying at the Wilkinses' Beach Resort while you're in town?"

"No, for privacy I'm staying in the Wilkinses' beach house," Slate answered.

Kendra met his gaze. "The beach house?"

"Yes. You remember where it is, don't you?"

She swallowed deeply, not wanting to acknowledge all the memories the beach house generated. The Wilkinses' Beach Resort and her home were right down the road from each other, and the smaller beach house sat snugly in between the two, hidden behind the sand dunes. The proximity of the Wilkinses' Beach Resort—where Slate had lived during the summers he'd worked as a lifeguard—and her home was the reason they had become so intimate so quickly. Secret late-night meetings at the beach house had been the norm for them.

"Of course I remember," Kendra breathed. "That's where we first made love."

Six

"I still think we need to talk."

Slate's words recaptured Kendra's attention, and she took a calming breath. Being as detached as she could, she said, "I don't know if that's possible since I'm pretty busy most of the time. I've taken over the running of the shop now that Dad's gone."

Slate nodded. "I heard about your father, Kendra, and I'm sorry. He was a good man. I really liked him."

"Yes, he was, and he really liked you, too," she responded softly. That had been true. Her father had never said an unkind word about Slate, even when he knew how badly Slate had hurt her.

"I think it's wonderful that you're carrying things on the way you know he would have wanted. I'm sure he was proud of you."

Kendra nodded. "Yes, he was," she murmured, thinking of how happy her father had been when she'd decided to become an optometrist.

"And I'm very proud of you, too, Kendra." Slate's words reined Kendra's thoughts back in, and her focus was completely reclaimed by him.

"Thanks, Slate, and I'm proud of you, as well. I understand your internet sales business is doing very well. I always knew that you would be successful one day."

A jolt of grief went through her upon remembering that she'd always assumed that she would be at his side when that success came. During those summers she had often dreamed about him moving permanently to Fernandina Beach, building websites and computer databases while he waited for her to complete college. Then the two of them would marry and build a huge oceanfront home—their dream home—on the land his parents had left him, and live happily ever after.

So much for dreams, she thought. This was the real world, and in the real world dreams didn't come true.

"Well, I have to finish my jog so I can open the office on time," she said, feeling the need to move on and not let her thoughts dwell on what would never be. "Goodbye, Slate."

She took off running and refused to look back.

Slate stood rooted in place as he watched Kendra take off. His piercing dark eyes remained on her until she was no longer in sight. It was only then that he gave himself a hard mental shake. Kendra was determined not to give him any slack, but he refused to let her keep him at bay. She was saying one thing but her body was saying another, and for the time being he decided to go with her body language rather than her words.

A determined smile tilted the corners of his mouth as he began jogging again. No matter what, he intended to break down any walls she erected between them. If she thought she could avoid him while he was in town she was wrong. He was determined to do whatever it took to get her back, and if he had to conquer her body before he could work his way to her mind, then so be it.

Seven

"Why didn't you tell me that Slate Landis was back in town?"

Kendra lifted her head from eating her salad and looked across the table at her best friend, Cheryl Wilkins-Huffman. The two of them had been best friends for as long as she could remember, and for years they had shared everything. Kendra was the first to know when Cheryl had fallen in love with Carl Huffman at sixteen, and was godmother to their two-year-old daughter, Carly.

"The reason I didn't tell you is that I just found out myself this morning." After taking a sip of iced tea she added, "Besides, I should be asking you the same question since he's living at your grandmother's place."

Cheryl bunched her eyebrows. "The resort?"

"No, the beach house."

Cheryl's face broke into a grin. "No wonder Grandma was acting so secretive a few days ago when I dropped

Carly off. Evidently Slate told her not to say anything. I guess he wanted to surprise you."

"Well, he certainly did that. I saw him while I was out jogging this morning. At first I thought I was seeing things. He was the last person I expected to run into."

Cheryl nodded. "Carl is the one who told me. They ran into each other yesterday at Milner's Grocery."

Kendra took another sip of her tea. "Well, just about everyone has made a point of telling me today just in case I didn't know. I had at least four drop-ins at the shop this morning, people who suddenly needed their eyes tested, bearing news that Slate was back in town."

Cheryl chuckled. "People were counting on a wedding between you two. Your and Slate's love life held everyone's interest back then."

Kendra shook her head, remembering. "And if you ask me, they're too interested in it now, although Slate and I don't have a love life."

"Did he say why he came back after all this time?"

Kendra sighed deeply as she spread more dressing on her salad. "He claims he wants my forgiveness for the way he left."

"Will you forgive him?"

Kendra picked up her fork. "Cheryl, I understood why he left, so there's no forgiveness needed for that. What I couldn't accept then, and still can't accept now, is the fact that not once did he call me in seven years."

Cheryl nodded. "He talked to Carl, and from what Carl said Slate had a rough time dealing with Susan Conrad's death all those years."

Kendra shook her head. "But still, he could have called or something. I think I deserved that much since he claimed to have loved me."

Cheryl met Kendra's gaze. "Have you given thought to what his return could mean?"

Kendra raised an eyebrow. "And just what do you think it could mean?"

"The two of you burying the past and getting on with your lives."

Eight

"I understand that Landis boy is back in town."

Kendra couldn't help but smile as she adjusted the optometric equipment to put it in place. The person she had seen on the beach that morning was definitely not a boy. No boy had a body quite like that. "Yes, Ms. Martha, that's what I hear, too."

"You haven't seen him yet?"

Kendra decided to tell the truth. In this town a lie could come back to haunt you. "Yes, ma'am. I ran into him this morning while jogging."

"And?"

Kendra shook her head. At eighty years old the woman was still sharp as a tack and still kept her mind on everyone's business. "And it was good seeing him again."

Martha Bolden frowned. "That's all you have to say, young lady?"

Kendra adjusted the lighting overhead to have a clear

view of Mrs. Bolden's shrewd eyes. "Yes, ma'am, other than to say your eyesight looks just as good as it did last week when you came in for your annual eye exam."

The older woman had the decency to smile. "Well, at my age you can't be too careful when it comes to your sight."

Yeah, especially if you think you need to start seeing something, Kendra thought as she shut down her equipment. She glanced over at the clock. She had an hour left before closing time. After Martha Bolden left, Kendra went back into her office to make notations in several of her patients' charts. Unless she had another walk-in she was through for the day.

She couldn't help but remember her conversation with Cheryl at lunch and the comment her friend had made about her and Slate getting back together. At the moment she was trying not to feel anything for him, although her mouth was still tingling from the effects of his kiss. She leaned back in her chair and remembered how Slate had kissed her as though there had not been seven years of separation between them, and how easily her body had responded.

The tinkling sound of the bell over the front door rang out through the office and caught her attention. The young woman she'd hired over a year ago as her assistant had left after Kendra's last scheduled patient. Walking out of her office, Kendra stopped dead in her tracks when she saw who her unscheduled patient was.

Slate Landis.

She swallowed as their eyes met. He stood in front of her display window; in the ray of sunshine that illuminated his features, as well as his physique in the tank top and cut-off jean shorts he wore, he looked totally stunning.

An awkward silence hung over the room while she tried

to regain her composure. She cleared her throat. "Slate, what are you doing here?"

He stepped away from the window and gave her a warm, cheerful smile. "I'm here for an eye exam."

Nine

Kendra's face tilted into a frown. Not for one minute did she believe Slate needed his eyes examined, especially considering the way those eyes had checked her out this morning and were doing likewise now. She leveled her gaze on him. "And when was the last time you had an eye exam?"

He shrugged. "I can't rightly recall at the moment. Probably not since the last time your father gave me one."

Kendra sighed. "All right, then, follow me."

He gave her a huge smile. "Sure thing."

When they reached her office she closed the door behind them. "Please sit in that chair while I locate your chart. Do you know if glaucoma ran in your family?" When he sat down Kendra couldn't help but notice how well his solid frame fit the sturdy chair.

"As far as I know, it didn't."

She nodded as she pulled his chart out of the cabinet. "All right, but I think I'll give you a glaucoma test, as well."

"Whatever you think is best."

She raised an eyebrow. What she didn't think was best at the moment was the two of them alone in her office. "Just sit back and relax for a moment while I get the equipment in place."

"All right."

Kendra leaned close to him to bring the slit lamp near his face. Her head began swimming when she took a sniff of his aftershave. It was such a masculine fragrance. Already her body was responding to his smell, his proximity.

"Rest your chin here and please read the line farthest to the bottom that you can."

"All right. I believe I can read the letters on the very last line."

"Okay then go for it, left to right."

"Well now, there's an *E* for ecstasy, an *S* for sex, a *P* for passion, an *O* for org—"

"Just saying the letter will do."

"If you prefer."

"I do."

"Okay. The remaining letters are *T* and *F*." He smiled. "I had good words lined up for them."

She shook her head, grinning. "Yes, I bet you did." She pulled the optical machine away from his face and jotted some notes in his chart.

"So what do you think?" he asked.

She thought that if she didn't get him out of her office, and soon, she would lose her ability to think, at least rationally. She was trying to remain professional but he was making it downright difficult.

"I'll let you know after your glaucoma screening," she said, setting up the tonometer.

The procedure was over in a few minutes. "You have twenty-twenty vision, which is surprising considering the type of work you do. You evidently monitor the amount of time you spend in front of your computer screen, which is a very smart thing to do."

He nodded then stood. "Is the exam over?"

"Yes."

"Am I your last patient for today?"

She raised an eyebrow before answering. "Yes, why?"

"Because of this."

And for the second time that day she found herself being pulled into his arms.

Ten

For the second time that day she didn't resist him. With smooth precision he had pulled her into his arms and took her mouth with the ease and experience of a man who knew what he wanted and what it took to get it.

Kendra was helpless to do anything but follow his lead, especially when her body was rejoicing at being held so tight to a man it had an affinity with, and when she felt his firm erection touch her belly she opened her mouth fully under his.

He thoroughly explored her mouth with his tongue, making her weak with desire and her body consumed with need. She felt his hands touch her backside, bringing her even closer to him. She began giving him bold strokes of her own.

Passion, the likes of which she hadn't felt in over seven years, took over, sending her mind reeling and her body burning. His kiss was filling an empty space that had been hollow since he'd left. And now her body was saying just what it wanted and whom it wanted it from. When one of his hands left her bottom to cup her breast, teasing the tip with his thumb, she moaned deep within her throat. She remembered the first time he had touched her this way and how the feel of his hands on her breasts had heightened every nerve in her body—just like it was doing now.

The blasting sound from a car horn drew them apart and for endless moments they just stared at each other, trying to get their breathing under control.

Finally, Kendra spoke. "You can't just go around kissing me whenever you feel like it, Slate."

To prove he disagreed, he leaned over and kissed the tip of her nose and instinctively her body moved closer to his. "I can't?"

"No, you can't," she whispered softly, yet at the same time tilted her mouth up to his for another kiss.

He greedily obliged her, and she shivered from the onslaught of his mouth again. Reaching out, she captured the hard muscles of his shoulders beneath her fingers and reveled in the feel of his mouth working magic on hers. She had to be stronger the next time, her mind reasoned, but right now she needed this. She wanted this. A part of her had forgotten the pleasure a woman could find in a man's arms. Especially when those arms belonged to Slate Landis.

Moments later, he slowly pulled back his mouth and met her gaze. "Have dinner with me tonight, Kendra," he said in a low, husky voice.

It was on the tip of Kendra's tongue to deny his request. She suddenly felt the need to get herself together before she did anything else with him she might be sorry for later. But when he began placing butterfly kisses around her mouth, she lost the fight to resist.

"Yes, I'll have dinner with you."

Eleven

"If you're so against going out with Slate tonight, Kendra, then why did you agree to do it?"

Kendra turned away from her mirror, met Cheryl's gaze and frowned when she thought about the kisses she and Slate had shared that afternoon in her office. "Let's just say he caught me at a weak moment."

Cheryl chuckled. "Yeah, I can just imagine how he did it, too, since I know just how ripe you are for the picking."

Kendra placed her hands on her hips. "What's that supposed to mean?"

"Just what I said. As your best friend I know what you've been getting and what you haven't been getting, and the one thing you haven't gotten in over seven years is laid." Cheryl arched a dark, slanted eyebrow. "Unless you've been holding back and not telling me everything."

Kendra's frown deepened. "I've told you everything you needed to know. And you're right, there hasn't been anyone since Slate, which is why I'm so tense about our date to-night." She dropped down on her bed. "I want him pretty damn bad."

"Then get him. Seven years is a long time to be deprived."

A groan rumbled deep within Kendra's throat. "Yeah, tell me about it. But I can't let Slate think he can waltz back into town after all this time and pick up where he left off."

"And I agree, but what's wrong with letting him see firsthand what he's been missing all those years? I say you should fight fire with fire. Turn the tables on Slate and have him at your mercy for the next week."

Kendra leaned back on the palms of her hands, tipped her head and met Cheryl's gaze. "Are you suggesting that I engage in an affair with him?"

Cheryl grinned. "Yes, an affair of the most passionate kind, and when the week is over, just walk away. It's a fantastic idea unless..."

Kendra frowned. "Unless what?"

Cheryl regarded her speculatively. "Unless you're afraid that you won't be able to walk away because a part of you still loves him."

Cheryl's words struck deep, and Kendra swallowed as she felt a tight knot in her throat. "I'm not in love with Slate."

"Then you don't have a thing to worry about, but as your best friend I suggest that you make certain of your feelings. You and Slate had a very special relationship and although you haven't mentioned him much over the years, I'd always felt the reason you never allowed yourself to get involved with another man was because you still loved him."

Kendra lifted her chin. "If you thought that then you were wrong."

Cheryl nodded. "If you're sure, then there's nothing for

you to worry about. You'll get the sexual fulfillment you need and still walk away with your heart intact."

Kendra liked the thought of that, and the corners of her mouth tilted into a beguiling smile. "I can handle that. Let the fun begin."

Twelve

Slate knew he was in deep trouble the moment Kendra opened her door. His gaze took in the outfit she'd chosen to wear. It was a black, clingy number that flaunted everything it was supposed to conceal. The way the dress fit her body reminded him of just how enticing all of her body parts were, covered or uncovered. The dress ended way above her knees with slits on both sides showing long, gorgeous legs. He swallowed deeply. There was no doubt that tonight would be one he'd remember for a long time.

"Come in, Slate. I just need to grab my purse," Kendra said, reminding him that he was there for some reason other than to stand in her doorway and ogle her.

"Yeah, sure," he said, stepping inside then watching as she disappeared into the back. He wiped the sweat from his brow with his hand. Things were heating up already. He glanced up when she reentered the room.

"I'm ready," she said, placing the strap of her purse on her shoulder. "And you never did say where we were going."

He gazed into her dark eyes and responded. "I thought it would be nice if we drove to Jacksonville. I heard there's a nice seafood restaurant on the Intercoastal Waterway there. And I know how much you like seafood."

Kendra's smile widened. She was glad he'd decided not to take her to any place local. The town was already buzzing about them.

"Sounds great, but first I think we should get this out of the way," she said taking a step closer and wrapping her arms around his neck. "Since our day started out this way we may as well stay on a roll, don't you think?" she whispered silkily before joining her mouth to his.

She wanted to show him that he could get just as good as he gave. Closing her eyes, she settled her body against his, immediately feeling him get hard against her. When he opened his mouth beneath hers she slipped her tongue inside and decided to play "catch me if you can."

He caught her, snarling her tongue with his and feasting on her mouth like a starving man. The more he feasted, the more her body began overflowing in desire so thick she could almost smother in it. When he reached down and touched her hips to bring her more snugly against him, slanting his mouth across hers in the process, she decided to pull back before they ended up making love on her living room floor. And that was not how she intended their evening to end.

At least not yet. She planned to torture him for a while longer.

Fighting the heat erupting in her stomach, Kendra licked

her lips as if relishing the taste of him. Tilting her head up, she smiled brightly. "All right, then, I'm ready to go."

Incapable of speech, Slate could only nod and follow her out the door.

Thirteen

The woman was trying to torment him, Slate concluded as they finished off the last of their meal. After a steamy kiss began their evening, things had gotten even hotter on the thirty-minute drive to the restaurant. Kendra had sat in the car with her legs crossed in a way that blatantly showed the slit in her dress. He could barely keep his eyes on the road.

Then when their meal had been delivered, she had turned eating snow crabs into the most erotic sight he'd ever seen when she had taken her tongue and practically sucked and licked the claws dry. The motions she had made with her mouth while eating the crabs had him shifting in his seat. He could just imagine the things that she could do with that mouth, which was something they'd never got around to doing when they had dated years back.

"Do you think you're going to want dessert?"

Her question grabbed his attention and their gazes met

and held across the table. Yes, he wanted dessert, but what he had a sweet tooth for was definitely not on the menu.

He took several deep breaths before answering. "No, I think I'll pass, but you can order something if you'd like."

She smiled. "Thanks. I see on the menu that they have ice cream cones. I think I'll order one since I feel like licking something tonight."

His erection suddenly strained against his zipper with such brutal force that he nearly gasped in pain. "Then by all means order one," he said huskily, surprised that he was capable of speech.

Her smile widened. "I will."

Slate thought that in all his twenty-nine years he had never seen anyone lick an ice cream cone the way she did. Sitting across from her and watching her tongue at work was enough to tempt him to have more than one glass of wine, but since he was the one doing the driving he just sat there and let her torture him. Besides, he had a feeling he needed all his faculties to handle the rest of the evening with Kendra, and couldn't help wondering how she intended it to end.

After he'd taken care of their check, he stood. "Ready to leave?"

"Yes."

He nodded. He would find out soon enough.

When she stood, intense longing flared through him as he took a look at her dress. Seeing what he could of her dark, creamy flesh was enough to make him lose control. "Have I told you how good you look tonight?"

Even her chuckle turned him on. "Yes, four times tonight. Thanks. And you know what they say, don't you?"

He raised a curious dark brow. "No, what do they say?"

"They say that flattery will get you everywhere."

He tilted his lips in a smile when he thought of all the possibilities. "Everywhere?"

Fourteen

"Ahh," Kendra moaned throatily. "Move just a little lower. Ah, now move just a little more to the right—do it harder. Yes, oh, yes, that's it, harder still. Umm, that feels so much better."

After one last moan she looked over her shoulder and said. "Thanks for scratching my back, Slate. You can zip me back up now."

Slate's hand trembled as he slowly zipped up Kendra's dress. When he had pulled into her driveway she had suddenly begun twitching in her seat, saying her back needed scratching. He had been more than happy to oblige until his fingers had come into contact with her bare skin. The first thing he'd noted was the absence of a bra. The next thing had been how warm and smooth her skin was.

His hand had glided over the spot she'd indicated needed scratching. The throaty sounds she'd made when he'd finally found the spot had sent shivers of excitement racing down his spine. If she made those kinds of sounds from having her body scratched, he didn't want to imagine what type of sounds she would make when they made love.

"Are you sure your back feels better?" he asked once he had zipped her dress completely up.

She turned around in her seat. "Yes, I'm sure." She smiled and gave him a thoughtful look. "I'd almost forgotten what great hands you have."

Blood raced through his body at an alarming speed with the memories that suddenly came to mind. "I'm glad I was able to help you to remember," he said as his fingers absently stroked the steering wheel. "We shared some wonderful times together back then, didn't we?"

Kendra rested her head against the back of her seat as memories filled her mind. "Yes, we did. I couldn't wait to hear Dad start snoring each night so I could sneak out. I'll never forget how we used to meet on the beach under the beautiful night sky and talk for hours."

Slate nodded. Talking wasn't the only thing they did on those nights. To keep what they did private, he would drive into Jacksonville each week for his condom purchases to make sure he always had plenty on hand.

"Well, it's getting late and I'd better go inside," Kendra said softly, breaking into his thoughts. She tipped her head and looked over at him. "Thanks for such a wonderful evening."

He swallowed deeply and shifted in his seat, wondering if she really intended to send him home with a hard-on. Her next words let him know that she did.

"I hope you sleep well tonight, Slate."

He tried to downplay his disappointment and cast a grin over at her. "Yeah, I hope so, too."

She placed a warm hand on his thigh, pretty close to a

part of him that was aching. "I'd like to invite you over to dinner tomorrow night at seven. Think you can make it?"

The look in her eyes indicated she had more than dinner on her mind, and he didn't hesitate in responding. "Yeah, I can make it."

Fifteen

Three hours later and Slate was still awake. How on earth could he sleep when thoughts of Kendra filled his mind? Although they had enjoyed nice conversation at dinner, they hadn't discussed the things he wanted to talk to her about. It seemed she had intentionally steered clear of any discussion about the past. Instead they had talked about mutual friends and what was happening with local politics.

He wanted to tell her how his emotions had been shattered after Susan Conrad's drowning, and that he hadn't wanted her to see him that way. He had stayed out of college the following year just to keep his sanity and when he had gone back, things had been rough.

He wanted her to know that his love for her was the only thing that had kept him sane during that time, and that after seeking counseling and therapy he finally felt normal again and wanted to seek her out, but had thought because of the time that had lapsed, he no longer deserved her love. He'd believed that he would be doing the right thing by giving her up so she could find love and happiness with someone else.

Finally, he'd broken down and contacted Marcie Wilkins, and the older woman had convinced him that regardless of what he thought, Kendra did need him and he needed her. Ms. Marcie had told him of Kendra's father's death and how she had accepted a future of being an old maid by not dating any of the eligible bachelors in town.

Talking to Ms. Marcie had made him realize just how much he still loved Kendra. He knew now he would not be completely happy until she was a part of his future. Oh, yeah, he wanted her in his bed, too—but more importantly, he wanted her in his life.

He got out of bed and decided since he couldn't sleep and it was such a beautiful night, he might as well take a walk on the beach.

Half a mile away, Kendra couldn't sleep, either. She stood outside on her porch, thinking that she had laid it on rather thick tonight with Slate and had made the mistake of spreading some on herself in the process.

Her body was hot and there was nothing she could do to get cool. She had practically stripped down to the bare essentials yet she was burning up. She hadn't dared let Slate kiss her good-night. After he had accepted her invitation to dinner, she had opened the car door and raced into the house without looking back.

Thinking about him only made Kendra's body feel hotter. Knowing she was in a state where she would not find relief tonight, she walked back into the house and went into her bedroom. Taking off her robe, she quickly slipped into her bikini.

It was a wonderful night to go swimming, and she decided to go to her favorite part of the beach—the stretch of sand in front of the beach house.

Sixteen

The night air was cool and Kendra tightened the robe at her waist as she walked along the shoreline. The moon's glow seemed endless and bathed the beach waters in a sparkling hue.

She drew in a calming breath and inhaled the scent of the ocean. A number of stars sparkled overhead like diamonds in a dark velvety sky. A few minutes later she had almost reached her destination, when suddenly she made out a figure not far from where she stood. The reflection from the moon provided enough light for her to see the person who was standing less than twenty feet away, staring out at the ocean.

She gathered her towel against her chest when a voice inside her head told her to turn around and go back. Slate was the last person she needed to see, but she couldn't advance or retreat. She just stood there transfixed and watched him, knowing he was unaware of her presence.

The shimmering light cast his features into sharp view, and she thought that she had never seen a more beautiful specimen of a man. The only piece of clothing he wore was swim shorts, and the rich brown coloring of his skin seemed to glow. His bare chest, masculine shoulders and firm thighs displayed a physically fit body, one that was capable of giving a woman intense pleasure. She shuddered, remembering just what kind of pleasure it could deliver.

Heated desire thrummed through her already-hot veins as her body responded to the sheer essence of him, making it plainly clear whom it wanted and what it needed.

The seven-year wait was over.

She inhaled deeply and the sound seemed to alert Slate to her presence. He turned, and his gaze caught hers and held it. Heat flowed from his eyes to her and the desire there communicated to her, making every nerve in her body move between her legs. She shuddered against the sexual power he held over her from just looking at her and was tempted to close her eyes to shut him out, but couldn't.

His gaze said it all. He wanted her.

Kendra took a step forward, knowing that she wanted him, too. She bit her lip, remembering how things used to be between them, the heat and the intensity. At seventeen and eighteen, she'd had the desires of a young girl; now her body had the hunger of a woman.

She watched Slate take the remaining steps toward her, holding her gaze all the while. The expression on his face was intense, and, for a moment, she could only imagine what thoughts were flitting through his mind. Then suddenly, she read a few of them and her breath caught and her nipples hardened. He planned on doing a lot to her tonight, seven years' worth, and no matter how he tried, he still wouldn't get enough.

But, then, she thought when he finally came to a stop in front of her, neither would she.

Seventeen

As much as Slate wanted to pick Kendra up in his arms and carry her to the beach house and devour her, he didn't do it. There was a reason the two of them had met out here under the stars and facing the ocean.

For seven years he had grown to hate the sea because of what it had taken away from the Conrads and away from him. Now with Kendra's help, the last phase of deep-rooted guilt was being destroyed. From now on whenever he thought of the sea, it wouldn't be as a taker of life but as a giver. In Kendra's arms tonight, in front of the rolling surf of the ocean on its mystic shores, he planned to get his life back.

Without saying a single word, he leaned down and kissed each corner of her mouth before hungrily staking his claim and slanting his mouth over hers. He could feel her breathing quicken and the heat that flooded her mouth when he felt her body shudder. He felt it vibrate through every cell, every pulse, every pore.

Slate's tongue was in control, and Kendra's went where his led, seeking, devouring, eating away at her with a hunger that made her knees weaken and her heart race. She wrapped her arms around him, feeling the hardness of him, large and physical. His fingers slipped beneath the straps of her bikini top and pulled it down off her shoulders, and his mouth began devouring her breasts.

He was renewing his brand, reaffirming what had always been. His mouth moved back to hers, demanding her response as it greedily robbed her of any conscious thought other than how he was making her feel. And she matched him, passion for passion.

His hand moved to her hips and grasped her bikini bottom, and after one firm tug on the flimsy material it ripped. She broke the kiss, panting profusely. Her decision made, she took a step back and eased what was left of the bikini bottom down her legs and kicked it aside. She then pulled the bikini top over her head and tossed it away.

Naked, she went back into Slate's arms. "I want you," she whispered softly.

His mouth captured hers, and he picked her up into his arms and walked her to the area where he had spread a towel earlier. He placed her down on it, then proceeded to remove his swim shorts.

He heard her breath catch when he stood before her, gloriously naked and aroused. He had wanted to talk to her and explain everything before things reached this stage. He had wanted to tell her what had gone on in his life over the past seven years and why he had stayed out of touch.

Out of touch but not out of mind. He had loved her and had never stopped loving her. Loving her was what had kept him sane when he'd felt himself about to go off the deep end.

His entire body was tensed, wired, filled with desire. And when she reached out her arms to him, he dropped down beside her on the towel, aroused and ravenous beyond reason.

Eighteen

Passion grew to extreme proportions when Slate's fingers touched Kendra, skimming all over her body, noticing the differences the years had made. This was no longer the body of a young girl still coming into bloom, but was a flower fully opened. The curves, fullness and lushness he found absolutely extraordinary as he stroked her everywhere, beginning with her breasts before moving lower, between her legs.

There his hand found the treasure he sought. She was hot to his fingers, exceedingly wet, and the scent of her consumed him. He began stroking her while whispering just what he wanted to do to her.

When neither of them could take any more, he knelt before her, driven to taste her all over. He began spreading kisses all over her body, paying special homage to her breasts, flicking his tongue over the swollen nipples. And when he heard her soft, throaty breath catch, he was determined to go someplace where he'd never gone before with her.

Holding her hips firmly in his hands, he lowered his mouth past her navel and felt her body clench in surprise, then heard the sounds of shocked pleasure that erupted from deep in her throat when his tongue delved into the very essence of her, loving it, cherishing it.

"Slate!"

His name was a scream of gratification when his tongue began stroking her in a way it had never done before. Taking his hand he gently widened her legs, determined to get everything he wanted. With the heat of his mouth he showed her in a way he had never shown another woman just what she meant to him—what she'd always meant to him.

She screamed his name over and over as her nails clawed his back, and when he felt her body tense with her climax, he swiftly moved in place over her.

Their gazes met the moment his body entered hers, as his hands grabbed her hips and lifted her to go deeper.

"Ahh." He released a long sigh and a deep shuddering breath when her inner muscles tightened around him, clenching his throbbing erection, holding it captive inside of her. For a second he couldn't move; he just remained still in that position, savoring the feel of being inside of her, connected to her, one with her.

"Love me, Slate."

Her words broke him, destroyed the very last vestige of his control and restraint, opening a floodgate of desire. He began moving and the strokes increased. His thrusts became extensive when a need long denied ripped through him. His mind began spinning out of control. His body followed, and when he felt her body let go as an orgasm shook her to the core, he screamed her name and pushed deeper inside her as an orgasm tore through him, as well, making him explode.

Lowering his head, he consumed her lips, her mouth and her tongue. She was back in his arms, and he was back inside her body, and there was no way he could ever let her go.

Nineteen

Too weak to move, Kendra lay in Slate's arms, enjoying the feel of being there. When he shifted his body to stare down at her, she felt the intensity in his gaze. He leaned forward and captured her lips, and she gloried in what they had shared, but knew what was still between them— the doubts, regrets and anger. It was time they got everything out in the open.

When he finally broke the kiss, emotions she'd tried holding at bay came tearing through, bringing with them pain. "Why?" she asked softly.

Slate knew what she was asking him. "I went through hell, Kendra, and couldn't let you see me that way. Not being able to save that girl almost destroyed me. It didn't matter that everyone thought I had done all I could do. I was convinced that I had not done enough and was a failure."

Kendra had understood the demons that had made him leave Fernandina Beach that morning after the incident, but what she could not understand, nor accept, was that he hadn't tried contacting her.

"Why didn't you try to get in touch over the years, Slate? If only to let me know you were all right. Didn't you think I deserved that much?" she asked softly, remembering all the emotions she had endured during that time.

He ran a finger along her eyelids and saw the tears lodged there. His throat tightened.

"I literally lost my mind after that, Kendra. I didn't go back to school that year. Guilt consumed me, and I was eaten up with it. I finally pulled myself together to finish my last year of college but things didn't get better. Every night when I went to bed I saw Susan's face and how it had looked that day. I saw the look in her eyes, her hope that I would save her. I began drinking heavily, and one night was involved in a car accident. Luckily, no one was hurt. Since I didn't have a prior record, the judge sentenced me to a full year of community service at a hospital. That's when I started getting my life back. I met people who had endured more than I had and were fighting not only to get their lives back but to retain what life they had.

"I made up my mind to get myself together and that's when I sought counseling and underwent therapy for two solid years before I felt worthy enough of peaceful sleep. I also started my company, but soon discovered I still wasn't happy. There was something missing from my life. It was something I desired more than life itself, something that I had tried to give up. You. That's when I decided to come here and explain why I didn't stay in touch, and to tell you how guilt had made me feel unworthy of your love."

Kendra sighed. She had never imagined that Slate had been that consumed by guilt. Over the past seven years she had been hurting, but he had been hurting even more.

Reaching out, she pulled him into her arms. "Let's go

to the beach house, Slate," she whispered softly. She intended to prove to him that he was worthy of everything, especially of her.

Twenty

After taking a shower together to wash the beach sand from their bodies, Slate and Kendra got into bed and made love again. This time she showed him just what he meant to her and just how lonely her life had been without him for seven years.

Slate leaned over in bed and tenderly cupped Kendra's cheek in his hand. "There wasn't a day that went by that I didn't think about you, even those days when I didn't feel I was worthy enough. I couldn't stop loving you because you were such a part of me, a part I knew that I'd have with me no matter what. For the past couple of years, I poured everything into my work and tried to get my life back right so when I did return I could have something to offer you."

A smile touched the corners of Kendra's lips. "And what do you have to offer me, Slate?" she asked teasingly, although the look in his eyes was serious.

"I want to offer you my love. I want you to be my wife,

my best friend and my lover. I won't ask you to leave here since I know how much this town means to you. In my line of business, I can set up shop anywhere. I want to recapture that dream we first had of being together forever." He pulled her closer into his arms. "I love you. Say you'll marry me, Kendra. Please say it."

A sense of overwhelming happiness brought tears to Kendra's eyes. She loved him, too, and had never stopped, even when she thought he no longer loved her. "Yes, Slate, I'll marry you. I never stopped loving you and now that you're back, we have a lot of catching up to do. Seven years' worth."

She reached up and caught the back of his head in her hand and pulled his mouth down to meet hers. He groaned when their mouths made contact, and his arms automatically closed around her. Heat poured through every part of him as he gladly took what she offered.

Moments later, he drew back and broke off the kiss, dragging in a deep breath. He felt his erection get heavy with the need to be inside her. "Look at me," he whispered huskily. "I want you to see just how you make me feel when I'm making love to you."

She gazed up at him when he placed his body over hers. His features revealed the intensity of how he felt when he was inside her. She wrapped her arms around his neck and smiled.

"There's nothing like a lover's touch," she said breathlessly when he began setting a rhythm and igniting their passion once again.

As he made love to her, he knew that her love and her touch were all he would ever need.

* * * * *

PASSION

Harlequin® Desire

COMING NEXT MONTH
AVAILABLE APRIL 10, 2012

#2149 FEELING THE HEAT
The Westmorelands
Brenda Jackson
Dr. Micah Westmoreland knows Kalina Daniels hasn't forgiven him. But he can't ignore the heat that still burns between them....

#2150 ON THE VERGE OF I DO
Dynasties: The Kincaids
Heidi Betts

#2151 HONORABLE INTENTIONS
Billionaires and Babies
Catherine Mann

#2152 WHAT LIES BENEATH
Andrea Laurence

#2153 UNFINISHED BUSINESS
Cat Schield

#2154 A BREATHLESS BRIDE
The Pearl House
Fiona Brand

REQUEST YOUR FREE BOOKS!
2 FREE NOVELS PLUS 2 FREE GIFTS!

Harlequin® Desire

ALWAYS POWERFUL, PASSIONATE AND PROVOCATIVE

YES! Please send me 2 FREE Harlequin Desire® novels and my 2 FREE gifts (gifts are worth about $10). After receiving them, if I don't wish to receive any more books, I can return the shipping statement marked "cancel." If I don't cancel, I will receive 6 brand-new novels every month and be billed just $4.30 per book in the U.S. or $4.99 per book in Canada. That's a saving of at least 14% off the cover price! It's quite a bargain! Shipping and handling is just 50¢ per book in the U.S. and 75¢ per book in Canada.* I understand that accepting the 2 free books and gifts places me under no obligation to buy anything. I can always return a shipment and cancel at any time. Even if I never buy another book, the two free books and gifts are mine to keep forever.

225/326 HDN FEF3

Name	(PLEASE PRINT)	
Address		Apt. #
City	State/Prov.	Zip/Postal Code

Signature (if under 18, a parent or guardian must sign)

Mail to the **Reader Service:**
IN U.S.A.: P.O. Box 1867, Buffalo, NY 14240-1867
IN CANADA: P.O. Box 609, Fort Erie, Ontario L2A 5X3

Not valid for current subscribers to Harlequin Desire books.

Want to try two free books from another line?
Call 1-800-873-8635 or visit www.ReaderService.com.

* Terms and prices subject to change without notice. Prices do not include applicable taxes. Sales tax applicable in N.Y. Canadian residents will be charged applicable taxes. Offer not valid in Quebec. This offer is limited to one order per household. All orders subject to credit approval. Credit or debit balances in a customer's account(s) may be offset by any other outstanding balance owed by or to the customer. Please allow 4 to 6 weeks for delivery. Offer available while quantities last.

Your Privacy—The Reader Service is committed to protecting your privacy. Our Privacy Policy is available online at www.ReaderService.com or upon request from the Reader Service.

We make a portion of our mailing list available to reputable third parties that offer products we believe may interest you. If you prefer that we not exchange your name with third parties, or if you wish to clarify or modify your communication preferences, please visit us at www.ReaderService.com/consumerchoice or write to us at Reader Service Preference Service, P.O. Box 9062, Buffalo, NY 14269. Include your complete name and address.

HDES11B

Harlequin Blaze

red-hot reads

Sizzling fairy tales
to make every fantasy come true!

Fan-favorite authors
Tori Carrington and Kate Hoffmann
bring readers

Blazing Bedtime Stories, Volume VI

MAID FOR HIM...

Successful businessman Kieran Morrison doesn't dare hope for
a big catch when he goes fishing. But when he wakes up one
night to find a beautiful woman seemingly unconscious on the
deck of his sailboat, he lands one bigger than he could ever
have imagined by way of mermaid Daphne Moore.
But is she real? Or just a fantasy?

OFF THE BEATEN PATH

Greta Adler and Alex Hansen have been friends for seven years.
So when Greta agrees to accompany Alex at a mountain retreat
owned by a client, she doesn't realize that Alex has a different
path he wants their relationshiop to take.
But will Greta follow his lead?

Available April 2012 wherever books are sold.

www.Harlequin.com

HB79679